SECRET OF THE SASSAFRAS

OLIVIA SPARROW

Happy reading!

BRODEN PUBLISHING

Happy reading!

Copyright © 2023 by Olivia Sparrow

This novel is a work of fiction. Unless otherwise indicated, all names, characters, businesses, places, events, and incidents in this book are either the product of the author's imagination or used in a fictitious manner. Any resemblance to actual persons, living or dead, actual companies or organizations, or actual events is purely coincidental.

All rights reserved.

No part of this book may be reproduced in any form or by any electronic or mechanical means, including information storage and retrieval systems, without written permission from the author, except for the use of brief quotations in a book review.

For CB
My love and solace, forever the one.

HB & BB
My greatest gifts, every day you make me proud.

sassafras. noun. sas sa fras ˈsas-(ə-)ˌfras.

Easy to identify by its leaves, the American Sassafras Tree is unique in that it displays three different leaf shapes—all of which can be found on the same tree.

ONE

GEMMA

"If you could make one wish, what would it be?"
"I wish she was still here—right next to me."

The sound of screeching tires erupts somewhere behind me and my body recoils, bracing for impact. A rush of adrenaline prickles my skin as I peer over my shoulder to survey the wreckage—there is none. Another false alarm.

Breathe. You're okay.

I shake it off, annoyed at my quick-fire nervous system. It wasn't always this way. I wasn't always sent into fight-or-flight with every sudden loud noise. You'd think after living here for three years my phonophobia would have gotten better, not worse.

I pick up my pace as the crisp air fills my lungs, a welcome relief from the summer's relentless humidity. Central Park's high-rise speckled skyline comes into view, reminding me of the first time I set foot in this city.

Since I was a little girl, fall has always been my favorite season. Mom used to call autumn nature's version of the Fourth of July. Jewel-toned leaves burst with every shade of unfiltered seasonal magic as they declare their short-lived independence. I look to the blue sky, captivated by the abundance of brightly decorated tree limbs. *She would have loved everything about this moment.*

I can still hear the sound of her laughter when she would sneak up on me and jump into piles of my carefully raked leaves, sending them flying in every direction. The blissful, yet guilty look on her face instantly erased any annoyance I felt about her ruining my attempts to clean up our yard. Sweet, yet painful memories.

I'm envious of the leaves and their promise of a new start. Every spring they have an opportunity to rewrite their history and come back as newer, potentially better versions of themselves. *What I would give to go back and rewrite just one single day.*

Glancing down at my watch to check my pace I suddenly realize I'm late. "Shit!" I mutter out loud. I turn and race the 1.5 miles back to our brownstone. I was supposed to meet my roommate, Mikayla, twenty minutes ago, to go over details for our annual Halloween party this Saturday. It's been almost impossible to find a time for us to meet between Mikayla's residency at Mount Sinai, and my last year of law school.

I can already hear what she's going to say. She's going to think I intentionally forgot about our meeting in an attempt to cancel the whole thing. Not that the idea of canceling doesn't appeal to me: it does. I'd much rather have a quiet night at home, like all my other Friday and Saturday nights. Mikayla thinks I avoid people and never do anything that isn't school or dance related, and if I'm being honest, there might be some truth to that.

I can't handle letting her down, especially not today. Mikayla doesn't know the significance of today's date: how could she? I decided to leave that part of my life behind when I moved to New York. She doesn't know the crushing weight of responsibility I still carry. For years I've tried to break free from my shackles of regret, but they always return and drag me under, deep into my ocean of sorrow.

A sudden breeze sends shivers down my spine, making me wish I'd dressed for cooler weather. Seemingly confused about which direction it's heading, a dry, tattered leaf floats toward me. It stalls and then stops directly in my path as my foot stomps down, sending a destructive yet oddly satisfying crunch into the cool air. Remnants of its fragile, skeletal frame scatter on the pavement, leaving its irreparable brokenness behind me. The kind I know all too well.

I exit the park at 72nd St. and 5th Ave. and weave my way through the crosswalk's perpetual sea of people. It never gets old running down these tree-lined, Lenox Hill streets. I've lived with Mikayla in her family's three-bedroom brownstone for almost three years. It's not lost on me that there's no way, outside a hefty trust fund, that a twenty-three-year-old law student could afford this place.

The front of our house comes into view, and I bound up our terracotta front steps, gripping onto the black iron railing that leads to our front door. I cup the sides of my face, shielding my eyes from the light and peer inside. Through the double glass doors, I can see that her shoes and backpack aren't by the front door. She's not home. I sigh a small breath of relief and let myself inside.

Kicking my sneakers off, I head to our kitchen. The sleek black cabinets and edgy, contemporary tiles makes me feel like I'm in one of those upscale cookware and cutlery stores. The thrill of living here will never wear off. I pick up the note on our gray-and-white marble island:

Sorry! Working late tonight. We'll figure out the party details—don't stress!
Xo, Mika

Who leaves notes anymore? Mikayla. So old-school. She could have just texted, but instead leaves a note with the cutest bouquet of flowers drawn at the bottom to brighten my day. So thoughtful, and good at everything—even drawing. She knew ahead of time and was considerate enough to leave a note for me before she left for work. On the other hand, I simply forgot. Oof. Mental note to myself—I can't let school take up so much of my life that I forget the little details. More often than not, it's the little details that end up mattering the most.

I head upstairs for my favorite part of every run. The promise of a hot shower is the only thing that keeps me going mile after mile. Mikayla and I each have our own floor with a bedroom and a private bathroom. It's a dream setup and a rare find in Manhattan, so I'm told. For most of my childhood, I never had my own room, let alone my own floor, and I'm not sure I'll ever get used to it. Fleeting memories of home slip down the drain, along with the grime of the city.

I pull on my old purple robe, the one Mom wore when we were young, feeling the warmth of her embrace as I tighten the belt around my waist. Tattered and frayed from age, it's my version of a security blanket. I trace the threadbare elbows, the well-loved fabric never fails to comfort me. I read through the small mountain of torts that have accumulated on my desk and before I know it, I'm rubbing my eyes. Glancing at the clock on my nightstand, I text Mikayla.:

> Early dance class tomorrow, going to bed.

She texts back immediately:

> Sweet dreams. Not sure when I'll be home.

Five-minutes later, she texts again:

> BTW I called a private chef who owes my parents a favor—they're catering our party. We just have to choose from their menu and send the list. ✅

Sure, of course. We'll just order from a private chef. *What even is this Manhattan world I now call home?* Private chefs weren't—and still aren't—a thing in rural Indiana as far as I know.

My mind drifts back to those happy-go-lucky days. My far-from-Manhattan modest upbringing consisted of late-night games of tag or ghosts in the graveyard, pausing only for a quick sip from the garden hose to quench our thirst. I can still hear the echoes of Mom's voice calling us through the screen-door: "Girls, time to come inside!"

I remember wishing those nights would last forever. Memories of my childhood stir within me, and I wince, recalling what happened on this night, ten years ago. *I can't believe it's been ten years.*

Don't think about that now. You somehow managed to tiptoe around that emotional landmine all day, and now isn't the time to set it off. I wearily crawl into bed, desperately trying to block out the memories that claw at the back of my mind. That night haunts me, like a nightmare that won't sleep.

TWO

GEM & EM

"I'll race you. First one home wins!" I scream over my shoulder at Emmeline, three paces behind. Em is my twin, older by two minutes—something she never lets me forget. The two of us are inseparable. Best friends from the moment we took our first strangled breaths. There are several cool things about being a twin, but if you ask me, the best thing is: never being alone.

Her footsteps trail off and I turn to see where she went.

"Look, Gem, a sassafras tree," she shouts, running down the embankment to the edge of the woods. Standing on her tiptoes, she pulls off two giant, mitten-shaped leaves.

I run down to her, taking one from her extended hand. "Mother Nature's favorite."

She tilts her head to the side. "How do you know?"

"Because it tastes like root beer," I reply, twirling the stem in my mouth.

"Can we sit down for a sec? I'm tired." She brushes her hair back from her beet-red face.

"C'mon, we're almost home."

A red-tailed hawk circles overhead as we dash between the steel rails of the tracks. The smell of tar clings to the inside of my nose, leaving the slightest taste of gasoline in my mouth. Sweat trickles down my back as we race up a small hill where I can just start to see the dirt road that leads to our house. I slow down so Em can catch up. The tracks bend sharply to the right as I pass our neighbor, Mr. Paul, on his tractor. We wave to each other as my feet hit dusty gravel, kicking up a wake of chalky plumes.

Em sprints at the very last minute, beating me to our front steps where Mom sits every day, awaiting our return from school. Sometimes Grandma Vivian waits with her too, and if we're lucky, a big pitcher of lemonade and fresh batch of chocolate chip cookies.

"My little moon and sun. I've missed you."

"Hi, Mom!" we call to her.

"She beat me," I say, defeated, as Emmeline adds, "It was a close race, though."

"I bet it was. Your faces look like little tomatoes," Mom says.

I wipe my forehead with the back of my hand and drop my backpack at my feet. "It's roasting out here. Will you set the sprinkler up for us?" I ask.

"Sure, but first come cool off in the shade."

Out of breath and panting hard, we fall onto our front porch. My legs twitch with crackling fireworks beneath my skin. Mom sits quietly, waiting to hear our stories from the day. She listens intently, like she's trying to memorize each word.

"Do you have any homework?"

"A little bit of math," I say.

"Anything you need help with before I leave for work?" she asks.

"No, we're still working on multiplication tables. They're pretty easy," Em says.

"Okay. Why don't you two get a snack while I set up the sprinkler." Mom walks around the side of the house to the shed.

Em follows me into the kitchen, grabbing a bag of pretzel rods. We watch from the kitchen window as Mom sets up the sprinkler in the shade, under our giant climbing tree.

"It's ready for you: just turn on the hose. When you're done, please make sure to turn it off all the way."

"We will, Mom."

Mom washes her hands, taking a pretzel from Em. "I'm going to start supper so we can eat together before I leave."

When we're at school, Mom takes classes at college for her master's in social work, and at night she waitresses at a restaurant near our house. Em and I are asleep when she gets home, usually not until the early morning.

We change out of our school clothes and run outside. The dry, yellow grass feels like hay beneath our feet. I turn on the hose, letting the slow-moving, rainbow-shaped streams drench our skin.

"Em, hop on," I say, running to our back door.

She climbs to the top step as I wrap my arms around the back of her knees. "Hold on tight!" I shout, as she grasps her elbows in front of my neck.

I wait until the rows of water point toward the sky and run as fast as I can, jumping over the sprinkler. Our shrieks fill the air as we burst through jets of cold water.

"My turn!" I climb on Em's back and she runs full force, stopping just before she clears the sprinkler. She stands still as a statue as the wall of water rotates toward the ground, slowly spraying us from head to toe.

"It's so cold. Run!" I squeal, kicking my legs.

She giggles as the frigid sprays blast our skin. The sprinkler moves toward the sky again, dousing us, but she doesn't budge.

"It's freezing, Em! Come on, move it!"

I wiggle, trying to break her grasp and we both tip over onto the wet grass, sprawled out like turtles on our backs.

"Why'd you just stand there?" I ask, staring up at the sky.

"Because it helped us cool off faster."

"I'm cold now."

"Me too," she says.

I hold my hand out to her, pulling her to her feet. "Your lips are turning blue, I'll go turn off the hose."

"I thought you might need these," Mom says, hanging two towels over the railing by the back door.

"Thanks, Mom."

"Dinner will be ready soon, time to come in and shower."

AFTER DINNER, Mom kisses us goodnight and rushes out the door. Emmeline and I clear the dishes and quickly finish our math homework before running outside.

"Gem, look! There's so many of them tonight," she shouts, pointing at the flashing yellow dots hovering in the shadows of our backyard. I grab our mason jar, air holes punched through the metal lid, and we gingerly fill it with fireflies until the jar glows like a nightlight.

"It makes me sad seeing them trapped in there," Emmeline says, unscrewing the lid so they can continue their end of summer dance.

She lies down on the grass next to me, beneath our tree. The day's remaining light dwindles, clearing the slate for the new colors that will take their place tomorrow. We listen in hushed silence while nature whispers secrets into the black velvet sky—the sky answers back in twinkling jewels. Their language for thousands of years.

A shooting star streaks across the sky, leaving a trail of glitter in the corner of my eye. "Did you see it?" I shriek, pointing upwards.

She shakes her head, still searching. I can tell from her grin she's happy for me that I did.

There are thousands of stars—too many to count, and we tire trying. Emmeline and I go back inside, closing and locking the door behind us, like Mom taught us. We turn out all the lights, except for the one on the front porch.

I follow Em to the bathroom to get ready for bed. As we brush our teeth, I stare at Emmeline's blue eyed, freckle-faced reflection—a perfect likeness of mine. I hold her long-blonde hair as she bends down to rinse her mouth from the faucet and then we trade places.

"Back-to-back," I say, turning my back to hers. The mirror offers proof that she's the tiniest bit taller than I. I don't understand how people can't tell us apart. It's easy: Emmeline has dimples, and I don't. Mom calls us her mirrored souls. She says we're identical in looks and spirit.

We run down the darkened hallway to our pale lavender bedroom where our twin beds sit beneath a big picture window. Dark green curtains with little white pom-poms made by our mom, billow gently in the night breeze, bringing in cool air from outside. When it's really hot and there's no breeze, Em and I soak a washcloth with cold water and lay it over our foreheads. It's a trick Mom taught us that works every time.

Tucked into the corner by our closet is Mom's desk from when she was little. One of our greatest discoveries was when we climbed underneath to build a fort one rainy day and saw she'd carved her name into the bottom. Em and I added our names on each side of hers, that way the three of us can always be together.

"Whose night is it to turn off the light?" Emmeline asks.

"Yours. I did it last night."

"Okay," she says, begrudgingly.

The walk back to bed is the scariest part; that is, until we are close enough to jump, saving ourselves from any monsters lurking underneath. Em waits for me as I turn on the fan and pull my top sheet under my chin. I watch from the safety of my bed as she gets ready to turn off the light and run. Finger on the switch, she stands chewing her bottom lip, eyeing the dark space beneath her bed.

"If you could make one wish, what would it be?" I ask, trying to distract her.

"Anything?"

"Yep, anything."

"That's easy."

"What is it?"

"I wish I could fly. Then I wouldn't have to touch the ground near the edge of my bed," she says, before flipping the light off. Her feet shuffle over the wood floor before she dives onto her bed.

"How about you?"

"I wish Mom was here, reading to us."

"Oh, that's a good one, Gem."

We tuck ourselves in under our green and white checkered bedspreads and even though it's dark when the light's off, we aren't scared that Mom isn't here. We have each other and honestly, there's no safer feeling in the world.

"Goodnight, Moon," I say, sleepily.

"Goodnight, Sun."

A hushed silence takes over our room, leaving us to our star-filled dreams.

THREE

GEMMA

I'm finishing up in the powder room near the front door when I hear footsteps on the stairs.

"I haven't seen you all week," I say, a little too excitedly to Mikayla's exhausted face. Her brown skin gleams softly in the morning light against her satin turquoise bonnet. She grumbles something back, but I can't make out the words.

"How'd you sleep?" I ask.

"I'm not totally convinced I'm awake yet. Why are you wearing yellow plastic gloves?"

"I wanted to get some cleaning done before the party," I say, as she grins. It's good to see her smile.

"You didn't have to do that, thanks."

"I know you need coffee before any serious questions—so how about a borderline-serious one?" I ask.

She stops before the last step and stares at me, dark circles under her eyes, a hand on her hip.

"I'm fairly sure I can't even handle borderline-serious right now."

"Rough night?"

"I don't even know where to begin." She shakes her head.

"You work so hard. Are you feeling okay?"

"I'm fine, I just need coffee. And food. Go ahead—"

"Seriously, I worry about you. When is the last time you had a full night's sleep?"

"You sound like my mom, Gemma. I'm fine."

"You sure?"

She lets out a sigh, my cue she's over this topic. "Moving on."

"Okay, but it's only been two weeks. If you faint again, I'm taking you to get checked out myself," I say, eyeing her carefully. "Doctors—you make the worst patients."

She rolls her eyes. "Now, what did you want to ask me?" she says, rubbing the back of her neck.

"Did you decide on a costume?"

She groans. "I honestly haven't even had a chance to think about it."

"No worries, we'll find something in my closet," I say.

I'm sure my obsession with costumes is a way for me to hold on to the bright spots of my childhood. *The before.* Picking out our costumes was an exciting annual tradition at our house. We never had extra money to buy costumes, so Mom taught herself to sew and would make ours every year. Last time I was home I found them all tucked away in the attic, a treasure box filled with handsewn memories.

Mikayla walks groggily to the kitchen, and I follow her, taking off my gloves. I sit down at the island while she measures heaping spoonfuls of beans into the coffee maker.

"I got great news yesterday. I was so busy last night I didn't even have a chance to text you," she says, waiting for the coffee to finishing brewing.

"What's up?"

"I've been chosen to speak at Columbia's tenth annual Black Women in Medicine Conference."

"Look at you! That's awesome, congratulations. When?"

"It's in May, I'm not sure of the exact date, but I'll let you know," she says.

It's clear to everyone who meets Mikayla that she's a star on the rise. Not only is she brilliant, beautiful and hard-working, she's just one of those people who the second you meet her, moves right into your heart. She inspires everyone around her with her kindness and passion for community work. In addition to her hectic workload, she always somehow finds time to organize toy, coat and food drives for the hospital as well as the underserved public-school systems throughout the five boroughs.

On days I've met her at the hospital, we can't walk 20-feet without someone stopping her to say hello. Her patients are constantly giving her hugs and introducing her to their families. There's no greater gift for someone who is ill than to be under her clever and good-natured care. She's pure sunshine and can warm an entire room with her smile alone.

We sip our coffee, catching up on the best and worst parts of our weeks when my stomach growls.

"Was that you?" she asks.

I cross my arms tightly, gripping onto my sides. "You heard that?"

"How could I not?"

"I skipped dinner and went to bed early last night," I admit.

"Let's go get something to eat. We can continue this conversation on the way," she says.

Mikayla runs upstairs to change, and I grab my vest from the front closet, and we head out into a bright yet windy autumn day.

"Are you excited for tonight? Or were you secretly hoping the hospital would need me and we'd have to cancel?" she asks.

"Of course I'm excited. I'll take any reason to play dress up."

"I know your love of costumes, but excited might be a stretch. Tolerating it, more likely," she says, narrowing her eyes.

"That's so not true," I say, stepping off the curb to let two joggers pass by. "Okay, maybe it's a little true. I know—these things are good for me. I'll say it so you don't have to."

"If it weren't for our Halloween and New Year's Eve parties, I wouldn't have met any of your classmates. Isn't there anyone you've met at school that's become more than just an acquaintance?" she asks.

I shake my head. "Not really. I honestly don't have the time."

"Really?" she says, giving me a look.

"Listen, I know even *you* find the time to go out. It's just not a priority for me like it is for you." I stop to look at the vibrant orange and brown window display of my favorite bookstore, hoping she'll take the hint and drop it.

"Gem, I've never understood why you'd move to NYC if going out and meeting people wasn't one of the main reasons for coming here?

Isn't that the whole point of moving to a big city like Manhattan? What is it you're afraid of?" she asks.

I swallow the lump in my throat. "I'm not afraid of anything, I just haven't met anyone as friendworthy as you. You should take it as a compliment." I turn and face her as she makes a face, clearly not buying what I'm selling.

"In the almost three years we've lived together, you've rarely brought a friend, let alone a guy back to the house. With my new schedule I'm hardly home. Doesn't it ever get lonely?" she asks. Her question stings my eyes and I continue our walk, past a row of carriage houses, so she can't see I'm blinking back tears.

Desperately lonely. But it's been that way for years.

"You act like I'm a recluse and I'm not. School, dance and community work takes up my entire life. As far as dating, you know I'm not looking to meet anyone. I truthfully don't have the time right now," I say, matter-of-factly. A cab cuts the corner a little too close as we're waiting for the light, and I protectively pull her out of harm's way.

"I'm good," she says, gently pulling her arm away. "I'm just saying for someone who is only twenty-three, your social life is non-existent."

"Living in NYC is all the social interaction I need. Even if they aren't friends, you can't discount the fact that I'm constantly surrounded by crowds of people. On campus, on the subway, running in the park. I promise you I get my daily recommended dose of people, Doctor Williams," I say, teasingly.

"All I'm saying is that it'd be good for you to get out. I know you get offers, how about saying yes once in a while?"

"Heard. Okay, I'll try to say yes more, can we change the subject, please?" I'm relieved to see the bright red and yellow faux flower boxes of our favorite creperie.

She puts her arm around me and pulls me to her. I know she only wants what's best for me. We find an open table in the cozy dining shed and sit beneath cheerful string lights, as a waiter comes to take our order.

"I've been looking forward to tonight all week," she says.

"Believe it or not. . .so have I," I sigh. "I've been feeling out of sorts all week. I'm glad it's over."

"What's going on? Is it school?"

I nod, feeling guilty for never having shared my story with her. It would explain my antisocial tendencies. I trust her completely and know she would never judge me for not telling her sooner. I've come close many times but—I just can't. *Some things are better pushed down deep and never talked about.*

"You're in your final year, just think about how different your life's going to look a year from now," she offers.

"I remind myself of that—all—the—time."

Mikayla devours her egg-white and spinach crepe with ravenous bites as I dive into my strawberry and fresh whipped-cream.

"I've been meaning to tell you, some of my friends from med-school are coming tonight," she says.

"No way! I'm finally going to meet your Columbia crew?" I nervously tap my foot under the table. "I'm not sure if I like having to share you," I say, teasingly. These are Mikayla's closest friends, I'm already feeling pressure for them to like me.

"I know you're going to love them and vice versa."

"Remind me of their names again," I ask.

"Nina, Owen, Sarika and Miles are all coming into the city tonight. I told them they can crash at our place if they want."

"Totally. I can't wait to meet them."

She smiles, but there's something more.

"Oh, and just a heads-up, I've been wanting to introduce you to Miles. He's ridiculously handsome, brilliant, and one of the nicest—"

I shake my head. "No. Absolutely not. I appreciate the heads-up, but no thank you," I say, my tone stern. *I'm never risking getting close to someone, just to have them taken from me again.*

She shrugs like she can't help herself.

"I don't have time for anything in my life that doesn't contribute to the following three things: focusing on my final year of school, studying for the bar and staying single."

"Should I write those down so I don't forget?" she asks, playfully.

"No need, I'm happy to remind you," I say, folding my arms across my chest. "By the way, if he's so awesome, maybe you should date him."

"Ew, no. He's like a brother to me. But you are his type so don't say I didn't warn you," she says, as her phone rings. She checks the number and picks up right away. *Must be work.*

"Hello? Yes, this is she."

Her face falls.

"You can't be serious. The party's tonight!"

I lean in and mouth the words "What?" raising my hands in the air. She mouths back to me "Caterer."

"This is completely unprofessional. You're leaving us with absolutely no alternative and less than eight hours before our guests arrive," she says, before hanging up.

"That didn't sound good," I say, my eyes wide.

"So irritating! We're going to have to find another caterer for tonight. So much for my parents' friend doing us a favor," she growls.

"This is NYC. We'll be able to figure something out, and it'll be great," I say.

She shrugs, unconvinced.

"We better go home and start calling around." Mikayla waves to our waiter so we can pay the check. We walk home feeling the stress of the ticking clock. After striking out with every call, desperation starts to set in.

"I have an idea. Why don't we just order pizzas from Joe's on Broadway and be done? It's our favorite and you know it's always a crowd pleaser. I'm sure people do it all the time," I say.

She gives me a blank stare. I can tell no other solution is coming to mind.

"Joe's it is!" I declare victoriously.

FOUR

GEM & EM

"Try it again! This time, Gemma, hold it steady and, Emmeline, keep running until I say let go. Run hard, I promise the string isn't going to break," Mom assures her.

Emmeline, Mom and I have been trying to get our kite in the air, and just when it looks like it's taken off, it makes a sharp turn and nosedives back to earth leaving bits of grass and mud caked to the tip. It crashes so hard I'm surprised the plastic sides haven't snapped in two. I don't understand why it won't stay in the air. We run as hard as we can when Mom says go, but the second we turn back and look, it rockets toward the ground and lands with a thud.

"Don't look back after you start running, just keep going. The string is strong, I promise it's not going to break," Mom says.

Not fully convinced, I hand the plastic green spool to Emmeline so she can have another try at running.

I grip the sides as she starts to run and when Mom says 'Go!' I throw it up at just the right time. It snaps out of my hands, up and into the wind. This time Emmeline never looks back, she just keeps running faster and faster, her long blonde hair flying wild in every direction. I squeal with delight, watching as our kite soars high into the vibrant blue spring sky.

"We did it, Mom!" I yell.

Mom's smiling face turns upwards, following as it climbs higher and higher. It floats toward the clouds, bound only to earth by Emmeline's small hand, still clinging tightly to the spool of string.

"Gemma, sweetheart..."

"Gemma."

I hear my name somewhere in the distance. Again. Someone's calling me. I feel like I'm stuck in a wave that keeps crashing onto the shore. My body topples over itself again and again until there's no telling which way is up.

I check the kite, still floating high above our heads. The yellow and green tail waves back and forth like a serpent slithering its way to the heavens.

"Gemma. Gemma, my sweet girl. I need you to wake up."

My eyelids fight to stay shut. I'm afraid if I open them, our kite will break off and be lost forever. Through tiny gaps in my eyelashes, I can see the outline of a figure standing above me. *It's not Mom.* My heart hammers in my chest. I'm afraid to move. I'm afraid to even breathe. There's a flash of recognition and I sit up so fast my head spins.

"What is it?" I whisper.

I rub my eyes with the backs of my fists, trying to pry open my heavy eyelids.

"Grandma? Is that you? Why are you here?" I ask.

I push the hair out of my eyes and look over to Emmeline's bed. She's sitting up, rubbing the sleep from her eyes.

"I'm sorry to wake you, but you need to get dressed right away."

"It's not time to wake up yet. It's still dark outside," Emmeline mumbles.

"Is Mom home yet?" I ask.

"What time is it?" Em asks.

Grandma struggles to find the right words. "My sweet girls... it's your mom. She—I need you to..."

"I just got a call... there's been... your mom was in an accident on her way home from work tonight," she says.

I can barely hear her. Her words sound like the air's being let out of them, like a slowly deflating balloon. Grandma takes a deep, shaky breath before walking over to turn on our bedroom light. Emmeline and

I shield our eyes, giving them a second to adjust to the sudden and unwelcome change.

"We need to get to the hospital as fast as we can," she says.

"Mom?" I reply groggily, sleep trailing the edges of my voice.

Grandma's eyebrows furrow, deepening the lines on her face. *She's trying to hold back her tears.* Seeing Grandma this upset makes my heart squeeze so hard in my chest it hurts to breathe. Emmeline and I quickly jump out of our beds as Grandma hands us our shirts. Sleep tugs at my eyelids as I stumble to my dresser and open the top drawer, searching for a pair of socks.

"What about our kite?" I ask, softly, to no one in particular. "We were just holding on to our kite."

FIVE

GEMMA

I get back from my run to find Mikayla in my closet rummaging through my costume trunk. She's pulling on a pair of black and white harlequin tights when I clear my throat, startling her.

"You scared me! I didn't even hear you come up the steps," she says, turning and holding out her arms. "What do you think?"

She's wearing a long brown wig with a black velvet bow on top, a short blue dress, and tied around her waist is a white, lace-edged apron.

"I think you make the perfect Alice. I have to admit, it kind of makes me wish I was going less Black Widow and more Mad Hatter. I'd follow you down the rabbit hole any day."

She takes off her wig and tights. "Backing out of the rabbit hole for a second—while you were on your run, I finished the decorations. That was the last thing on our list."

I dig through the costumes to find my wig. "Downstairs looks great. Let's get ready and hopefully we'll have a minute to sit and chill before our guests arrive?"

"It's New York, everyone will be at least thirty minutes late if not more, we'll have plenty of time," she says, like it's a known fact.

Mikayla leaves with her costume under her arm, happy with her choice. I typically underestimate how much time it takes for me to get into costume, so I take a quick shower. My wig takes forever, I'd forgotten how hard these things are to put on. I pull on my skin-tight Black Widow costume and as I start tugging up the front zipper, I'm suddenly grateful for my four-mile run. I head downstairs and find Mikayla in the kitchen.

"You, and our haunted wonderland, look amazing." I say, giving her a twirl.

"Red hair looks good on you."

"How long did all of this take you?" I ask, pointing to the cobwebs and tombstones lining the perimeter of the room.

"Those were easy. It was switching out all the lightbulbs with black lights that took so long. Oh, and I pulled out the fog machine from the basement and put it under the bar for a true haunted house effect," she says, pouring a glass of wine for each of us.

"The last time we had a drink together was the night I got my offer, and that was almost two months ago. This is nice," I say, taking a seat next to her at our bar, careful not to let my wig get close to the candles.

IN LESS THAN an hour our living room quickly fills with people dressed in their Halloween best. It's packed in here. *How many people did she invite?* I'm talking to Dracula and The Little Mermaid when Mikayla calls from across the room.

"Gemma!" she shouts, waving me over.

I pardon myself from my blood-sucking friend and his date and walk to her. The room's so crowded, I don't make much progress before one of my dance classmates grabs my hand.

"Gem, come dance with us!"

I follow her up onto our kitchen island, giving me an aerial view of the party. Our living room looks like a scene straight out of The Rocky Horror Picture Show. I'm impressed how seriously people have taken their costumes this year. Costumes in New York are next level. Who am I kidding, I've lived here long enough to know that it doesn't stop at costumes. Everything in this city is next level.

It feels good to let my stress from the week go. Dance has always been my escape. It's what helped save me so many years ago. I think back to my younger self, thankful I was introduced to dance at a time when I needed it most.

My eye catches Mikayla's—she's heading my way. She motions for me to come down while a mummy helps clear a spot so I can jump down. I grab my drink off the counter and follow her.

"Come meet my friends," she says, taking my hand and leading me through the crowd. My stomach knots and I pull her back.

"You didn't say anything to your friend about potentially setting us up, did you? Please tell me you didn't—or I'm turning around and going upstairs."

"Gem, relax. I didn't say a word. I know the rules, I heard them loud and clear: school, study for the bar and you plan on staying single—maybe forever."

Of course she wouldn't say anything. Instantly relieved, I hug her. "I never said forever, but definitely for the foreseeable future." Meeting her close friends is anxiety-inducing enough, I don't need any added pressure to make me feel even more self-conscious.

We serpentine our way through the room and she puts her arm around me waving her hand toward a small group of people standing in front of us.

"This is my friend Gemma you've all heard so much about. Gemma, these are my friends I've been wanting you to meet."

"It's nice to meet you," I shout, over the music.

As she's trying to introduce them individually, people keep bumping into us on their way to the bar. Sensing we need a little more space, Mikayla motions for us to go out onto our patio. We slowly squeeze our way through the crammed room until we've filed out the back door. I hadn't realized how hot it had gotten inside, the fresh air feels good. I touch the hairline of my wig making sure it's still in place.

"Let's try this again. Gemma, this is Nina and Miles. I guess we lost Owen and Sarika on the way out here. Nina and Miles, this is my roommate Gemma," Mikayla says.

"Black Widow, it's a pleasure to meet you," Nina says, raising her glass.

"Likewise, Velma," I clink my glass to hers and turn to Miles. "I take it from your suspenders and the giant red S that you must be Mr. Kent?"

"Please—call me Clark." He shakes my hand with a firm and steady grip and then leans in to give me a kiss on the cheek hello. When his skin brushes mine, the whole side of my face tingles and I flush, puzzled by the heat rising in my cheeks. *What in the world?*

The four of us exchange small talk and when Nina and Mikayla start discussing one of their classmates, Miles turns to me. I watch as the words come out of his mouth but the only thing I can focus on are his sparkling, perfectly straight teeth. *Whoa.* Teeth are always the first thing I notice—about anyone. I'd go as far as to say they're my kryptonite. It's hard to pull my eyes away from them and when I do, I realize I've missed his question. I panic slightly, knowing I can't blame the noise from the party.

"I'm sorry, I thought I heard someone inside calling me. What were you saying?" I ask, turning my back to our patio doors.

"No worries. I was just asking where you learned to dance. It looked like you were having a lot of fun up there," he says.

"Oh—right. I love to dance, I started when I was young. I take classes at Tisch's School of the Arts."

"So you're a dancer?" he asks.

I shake my head. "Not exactly. I take non-major classes to decompress from the stress of my schedule. I'm in my final year of Law School at NYU."

"Oh okay, so you're a dancing, soon-to-be lawyer?"

"Something like that," I say, casually.

"One of my friends is also in his last year of law school at NYU. I wonder if you know him?"

"It's a big school but you never know. What's his name?" I ask.

"Levi Friedman."

My face lights up. "That's so funny, yes, I know Levi. He's in my Stats and Data Analysis class. Great guy."

Miles nods.

"Levi and I've been friends since I moved to New York. We grew up down the street from each other."

"That's so random. I didn't think 'small world' ever happened in a city as huge as this one," I say.

"You'd be surprised." Miles scratches his scruff in thought. "You say that like you're not from around here."

I shake my head. "I'm from a small town in Indiana."

"Indiana? That's something I don't hear very often. Or ever." His bluntness makes me laugh. There's something unnerving about his eyes and I look away.

"I can't imagine you do."

"You're a long way from home. How'd you end up in the city?" he asks.

"I get that question a lot. It's a long, and honestly, not a very interesting story," I say, trying to avoid getting into it.

He takes a sip from his bottle of beer. "I've got time. Try me."

I take a beat, reading his expression. I search for one of the many versions I've told before, none of which are the real reason.

"Growing up I was obsessed with New York City. My bedroom walls were plastered with pictures of the skyline. There was always something so mysterious about it. I don't know why, but I've been drawn to this city ever since I can remember. Living here is a dream come true," I say, suddenly cringing inside.

Ew, gross—dream come true? Why did I just say that? I've never told that story to anyone. Since when do I talk about my dreams with a total stranger? Not even Mikayla knows about those posters. The mere mention of home makes my throat feel tight.

"Where are you from?" I quickly ask, before he has a chance to jump in with more questions.

"I was born in Los Angeles, but my parents divorced when I was young. My mom, brother and I moved to Brooklyn when I was six. I've lived here long enough that I consider myself a New Yorker, but I miss LA. I'll always love it out there," he says.

Mikayla and Nina hop back into our conversation and I'm thankful for the interruption.

"How did you and Mikayla meet?" Nina asks. I glance over at Mikayla.

"Do you want to tell the story or should I?" she asks.

"You go ahead, you tell it better," I reply, needing a second to wrestle with my sudden willingness to share details from my childhood with someone I've just met. *Something I've never done before.*

"About three years ago I was home visiting my parents for the weekend. My dad and I were walking in the park when a cyclist swerved and crashed into Gemma. He picked up his bike and sped off; not even stopping to see if she was okay. She couldn't put pressure on her ankle, so we helped carry her to a bench. She told us she'd just moved here and was on her very first run in Central Park."

"Welcome to New York," Nina says, making us all laugh.

"We felt so bad for her that we ended up walking her back to our house so I could bandage her ankle and my mom asked her to stay for dinner," she says.

"Seriously? Two New Yorkers meet a stranger in the park, invite them back to their house and then ask them to stay for dinner?" Nina asks, as Mikayla and I nod.

"My parents and I fell in love with her, and we've been close friends ever since," she says, squeezing me around the waist.

"File that under things that never happen in New York," Miles says.

"You know, I have to say, New Yorkers get such an undeserved bad rap. Except for the cyclist, everyone in this city has been so generous and kind. I wasn't expecting that when I moved here. It's been a nice surprise," I admit.

"When it comes down to it, we're good people at heart," Miles says, with a warm smile.

"From my experience, that seems to be the case." I nervously tuck my fake hair behind my ear and look at Mikayla to distract myself from him and his Hollywood teeth. *What is with me right now? Wasn't I just reminding Mikayla of rule number three?*

"It's getting chilly out here, let's head back inside," Mikayla says, shooting me a questioning glance before walking inside. I follow closely behind, wondering what she just meant by that look. It suddenly feels like a good idea to put a little space between Mr. Kent and me.

SIX

GEM & EM

The hospital lights are so bright, you'd never know it was the middle of night. The hallway glows a dingy-yellow as Grandma ushers Emmeline and I into a room with several rows of chairs and a big TV mounted in the corner. Except for a sleeping man propped in the corner, there's nobody here. It looks like he's been here a long time.

Emmeline and I keep looking to Grandma for any kind of sign. It's scary not knowing what's happening. She's putting on a brave face for us, but it's obvious she's in a lot of pain too, and there's no one to comfort her. I turn away, giving her a moment to her thoughts.

The knot in my stomach keeps getting bigger by the second. I just want to know if Mom's okay. *She has to be.* I reach over and hold Em's hand. She looks back, fear in her eyes. She blinks and a gush of tears spill over the edge of her lower lids, leaving tiny puddles on her green corduroys. She wipes them away with her sleeve, but the dam has broken, and they fall in a steady stream.

"Mom's going to be alright," I say, wanting with all my heart to believe my own words, but I've had a sinking feeling I haven't been able to shake since Grandma woke us up. A woman in a matching blue outfit comes out from behind two swinging doors.

"Is the family of Willow Ellsworth here?"

It's strange hearing Mom's name announced so formally. Grandma jumps up and we follow her.

"Yes, I'm her mother and these are her two daughters," she says, her voice cracking at the mention of Emmeline and me. Every muscle in my body tenses as the woman looks down at us. She smiles tightly and then asks Grandma to follow her, motioning to a room down the hall.

"Girls, go sit down. I'll be right back," she manages, before turning away.

Emmeline and I want to go with her, but we do as we're told and go sit quietly in our seats.

"What do you think she's going to tell her?" Emmeline whispers.

"I don't know. We have to think really hard that the doctors can fix whatever needs fixing," I say, reaching over and grabbing her hands. Her chin starts to quiver as she squeezes my hands.

"Mom can always hear us—you know she can. Even when we don't want her to, she always hears. Right now, we just have to keep talking to her and telling her to get better," I say.

"Okay."

I've never seen her look this sad before. *She looks like she might break in half.*

"If you could make one wish, what would it be?" I ask.

"I don't want to play that game."

"Come on, it might make you feel better."

She gives me a look that says she's not convinced, but being the good sport she always is—she plays along.

"Anything?" she says with a sniffle.

"Yep, anything."

"That's easy."

"What is it?"

"I wish we weren't here right now," she says, as her eyes well up. "How about you?"

"That's my wish too," I say, softly.

Emmeline can't hold it in one more second, she bursts into tears. I put my arm around her and our cries eventually give way to sobs, filling the entire room with sadness. The sound wakes the sleeping man who stirs, looks over at us, and then falls right back to sleep. *Crying must be common around here.*

It seems like an eternity before Grandma reappears down the hallway. I hold my breath as Emmeline and I jump off our chairs and run to her. She bends down and scoops us both into a giant hug. *Grandma usually gives the best hugs, but tonight her arms feel like bad news.* My heart pounds and I hold on to her as tightly as I can.

"Grandma, is Mom okay?" I ask.

I can tell by the pained look on her face something's really wrong. She pauses and then rests her hands on both of our shoulders and whispers, "The doctors are taking good care of your mom," she says, squeezing her eyes tight as if that might make her tears go away. Grandma's mouth is forming words but it's hard to hear them because the buzzing in my ears is too loud. I can tell she's trying to hold in her cries, but the inside cries are much scarier than the loud ones. The three of us stand holding on to each other, as if Mom's life depends on it.

"Grandma, what if. . . will she. . ." I can't even get the words out. I'm crying so hard my chest burns. Em and my tears soak the back of her jacket.

"Girls, your mom is strong, she always has been." Grandma blots her eyes. "She'll fight hard for the two of you. For all of us." She clears her throat.

"She'll be okay, though, right? The doctors will be able to make her better, won't they?" I ask.

Grandma's eyes fill with more tears, and she pulls me to her.

"The doctors are doing everything they can right now. She said these next twenty-four hours are important, so keep talking to your mom. Let her know how much you love her and want her to get better. She can hear you. You have to believe that."

"Okay," Emmeline manages through her sniffles.

"We will, Grandma," I say, reaching for Em's tear soaked hand.

SEVEN

GEMMA

Mikayla and I huddle inside our foyer trying our best to quietly say goodbye to our last guests so we don't wake the neighbors. The party was so much fun, I'm honestly a little sad it's over. Everyone said as they were leaving, tonight was the best party they'd been to in a long time.

It's time to call it a night. The only thing I'm looking forward to right now is taking off this wig and sleep. We close and lock the door behind us and head into the kitchen where Nina and Miles are cleaning up.

"Thank you, but cleanup is going to have to wait until tomorrow. It's way too late," Mikayla says.

"It was great finally meeting you both. But now it's time for Black Widow to put herself to bed," I say.

"I'm right behind you," Mikayla says, through a long, drawn-out yawn.

"Tonight was a blast. Thanks again," Nina says.

"It was nice meeting you too, Gemma," Miles says. My stomach tightens hearing him say my name, and I tell myself it's just hunger. As I'm heading for the stairs, I overhear Miles telling Nina to take the spare bedroom, he's going to crash on the couch.

"There are blankets and spare pillows in the closet." I motion towards the front door.

"Got it, thanks," he says, waving goodnight. I smile at him and then turn and hurry up the stairs. Mikayla follows me into my room, closing the door behind us.

"What did you think?" she says.

"I think it's four a.m. and we need to go to bed."

"We will, but first you have to tell me," she insists.

"Tell you what?"

"Oh come on. You know what," she hisses.

"Oh. . . you mean, if there wasn't a rule number three—what did I think of Miles?" I ask coyly.

She nods, impatiently. "Of course that's what I mean."

"He seems like a really nice person and yes, I happened to notice how ridiculously handsome he is."

"Mm-hmm. Don't say I didn't warn you," she says, batting her eyelashes.

"Goodnight," I say, prodding her gently toward my door.

"Sweet dreams." She winks before lowering her eyes to the floor below us.

"Staaahhhhp." I lean in and give her a hug before she opens the door and takes the stairs to her room.

It takes what feels like an eternity to pull out all my bobby pins, freeing my scalp at last from my synthetic mane. I'm lightheaded from all the social interaction, and I walk over to my bed, falling face first onto my pillow. I close my eyes and drift off quickly before any thoughts of the guy sleeping just one floor below me have a chance to creep in and keep me up.

RAZOR GRASS SLASHES my arms and I push it out of my way to clear a path. Something's chasing me. Every step I take, my feet sink further into the soggy earth. It takes all of my strength to pull them from the muddy suction cups. Pointy tree roots poke out from the ground and slither after me like snakes hunting prey. I scream but no sound will come out. A cyclone of hissing vultures swirls above my head waiting to pounce while thick, twisting vines leap from the ground. Their thorny ropes wind around my ankles, biting into my flesh as they tighten their grip. I trip and fall to the ground as the earth opens and I plummet into the murky abyss. Echoes of my cries slice through the night like a guillotine, as my lungs fill with fire.

THE SOUND of chirping birds outside my window wakes me up. I try pulling the pillow over my head, but it's no use. I grab my phone and text Mikayla to see if she's awake.

Four hours of sleep is going to have to do it for me today. I crawl out of bed and pull on a pair of running tights and my favorite sweatshirt. When I get downstairs, I find Miles in our now spotless kitchen.

"Are you kidding me right now? Thank you so much," I say, as he leans against our island, smiling.

"It's the least I could do. I'm kinda hoping this might snag me an invite for next year."

I shrug, giving him a smirk. "The party committee will have to vote on it, but I'll be sure to put in a good word."

"So kind of you, thanks." A smile creeps across his face.

I feel his eyes on me as I turn to get coffee mugs from the cabinet.

"Your hair. It's not red," he says.

"Ha, no. The real Black Widow wanted it back."

"It's so long... and blonde—it's... nice."

"Um... thanks?" I say, feeling myself blush. Now it's awkward. Or at least—I'm awkward. I turn my back to him as I walk to our coffee maker.

"Would you like some coffee?" I ask, pulling it together.

"That'd be great, thanks."

Nina and Mikayla join us in the kitchen as the coffee brews.

"Wait a minute, did the cleaning fairy come last night?" Mikayla asks.

I point to Miles, who just shrugs.

"You're the best. Thank you. I was dreading clean-up," she says.

The four of us sit around our dining table, recounting all the costumes from last night.

"Hey, did anyone hear those screams last night?" Miles asks.

Mikayla slowly looks over to me and I try my best to act normal. *Oh no. My heart sinks. It happened again.*

"Nope, I didn't hear anything," Mikayla says.

"Me neither," I add.

"I bet you it was one of our neighbors, we've heard them a few times before," she adds.

"It sounded like it was right above me, but I guess it could've been coming from next door. It woke me out of a dead sleep. I got up to check out where it was coming from but just as I got off the couch, it stopped," he says.

"I didn't hear anything, but I was all the way up on the fourth floor," Nina adds.

"Maybe our neighbor was paying us back for the noise from the party. Is anyone hungry by the way? There's a cute brunch place a few blocks away," she says.

I shoot Mikayla a look of thanks.

"I need food," Nina says.

"Me too," I add.

Nina and I walk behind Miles and Mikayla until Hokusai's The Great Wave mural, painted on the side of our brunch spot, comes into view. We're all thrilled there's no line.

"The only good thing about those birds and their early wake up call — there's no wait," Mikayla says, holding the door open.

The four of us grab a booth in the back and I listen as the three resident doctors share stories from their respective hospitals. I can't remember the last time I've laughed this hard. It's obvious they've managed to remain close since medical school. It's not surprising Mikayla would surround herself with kind, super-bright overachievers who aren't boastful in the least.

After brunch, Mikayla and I walk them to the closest subway station so they can catch their trains. Nina, Miles and I exchange Instagrams before saying goodbye. Mikayla and I walk back to our house and spend the next few hours taking down the party decorations, bringing our house back from the dead.

"By the way, I owe you for covering for me and my early morning screams. So embarrassing." I squeeze my eyes shut, shaking my head.

"I didn't hear you, but as soon as he said it, I knew. What were you dreaming about this time?" she asks.

"Oh, I don't know—the usual," I say, folding a giant skeleton in half.

"Do you think there could be a reason for your nightmares?"

"Not that I can think of. They're just your typical bad dreams."

She looks at me quietly nodding, before turning and carrying a box of tombstones down to the basement. *She knows there's something more to this.*

EIGHT

GEM & EM

I lean over and rest my head firmly on Emmeline's pillow, trying to wake her without it seeming like I'm trying to wake her. She rolls over, groggily rubbing her eyes. A confused look crosses her face. "I forgot where I was for a second."

"I did the same thing when I woke up." I reach over, brushing the hair out of her eyes.

"We should push our beds together when we get back home. I like not having to walk all the way over to your bed," I say.

"Do you think Mom's okay?" she asks.

"I hope so. I'm scared, Em."

She looks at me, terror in her eyes. "I am too. But. . .she. . . she'll be alright, won't she?"

I nod slowly, feeling uneasy. "I think so."

"Do you think we'll get to see her today?" she asks, sitting up.

"Grandma told me kids aren't allowed because of all the machines. That's why she couldn't take us with her yesterday," I say.

She bends her head down folding her hands in her lap.

"Are you hungry?" I ask.

"A little. You?"

"Yeah. Let's go downstairs and see Grandma."

We hop down from our bed and run down the hall. It feels funny taking the stairs; we don't have them at our house. The railing is smooth and cool beneath my hand as it guides me to the last step.

"Hi, Grandma," we call out when our feet touch the landing. We follow her humming to the kitchen where we find her in front of the stove, wearing an apron, a spatula in her hand.

"Good morning, sleepyheads. Are you hungry?"

She looks tired but her smile is warm. Her smile has a way of making me feel better no matter what kind of day I'm having.

"Starving," Em says, pulling herself onto a chair.

"Chocolate chip pancakes are on the menu today. I made some special shapes; do you want you to guess what they are?"

"Yes, don't tell us!" we say.

Grandma puts a finger to her lips. "I wouldn't think of it."

She sets the syrup between our plates and takes a seat next to Em.

"Mine's a flower," Em says.

"I have a sun. I'm Mom's sun," I say, looking to Grandma.

"That's right. Your flower was supposed to be a moon, Emmeline, but my hand slipped so I made petals instead. There's more if you're still hungry after these."

"Thanks, Grandma," I say, pouring my syrup.

"While you were sleeping, the doctor called with an update on your mom."

I hold my breath as I wait for her to continue.

"She woke up and is talking," she says, tears forming in the corners of her eyes.

"That's great news, right?" I ask.

"Mom's getting better!" Emmeline shouts.

I watch her response closely. *There's something she's not saying.*

"Will we be able to see her today?" I ask.

Grandma shakes her head. "Not yet."

Our hearts and hopes fall in unison.

"The doctors want her to rest. She gets tired easily, but you'll be able to see her soon."

"It's been five days, we've never gone this long without seeing her," Emmeline says quietly.

I take my fork and run it through the small pool of syrup left on my empty plate.

"She misses you just as much as you miss her. Why don't you go upstairs and get a brush? I'll braid your hair for school. We have to leave here in about twenty minutes."

We jump down and race each other up to our room. I dig out our brush from our suitcase, and Emmeline unzips the front pocket, fishing out purple hair ties for our braids.

"Mom's favorite color, maybe it will bring her good luck if we wear them," she says, handing me two

"I hope so."

We turn to walk downstairs, and I put my hands on Emmeline's shoulders giving them a squeeze.

"If you could make one wish, what would it be?" I ask.

"Anything?"

"Yep, anything," I say, our feet moving in tandem as we tread down the darkened hallway.

"That's easy."

"What is it?"

"I wish we could see Mom today. How about you?"

"I wish none of this had ever happened and we were at home right now," she says, her shoulders sagging.

I nod sadly, commiserating with her heavy heart. "I love you, Em."

She turns around, managing a thin smile.

"Love you right back."

NINE

GEMMA

I rub my temples and shake my hand before handing my exam to my professor. Needing a respite from the last three hours of intense focus, I walk to Washington Square Park and find an open bench. I sit down to mindlessly scroll Instagram and catch up on emails. Sitting in my inbox is a message from Miles, sent yesterday. Seeing his name in my DMs sends a flutter of excitement through me, yet at the same time, floods me with anxiety.

Hey Gemma! I had a great time Saturday. It was nice to meet you.

That's nice. *Keep it friendly.*

We're glad you could join us. It was nice meeting you too.

He must be scrolling too, because he messages me right back:

I'm coming into the city Saturday for opening night of my friend's Broadway show. Any chance you and Mikayla want to join me?

I read his message again. My heart does a somersault and doesn't know which way to turn. I can't get distracted with someone right now. Nothing can get in the way of staying focused on school and my future.

That sounds fun, thank you. I'll talk to her and get back to you.

A visual of him standing in our backyard in his suspenders pops into my head and I shoo it away, reminding myself of the three rules.

Needing to distract my mind from Miles and his perfect smile, I tap Grandma's smiling face from the short list of favorites on my screen. She picks up on the third ring.

"Hi, my love, I was just going outside to shovel. It's snowing like crazy here. How'd your test go?"

"Pretty well. I'm glad it's over. It's snowing already? That's early, even by Indiana standards. You're not shoveling your driveway by yourself, are you?" I ask.

"Of course I am. I've got to stay in shape somehow."

I shake my head, feeling anxious. "Please be careful. There must be someone in your neighborhood who can help you."

"I'm fine, Gemma, it gives me something to do. These winter nights can get awfully boring. Before I head outside, what's on your Christmas list this year? You know I like to get my shopping done early."

Right—I forgot that's right around the corner. "I haven't even thought about it. You don't have to get me anything, Grandma."

"Hush now, I love putting your presents under the tree," she says.

"Well now that you mention it, do you think you'd have time to knit me another blanket? The one you made me when I graduated high school is worn in spots. I sleep with it every night and I'm afraid it's going to tear."

"That makes me happy. I was just thinking I needed a new project. It will give me a reason to go buy some new yarn."

"Thanks, Grandma."

"I'd love to talk but I better run. The snow is piling up fast and I want to clear it before it gets too heavy."

I bite my lower lip. "Please be careful—you make me a nervous wreck. I love you."

"You worry too much. I'll be fine. I love you too. Bye-bye, my Gem."

"Bye."

The sound of her voice instantly transports me back to her kitchen table instead of a cold park bench hundreds of miles away.

My thoughts are filled with home as I walk down the subway stairs for my ride uptown.

"Hey, stranger! How was your day?" I ask, as I walk in the door.

Snuggled on the couch under a blanket from her chin to her toes, sits Mikayla. In between bites of Twizzlers, she lets out a long, exasperated sigh.

"That good, huh? I know it's bad when you're eating junk food."

She leans back, pulling the blanket tighter. "I've never been happier to be home. I'm not moving from this couch. Maybe ever."

"Well then, I'll help keep you company. Move over," I say, taking a seat next to her. "Hey, one of your Columbia friends reached out to me."

"Really?" she replies, raising her eyebrows. "What did Miles have to say?"

I narrow my eyes. "I never said it was Miles. It could have been any of them."

"You're not serious, are you? Please. Miles couldn't take his eyes off you at our party, and at brunch too."

"That's not true," I say, shaking my head.

"Gemma. Come on. Before I introduced you, when you were dancing on the island—he asked me who Black Widow was." My pulse quickens at the thought of him asking about me.

"Really? I honestly didn't pick up anything from him."

She slides her glasses down her nose and gives me a look over her bold, tortoiseshell frames.

I push my shoulder into her. "What? It's true!"

"Okay, you see what you want to see, and I'll just sit over here not acting surprised when he asks you out," she says, rolling her eyes.

"You're right about a lot of things, but not this time. He's a nice guy, there's nothing more to it. Speaking of going out, what are you doing Saturday night?" I ask.

"I'm working. My turn to take the long shift. Why?"

"Because Miles invited us to opening night for his friend's Broadway show."

"That's this weekend? I used to date his friend, he's the director. This show has the entire city buzzing," she says.

"You did? Then you have to come with me. You know I've never been to a Broadway show, right?" I ask.

"That's right! Which is so wrong. You have to go, you'll love it."

I pause, unsure about going without her. "Is there any chance your schedule might change?" I ask.

"No. I switched weekends with a colleague. Let's be real though. He said 'we' but he 100% meant *you*. You should absolutely go."

'Hmm, I'll think about it," I say in my non-committal voice.

"Gem, seriously. Go. You'll regret it if you miss this show. Especially opening night. There are a million New Yorkers who would give anything to be in your shoes. Getting tickets is nearly impossible."

"Like I said—I'll think about it." She glares at me.

"It's a firm maybe," I say, glibly.

She laughs and starts to say something, but instead bends forward, grabbing her throat.

"Are you okay?" I ask. "These dramatics aren't going to convince me to go, you know."

The bag of licorice falls to the floor and she scoots to the edge of the couch not saying anything. Her other hand flies up to her throat and she holds her neck, her eyes wide with terror.

"What's wrong?" She closes her eyes as the color starts to drain from her face. "Oh my God, are you choking?" I shout, the gravity of the situation hitting me all at once.

Ice runs through my veins. "Oh no, oh no, no. NO!" This can't be happening. I feel like I'm going to be sick. She grabs my arm, snapping me out of my trance and I thump her several times on the back but nothing happens.

"Breathe, come on, please breathe! Mikayla, you have to breathe!" My adrenaline surges as I whisper the word no over and over. She slumps forward as the blanket falls to the floor. I jump up, pulling her with me while I move in behind her. I wrack my brain, desperately trying to remember the CPR class we took last year when she had to renew her certification.

"Mika, breathe!" I beg. I feel for her ribcage and ball my fist just below, thrusting as hard as I can into her abdomen three times before she finally coughs and throws up. My legs go weak at the sound. I break out in a cold sweat and my knees buckle, dropping me to the floor. I rock back and forth as tears fall down my face. She wipes her mouth and sits beside me, on the floor. I can't tell if the look on her face is from her near-death experience or my reaction. Maybe both.

"That was scary," she says, clearing her throat. "I'm okay though."

I grab her water from the side table and hand it to her. "That scared the shit out of me! I thought you were going to die," I say between sobs. She rubs my back while I lean against her, listening to her breath, making sure it's still there.

"That'll teach me to eat junk food again," she scoffs, trying to lighten the mood.

"It's not funny," I say, sniffling. Completely wrung out, I wipe my eyes with my sleeve. "What if I hadn't been here?"

She puts her arm around my shoulder and squeezes me to her. "You were here, and that's all that matters. You did great. You remembered everything from our class—I'm impressed. You saved my life."

I shake my head, fighting my growing nausea. "Don't ever do that again."

"What—eat licorice?"

I make a face. "You know what I mean. How are you so calm right now? You almost just died," I say, shocked by her cheery demeanor.

"Gem, I didn't almost just die. I knew you'd save me," she says, walking to the kitchen for a towel.

But I couldn't save *her*.

Triggered and unsettled, I let out a heavy sigh and rest my head in my hands. My mind floods with flashbacks of that tragic night, painfully reminding me how helpless I felt. Before Mikayla gets back from the kitchen, I run upstairs to go cry my eyes out in the shower.

This is what happens when I let someone get too close.

TEN

GEM & EM

"Gemma, get off of meeeeeeeeee!" Emmeline squeals as I climb over her in the back seat of Grandma's car. We both fasten our seatbelts before she even has to tell us.

"Let's go see Mom!" I shout, unable to contain my excitement.

"I can't believe we finally get to see her," Emmeline says, holding onto the get-well card she drew last night.

Grandma said the reason Mom had to stay in the hospital so long was because there was swelling in her head. She also fractured a few ribs and broke her leg. The doctor said Mom was lucky, but it doesn't sound like the lucky I know.

The summer sun feels warm on my face, and I roll my window down, letting in a cool breeze. *I get to hug Mom today.* My heart beats faster at the thought of seeing her. This morning Emmeline and I picked some flowers from the field behind Grandma's house. We picked as many purple ones as we could find.

I reach over and squeeze Emmeline's arm as Grandma pulls into the hospital parking lot. The hospital looks a little less scary during the daytime. We jump out and Grandma takes both of our hands, leading us through a wall of glass doors.

I wrinkle my nose. "It smells like band aids in here," I whisper to Emmeline behind Grandma's back.

Our worn-out soles squeak against the glossy floors. I've decided that everything in here looks way too bright for all the gloomy faces. I sneak a few peeks from behind Grandma's arm, but it feels like I shouldn't be looking. When someone looks down at me, I quickly turn my eyes back to the floor. We pass through several sets of swinging doors until Grandma finally points to Mom's room three doors down on the right. Just the sight of her room makes my arms and legs tingle. Grandma pauses, pulling us over to the side of the empty hallway and bends down so we are eye-level with her.

"The doctor said we can only stay for a half hour, and we need to use our whisper voices because your mom could get a headache. If she gets sleepy, we'll have to leave so she can rest."

We nod our heads, promising our best behavior. A door opens and I look toward her room as a woman in a fancy yellow plaid suit walks out. She looks down and smiles as she passes Em and me, dabbing the corners of her eyes. *I don't like hospitals, they're filled with sad people.* She whispers hello to Grandma and then passes by quickly, clicking her heels all the way down the desolate hallway.

When we get to Mom's door Em and I stand on our toes trying to peer through the rectangular window. It's dark inside.

"I don't want to wake her if she's sleeping," Grandma whispers, peering through the window above our heads. She gently turns the knob and the three of us tiptoe into her room.

I freeze when I see Mom. She's surrounded by lots of beeping equipment; the digital numbers glow in the dark like tiny white nightlights. Mom's in her bed, slightly reclined, dressed in a blue and white diamond hospital gown. Her cast sticks out from beneath the covers, elevated by a stack of blankets near the foot of her bed. As my eyes adjust, I can see she's been crying.

"Mom?" Emmeline and I whisper hesitantly. She startles at the sound of our voices.

"My babies. Come here so I can hug you," she cries out, pain in her voice. "I've missed you so much."

"We missed you too," we say, trying our best to remember our whisper voices. *We don't want to give Mom a headache.*

Wanting to be as close to her as possible, we rush to her side. Dark bruises cover her face and arms, making my stomach turn. I stare at a tube that's taped to the back of her hand. She has wires hooked up to every bit of her.

I'm afraid to touch her.

Mom must sense our hesitation because she holds out her arms grabbing Emmeline's free hand and then mine.

I touch her soft, pale skin. I want to hold on to her and never let go. Seeing her makes me realize just how much I've missed her and despite having to look at her bruises, something in me feels whole again. Grandma leans over, giving Mom a kiss on top of her head.

"My brave and strong girl," Grandma says as Mom takes Grandma's hand and presses it gently against her cheek. Emmeline and I put our cards and flowers on her side table and then lay our heads down on each side of her bed. Mom's been here so long she smells like the hospital—not like our mom. I want our old Mom back. The one that smells like lavender and sits on our beds in her purple robe and fuzzy slippers. She runs her fingers through our hair and it's like we're back in our room, and all of this was just a bad dream.

"Tell your mom about the game we play every night at dinner," Grandma says, taking a seat in a chair by the window.

Emmeline and I perk up. "When we're sad and missing you, Grandma taught us a game that makes us remember the little things about you so it's like pieces of you are with us," I say.

"She did, did she?" Mom smiles over at Grandma.

Emmeline and I carefully crawl up on the bed beside Mom, trying our best to contain our excitement at getting to be this close to her. I make sure not to get too close to her sides where her ribs are broken.

"We call it the mom game," Emmeline whispers.

"Can we play it now?" I ask.

Mom nods ever so slightly. "Of course, my little loves."

My heart leaps. It's been so long since I've heard her call us that.

"Mom loves planting in her garden," Em begins.

"Mom's favorite blanket is the yellow one Grandma made for her."

"Grandma, it's your turn," Em and I say.

"Your mom loves reading to you."

"Mom loves rainy days but only from the inside," Em says, as we all laugh quietly in agreement.

"Mom doesn't like getting sand between her toes," I say, as Mom wrinkles her nose.

"Mom loves it when we brush her hair."

"Mom doesn't like tomatoes or green peppers." Mom shakes her head, scrunching her face.

"Mom's favorite necklace is her locket with our initials on it. E,G,F—Emmeline and Gemma Forever," Em says.

"That's true. I never take it off," she says, wearily. "I asked the nurse to put it back on after my surgery." Her fingers delicately trace the gold heart-shaped locket dangling from her neck.

"Are you tired, my sweet girl?" Grandma asks.

Mom insists she's not, but all of a sudden, she looks worn out.

"We should let you get some rest, Willow. I saw you had a visitor before us."

Mom and Grandma exchange a look, but I'm not sure what it means. *Usually I can tell.*

Emmeline and I gently slide off Mom's bed and stand next to her, not wanting to leave her side. Grandma joins us at her bedside and the three of us take turns kissing her goodbye.

Mom rests her head back on her pillow, her voice sounds tired. "You and your smiles made me feel so much better. Today is the first day I've felt like myself."

"Feel better, Mom," we both say.

"You get some rest, darling, and soon we can take you home with us," Grandma says.

Mom nods, her eyelids suddenly heavy. She reaches out for Grandma's hand and whispers to her.

"Thank you, Mom. For everything."

ELEVEN

GEMMA

"It's open," I say, as Mikayla gently knocks and pushes my door the rest of the way open. She sits on the edge of my bed, scanning my face.

"I wanted to make sure you're okay."

"Isn't this reversed? Shouldn't I be the one checking on you? You were, after all, the one who stopped breathing."

"Yes, but I'm fine. Look," she says, sweeping her arms up and to the side. "You were so upset..."

"I wasn't just upset Mika, that was terrifying. I thought I was going to lose you," I say, choking on my words.

"But you didn't. I'm okay and I'm not going anywhere. Gem, I know that was a frightening situation, but thankfully, most of the time things like that end up fine rather than in tragedy." She leans back on her hands, gauging my reaction.

"I can't tell you how many random accidents I've witnessed. Trust me when I say that for the most part, people usually walk away from them. Not every serious situation ends in catastrophe. You know that, right?"

I shrug, looking at her dismally. "It seems like it happens more often than not. I worry it's more frequent than you're admitting."

"Well, I can confirm it's not. By the way, it's been clinically proven that worrying has zero effect on an outcome, the only thing it does is cause undue stress."

I shake my head defiantly. "Not for me. I've learned if I worry about something it's less likely to happen. It's how I safeguard everyone in my life from danger. You're welcome," I say, smartly.

She rolls her eyes. "I hate to be the one to point out a flaw in your logic, but it looks like you should've been worrying about me choking on Twizzlers."

"Yeah, I missed that one. Sorry," I quip. "Listen, I just have this terrible fear of being blindsided. I'd rather worry about something and have it never happen, than never worry about something and have disaster strike."

"You're hopeless, you know that?"

I tilt my head and shrug. "Maybe. I don't know."

"Worry or not, there are two certainties in life. One, life is short and two, second chances aren't always promised. My choking incident downstairs is a perfect example of why we need to be out there living our best lives."

"Wait—you just said things usually don't end up in traged. . ."

"This isn't court." She smiles and nudges me with her foot. "Listen, we need to make the most of every day, especially while we're young. And for you—making the most of this weekend means going to see your first Broadway show. And not only any Broadway show, *this* Broadway show."

I lean back on my pillows and sigh. "Not this again. You know that's how this whole thing started, right?"

She shakes her head. "Me choking had nothing to do with our conversation."

"I'm pretty sure it was a sign," I say, crossing my arms.

"Listen, it's your decision. But why not just go as friends? You'd be crazy to turn down an opportunity to see this show. Plus, Miles told me at our party that he just got out of a serious relationship a few months ago and things did not end well," she says, her eyes widening.

"What happened?" I ask.

"Too much drama to go into, but trust me, it wasn't pretty." She shudders. "For all we know, getting into another relationship might be the last thing on his mind. There *is* a good chance he just doesn't want to go alone."

"Is that what you really think, or are you just saying that so I'll agree to go?" I ask.

"There's only one way to find out."

AFTER FINISHING my homework I sit thinking about what Mikayla said. She's right. I'm young, I'm living in this incredible city with so many amazing experiences at my fingertips. It feels like a waste not to take advantage of Miles's offer. I am well aware that not everyone gets a second chance. And—it's not like I have anything else planned.

I gather the courage and DM him:

Mikayla's working, but I would love to see the show. Please let me know how much I owe you for the ticket.

Send.

My stomach flips as soon as I hit that little blue word. *I hope I don't regret this.*

TWELVE

GEM & EM

"Girls, can you get the door?" Grandma shouts from the laundry room when the doorbell rings for the second time. We race down the stairs and open the front door to find a man standing there, a tinfoil wrapped dish in his hands. A surprised look spreads across his long and mustached face.

"Well—whoa, hello there. You two must be Gemma and Emmeline," he says, clenching his jaw. "Is your grandma here?"

"She's upstairs," I reply.

"Can you please tell her Evan's here to see her?"

"I'll go get her," Emmeline offers, running upstairs. He shuffles back and forth on his feet, looking at the sky to pass the moments of our uncomfortable silence. *It looks like he's trying to remember how to stand.*

"You two look so much like your dad," he finally says, softly.

"We do?"

He nods slowly, sadness moving into his eyes. *Mom gets that same look when she talks about our dad.*

"You knew him?" I ask, locking my arms behind my back. I quickly look away when he catches me staring at the melted, lumpy red scars on the side of his face and neck.

"I did. He was, err. . .he was—my best friend," he says, drawing his lips in a tight line.

"What was he like?"

"Your dad? Oh, gosh. Harrison... well, he was a good man. Funny and kind. He was always the smartest person in every room. He dreamed of being a lawyer one day. No doubt he'd have made a great one."

"Evan? My goodness, it's been years," Grandma says, rushing up behind me, a look of concern on her face.

"Hi, Mrs. Ellsworth," he says, tapping his foot on our doormat. "I know... it's been—well quite a while I guess."

"It's good to see you."

"You too," he says, lifting the dish slightly in his hands. "Ivy made you and the girls some of her home-made macaroni and cheese."

"That was so kind of her. Please—come inside," she says, opening the door further. "Girls, why don't you run upstairs while Mr. Evan and I talk."

"Okay, Grandma. It was nice meeting you," I say, wishing I could stay and hear more about our dad. Emmeline grabs my hand and we run through the kitchen to the stairs. "Let's stay down here. I want to hear what they're talking about," I whisper, as we round the corner.

Em frowns. "Grandma told us to go upstairs."

"We'll just sit on the bottom step. They won't even know we're here," I say, putting a finger to my lips.

"Here, let me take that from you, this is one of the girl's favorite dishes," she says, as the refrigerator door squeaks. "Please, have a seat. Would you like some coffee? It's about time for my second cup."

"No, thank you. I won't take too much of your time." Evan's low voice drifts toward them, as a chair slides across the kitchen floor. "I just wanted to stop by and let you know I'm sorry to hear about Willow's accident. I haven't been able to stop thinking about her. We're all so worried about her—the whole town is."

"It's been a tough couple of weeks, but she's improved considerably, thank goodness. The doctors think she'll be able to come home soon."

"What a relief, that's great news."

"It is." Grandma lets out a long sigh. "It was touch and go for a while there. I haven't slept much since her accident. I close my eyes and all I see is her lying in that hospital bed, fighting for her life."

I look over at Emmeline, elbows on her knees, covering her ears to block out Grandma's words.

"I can't imagine. I'm sorry for the pain you and the girls have been through," he says, his voice almost a whisper. "Ivy and I want to know if there is there anything we can do? Check on her house or take the girls for a few hours to give you a break?"

"That's so nice, Evan. Thank you. Willow's neighbor Paul has been looking after her house for her. He's always so helpful to her and the girls. It's comforting knowing he and his wife live so close to them. I worry about the three of them living so remote from everything. But you know Willow, she's always loved the woods."

The two of them chuckle.

"As far as having the girls, they help to keep my mind off of this whole nightmare," Grandma says.

"Well, if there's anything at all, you have our number. Please don't hesitate."

"Willow and I both appreciate it." Everything goes quiet for a moment. "Is there something else?" Grandma asks.

A long sigh floats out from the kitchen. "There's something that's been on my mind. It's just—this is hard for me to say," he says, clearing his throat.

Grandma's voice goes higher. "What is it? About the accident?"

"No, it's um—not related. It's just that I've been thinking a lot about him lately, what with Willow's accident and all."

"Thinking. . . about who?"

"Harrison." Evan's voice cracks. Dad's name hangs in the air, between the lingering smells of coffee grounds and Grandma's pancakes. "I still feel responsible for his death. Maybe I always will. I've never been able to shake the feeling that I was the reason he didn't leave that night. Willow, the kids—they deserved a life with him."

I look over at Emmeline, knowing my eyes are as wide as hers.

"Evan. . . no. You mustn't think like that. What happened to Harrison wasn't your fault. It wasn't anyone's. That old house had faulty wiring. Everyone knows that's how the fire started," she says reassuringly.

"But he wasn't even supposed to be there," he says, his words tight.

"He was doing me a favor. If I had just called out of work that night instead of having him change his plans—"

"Oh no. . . that's. . ." she says, searching for the right words, "That's far too much guilt for any one person to shoulder. Willow wouldn't want you to feel this way."

There's a long pause. "If only I could've gotten to him in time. I tried, I just. . ." he says, shakily.

"Everyone knows how hard you tried, Evan. You were hospitalized for weeks. You did everything you could to save him, and in the process, almost lost your own life." Grandma croaks.

"I just wish things were different," he admits, pain in his voice.

"What happened that night was a tragic accident, nothing more. Please, you owe it to yourself, to your family, to finally lay down this guilt you've been carrying. I promise when you do, you'll find there's more room for the good things in your life. Like Ivy and those beautiful boys of yours. That's where your energy belongs. Put it towards something good instead of tormenting yourself with the past. You have no control over what is behind you," Grandma says encouragingly.

A chair creaks. *Evan must be sitting in the squeaky chair.* "I know you're right. I've tried. It's just. . . it's hard. I'm sorry for dropping all of that on you, I know you have a lot on your plate right now. Thank you for listening."

"I think it's me who owes you and Ivy a thank you. You've saved me from having to cook dinner tonight and you've been keeping my Willow in your thoughts. She'll be so happy to hear you stopped by."

The carpet is starting to itch my legs, but I can't move. It's like all the words I've just heard have me stuck to the step.

"Well, I've probably outstayed my welcome. Please—give my best to Willow."

"Will do," she says, brightly. "Promise me something, Evan."

"What's that?"

"Promise me you'll think about what I've said. There's no point in holding onto the pain of the past. Trust me, I've been there a time or two myself. It's wasted effort."

"I didn't come here for a pep talk, but I guess it's something I've needed to get off my chest for a long time." The scraping of the chair against the kitchen floor makes me jump.

I squeeze Emmeline's arm and we tiptoe up the stairs as quietly as we can so Grandma won't know we've been listening.

Why do grown-ups hold in all their sad stuff? I hope I don't do that when I'm older.

THIRTEEN

GEMMA

I exit the station onto 42nd St. as the sun dips just below the horizon, painting the streets of Manhattan in a golden glow. Several people are gathered in front of the theater, and I scan the crowd for Miles. My pulse picks up when I see him leaning against a tree staring into his phone. He's wearing a stylish, mid length charcoal overcoat, black jeans and lace-up suede boots. My breath catches and I take a moment to steady myself before walking to him. *Relax, this isn't a date.*

"Hey," I say, surprising him from behind.

He smiles, dimples flashing. *Damn.*

"Hey Gemma!" He pulls me in for a kiss on the cheek and I fluster, returning his kiss with an awkward pat on the back. I'll never get used to this kiss hello thing New Yorkers do. His medium-length chestnut hair falls in wavy layers just below his ears, and those perfect teeth—they're still there.

"You look nice," he says.

"Thanks. No giant S and suspenders tonight?"

He laughs, shaking his head.

"The man of steel had other plans. Want to head inside?"

"Sure." My stomach stirs with excitement. "This is my first Broadway show by the way," I say.

"No way. You've never been to a Broadway show?"

I shake my head.

"Be prepared to have your mind blown."

"I've heard. Mikayla told me that getting tickets is almost impossible." I reach into my bag. "Which reminds me, what do I owe you?"

"Not a thing. I read somewhere it's a New York tradition to treat people from Indiana to their first Broadway show."

The glint in his eye makes my stomach flip, and I glance toward the theater entrance while my internal dialogue loudly reiterates rule number three.

"Ha, I'm not sure what you've been reading, but thank you."

He smiles and shakes his head. "My friend Oliver gave me the tickets. Tonight's a huge night for him. He started writing this musical when I met him," he looks up, counting. "That was ten years ago."

Miles motions for us to get in the fast-moving security line. The usher leads us to our seats, stopping near the front row of the theater. I peer over the half wall surprised to find an orchestra beneath the stage.

"Broadway shows have live music? They play right down there?" I ask, gawking at the musicians and their instruments.

Miles nods, watching me as I study the pit.

We take our seats and my head swivels in every direction, soaking in the plush, red carpets, velvet curtains and sparkling crystal chandeliers that dangle from an ornately carved golden ceiling. *I wish Mom and Grandma could see this.*

"There's so much beauty in one place," I say, my eyes welling up. I sense Miles looking at me and when I turn toward him, he smiles comfortingly, as if sensing my vulnerability.

"So far so good I guess." He winks, making me feel at ease.

The curtain goes up and for the next hour, I sit mesmerized as the moving stage comes to life before my eyes. Miles keeps glancing over at me and my expressions from time to time, but I'm too caught up in the wonder of the moment to worry about what my face is doing.

The curtain drops for intermission and we stand to stretch our legs.

"What do you think?" he asks, a smile on his face.

Flabbergasted, I quickly assemble my swirling thoughts. "Oh my... I don't know where to start," I say, as Miles and I excitedly begin discussing the show. I'm talking a mile a minute when a gorgeous, leggy brunette hastily brushes past me, interrupting us.

"Miles, can I talk to you for a second?" she says curtly, eyeing me up and down.

Oh no, it's not what . . . I'm not—

Miles flusters. "I'll be right back." He follows her to the side of the theater while I sit back down in my seat, heat rising in my cheeks.

That was awkward.

I pick the playbill off the floor and read through the names of the actors, trying not to feel weird about what just happened. When I reach the back page, I rest it on my lap eagerly awaiting the curtain to go back up. The lights flicker as people once again fill their seats.

"Sorry about that," Miles says, quickly ducking into his seat before the curtain rises.

"No worries," I say, unfazed.

Whatever that was, it's none of my business.

The second half of the show is even more spectacular than the first and I try not to blink so I don't miss anything. The curtain falls and then rises one last time for the cast to take their final bow while a thunderous ovation fills the theater.

Miles and I head towards the exit. It feels like I'm floating, strangely suspended between the anguished, yet inspiring musical performances and the here and now. Witnessing the characters pour every ounce of their wounded selves into healing after suffering such tragedy and loss, spoke to something deep inside of me.

Miles looks over at me after we break from the crowd. "You look like you're in your own world right now."

"I feel like I'm in my own world right now. Your friend's production was so raw, heartbreaking and so beautifully profound," I say, adding, "This might sound crazy, but watching Oliver's production and witnessing the struggles his grandparents faced immigrating to this country, feels like one of those life-changing moments."

A proud grin breaks out on Miles's face. "Ollie would be so touched to hear you say that. His family has gone through so much. He really put himself out there sharing his story."

I nod, hovering between the two worlds.

"Do you want to go get a drink and talk about the show?" he asks, "You were so excited earlier—I'd love to hear more of your thoughts, this time without any interruptions." He pushes his hands deep into his pockets.

"Oh... right." I nod and wait for him to expand and when he doesn't, I glance at my watch, stalling. I'm unsure of what saying yes might imply. "I have a full day of studying tomorrow, but one drink couldn't hurt. There's so much to discuss. Do you want to find a place around here?"

Miles chews on his lip as if he's considering something. "This area gets so crowded after all the shows let out. I'd love to find somewhere a little quieter."

That sounds a little too intimate.

I swallow, flooded with a rush of uncertainty. "There's a place closer to my neighborhood that Mikayla told me about. I don't think it's necessarily quiet, but she loves it there. Do you want to go check it out?" I ask.

Miles nods. "Sure. She always knows the best spots."

Relieved to be going somewhere closer to our house, we take an uptown train to 86th St. and walk a few blocks. The exposed brick and velvet bar is quaint and has live jazz. We find a table in the back and order two glasses of pinot noir.

After a few sips of wine my shoulders begin to relax. The conversation flows back and forth with ease. Hearing his unique perspectives and insights about the show makes my Broadway debut even more memorable. I'm caught off guard at how comfortable I feel with him. He's a great listener. So many people just want to hear themselves talk. After discussing the show at length, he tells me about his work at Greenwich Hospital and I share details of my law-school life.

"Moving here must have been a big change for you," he says.

I nod and raise my eyebrows. "Big change is an understatement."

"What was it like growing up in Indiana? Do you come from a big family?"

I flinch at the mention of my family. Ignoring the ball of dread spreading inside of me, I force some normality into my voice and respond with my go-to script.

"No. My father passed away before I was born, and I was raised by my mom and Grandma. I'm an only child."

The words fly out of my mouth and my heart sinks. *I hate myself for how easily that was to say.* The rotting pit festers in my stomach.

"What about you? Do you have a big family?" I ask, changing the topic.

He shakes his head. "I have a brother who's two years younger than me. Amos moved out to Los Angeles recently for work and lives near our dad. With medical school and now my residency, I don't see him as often as I'd like, but we get together a few times a year. My mom lives in Brooklyn."

"That's right, I remember you saying the three of you moved here when you were young. It must be nice having her close by." I slowly trace the top of my glass with my fingertip.

"The best. She got into real estate when we moved here and ended up starting her own business. It's grown so fast and with my insane hours, we don't see each other as much as I'd like. I'm proud of her and how hard she's worked to get where she is."

I nod, feeling a pang of something inside at the soft tone he uses when he talks about his mom. "Good for her for going for it. Especially as a single mom with two small boys. That couldn't have been easy."

"You know first-hand how strong and hardworking single moms are," he says, as I nod in agreement.

"I have so much respect for my mom. My grandma, too. I miss them so much, I wish they lived closer," I say. "How about your dad? Do you see him often?"

He pauses a few seconds, taking a sip of wine.

"Not lately. My dad and I, um, we aren't on speaking terms right now," he says, glancing out the window. "Family—well, it can be difficult sometimes."

Everybody has their stuff Gemma, it's not just you.

Sensing he doesn't want to talk about it, I look down at my watch.

"How is it already twelve-thirty a.m.?" I ask, shocked at how much time has passed. "We've been sitting at this table for two hours and never even ordered a second round."

"Let's get out of here before they throw us out." He laughs and motions that we'd like to pay our check.

"Drinks are on me," I say, handing my credit card to the waiter.

"You don't have to. . ."

"I read somewhere it's an Indiana tradition to pay the bill after a New Yorker treats them to their first Broadway show."

"Touché." He smiles a wide and gorgeous grin and my traitor of a stomach tenses.

"The people standing behind you are waiting for this table." I motion behind him as we get up. "Are you meeting up with Oliver and the cast to celebrate their big night?"

"I told him I'd meet up with them at some point since I'm staying at his place tonight." He pauses. "You're welcome to join us, but I know you have a busy day tomorrow."

"I do. I've got two big exams this week, I should probably call it a night."

"How about if I walk you home?"

Yikes.

My heart flutters. I'm conflicted at how well tonight has gone. Part of me doesn't want it to end, while the other part wants to run so I can hold fast to the rules. I look around, the neighborhood is quiet.

"I don't like walking alone this late at night, that would be great," I say.

About ten minutes into our walk, I grimace at the blisters forming on the back of my ankles.

"Ow," I say, under my breath.

"You okay?"

I nod, looking ahead. "I'm fine, it's my boots. They haven't been broken in yet."

I take another step as the leather bites into my heel sending a shiver down my legs, and I grip onto his arm.

A look of concern crosses his face. "Do you want to sit down?"

"Sure, I just need a second. Blisters are nothing new. I get them all the time from dance."

We sit for a few minutes as several cabs pass by. Miles offers to hail one of them.

"Please, go meet up with your friends. It's such a short walk, I can make it."

He shakes his head. "No, that's alright. I ran track in high school. Blisters are no joke."

I stand up and take a step and shudder from the pain.

"I have another idea," he says as he pats the ledge we were just sitting on.

"Hop up here."

I turn to look at what he's talking about.

"Um, why?"

"So I can carry you the rest of the way home."

I laugh so loud, a couple passing by turns to look.

"Miles, no! I'm not letting you carry me on your back."

"Ask Mikayla how many times I've carried her home from a bar. Seriously, it's no big deal."

Mortified. I'm in a dress, how am I supposed to climb onto his back? I weigh my options and decide there's really no use arguing with him. He seems determined, plus my feet are killing me.

"Besides, aren't you dancers used to having people carry you around?" he asks.

"Well, yes, but that's—"

"Let's go," he says, cutting me off.

I take his hand and step up onto the cement ledge. Humiliation stings my face as I hold on to his shoulders while he backs into me.

"Oh God—we're really doing this." I can feel my face turning bright red.

"Yep. Hold on."

I lean into him as he reaches behind my knees and pulls me onto his back. I can only imagine how ridiculous this looks. We limp along slowly, talking and walking.

"Mi-iles, if this is t-t-oo much, j-j-just tell me!"

"It's nothing, besides, you're meant to be carried," he says, sounding giddy.

He's enjoying this.

He attempts a twirl and I almost lose my grip around his neck.

"Miles!" I scream, tightening my grip around his neck. He smells of cedarwood and citrus. I'd be really embarrassed about this whole thing, if his act of chivalry wasn't so damn charming.

"We're almost there, o-o-nly three more blocks to go-o," I say, encouragingly.

He hikes me further onto his back and we giggle the rest of the way home. When we finally make it to our place, he bends down, his hands sliding up the backs of my legs, as he sets me on the step.

"I haven't had a piggyback ride since. . ." My eyes sting thinking about the rest of that sentence. "Um, well—it's been a really long time," I say, pushing my nostalgia aside.

He turns so he's eye level with me.

"You think I'm ready to audition for the American Ballet?" he asks, slightly out of breath.

"One of the most prestigious ballet companies in the world? Absolutely." I nudge him backward as a car pulls up to our house.

"Aww, are you two waiting up for me?" I hear Mikayla's voice before I see her.

"Are you just getting home from work?"

"Yep. Thirty-two hours from when I last saw you," she says as Miles groans.

"Hey, MK. Your turn for the long weekend, huh?"

"Yep. Hey, how was the show?"

My face beams with excitement. "Oh my God, there are no words to explain how good it was. You have to see it!" I say.

"Oliver knocked it out of the park. The whole team put together a mind-blowing production. Gemma's right—you'd love it," Miles adds.

"I can't wait. Tell Oliver I've heard incredible things. I haven't seen him in forever. Are you two just getting back?"

"Yep. We went to the Purple Fig after the show," I say.

"I love that place," Mikayla says, as her car pulls away.

"MK, tell Gemma how many times I've carried you home after a night at the bars when we were at Columbia."

"More than a few. Why?" she asks.

I plant my palm on my forehead. "Shoe malfunction. He had to carry me on his back from the bar."

"You carried her all the way from Purple Fig?" she asks, incredulous.

"Only halfway. Can't have the ballerina injuring her feet now, can we?"

We laugh until silence settles around us.

"I've got to go to bed. I'm also pretty sure our neighbors would be happy if we moved this party inside," she says, walking up the stairs.

"I'm actually going to meet up with Ollie and the cast," Miles says, pulling out his phone to send a quick text.

"I'm right behind you," I say to Mikayla.

"Goodnight, Miles, always a pleasure. Come say goodnight before you go to bed, Gem."

"G'night. Great to see you too."

Mikayla waves and then lets herself in, leaving us on the landing below.

"You can go inside with her if you want. I'm just waiting to hear back from Oliver about where to meet them."

"I'll sit with you until he responds," I say, sitting down on our steps. He takes a seat next to me.

"I had a great time tonight, thank you," I say, thinking about how much I would have missed if I hadn't joined him.

"I did too. I'm glad you could join me."

His phone lights up, illuminating his chiseled jawline and the peak of his full lips as he reads his incoming message. I look away before he catches me looking at him.

"They're at a bar on Lexington."

"That's only a few blocks from here," I say.

We stand and my heartbeat triples in speed. I nervously glance down the street as he leans in for a hug, giving me a quick kiss goodbye on the cheek.

"Goodnight. My first Broadway show was unforgettable." A smile crawls across my face as I turn and walk up the stairs, his eyes trailing me with every step.

"You know what the best part of tonight was for me?" he says, after a few beats of silence.

I turn and look down at him.

"What?"

"Watching you watching the show." He holds my gaze as his smile lingers. "Goodnight, Gemma."

He strides down the sidewalk, his silhouette fading with every footstep, until it finally dissolves into the city's early morning shadows.

FOURTEEN

GEM & EM

"Grandma, whose car is that? Is someone here?" I ask, as we pull into her driveway.

"Mm-hmm, it's an old friend of your mom's. They're probably just finishing up. I'll go let her know we're home."

I unclip my seatbelt and scoot to the edge of my seat. "Who is it? Is it someone we know?"

"No. It's someone your mom has known since you two were babies. She lives far away. I thought having some visitors might help cheer her up."

"Is Mom sad?" Emmeline asks, her face crumpling.

Grandma goes quiet as she reaches for her handbag in the bottom of the car. "It's frustrating for her to have to wait for her leg to heal. There are so many things she wants to do with the two of you before summer ends."

I play with my bottom lip. "When is she getting her cast off? It should be soon, right?"

She nods. "Every day it's a little better. We just have to be patient."

"Can we go play in the puddles? We already have our raincoats on," Em asks.

"Yes, go have fun, girls. I'm going inside, just make sure you stay in the yard."

"We will, Grandma."

Emmeline and I kick off our shoes and run through the wet grass. The mud squishes up between our toes, leaving a trail of sunken muddy footprints behind us. We tilt our heads to the sky, opening our mouths as wide as they'll stretch, trying to catch as many raindrops as we can.

"Look, Gem, a toad!" Emmeline screams, chasing it around to the side of Grandma's house. I run after her, watching as she gently captures it in her hands. She holds it out like a prize for me to see.

"Look at her eyes!" she says proudly. "They look like they're made of gold."

I lean in, nose to nose with the toad, studying its face. "They do. People talk about toads like they aren't cute, but they have the prettiest eyes of any animal I've ever seen."

Em nods. "She's cute. Touch her skin, it feels like leather."

I reach out and pet the bumps on its back.

"How do you know it's a girl?" I ask.

She shrugs. "I don't."

"I want my own," I say, running around to Grandma's side garden. Two toads are splashing near the downspout, and I pick up the biggest one.

"Em, come look at mine!"

She runs over so we can compare our little friends. We pet them, straining to hear their little chirps over the raindrops pelting the hoods of our raincoats. A huge bolt of lightning strikes nearby, followed by booming thunder.

Em jumps. "That was close!"

"Time to come in, girls!" Mom calls from the front porch.

"Awww, but we just found two toads!" we shout to her.

"That was too close; you can go back outside after the storm passes."

"Coming," I say, looking at Emmeline, still admiring the pots of gold in her toad's eyes.

"Hopefully they'll still be here when the rain stops," I say.

We gently return them to the garden and run to the front yard where Mom's standing on the top step, hands on her hips. As Emmeline and I duck under the shelter of the porch, a woman and her son walk down Grandma's sidewalk to the black SUV parked on the street.

The woman's wearing a bright yellow trench coat with a white belt wrapped tightly around her waist and a matching wide-brimmed hat.

"She must love the rain," Em whispers.

"How can you tell?"

"Because she dressed up for it."

I make a face. "She looks like someone who doesn't like getting wet, though."

A tall man runs around from the driver's seat to hold the back door open for them as they climb into the backseat. Before he closes the door, the boy looks out and waves to us. Emmeline and I wave back. I push the hood of my raincoat out of my face so I can see them better. I'm not positive, but the woman looks a little like the person I saw clicking her heels down the hallway of the hospital the first time we went to visit Mom.

"What's wrong, Mom?" I ask, glancing up at her.

Her frown fades. "Nothing, my love. I just wanted you two to come in from the storm."

"Who are they?" Emmeline asks.

She looks distracted and can't seem to pull her eyes away from their car. "Old friends of mine. Sorry they had to leave before you could say hi. They're on their way to the airport."

I nod and watch as the car slowly pulls away, wondering why we didn't get to meet them.

"Look at my two little rain lovers, you're soaked! Take your raincoats off and leave them out here so they can dry out."

We hang them over Grandma's rocking chair, wiping our grassy feet on her mat.

I put my arm around Emmeline's shoulders as we follow Mom inside. I love summertime, especially rainy days. The truth is, as long as the two of us are together, Em and I can find a way to have fun no matter what the season. That's what's so special about being a twin: having a built-in best friend for life.

FIFTEEN

GEMMA

I'm frozen. No matter how hard I try, I can't move. Clusters of tarantulas crawl out from my sheets, brushing against me as they flash their venomous fangs. Their webs spin tightly around my throat, trapping my breath like it's their next meal. Hundreds of them skitter up and down my arms. I thrash back and forth but can't shake them. My mouth opens to scream and several of them climb inside. I can't breathe—I'm drowning in fire. Someone's holding me down. "No! No! No!"

"Gemma... Gemma!"

I hear my name as I struggle against the darkness pulling me under.

"Gemma, wake up."

Someone's shaking me. I sit straight up and gulp for air like I've been underwater too long. My heart pounds against my ribs, searching for the way out.

"Gemma, it was a bad dream, you're okay."

I open my eyes to find Mikayla sitting in front of me, hands on my shoulders. I hold my throat, still aflame from my cries.

"You're drenched."

I look around my room, comforted by my surroundings. *Breathe. You're fine.*

"What was... did I wake you?" I ask, sleepily.

"No, I just got home from work and was in the kitchen when I heard you."

"That's a terrible thing to come home to." I guiltily fold my hands in my lap.

"It's okay." She stands and walks to my door. "It's two in the morning, go back to bed. You've got to be up in a few hours."

"HEY THERE! Good timing. I'm glad I get to see you before I leave for the day," I say, on my way out the door.

"Well good morning . . . again," Mikayla says, insinuatingly, on her way down the stairs.

I smile and nod before her words register. "Again?"

"Do you remember me waking you up this morning?"

The memory comes flooding back and I tilt my head back, taking a deep inhale, letting my heavy backpack fall to the floor with a thud.

"Now I do."

"What were you dreaming about last night?"

"I don't know. I remember darkness and trying to scream but couldn't. Oh, and spiders. Lots of them."

Mikayla makes a face. "Have you ever thought about talking to someone about these night terrors?"

"Talking to someone? You mean, like a therapist?"

"Yes, like a therapist."

I shake my head. "They stopped for a while, but recently they've come back with a vengeance."

"You had them before you moved in with me?" she asks.

"Yeah. I've kind of had them off and on since I was young."

"Gem, you can't live like that. Talking to a therapist might help get to the reason behind them."

I know exactly what's causing my night terrors. She's right, though. I can't live like this. Especially now that it's not just affecting me. "I'll think about it."

"Really? I can ask around at the hospital for a name," she says.

Persistent Mikayla, she always comes from the right place.

"Yes, really. Or at least—definite maybe."

She rolls her eyes.

"Okay, I gotta go, I'll miss my train," I say, picking up my backpack.

She shakes her head, waving me out the door.

I run down our front steps. I don't feel like talking about it with a new therapist, or with anyone for that matter. A text from Miles comes through as I'm walking down the stairs to the subway.

> I'm in the city today.

I nervously chew my bottom lip. It's been five days since our Broadway show and I've been wondering if I'd hear from him again. Every day when there's been no text, I've tried convincing myself that I'm not disappointed. That I'm fine to continue with my life as it was before I met him—after all, rules aren't made to be broken.

I find an open seat and stare out the window. I'm comforted by the sounds of the urban lullaby as the train glides along the tracks, rocking me back and forth. The sounds of the subway soothe me. I far prefer the continuous sounds of a city landscape to the stillness of my Indiana home. Hollow silence keeps me on edge, bracing me for the unexpected. I get a signal as I'm walking up the steps of my West 4th St. stop and text him.

> Where?

As I sit down at my desk, Miles texts me back:

> Conference at The Marlton. Do you have a break in your schedule?

> You're in my neighborhood! Only window is 1:30-2:30.

> I have a break at 1:30. How about Washington Square on the fountain side of the arch. 1:45?

Class is starting, and I anxiously drum my fingers on my desk, not wanting to make a hasty decision. My professor begins her lecture and I panic, not wanting to miss anything. I text back, quickly putting my phone away.

> Sounds good.

SINCE GETTING MILES'S TEXT, I've been going back and forth about canceling. It's totally believable my clinic could run long, and it's not like this has been planned for a long time. On the other hand, that night of the Broadway show was one of the best times I've had since moving to the city. Mikayla's words ring loudly in my ears. I owe it to myself to live my best life.

There's someone else I owe it to.

I walk to Washington Square Park and find an open bench in the sun. Today is one of those unseasonably warm November days. I take out my tofu wrap and pretzels from my backpack and sit facing the arch so I'll be able to see when Miles arrives. Famished, I devour my lunch, putting my reusable bags back in my backpack. The sun warms my face as I take in the newly independent leaves resting in piles on the ground.

"Someone looks deep in thought."

I hear Miles's voice and look up to find he's walking towards me.

"Hey there!" Just the sight of him makes my insides jitter. He smiles and leans down to hug me, kissing me hello on the cheek. I hug him back, this time without the awkward pat on the back. *Progress.*

"I can't believe you're only a few blocks away," I say, moving over on the bench to make room for him."

"Crazy right?"

"How's your conference?"

"It's going well. It's on neurodegenerative disorders. Fascinating stuff. I'm considering it as my specialty."

"Is that like Parkinson's and Alzheimer's?" I ask, as he looks around the park.

"Those are two of the most common, but also Multiple Sclerosis, strokes, cerebral aneurysms and epilepsy," he adds.

"What made you want to consider that for your specialty?"

His face turns serious. "My brother Amos had epilepsy as a child, and I remember the stress it caused my parents and their relationship."

My heart clenches. "I'm so sorry, Miles. That must have been hard for all of you."

He rakes his fingers through his hair. "It was. Thanks. He's been seizure free for almost fifteen years, but his early years were rough. The first time I ever thought about becoming a doctor was when I was seven. I remember wanting to figure out what it was in his brain that caused his seizures."

"The noble and protective older brother," I say, smiling.

"Something like that."

He blushes and averts his eyes. He clearly has a hard time accepting compliments.

"What made you want to go to law school?" he asks. I think for a moment. I don't know why, but something in me wants to give him the real reason—not the ones I've used for my interviews.

"Before my dad passed away, he was planning to go to law school. I guess this is my way of carrying the baton he was never able to hold."

He nods, contemplating my words.

"As far as choosing environmental law—I learned my love of nature from my mom. Growing up, the woods were my second home. I decided in college that I wanted to do what I could to make a positive impact on the environment and ultimately, people's lives."

"Critical work," he says, as I nod. A cool breeze blows and I pull my scarf tighter, tucking the ends into the collar of my jacket.

"Back in August, the firm I've been interning for the last two summers made me an offer and I accepted."

His eyebrows shoot up. "That's impressive, congratulations. Knowing you already have a job waiting for you must take some of the pressure off your last year."

"Maybe a little, but I still need to graduate and pass the bar."

My stress level rises thinking about all my work between now and graduation. I push it to the back of my mind, letting myself enjoy the moment. We sit quietly, side by side, watching as people pass by.

"What's that look on your face?" he asks.

I look over at him. "I didn't realize I was making a face."

"You look—oh, I don't know. Content."

"I usually sit out here by myself, having company is nice."

"I'm glad it worked out." He moves in closer, and my stomach drops as our shoulders softly brush. I shift my weight, inching further away from him.

"What are your plans for the holidays?" he asks.

"Mikayla and I are spending Thanksgiving together, and then at the end of December I'm flying home to spend the holidays with my mom and Grandma. It's been way too long since I've been home, and my grandma's getting older. I want to make sure I see her at least a few times a year."

"When was the last time you saw them?" he asks.

"They came out to visit me this past summer. It was their first time to the city and they loved it. I took them to all the fun spots I never go to because I live here now."

"You know you sound like a New Yorker when you say things like that," he teases.

I shrug and smile.

"My grandma's favorite spot was Little Island."

"She has good taste. I love that place."

A leaf lands on the bench next to me and I pick it up, twirling it between my fingers. "My mom loved the Guggenheim. We spent hours on each ring. She's always loved art and we don't have museums like that back home. It was nice to introduce her to artists she'd never heard of before."

Miles rests his arm on the back of the bench behind me. Instinctively, I sit taller, away from his touch. *Old habits die hard.*

"What are your plans?" I ask.

"I'm not sure what my schedule will be in December, so this year we're all getting together for Thanksgiving. My mom has a place out in the Hamptons and it's our tradition to spend holidays out there. Amos is flying out from LA so it'll be the three of us."

"That's a nice tradition. The Hamptons are incredible," I say.

"You've been?"

I nod. "Yep. Once. I went last summer with Mikayla. Her friend threw a Fourth of July party in Southampton. It's definitely a scene." I raise my eyebrows. "From the designer boutique shops to the people and their luxury cars, it was all a little intimidating to be honest. The homes were all so beautiful, the ones I could see at least. Most of them were behind tall walls of meticulously manicured hedges."

Miles laughs. "I know what you mean. Southampton has a totally different vibe than where my mom's house is. She bought a place in Amagansett over twenty years ago. She rents it out most of the year except for a few weeks in the summer and during the holidays. It's been a great investment for her. I think you'd like Amagansett—it's laid back and surrounded by nature."

I nod. "It sounds beautiful. How long has it been since you've seen Amos?"

"Not too long. I flew out to LA last summer. We try to see each other every few months."

A trio of musicians: a flutist, a violinist and a guitarist start playing softly to our right.

"New York is seriously the coolest place. This park is always packed with creatives of every kind. The energy is unlike any other place I've ever been," I say, moved by their harmony.

Miles looks at the musicians and nods. "This city's in my blood. No matter where I end up, this will always be home."

"Do you think you could ever leave?" I ask.

"I can't picture it now, but who knows. Ideally, I'd love to have a place out West and an apartment in the city. Best of both worlds."

I nod and look at my watch. Our time together is almost over. I feel the start of a knot tightening in my stomach.

"I hate to say it, but I should head back to class," I say, hesitantly.

"I gotta get back too, my break is almost over."

We walk wordlessly across the park until we get to Washington's arch.

"Thanks again for meeting up last minute," he says.

I pull my backpack up further on my shoulder. "It was great to see you."

He looks around, like he's waiting for something. "What are you up to this weekend?"

"Probably hanging out with Mikayla if she's not working. How 'bout you?"

"I just found out my schedule changed, and I'm not working

Saturday night. I realize it's the day after tomorrow—but I'd like to take you to dinner if Mikayla will let me borrow you."

I shift my weight to one foot, dragging the toe of my boot behind me. *Maybe I could bend the rules—just this once.*

"Dinner—that sounds nice." I smile cautiously as my insides wring together, wondering if I've just crossed over the point of no return.

Live your life.

He smiles at my response.

"Leave the details to me." He kisses me on the cheek and this time I lean into his kiss, inhaling as much as I can of his citrusy scent.

"Bye, Gemma."

"See you Saturday."

We turn and walk in opposite directions. I'm nearing the fountain and turn to look at him, wanting him in my sight one more time. He turns back at the same time I do and we both wave. My heart skips a beat.

I wish I could just let myself enjoy the feeling because it's really nice, but a cold dread creeps up my arms and I can already feel my guard going up. I've spent so much time and energy protecting myself from getting close to anyone again. It's a hard habit to break and I have to admit, it's getting old.

SIXTEEN

GEM & EM

Em and I slide down the banister and find Mom and Grandma sitting at the kitchen table. *They look so serious.* I pretend not to see when Mom wipes the tears from her eyes. She looks over at me and smiles, but it's not a happy smile. It's one of those smiles that comes with a lot of thoughts behind it.

Grandma stands, and I give her a squeeze around the waist. Her arms wrap around the back of my head, and I bury my face into her ruffled yellow apron. *She smells like maple syrup and home.*

"Grandma's taking me to my doctor's appointment. Do you want to come with us or stay here?"

I look longingly out the window. "Can we go into the woods? It finally stopped raining."

"Sure, but I don't want you going too far. You need to learn these woods before you go all the way to the river," Mom says.

"Your mom's right, not too far today. Make sure you watch for poison ivy too, it'll be everywhere with all the rain we've had," Grandma adds.

EMMELINE and I walk single file, trying not to touch the sides of the trail just in case there's poison ivy. We stay under the canopy of the trees, shading ourselves from the blazing sun. Birds chatter to one another above our heads as we follow the winding dirt trail deeper into the woods. The trail eventually widens, making it possible for us to walk side by side.

Em slows to a stop. "Do you hear running water?"

I stop and listen.

"Yep. The creek must be ahead."

We take a rock and dig an X into a tree at eye level so we can remember our turn off for home. Tiny river pebbles crunch beneath our shoes as we pad along the sides of the creek.

"Are you hungry?" I ask, as my stomach rumbles.

"A little. My feet are hot."

"Mine too. Let's take our shoes off on that log," I say, pointing ahead.

"How long do you think we've been hiking?"

I shrug, looking back in the direction we came from. "I don't know, maybe an hour?"

We climb onto the log and plunge our feet in the creek's steady stream.

"Ahh, that's better," Em says, reaching into the backpack handing me the pretzels Grandma left out for us, as well as our waters.

"If you could make one wish, what would it be?" I ask, opening the bag.

"Anything?"

"Yep, anything."

"That's easy," she says.

"What is it?"

"I wish summer could go on forever. How about you?" she asks.

"I wish we could get a puppy."

"Oh, that's a good one. I take mine back. I wish we could get a puppy too," she says.

"Did you hear that?"

She shakes her head. "No, hear what?"

"Shh, wait a second. Let me see if I hear it again."

We sit quietly, listening to the woods. The only noise is the sound of the bubbling creek beneath our feet.

"There it is again."

"I hear it. It sounds like laughing," Emmeline says.

I jump off the log. "Let's go check it out."

We put our shoes back on, carefully listening for the sound.

"It's coming from that way," Em says, pointing up ahead.

As we round a sharp bend, Emmeline looks up and gasps. Sandwiched between branches of an enormous tree is a fort, that looks more like a small house than a tree fort. I hear voices and pull her behind a tree to hide us.

"Do you think they've seen us?" Em whispers.

"Who's there?" a voice calls out from above. Emmeline and I hold our hands over our mouths, trying not to make a sound.

"We see you hiding behind that tree," the voice says.

Em's eyes go wide. "Should we run?"

I shake my head. Someone's climbing down the pieces of wood nailed to the tree's trunk. Emmeline's standing so close—I can feel her heart thumping into mine.

"What should we do?"

"Peek your head around and see who it is," she says.

I poke my head out and see a girl with fiery-red hair and freckles, staring at us, her hands crossed defiantly across her chest. *She's tall, she must be a few years older than us.*

"Who's there?" she demands.

I tentatively come out from behind the tree and hold up my hand.

"Just me and my sister," I say, as Emmeline follows after me.

Another voice calls out from inside the fort.

"Who is it?"

"Two girls," says red hair, sassily. She glares at us, a menacing look on her face.

"Do we know them?"

"No."

A boy that looks to be a few years younger than us, with the same red hair and freckles, pokes his head out from one of the fort's cut-out windows and waves down at us. We wave back.

The girl sizes us up. "Do you live around here?"

"No, we're staying at our grandma's."

"I've never seen a fort this big before!" Emmeline interjects, breaking the tension in the air.

"Do you want to come up and see it?" the boy calls from inside. Sassy red hair scowls at her brother.

"Um, maybe for a little bit," I say, eyeing her closely.

We walk past her to the base of the tree. "What are your names?" she calls after us.

"I'm Gemma and this is my twin sister, Emmeline."

"I'm Violet and my brother's name is Otis." She pushes past us and climbs the tree's makeshift stairs. "Make sure you hold on tight, it gets harder the closer you get to the top."

"Okay, thanks. We're pretty good climbers." I follow her up the tree, gripping onto each board tightly. Emmeline tightens the straps on the backpack and follows me up. We get to the top, pulling ourselves onto the platform.

"Wow, look how far up we are!" I say.

Emmeline mouths the words, "This is so cool!" but I already know what she's thinking because I'm thinking the same thing.

We follow Violet inside to where her brother's sitting in the middle of the floor, next to a stack of board games. "I'm Otis," he says, shuffling a deck of Uno cards.

"Hi, Otis," we say.

Em's mouth opens wide. "This place is huge."

"My sister and I come here all the time. We've never seen anyone else out here."

The walls are decorated with people's names and several drawings. I look over to the corner of the room that has a square cutout in the ceiling and a ladder leading to the roof.

"What's up there?" I say, pointing to the ladder.

"Follow me, I'll show you," Violet says.

We follow her up the worn rungs onto a deck that's completely enclosed by a railing made from thick tree branches.

"Whoa! Gem, you can see even further from all the way up here!" Emmeline squeals as she climbs onto the roof.

"Holy buckets, I've climbed a lot of trees, but I've never been up this high before. Do you ever come up here at night? I bet you can see millions of stars from up here," I say.

"No, our parents won't let us come here at night, but maybe one day we'll come and just not tell them," she says, her tone rebellious.

She turns and climbs down the ladder to where her brother is sitting, and we follow.

"I can't believe you got her to go up on the roof; she never likes going up there."

"Yes, I do, Otis! You don't know what you're talking about."

He rolls his eyes at us. "Do you want to play a game?" he asks.

"Mom said to be home by lunch, we have to go. Come on, Otis."

He grudgingly gets up, leaving the cards in a pile on the floor, and follows her down the tree. I lean over the deck to watch as they leave. "Maybe we'll see you up here next time!" I shout.

"Okay. There's a haunted graveyard nearby we can show you," Violet offers.

Emmeline looks at me, her eyes wide. We wave at them, excited to have the whole fort to ourselves. Em takes off the backpack and lays it down next to the stack of games. We climb back up the ladder onto the roof and shout as loud as we can into the sky.

"Hello. . .hello. . .hello. . ." our voices boomerang back to us.

"These woods go on forever," I say, my eyes searching in every direction.

Em gets a nervous look on her face. "Do you think we'll be able to find our way home? Maybe we should leave. Mom told us to be home for lunch."

"Let's stay a little longer," I say, wiping the sweat from my brow. The air is thick and sticky, our shirts cling to our backs.

"It's too hot up here, let's go back inside," Em says, her face bright red from the heat.

We climb down and walk to the bridge suspended between another giant tree and the fort. Through the gaps in the wooden boards I can see the ground far beneath us. The further out we go, the more the bridge rocks back and forth.

"Should it swing like this when we walk?" she asks.

"I think so. Hold on tight."

We spread out and take turns jumping, holding tightly to the sides. The bridge goes up and down like a seesaw and we squeal with delight the higher it goes. The branches groan like a creaky door hinge, as they resist the pull of the ropes.

We walk back to the room with the board games and sit down. Emmeline dumps everything in our backpack on the floor. Our snacks, waters and a few markers left in the bottom from school fall out.

"I have an idea, let's add some of our drawings on that wall over there," I say pointing behind the ladder where there's still lots of empty space. Emmeline and I take turns passing markers back and forth, slowly decorating the wall with flowers, trees and butterflies. Em adds several brown and green turtles—her favorite.

"Let's sign our names underneath so anyone up here will know we were here," I say.

Together in green marker we write:

Gemma and Emmeline
Sisters, explorers and best friends forever.

We stand back to admire our work as a gust of wind blows, rustling the leaves on the trees. I lean my head out the window to peek at the sky. An angry greenish-gray sky glares down at me. Dark clouds rush in as their feathery edges swirl toward the ground, trying to block out the remaining sunlight.

"Uh oh, storm's coming," I say, as a clap of thunder rumbles in the distance.

"Do you think we have time to run home?" she asks, nervously.

"No, it's going to start raining any second."

Another crack of thunder fills the woods, this time only closer. The wind picks up, blowing back the smaller branches on the surrounding trees. I look over to Emmeline, her face floods with worry.

The first drops pelt the roof and I walk over to her, joining her on the floor.

"We'll be okay in here, let's move away from the hole in the roof so we don't get wet," I say.

"I didn't even hear it coming."

"Me neither. Hopefully it leaves as fast as it came in."

"I hope so," Em says, scooting closer to me as a crack of thunder explodes, making us jump. *It's on top of us.* Em and I sit shoulder to shoulder with our knees up and our arms clenched tightly around our shins. The cool air blasts in, raising all the hairs on my skin.

"It feels like someone just turned on the air conditioning," Emmeline says.

Pinging thuds bombard the roof and I watch through the window as hail the size of golf balls falls from the sky and into the fort. We cover our ears trying to shield them from the noise, but it's no use. The wind blows so hard the fort sways back and forth with every gust. Emmeline and I hold onto each other as if the tightness of our grip might calm the storm.

"We need to get home. Mom and Grandma are going to wonder where we are," Emmeline shouts, over the hail battering the roof.

"Don't worry, it will end soon," I say.

"Pinky promise?" she asks, holding out her hand. I wrap my pinky finger around hers, and we shake on it.

The thunder and lightning take turns terrorizing everything in its path, including us. We sit panic stricken, counting the seconds between their attacks, like our teacher taught us.

A crooked streak of lightning flashes, brightening the inside of the fort.

"One, one thousand, two, one thousand."

BOOM!

"It's close which means the worst is almost over."

"I hope so," Emmeline says, looking terrified.

"Listen—the hail stopped."

Emmeline looks up at the ceiling, relieved. It's still pouring, but at least it doesn't sound like the ceiling's going to break in half.

"You don't think the wind could blow the tree fort out of the tree, could it?" Emmeline asks.

I swallow. "No, it's probably been here a long time."

"Oh, okay."

There's doubt in her voice and I reach over and hold her hand. We sit listening to the storm and counting lightning and thunder strikes for the next ten minutes. The patter of the rain on the roof slows until it eventually stops and is replaced by the sun. *The storm is over.*

"That was a bad one," Emmeline says.

"We should get back home just in case another one's coming," I say.

Em and I quickly pack up our markers and snacks and climb down the ladder. The boards are soaking wet from the storm so we take our time. We each breathe a sigh of relief when our feet touch the soft, muddy ground, littered with melting marbles of ice.

"We better hurry," I say, as we run along the banks of the swollen creek. Our trek home is a slick and muddy slip-and-slide, and we fall several times, soaking our clothes and shoes with mud. We move further away from the edges of the creek, hoping to gain better traction near the grassy edge. A massive fallen branch lies in our path, and I climb over it, knocking my shin on the mossy bark.

"Careful, Em, it's slippery."

She takes her time and once she's over it, we pick up our pace. I'm relieved when I finally spot our X near the trail entrance and run toward it as fast as I can.

"Gem, the backpack's soaked, it's too heavy," Em shouts, as I turn and run back to her.

"Here, give it to me, I'll carry it the rest of the way."

We stop briefly for her to take it off as more thunder rumbles.

"We have to get home," I urge.

"I'm scared," Emmeline cries out, tears falling down her cheeks.

I put my hand on her shoulder. "Don't cry. It's going to be okay. Can you go a little faster?"

She nods, sniffling. "I'll try."

Our shoes and socks are caked with mud and sand, making it hard to run.

"Emmeline, Gemma!" Mom's voice calls out in the distance.

My shoulders sag with relief at the sound of her voice, despite the fact we're probably going to be in big trouble. "It's Mom, she's out looking for us. Hurry, Em!"

"We're here!" I shout as loud as I can. Emmeline and I stumble along the wet grass until we see Mom way up ahead leaning on one crutch, wearing her oversized orange raincoat. We try our best to run to her, but our shoes are suction cups in the mud.

"Girls! Oh my goodness where in the world have you been? Grandma and I have been worried sick."

"We're sorry, Mom," Emmeline calls out.

She reaches out with one arm and pulls us into her in a protective embrace, smearing her with mud.

"We didn't know there was going to be a bad storm or we wouldn't have gone in the woods," I say, trying not to look directly at the agonizing worry all over her face. My guilt spreads from my chest into my stomach.

"We didn't mean to make you worry." Em starts to cry.

"I'm just so glad that you're home and you're both okay," Mom says, putting her arms around us.

"We knew we couldn't outrun it, so we just stayed where we were," I say, holding onto her.

"Where were you? Did you find a place to wait out the storm?"

I open my mouth to speak.

"Willow?" Grandma's voice calls from her backyard.

"I'm over here, Mom! I found them," she shouts.

"Thank heavens!" Grandma says, hurrying toward us holding her hand over her heart as she makes her way down the grassy alleyway behind her house.

"I hope you weren't out in this storm the whole time," Mom says.

Emmeline and I guiltily look at each other and put our heads down.

"We got stuck. We found a big tree fort in the woods and hid there while the storm passed," I say.

"What tree fort? You two were up in a tree during this storm?" she asks, her eyes wide with horror.

Emmeline sobs. "There was nowhere to go. The storm was right on top of us before we realized it was even coming. The hail was so loud we had to cover our ears."

Grandma pulls us into her arms, hugging us tight. She also doesn't seem to mind the streaks of mud we leave on her.

Another clap of thunder sounds, closer this time.

"Let's get inside, another storm is on the way," Grandma says, "I can't imagine how scary that must have been for you."

Mom shakes her head. "I hate to think of you out in this storm. A tornado touched down on the other side of town. We got home from my appointment and were worried sick when we saw you weren't back yet."

"A tornado?" we say, our eyes wide.

"Wait. Look, Gem. Mom got her cast off!" Em wipes her nose and points to Mom's bare foot.

"What did the doctor say?" I ask.

"My ankle is much better. I have to use this crutch a little longer until it gets stronger," she says, with a thin smile. "C'mon let's get inside."

"I'm glad it's off, Mom," I say, as we turn and head for Grandma's backyard.

"Me too, sweetheart. Listen, I don't want you girls going to that fort anymore. That was a dangerous storm and you two could have been hurt," Mom says, as Emmeline and I hang our heads.

"Let's go inside and get you into some dry clothes. Take your sneakers off and leave them at the back door," Grandma says.

"Okay," we say, sadly.

The four of us walk to the back of the house as the skies grow darker. Mom leans on her crutch for support, the wet grass making it difficult for her to walk.

"Be careful, Mom. It's really slippery. I'm sorry we made you come out looking for us," I say, guiltily.

"It's okay, sweetheart. I'm just so thankful nothing bad happened to you."

SEVENTEEN

GEMMA

I jog to the park entrance to get warm, bursts of breath clouds trailing me. *Winter will be here soon.* My fingers are numb, and I rub them together, already dreaming about my post-run shower. The park is bustling with Saturday afternoon runners, rollerbladers and coffee drinkers, all bundled up, carelessly strolling around the park.

The sound of crushed gravel under my feet keeps me company as I run my four-mile loop around the reservoir and Boathouse. Mikayla was the one who told me about this running path. It has some of the best views (and people watching) the city has to offer. To say I've fallen in love with Manhattan is an understatement. Maybe it's because I grew up in such a different environment that I appreciate it so much. Or maybe it's because since the first day I moved here it's given me hope for a new start.

My reward for putting in the miles is ending every run at the Model Boat Pond. I stretch and watch from the sidelines as families hover over their remote controls, navigating their miniature sailboats through the pond's murky water. This place reminds me of the small pond near our house where Mom, Emmeline and I would spend hours skipping rocks, floating on inner tubes and searching for tadpoles when they were in season. During the winter when it would freeze over, the three of us spent almost every weekend ice-skating.

What an untroubled life it was, back when my biggest fear was having to face Mom, her tweezers and a cotton ball of rubbing alcohol as she pulled a splinter from the bottom of my foot. My phone vibrates and I take it out of my waistband. It's a text from Miles:

> Looking forward to tonight. I'll pick you up at 7:30.

I read his words and get a sinking feeling. I don't know if going out with him tonight is such a good idea after all. Sour indecision swirls in my belly. I only said yes because he was standing in front of me with that perfect smile of his. It's not yet past the point of no return. There's still time to cancel.

This time of year I can't help but think of Thanksgiving at Grandma's house. Mom's famous triple chocolate pecan pie and sweet potato casserole. But nothing comes close to Grandma's biscuits. Fresh out of the oven, Em and I would slather them with butter and then be so full there was no room for much of anything else.

Grandma's entire basement was stacked to the ceiling with toys, records, books and old photo albums. Em and I would always lose track of time, happily immersed in our twin world. *The holidays haven't felt like the holidays in a long time.* I hope I don't regret my decision to not go home this year. It never feels right being so far away, especially at this time of year.

Two dogs bark at each other, snapping me from my thoughts of home. I finish stretching and walk back to our place, stopping to pick up some fresh bagels. While I'm waiting for my order, I text Miles:

> I'm not going to be able to make it tonight. I'm sorry.

My finger hovers over the send button while apprehension plays tug of war with my emotions. "Gemma!" A mountain of a man shouts from behind the counter, startling me. I hit send and scoot past a long line of waiting customers. He hands me a large brown bag and I hurry out of the crowded store.

After a hot shower I sit at my desk to start my homework, convinced I made the right decision. I'm doing us both a favor bowing out now.

Getting close to someone is something that can't be undone. *There's no reverse when it comes to matters of the heart.*

A few hours later I'm finishing homework when I hear Mikayla's feet on the stairs.

"How was work last night?" I call out.

She sticks her head in my door. "Busy as always. This week I worked the pediatric unit. It was challenging in a way I haven't gotten used to yet. Not that you ever get used to it, just more experience with it, I suppose." She lets out a long sigh. "Some weeks are really hard. Needless to say, I don't foresee peds becoming my specialty."

"I can't imagine. I know you're a comfort to every one of those kids and their parents, if it's any consolation."

She shrugs, rubbing her forehead.

"What time's Miles picking you up?" she asks, changing the topic.

"Yeah, about that . . ."

She glares at me. "Don't tell me you canceled." I wrinkle my nose and nod.

"Gemma Ellsworth. Are you serious?"

"I just can't get into a relationship right now. There's no point in going out with him if I have no intention of dating him. He's a great guy who *also* happens to be one of your closest friends. I don't want to lead him on." She leans against my door frame and I can tell from her posture she's irritated with me.

"What did you say to him?"

"Here, read the texts." I hand her my phone. She types in my password and searches for our conversation.

"He hasn't responded and I doubt he will," I say, turning back to my laptop so I don't have to see the disappointment on her face.

"I'm telling you right now, you're making a mistake." She walks over and hands me back my phone.

"You know what they say—if it's truly meant to be, it will find a way. Maybe somewhere down the road after graduation . . ." I say, tilting my head the side.

"You're impossible, you know that right?"

"I know. I'm sorry. I hope you're not upset with me."

"No, I'm not upset. But you are *not* sitting at home alone tonight. A group of friends are coming over to pick me up around seven p.m. We're going out for dinner and dancing and you're coming with us," she says, like it's been decided.

"Dancing? You know I'm in! I was feeling bad I agreed to go out with him when you have a night off anyway. I'd much rather spend it with you."

"Okay, get ready. They'll be here in an hour." She turns and walks out, heading downstairs.

Guilt starts to creep in for canceling on Miles, but I push it away and go to my closet to find an outfit. I pull out my favorite pair of high-rise black jeans, a lavender blazer and several delicate gold layering necklaces. And most importantly, comfortable wedge-heeled boots. My blisters have finally healed, and I'm not about to risk more.

I'M UPSTAIRS FINISHING GETTING ready when our doorbell rings at seven-twenty. Mikayla rushes past my room down the stairs and her friends' voices fill our living room.

"You almost ready?" Mikayla shouts up to me.

"Be down in a sec."

The doorbell rings again at seven-thirty and I grab my purse, not wanting to keep everyone waiting. As I'm coming down the stairs, I see Miles standing by our front door and I stumble, grabbing onto the railing to keep from falling. *Why is he here?*

Mikayla pauses introducing Miles to her friends and they both look up at me. "Hey, Gemma," he smiles warmly. My face goes hot and I immediately start to sweat. *Why is he here?*

"Oh... Miles. Hi," I reply, shakily, trying to hide the fact I'm totally confused. I shoot Mikayla a bewildered look and she just smiles. Not wanting to embarrass him in front of her friends, I walk over to the two of them. "Did you get my text?" I ask him, quietly.

"Yep. Are you ready? The car will be here any second," he says, ardently. *What the?* Feeling as if I've been swallowed by an alternate dimension, I look to Mikayla for any kind of clue that might help explain what is happening right now.

"Um—yes. I just have to talk to Mikayla for a second, I'll be right back," I say, grabbing her arm and leading her to the kitchen.

Out of earshot I whisper, "What is he doing here?"

"Don't be upset," she says, a look of uncertainty on her face.

"Upset about what? What's going on?" I ask, seething. "Wait a minute, did you tell him to come anyway?"

"I would never do that! Look at your text to him—it never sent." She crosses her arms across her chest.

"What?" Panicking, I pull out my phone to see what she's talking about.

"I saw your message hadn't gone through and deleted it. I sent a thumbs up instead. Please don't be mad."

"You did not!" I shake my head, pacing back and forth. "That's so not cool. This wasn't your decision to make."

"You're right, I'm sorry. Just go out with him once. If you decide you really don't want to see him again—"

"I already decided that! Until you went and changed my response." We stare each other down in our dimly lit kitchen, neither one of us wanting to be the first to look away. His sweet smile flashes in my mind and I picture him standing there, awkwardly waiting for me.

"I really didn't think you felt this strongly about not going out with him and I certainly didn't think you'd get this upset. It was my mistake, I'll go tell him what I did," she offers, reticently.

If you only knew the reason I can't let someone in again.

I let out a deep sigh, annoyed at her for putting me in this position.

"Oh my God—no. That would be so embarrassing for him. I'll go. But don't ever do this again. I'm serious."

"I won't. I promise. Gem, I would never have interfered if I didn't feel as strongly as I do about you two," she says, pulling me in for a hug. I reluctantly hug her, shaking my head as I pull away.

"Let's go before he knows something's up," I say, walking back to the living room.

I PUT a smile on my face and grab my coat from the front closet.

"The car just got here," he says, opening our front door.

"Bye, you two, have fun tonight. Text me later if you want to meet up," Mikayla says, looking apologetic. I give her a disapproving side-eye as we turn to leave.

A black sedan is waiting for us at the bottom of our steps and we climb into the backseat. I try to calm myself, still angry with Mikayla for intervening.

"Everything okay with MK?" he asks, sounding concerned.

"Yeah, I just . . . I had to remind her that one of my tutoring students is coming over tomorrow morning," I say, trying my best not to sound annoyed. It's one night, I can deal with spending the next few hours with him. *There are certainly worse things in life.*

"You're a tutor?"

"Mm-hmm, mostly college essays, but I have a few U.S. History students too."

"That's cool. How long have you been doing that?" he asks. I take a deep breath, settling back in my seat. "About three years. It started with one of our neighbor's kids and has grown from there. Where are we off to?"

"To the best pizza place that is, not technically, in the city. My mom and I go all the time, it's a few blocks from her house."

"Brooklyn?" I ask.

"Yep."

Our car speeds down the FDR toward the Brooklyn Bridge and even though I'm irritated, I can't help but be wonderstruck as the metropolitan constellation unfolds outside my window. Shimmering lights dance across the East River, and I'm bedazzled by the powerful pulse of the city as it takes its first breaths of night.

"The energy of this city is intoxicating," I say, remembering all of the daydreams I had about this place when I was a teen. Like dance, this skyline was my escape.

Miles smiles thoughtfully. "This view never gets old."

I nod, feeling a little more relaxed. I gaze at the black sky, illuminated by towers of metal and glass in the distance. Their windows twinkle with big-city dreams. The flickering lights remind me of the spark that has ignited since meeting him. He's awakened something deep inside of me, and it both terrifies and excites me. I pull my eyes away from the skyline and glance over at him, grateful he isn't someone who has to fill every quiet moment with endless chatter.

"How was your day?" I ask, distracting myself from my invasive thoughts of flickers and sparks.

"I was at my mom's all day, it's been a minute with my new schedule. She's selling a house that needed staging, so I helped her move some things around."

The car slows in front of an old brick building that sits on the corner. Two red iron benches sit beneath a black and white awning and a large glass window. The neighborhood is a mix of both residential and commercial buildings with green bike lanes sprawling in every direction.

"This is such a cute neighborhood."

"I loved growing up here. The location's great—walkable to everything. My mom's place is only three blocks that way," he says, pointing behind me.

He opens the door, and the scent of baking wood-fired pizza dough makes my mouth water. The place is packed, and I can understand why. Miles leads me through the crowd to a table in the back, where two people are getting up. He holds my chair out as I sit down.

"How'd you do that?" I ask.

"How'd I do what?"

"It's packed in here and yet you find the perfect table. I would have turned around and left after looking at this group. A bunch of hungry New Yorkers circling for an empty table can be a tad intimidating."

"I've lived in NY so long, I guess my superpower has become finding the open tables."

I give him a lopsided grin. "I bet that comes in handy."

"In all honesty, I saw them paying the bill, so I knew they'd be getting up soon."

He winks and hands me a menu. *Oof. That wink.*

The restaurant is charming and modest. Exposed brick walls, string lights and red and white checkered tablecloths make for a casual and inviting space. Two enormous wood-fired ovens are built into the back wall behind the counter, making it cozy and warm. It's fun to watch as they stretch and toss the dough, while bubbling pies are pulled from the ovens on long wooden peels.

"What a sweet little spot."

"Wait until you taste the pizza. My mom and I have been coming here since I was a kid. Do you like classic or specialty?" he asks.

I look down at the simple menu. There are only a few options.

"I gotta go classic, I don't like toppings on my pizza. How about you?"

"I've never been a fan of toppings. Classic cheese and an extra side of sauce. What do you want to drink?" he asks.

I look at the options: beer, soda or sparkling water.

"Sparkling water is great, thank you." Completely sober is how I'll be staying tonight, thank you very much. Seriously—I've never known someone so annoyingly good looking in my life. *I already don't trust myself with him.*

I put my menu down and read through my emails as he walks up to the counter to place our order. He brings back two sparkling waters and a stack of napkins.

"Before I moved to the city, I never knew pizza was such a thing," I say, as he makes a shocked face.

"Pizza is a way of life here in New York."

"Don't get me wrong, I've always liked pizza, but in Indiana there isn't a race to be the 'original best' like here in New York."

"I hate to be the one to tell you, but if it isn't in New York, it isn't pizza."

"Oh, is that right?" I ask, shooting him a sideways glance.

"That's 100% right," he says, cementing his position. The kitchen calls our number and he jumps up, and heads for the counter. He returns with a bubbling, fresh-out-of-the-brick-oven-pizza.

I dab my slice with napkins as he folds his, as any respectable New Yorker does, and dives in. Our conversation is effortless, just as it was the night after his friend's show. In between devouring an entire pizza, we take turns sharing stories. Watching him eat surprisingly doesn't gross me out—red flag. It's odd how at ease I feel around him—another red flag. *One more flag and I'm out of here.* Several people walk by, eyeing our empty plates, as they hungrily wait for a table.

"I want to show you something," he says, looking under the table at my feet.

"What?" I ask.

"Just checking to make sure you're not wearing your pointe shoes."

I narrow my eyes at him. "Funny."

"You up for a walk?" he asks.

"Always."

We push our plates to the side and put on our coats. Miles weaves his way through the crowd and I follow him to the front door. He holds the door open as I step out onto a crowded Brooklyn intersection. The streets are filled with families and couples of every age out enjoying their Saturday evening, and we cross the street to a less crowded sidewalk. As we turn the corner, I'm stunned by the ethereal beauty of the Brooklyn Bridge.

"Whoa! I've never seen it all lit up from down here," I say, my eyes drinking in the view. Glowing orbs hang like lanterns, illuminating the entire bridge, as they stretch toward the shores of lower Manhattan on the other side. "Every time I think New York can't possibly get any more mind blowing. . ."

"This bridge is one of my favorite places—it'll always remind me of home." His eyes crinkle in the corners as he looks up and smiles. "I'll never forget the feeling I got the first time I saw it, right after we moved here from LA."

"I remember the first time I saw it in person, too. It blew me away," I say, keenly. "It still does."

"Have you ever walked across?"

I shake my head. "Surprisingly, with how busy school has kept me, I've never had the chance. It's been on my bucket list since I moved here."

"Come on, I want to show you the view from the middle," he says, taking my hand. Red flag number three. *Where's the referee anyway? Is she off duty or something?*

His warm hand feels nice as it squeezes against mine. He leads me up a set of stairs onto a pedestrian walkway. The wooden walkway spans the length of the bridge and is suspended by an intricate web of dangling cables. Granite keystone towers stand like powerful giants, their pointed arches beacons in the night sky. It's a little dizzying walking along as cars speed under us and I lean into Miles.

"The Brooklyn Bridge is anchored into bedrock far below the East River, which was an incredible feat considering the technology they had at the time. If you look way over there, you'll see Lady Liberty. She's a little harder to find at night."

As he points to our left, his arm brushes my back and my muscles tense. His voice is strong and deep and his enthusiasm for the little details of the bridge's architecture is endearing—but I'm having trouble concentrating on anything he's saying. *I think the referee realized this was a losing game and went home a while ago.*

When we get to the top of the bridge, we're surrounded by unobstructed 360-degree views of New York Harbor, Governor's Island and Lower Manhattan. I hold onto the railing as my jaw drops.

"What do you think? Pretty incredible, right?"

"I think this is one of the most magnificent views I've ever seen," I say, my heart beating faster.

"I can't tell you how many times I've been across this bridge, and it still gives me chills to stand in this spot," he says, moving behind me. He puts his hands on the railing, one on each side of me, and I tremble at the feel of our bodies being this close. He leans in closer, his cheek softly touching mine. We stand pressed together, taking in the majesty surrounding us. Talk about a romantic setting.

He turns me around to face him, wrapping his arms around my lower back. I shiver from the cold or from him—I'm not sure which. He's the perfect amount taller than me; my head rests at the hollow just below his chin. I press my ear to his chest to get warm, feeling his thudding heartbeat. I gaze steadily into his golden-flecked, green eyes.

He's watching me with an intensity that makes me lose my footing and he catches me, helping me regain my balance. My heart is fluttering so fast, I wonder if he can feel it through our jackets. He slowly drags his teeth over his bottom lip and I have to look away.

Even the best laid plans.

I hold my breath as he lowers his mouth, gently brushing his lips against mine before pulling away. My insides quiver and he gives me a smirk. I narrow my eyes. *He knows exactly what his whisper kiss just did to me.* He traces my bottom lip with his thumb, pulling me closer.

My body tingles from head to toe as he leans down and presses his full lips passionately against mine. My mouth parts as he eases his tongue inside, ever so tenderly, meeting mine before pulling back. I tilt my head as our kiss deepens, lighting a fire inside me. An electric current pulses through my every cell as we greedily explore each other.

There's such an unexpected softness in his kiss. He's a man whose gentleness shows through even in the hungriest moments of his desire.

His mouth is eager—yet patient. From the second our lips touched, they molded together and found a perfect rhythm of what is most definitely, the best kiss I've ever had in my life. I pull away lightheaded, needing a breath from our heated exchange. It feels like he just taught me what it's like to be kissed. I don't know what I've been doing all these years, but it's never felt like this before.

"Damn. You're an incredible kisser, Gemma," he whispers in my ear, turning my insides upside down.

He smiles and I'm unhinged. This isn't like me to feel such a flood of intense emotions. It's taking every ounce of me to not fight it and just let myself enjoy our first kiss.

We stare longingly into each other's eyes as he holds my face, trailing his thumb along my jawline. I could stand here with him, in this moment, all night. Being with him feels so good. Like a curious moth, it feels dangerous how drawn I am to his flame. The smell of him, the views of Manhattan and the full moon collide in a sensuous and powerful storm, leaving me breathless and wanting more.

EIGHTEEN

GEM & EM

Our room is blanketed in darkness. I peek at the clock on the nightstand and see it's still early. I look over at Emmeline, still fast asleep. The soft sound of her breathing comforts me. I rest the side of my face on my pillow close to hers and watch as her eyelids move back and forth. I wonder what she's dreaming about. *I bet she's on an adventure with a sea of turtles.* I wish I could join her in her dreams so we could go exploring together.

She flinches. Her breath's tranquil cadence stops, turning into a string of whimpers as her feet twitch back and forth. Raspy and rapid breaths come from the back of her throat, like she's trying to cry out, but something is stopping her. I place my hand over hers, rubbing gently until the noises stop and her soft and slow rhythm returns.

"It was just a bad dream," I whisper, falling back to sleep beside her.

"GIRLS, come on down once you're dressed and please finish packing," Mom calls up to us.

"Okay, Mom. I'm finishing Emmeline's hair."

Em fidgets impatiently. "I forgot to pack my toothbrush. Are you almost done? We need to make sure we get everything out of the bathroom."

"Almost. Hold still, I want to make sure they're even." I let out a sigh. "I'm a little sad to be moving back home, it's been fun living at Grandma's."

"Yeah, me too."

"Okay. All done. Don't forget Lenny," I say, pointing to a lump near the bottom of our bed.

Em shakes her ponytails and dives under the sheets, pulling out her turtle. "Oh my gosh, I almost forgot him. I wouldn't have been able to sleep tonight."

She puts him on top of our clothes next to Louie, my beloved lion. Mom bought us these stuffed animals before we were born; they go everywhere with us, their patched holes proof of their adventures.

We finish packing and help each other carry our suitcases downstairs, sitting on the couch where Mom's bed once was. The pictures we drew are still taped to the walls.

"Grandma?" I call out.

"I'm in the kitchen, love."

"Do you want us to take down the pictures we hung on the walls for Mom?"

"No, leave them up. Your artwork brightens the whole room," she says.

"Okay." I whisper to Em, "We'll make her some more when we're home."

"Is everyone ready?" Mom asks, carrying her toothbrush and a few other items, placing them in her maroon duffle bag.

"Yep," Em and I say together.

The little seed of sadness sprouts in my stomach. It's been nice seeing Grandma every day. *I'm going to miss her.*

NINETEEN

GEMMA

"You awake?" I ask, softly tapping on Mikayla's door.

"Only if you're not mad at me. If you are—I'm still asleep." She rolls over, pulling her duvet over her head as I open the door.

"How did it go last night?" she asks, from beneath her covers. I stand quietly, at the end of her bed, waiting for her to reappear. When I don't respond, she peeks one eye out.

"Uh oh, not good? I figured when I didn't get a text from you to meet up that things were going well." She sounds concerned. I faceplant onto her bed as she sits up.

"What happened? Why aren't you saying anything?" she asks, starting to squirm. "Was it bad? How could it not have gone well? Oh no. I'm sorry. Okay, I'll never do that again."

"Are you finished?" I ask, flatly, rolling onto my side.

"Mm-hmm," she responds, biting her cheek.

"I'm still not happy with the way that went down—but you were right."

"I was?" she asks, apprehensively.

"You were. He's incredible," I say, unable to control my smile.

"I knew it! You two are perfect for each other. There's no way I was going to miss on this one."

"No. Don't say that—don't put pressure on it. It was one date. A date that went really well—but still."

"Where did he take you?" she asks, ignoring me. She curls her legs under her like she always does for our morning story times.

"He took me to dinner in Brooklyn near his mom's house. The pizza was a 10/10. I have to take you sometime. Then we walked over the Brooklyn Bridge into lower Manhattan, I've never walked across before. Have you done it before?"

"Of course. I'm a New Yorker—it's mandatory. Not in years, though," she admits.

"Oh, Mika—everything about last night was perfection," I say, still reeling from our date. "He kissed me on the midway point at the top of the bridge and it was—aah there are no words! Which is why I'm so mad at you."

"You're mad at me because he kissed you?"

"I'm mad at you because he kissed me and I kissed him back. No, it's worse than that. It was the best kiss I've ever had," I say, hopelessly, putting my head in my hands.

"Uh-oh, look at you. This sounds like the witness is pleading guilty to breaking rule number three."

I glare at her. "Maybe you'll make a better lawyer when I fail out of law school," I say, miserably.

"You're not failing out of law school. Here, let's review the evidence," she says, in her best judge voice, as I roll my eyes.

"You are graduating from law school in May, which is roughly—six months away. Is this correct?"

"Yes, Your Honor, if I remain diligent about my studies and don't get distracted," I reply.

"Miles lives an hour away in Greenwich, is this also true?"

"That is true, Your Honor."

"Miles is a resident doctor who also has a demanding schedule and thereby does not have a lot of extra time on his hands to distract you from your studies, is this again, also true?"

"Objection, Your Honor. The question calls for speculation," I say, smugly.

"Overruled. This is my courtroom and I'll speculate if I want to."

I throw a pillow at her and it misses.

"Order in the court!" she shouts, as we both roll on her bed laughing. "Seriously, though. Miles couldn't distract you from your studies, even if he wanted to. If the two of you start dating, you'd be lucky to see each other twice a month."

"You're right. I hadn't really thought of that." I give her a dirty look. "Probably because I was too busy trying to never see him again."

"Um, you're welcome," she says, snarkily.

I roll onto my back, staring at the ceiling, conflicted. "No, he's great and all, don't get me wrong. It's just that every time something good in my life happens, I worry that something bad will happen, you know, to balance it out."

"Why would you think that? Have you always thought that way?" she asks.

"No. Maybe. I don't know," I say, thinking back to when I started carrying this fear around. *I know exactly when it started.*

"It's just a date, Gemma. Nothing bad is going to happen because you like him," she says.

Except for the fact bad things happen to people I love.

"I have such a hard time letting people in. It honestly terrifies me," I admit, as she listens carefully, giving me time to find the right words.

"The few times I've started dating someone, I pull away and find a reason to end things no matter how great the person is. I don't want to do that to Miles, he's such a sweet guy," I say.

"What do you think it is that's keeping you from letting yourself be happy?"

There it is, the loaded question.

The one I can't answer because there's still so much I haven't told her.

"Is there a terrible breakup you went through that I don't know about? I don't remember you ever telling me about a breakup that wounded you so deeply it left you with lasting trust issues," she says.

I shake my head.

"No. I never let myself date someone long enough. I always end up breaking things off at the start to protect myself from ever feeling any kind of loss."

I would give anything for my issues to have stemmed from a bad breakup. I sit up and fold a sweater on the end of her bed, the weight of the true source of my pain sitting heavy in my chest.

"Miles isn't someone who would ever hurt you if that's what you're worried about. Even if things didn't work out between the two of you, he would never be rude or disrespect you. As far as I know, he's still on good terms with all of his ex-girlfriends. Well, except for the last one."

"All? How many has he had?" I ask, suddenly skeptical.

"Enough. He's not a player if that's what you're worried about."

"No. He doesn't come across that way—at all. It's actually not Miles I'm worried about," I say.

"Oh—I get it. Gem, sometimes things don't work out and it doesn't necessarily have to be someone's fault. Maybe you just haven't found the right fit yet, but you'll never know unless you try. Having a relationship that doesn't work out isn't a bad thing. Past relationships are a great way to learn what you want or don't want so you can do better with the next one. I know you've said before that you have a hard time trusting someone enough to let them in, I wonder where that comes from. You don't seem like someone who believes everyone's out to hurt you."

No, not everyone. I don't like where this conversation's headed and I'm the one who started it.

"Enough about me, how was your night? What'd you end up doing? Did you end up going dancing?" I ask.

"We did. But this conversation is important. Just know I'm always here if you want to talk more about it," she says, patiently.

"Thanks, I appreciate you." I want so badly to open up to her. "Tell me about your night."

"We went out for dinner and then to a comedy club. My sides still hurt, we laughed so hard. After the show we went dancing. I didn't get home until after three," she says, stretching her arms over her head, yawning.

"Aww, I'm sorry I missed it. You haven't had a night like that in a long time. You deserved a fun night after the week you had."

She nods. "I'm so glad I had this weekend off. I needed a break from the hospital."

I pick at my cuticle, looking down.

"What?" She knows me so well. "There's clearly something on your mind. Don't take it out on your poor cuticles. They're a mess lately."

I drop my hands, hiding them under me. "Gee, thanks. It's nothing. Tell me more about your night."

"I told you everything, spit it out," she says.

"It's just that Miles is such a great person, and on top of that he's one of your closest friends. I'd never want to hurt him," I say.

"Listen, Miles is someone who fully understands that life isn't perfect, and things don't always go as planned. I know him well enough to know he wouldn't want you stressing over any of this. He's a grown man who can totally handle what may or may not come of your relationship, so why not put the 'what ifs' away for a moment and at least try with him? If it doesn't work out, it doesn't work out. No hard feelings—from either of us."

I make a face. "I don't like the way that sounds."

"I think your feelings for him might be deeper than you realize. Maybe it's time to let your guard down and see what happens."

"Thanks. I know you're right. I'm going to keep an open mind and try and let all of my intrusive thoughts go."

"I think you'd regret not giving it a chance."

I nod as a text comes in, it's Miles.

> GM, Gem

I look at my phone and smile. *Gem.*

Mikayla grins and shakes her head.

"Let me guess, Miles?" She clasps her hands in front of her chest, a lovesick look on her face. "Text him back—he probably knows we're talking about him anyway."

> GM. I had a great time last night, thanks again. Talking to Mika. Catch up later?

> Sure. I had a great time too. Can you ask MK what her Wednesday schedule looks like?

"Are you working Wednesday?" I ask.

"I think so—why?"

"Miles wants to know."

"Okay, tell him I'll text him later," she says, getting up to change. I nod and get up from the end of her bed.

"Thanks, I really needed to hear this."

"You know I'm always here for you," she says, with a warm smile.

"I'll meet you downstairs," I say, closing her door behind me.

What might Miles want to talk to her about? Probably just two old friends catching up over coffee.

TWENTY

GEM & EM

Grandma's car pulls into our gravel driveway that runs alongside our house. Our once-green grass has been taken over almost entirely by yellow patches, scorched from the sun. Dry, withered stems hang over the sides of Mom's window boxes, they've given up every last hope of survival. It makes me sad to see them in such a state, knowing just how many hours Mom spent watering and caring for them. It's been so long since we've been home, I almost forgot what our house looks like.

"I missed our house," Em whispers in my ear. We hop out of the car and run to our cheerful yellow front door. I stand on my tiptoes trying to see through the square glass windows, impatiently waiting for Mom to unlock the door.

"Girls, please come and get your things," Mom says, leaning on her crutch as she gets out of the car. In our excitement we'd forgotten about our suitcases. We run back while Grandma pulls them from her trunk. We put them on the front porch and go back to help Mom with her things.

"My little helpers, thank you. Here, can you go and unlock the door for us?" she asks, handing me the key.

Emmeline and I take off for the front porch. It takes me a few times to put the key in the right way but finally, the lock turns and I push the door open. It's dark inside. The air is hot, and smells like it's been trapped inside Grandma's old suitcase; the one we stuff our dolls into when we play in her basement. Em and I run down the hallway, eager to see everything.

"I've missed our room. And our desk," I say, jumping up and down on my bed.

"Me too!" Emmeline reaches up and opens the window above our bed to let in some fresh air.

"Let's go get our suitcases so we can unpack," I say.

We jump off our beds and wheel our suitcases down the hall. The sound of the wheels against the wooden floors reminds me of the night we left in a hurry for the hospital. I shudder, trying to forget everything about that night.

"Mom, can we go outside?" I ask.

"Of course. Don't go too far because Grandma's leaving soon and I want you to get ready for bed. Today's been a long day for all of us."

"Okay." Emmeline and I kick our shoes off and run outside into our backyard past Mom's overgrown garden.

"Let's watch the sunset," Emmeline says, climbing onto the lowest branch of our giant sassafras tree.

My fingers grip the deep, old grooves of the bark while I wait for her to heave herself up. I follow, sitting beside her. We dangle our legs in the twilight, listening to the crickets and frogs sing their nighttime melodies.

"Hey, if you could make one wish, what would it be?" Em asks.

"Anything?"

"Yep, anything," she says.

"That's easy."

"What is it?"

"I wish we could've seen those little blue eggs hatch," I say pointing to the empty nest we found a few months ago in a branch over our heads.

"How about you?"

"I wish we could start summer over again," she says.

AFTER OUR FIRST dinner back home, Emmeline and I finish unpacking and head to the bathroom to brush our teeth and get ready for bed. We stand shoulder to shoulder, happy to see our freckled reflections once again in our bathroom mirror.

"Look at your dimples," I giggle, pointing at her.

She opens her mouth in a goofy smile showing both rows of teeth, deepening the pockets of her dimples. Her silly face makes us laugh.

"During class I use my pencil's eraser to twist my cheek trying to make a dimple so I can match you, but as soon as I let go, it always disappears."

Em looks at my cheeks. "You don't need dimples. You're perfect just the way you are. Back-to-back."

I pat her on top of her head, showing a level hand between us.

"We're even! I must have grown at Grandma's," I say.

We brush our teeth, holding each other's hair while the other rinses and then run down the hall to our bedroom, jumping into bed.

"Mom, we're ready for our bedtime story!" Emmeline and I call to her.

We listen to her footsteps, paired with the thumping of her crutch as she slowly hobbles down the hallway.

"Whose bed am I sitting on tonight?" she asks.

"Mine, mine!" we both call out.

"How about birth order? Emmeline's bed tonight and Gemma—yours tomorrow."

"Okay," I say, sticking out my lower lip before joining them on Em's bed.

Mom reading us a bedtime story back in our room feels like a fairy-tale ending. I push down the scary parts of our summer, not wanting to invite those memories into our sacred bubble. Listening to the sound of Mom's voice as I lean against her is like hearing my favorite song. One I haven't heard in a long time.

"Hey, Mom?" I ask, as she finishes the story, tucking the book into the shelf near Emmeline's bed.

"Yes, love?"

"Can you tell us a story about our dad?"

She pauses, looking down at me. "Of course." Her smile fades to the faraway look she gets when we ask about him. She takes a deep breath. "Let's see. . . your dad loved you both more than anything in this whole world. He was so excited to be a father."

I can tell the words sting because her eyes get misty.

"When I was pregnant with you, he would always put his hands on my belly and lean down and whisper 'I love you more than the moon, the sun and the stars'. That's why I call you that; they're nicknames from your dad." she says, her eyes welling up.

My chest goes tight. "I'm sorry, I didn't mean to make you sad," I say, hugging her around the waist.

"It's okay, sweetheart. You didn't make me sad. I just miss him. I want you to always feel like you can ask questions about him–okay?" Emmeline and I nod.

"Time for bed, my sweet girls." She stands, and I hand her the crutch leaning against the wall under our window.

I jump over the rug between our beds and land with a bounce on my bed. Mom gently tugs our curtains closed as I pull the top sheet under my chin.

"I'm glad we're home," Emmeline says.

"I missed our room." I add.

"You two," she says, a proud smile on my face. "You're the best thing that ever happened to me."

Every time she says that it makes my insides smile.

"Dream big dreams, my moon and sun. Fill your pockets with as many stars as you can gather—and show me in the morning. I love you so much."

"Goodnight, Mom. We love you."

Mom switches off the light and pulls our door closed behind her. I let out a long exhale, one I've been holding in for weeks. Sleep pulls at my itchy eyelids, and I rub them with the backs of my fists.

"Goodnight, Sun," Emmeline whispers.

"Goodnight, Moon."

Em and I float up and up, into the pitch-black sky. Bright yellow stars of every size twirl around us and we run hand in hand among them, gathering as many of them as our pockets will hold. A peace-filled quiet creeps into every nook of our room. My heart smiles. *We're home.*

TWENTY-ONE

GEMMA

It's a gray and chilly Wednesday morning and I'm late for my train. Again. I close the door and drop my keys as I'm trying to lock up. I pick them up and drop them again. Ugh! *I hope this isn't a sign of how my day's going to go.* After the third try, I manage to lock the door and run down the steps to make up for those few seconds I just lost.

It's morning rush and the sidewalk is filled with people as I hurry toward my subway entrance. I dart through myriad briefcases, backpacks and lunch boxes while checking my watch to see how many minutes I have to make my train. Crashing metal hits the sidewalk behind me. I jump, covering my ears.

Breathe, it was just a loud noise. You're fine.

Annoyed at myself for flinching so hard, I start to jog when a small voice calls after me.

"Excuse me, you dropped this."

Something tells me she's talking to me. I feel around to the side pocket of my backpack where my water sits to find it's empty. I turn around and see a small girl holding my bottle in the air. She's standing at the base of a red stone and iron staircase, wearing a fuzzy pink fleece jacket. Her other arm is hooked through her sister's.

Just like Gem & Em.

My breath hitches in my throat and I walk back to the girls, taking in their matching clothes and braids as their mom descends the stairs. I look down into their little faces and smile.

"That was so nice of you," I say, their steely blue eyes studying me. I reach out and take the water bottle from her small hand.

"Twins?" I say to the mom as she steps onto the sidewalk beside the girls, out of breath.

"Yes. Mornings are always an adventure for us."

I smile and nod, knowingly.

"I'm older by three minutes!" the girl who handed me my water says proudly as her sister tugs on her arm.

"Ahh, the older twin. I was a. . . I'm a twin too," I say.

"You are?" The girls giggle together, the way only twins do.

"I am," I whisper, feeling the heavy weight of those two little words.

"Thanks for my water," I say, turning away as tears fill my eyes. I run for the subway station, needing to put as much space as I can between the twins, their mother and me.

TWENTY-TWO

GEM & EM

"Mom? Emmeline? Where are you?" After searching the house, I find them picking vegetables in the garden. I swing our screen door open, noticing a flurry of movement out of the corner of my eye.

"Look at the butterflies," I say, pointing to the hydrangeas and milkweed Mom planted to welcome our little flying friends. Dried dirt crumbles under my feet as I run between our garden rows trying to catch one.

"I got one!"

Em runs to me, and I make an opening with my thumbs wide enough that she can peek inside, yet small enough so the butterfly can't escape.

"It's a zebra!" Em squeals. "Mom, come see!"

Mom looks up from pruning her rose bushes and as she starts to stand, she stops. "Ouch!"

"What is it?" Emmeline shouts.

"It's nothing. I just got too close to the thorns." She drops her shears dabbing the back of gardening glove against her cheek. Em and I run to her; my butterfly still cupped in my hands.

"You're bleeding!" I say, as two rows of tiny red droplets grow on her cheek.

"It's just a scratch." Mom smiles and wipes her cheek. "Now, let me see your butterfly," she says, peeking into my hands. "Ooh, it's a Zebra Swallowtail. It must be your lucky day, Gem. I haven't seen one in years."

I slowly peel my hands apart, the butterfly pauses a beat and then leaps into the air, flapping its black and white striped wings to freedom.

"I couldn't even feel it in my hand, it was like holding air," I say.

"Can you two help me carry these inside?" Mom asks, pointing to the piles of vegetables at the edge of our garden. "Make sure you wash your feet off after me, so we don't track dirt in the house."

Mom likes going barefoot in the summer, just like we do. She's walking without a crutch now—but still has to be careful. Em and I take turns carrying load after load of cucumbers, zucchini, sweet corn and green beans inside.

"Is it okay if we go into the woods? We want to press a few more pennies for our summer artifact project. Em and I are going to win this year!" I say, with unabashed certainty.

"Of course. When you get back, we'll make snickerdoodles. That way you can take them as a snack in your lunchboxes next week."

"Nooo. I can't believe this is our last weekend of summer," Emmeline says, hanging her head.

I put my arm around the back of her shoulders and start for the front door.

"Wait, I need to go get some pennies," Em says.

"I already got some from our desk. Here," I say, reaching into my pocket, handing half to her.

We walk down the winding gravel road until we get to the sharp bend by Mr. Paul's house and pick up the railroad tracks. The tracks ahead look shimmery and blurry. Mom says that's called a heat haze.

"The tracks are hot; make sure you step all the way over, so you don't get burned like last summer."

"I still have a scar," Em says, looking down at her left shin.

I step over the rust-colored track closest to us and Emmeline follows. We walk down the middle of the tracks side by side, just like we'll do next week on our walk to and from school. A warm breeze blows, mixing dusty gravel, fresh cut hay, and creosote—all familiar scents of a hot summer day.

We each pick a track and spread our pennies in a long row. I stand off to the side inspecting my shiny Abraham Lincoln heads, feeling good about the space I made sure to leave between each one.

"Ouch!" Emmeline screams.

"What?"

"I just burned my finger."

"Oh no. Are you alright?"

"Yeah," she says, putting it in her mouth.

"Is it bad?"

"I don't think so, but it hurts."

I cross over to her side of the track so I can look at her finger. There's already a blister forming. I give it a kiss like Mom always does.

"Feel better?" I ask.

"A little."

Off in the distance a train whistles.

"Train's coming," I say, as Emmeline and I scurry down the hill to watch from the shadows as it races by. The whistle sounds several times, slicing through the stillness, warning anything in its path. The blasts grow louder with every second. Em and I push our backs against a tree near the edge of the woods and wait. Being this close to a train going full speed is both scary and exciting.

A drum pounds inside my chest to the beat of the wheels as they glide over the tracks. Green, blue and brown boxcars whiz by in a blur, rushing off to their destination. And then, just as quickly as it raced in, it's gone, swallowed by miles of track and forest. The woods blanketed once again in silence.

Like two hidden mice checking if the coast is clear, we creep slowly from the edge of the tree line and run up the steep, rocky embankment to check on our pennies.

"Mine all stayed," I say, victoriously.

"Mine too!"

We wait for them to cool before picking them up. When we've collected them all, we spread them out in a grassy patch to the side of the tracks so we can compare our favorites. Em looks over at me, a proud smile on her face. "Now we'll be able to finish our wind chime before summer's over."

TWENTY-THREE

GEMMA

I'm on the train heading uptown thankful I don't have to be back on campus for the next four days. I get off at my stop and walk to the store to pick up a few things as my phone rings.

"Hey, Mom!"

"Hi, sweetheart. I've been thinking about you. You sounded so stressed when we spoke on Sunday. Did you finish everything?"

"Everything's done. The last few weeks have been my toughest yet between school and my tutoring schedule."

"You've been working so hard, I'm glad you have a break."

I grab a basket and start down a crowded aisle. "That makes two of us. Did I tell you Mikayla and I are helping serve the annual Thanksgiving dinner at the Neighborhood House tomorrow?"

"That's the place you volunteer teaching kids to dance during the summer, right?"

"Yep, same place. I'm hoping to see some of my students when we're there."

Sharing my love of dance has helped heal a younger piece of myself. I can't wait to get back to it after graduation.

"I'm sad I'm not coming home this year. You realize this is the first Thanksgiving we won't be together?" I ask.

"I know, we're going to miss you too."

"Sorry—excuse me." I step out of the way of someone reaching for yams. "What are you and Grandma doing?"

"We're hosting our very first Friendsgiving. If all goes well, it might become a new tradition for us."

"Friendsgiving—you two are the cutest. Who's coming?"

"The Baxters and the Wilson family from down the street, and you remember Mr. Collins, right?"

"My old grief counselor? I haven't heard his name in years."

"Yep, he's joining us too. I'm looking forward to it. Work has been so busy lately—I need a break too," she says.

"I bet. The holidays can be a hard time for a lot of people," I say, as silence takes over the line. *Those first few holidays were brutal.*

"Hey, how'd that date go with—what was his name again?"

I let out a breath, grateful for her change of subject.

"Miles. It went well. I don't know. We're both so busy. I was hoping to see him this weekend but he's spending Thanksgiving in the Hamptons with his mom and brother. It's a few hours from the city."

"Oh, I see. From what little you've told me, he seems nice," she says.

"He is. I haven't been interested in dating anyone since moving to New York and—I don't know. We'll see."

"You're young, have fun," she says, her voice full of warmth.

Something's different in her tone.

"You sound happy, Mom."

"I do?"

I turn down the canned goods aisle and grab one of the last cans of pumpkin, putting it in my basket before they're all gone. "You do. I hear it in your voice."

"You never miss a thing, do you? I got a letter in the mail recently from someone I haven't heard from in a long time. Reconnecting with them has—well... it's made me really happy," she says.

I pull my backpack up higher on my shoulder, trying not to bump into anyone. "Who is it?"

"It's no one you know. They moved away when you were a baby."

"Well, they have great timing—with Thanksgiving and all. I'm glad it's made you so happy."

"It has. I have so much to be thankful for this year. You are, once again, at the top of my list," she says.

"And you and Grandma are at the top of mine. I hope you know I feel like I won the lottery being raised by you two."

"That's nice to hear, sweetheart. Where are you right now? I keep hearing noises in the background."

"I've been walking in circles at the grocery store with a basket in my hand. I need to pick up a few ingredients for Mikayla and my Thanksgiving dinner tomorrow and right now it looks like we'll be splitting a can of pumpkin."

"Okay, love, let me let you go so you can focus."

"Thanks Mom. Talk to you tomorrow."

"Sounds good. Please say hi to Mikayla for me. I love you, Gem."

"Will do. Love you too, Mom."

I stand in the middle of the aisle, a nearly empty basket in my hand, smiling at nothing in particular. *It makes my heart happy hearing her sound so cheerful.*

THE SMELL of something delicious wakes me. I grab my robe and walk downstairs to investigate.

"What a nice way to wake up on Thanksgiving morning. It smells amazing down here." I hover over our kitchen island and inhale deeply.

"Hey there! I hope you're hungry," she says.

"Famished. What're you making?"

"I broke out our old waffle iron. I'm making homemade Belgian waffles with whipped cream and fresh cut strawberries; your favorite."

My heart swells in my chest. "You're the best, you know that?"

I reach into the cabinet behind her and pull out a large coffee mug pouring myself a cup. "How can I help?" I ask.

"Just sit and talk to me while these last two finish cooking."

I sit down at the island and take my first sip of coffee, savoring every drop.

"Before I forget, I'm thankful for coffee," I say.

Mikayla nods exaggeratedly. "You and me both."

"What time do you want to head over to Neighborhood House?" I dip my finger into the whipped cream, remembering how we used to steal spoonfuls of Grandma's.

"I'm thinking as soon as we finish eating, we could walk over. Did you finish all your projects? I know you had a lot going on with your clinic," she asks.

I nod. "And now I'm so glad to turn off my lawyer brain for a few days."

"I'll bet. Are you seeing Miles over break?"

I shake my head. "He's working today and then heading out to the Hamptons," I say.

"Oh, that's right. His mom has an amazing place out there. I forgot they typically go there for the holidays."

I sit up straighter and take a breath, trying to find the right words so I don't sound too nosy. "I've been meaning to ask you but haven't seen you —how was your coffee with him last week?" I ask, in my most casual voice.

"It's always good to see Miles. That morning was especially chaotic for me, so it was short and sweet. I can tell he really likes you," she says.

"Really?" I try but fail to stop the grin crawling across my face.

"Yes, really. You say that like it's hard for you to believe. Dude seriously likes you. You have to know that, right?"

I smile at the thought of Miles talking to Mikayla about me. "I guess so. Maybe I'm just needing some reassurance. It's so sudden, I'm still surprised by all of it," I say.

"You two are a good match. I've wanted to introduce you for a long time."

"I hate to admit it, but I'm glad you did. So much for sticking to the rules." I put my head in my hands as she shrugs.

"Do you think he's easy to talk to?" She plops two more waffles onto a growing pile.

"Miles? Of course. I could talk to him about anything. What makes you ask?"

"He mentioned something that I think is just a New York/Midwest thing."

I tilt my head to the side. "Like what?"

She hesitates and the beat of silence seems to go on forever. "He said it feels like you hold back sometimes when you're talking to him."

I stiffen. "He did? Holding back about what?"

"Like when he brings up your family."

My pulse speeds up. *I was afraid of this.* I try to cover the fact that I'm immediately defensive. I shake my head as indifferently as I can. "I can't think of anything," I reply.

"I told him it could just be the differences between the way New Yorkers and people from the Midwest communicate. Not to generalize, but we New Yorkers tend to talk a lot and can over communicate—if there's such a thing. Midwesterners, in my limited experience, seem a bit more—I don't know. . . reserved. Since getting to know you I've noticed that you'd much rather be the one asking questions than the one talking about yourself," she says.

I nod. "That's true. Did he seem concerned?"

"I wouldn't say concerned, he was just wondering if there was something significant in your past that you don't feel comfortable talking about," she says.

There it is. My guilt surges. *I'm such a liar.*

"I told him to ask you about it when, and if, it comes up again."

I manage a smile. "Of course, I hope he does. I think it's just me getting used to the idea of letting someone in. You know, like we talked about the other day."

"Totally," she replies, keeping her eyes on the waffles.

I hate lying to her, it makes me feel even worse. I need to tell her. I don't know why I keep putting it off. It's never going to be easy.

Beep—Beep—Beep! The timer goes off again. "That was the last batch. Let's eat!" She takes off her apron.

"I can't believe you made whipped cream too. My grandma would be proud," I say, smiling.

"I love to cook, I just never have the time. I wanted to make something special today."

"Thanks, Mika. I'm so thankful for you and your friendship."

"Right back at you. I'm also thankful for the A-hole cyclist who crashed into you in the park because without him, we never would have met," she says.

"Ha! You're right. Cheers to the A-hole!" I say, as we clink coffee mugs.

MIKAYLA and I finish serving Thanksgiving dinner and sign out at the front desk. It was great seeing so many of my dance students and their families.

"We left just as the dance floor was heating up," I say, feeling good about all the smiling faces we just served. The streets are eerily quiet as we walk home. Even the city feels like it's taking a moment to catch its breath. As we turn the corner, Mikayla bends at the waist grabbing my arm to stop herself from falling.

I hold on tight, helping her find her footing. "What's wrong?"

"I don't know, I just saw stars. That was weird," she says, taking long, drawn out breaths.

"Come here, sit down." I pull her over to the side, sitting next to her on someone's front steps. I search her face. "You look pale. When was the last time you fainted? Has it happened since that morning in the kitchen, what was that—a month ago?"

She nods. "A few times."

I rest my forehead in my hand. "What? Why didn't you tell me?"

"Because you worry too much about me as it is. I didn't want to make you even more neurotic." Her words bite and I blink several times to stop my eyes from welling.

There's a reason I worry about the people I love.

"The last thing I need is you following me around, like I'm going to fall over at any minute. I'm scarred from the time I woke up and your hand was on me checking if I was breathing."

Humiliated, I stare at the sidewalk. "You need to go to the doctor. This has happened too many times."

"I will. But I know I'm fine. My blood sugar is probably low."

"We had waffles and whipped cream a few hours ago, how is that possible?"

"One of us is an actual doctor. It's possible."

I shake my head. "I'm worried about you," I say, a fretful look on my face.

"I had some labs drawn a few days ago just to rule anything out. I'm sure they'll come back normal. C'mon, let's go. I'm already feeling better," she says, standing up.

I get up with her and hold onto her arm so she can't turn away. "Promise you'll let me know as soon as the labs come back. I don't want you to hide this from me. I won't follow you around compulsively asking if you're okay," I say, trying to hide my hurt.

"I'm sorry. That was mean. I shouldn't have said that. I know you worry about me, I'd worry about you too if this situation was reversed. I'm just frustrated, I don't know why this keeps happening." She says, as her eyes mist over. I put my arms around her and hug her tight.

Please let her be okay.

I BRUSH my teeth and just as I'm about to wash my face, my phone rings.

"Hey Miles, Happy Thanksgiving," I say, sitting down on the edge of my bed.

"Thanks, you too. How was your day?" he asks.

"It was good. Mikayla and I just finished watching *It's a Wonderful Life*—our holiday tradition. That ending—it gets us every time," I say, sniffling.

"I know the scene you're talking about. Good ole' George Bailey will do that to you."

I grab a tissue from my nightstand to wipe my nose. "Right? I could watch it on repeat the entire season. How was your day? I bet your mom and brother are happy to see you."

"They are. It's been great, I'm glad we could all be together tonight. You aren't going to believe this, though."

"That doesn't sound good." I fall back against my pillows, pulling the sides of my robe tighter. I need to turn up the heat, it's chilly in here. I glance at my windows to make sure they're all shut.

"My mom has a closing in the city so she's driving back tomorrow afternoon and taking my brother with her. He's been out here all week and needs to get back to LA for work."

"Oh no! You just got there," I say.

"I know."

"Are you coming back with them?" I ask, trying to contain my excitement at the possibility of seeing him over break.

"I considered that and then I had another thought—"

"...Which was?"

"Do you and Mikayla have plans for the weekend?"

"She's working all weekend. Why?"

"Well, I was going to ask you both, but since she's working—what do you think about coming out here tomorrow? I'm not working again until Sunday night and your classes don't start back until Monday, right?" he asks.

I nervously trace the worn elbow of my robe. "That's right. Oh...wow." My palms start to sweat at the thought of a weekend alone with him. What about Mikayla though? I can't leave her right now.

"Is that a good 'oh wow'?" he asks.

"I mean, I'd love to see you. I was hoping we could see each other at some point this weekend. The only thing is, I have a few tutoring sessions tomorrow and then one on Saturday."

"Are they in person or online?"

I open the planner on my nightstand. "My morning sessions tomorrow are all in person and so is my session on Saturday."

"Any chance you could switch your session on Saturday to online?"

"I could ask," I say, hesitantly. "We've always met in person, but I could see if they wouldn't mind switching this once."

"Does that sound like it's a maybe then?"

I hear the smile in his voice.

My heart hiccups. "Um, I think so. I mean, I'd love to. I'll text them first thing in the morning."

"Sounds good. I hope it works out...because...I'd really love to see you."

Our kiss on the bridge flashes in my mind.

"Well, my mom and brother are waiting for me downstairs, we're three Scrabble games deep. I want to spend as much time with them as I can before they leave."

Awww, they play Scrabble together.

"Yes, go squeeze in as much family time as you can."

"Goodnight. I hope I'll see you tomorrow," he says.

"Me too. G'night."

My skin prickles with goosebumps, and I slide under my comforter to get warm. Why am I so nervous?

I can't leave Mikayla, not after she almost fainted. But she *is* working all weekend. This is exactly what she means about obsessing over her. She would insist that I go. Going might even prove to her that I can handle whatever it is she's facing. Maybe then she won't feel like she has to hide things from me. I turn out the light and chew my cuticles, wondering how this is all going to play out. *A whole weekend?*

TWENTY-FOUR

GEM & EM

It's autumn, my favorite season. Pumpkins, corn mazes, and Halloween. The leaves have changed into their fall colors and are piling up on the ground as the weather turns cold. Emmeline, Mom and I have all settled into our school routine. Mom's driving again. She goes to her classes during the day and is slowly picking up night shifts at the restaurant. When she graduates from her Masters' program in December, she's going to quit the restaurant so she can spend more time with us.

A cool wind blows as Em and I sit perched on a low branch of our climbing tree, dangling our feet while we take a break from raking. Mom opens the back door, our penny wind chime in her hands.

"You finished it!" Em shouts.

I clasp my hands together. "I think we're going to win!"

"I think you have a good chance, you've been working on it for months. I thought you'd be excited to see how it turned out. How's the raking going back here?" she says.

"We were almost done and then she jumped into our pile, and they went everywhere," I say, looking over at Emmeline who shrugs her shoulders.

"I couldn't help myself, Mom, you should have seen our leaf mountain."

"Jumping in the leaves is the best part of raking. I'm sure Em will help you rake them all back into the pile," Mom says.

Em looks at me, shrugging one shoulder. "After a few more jumps?"

I sigh and let out a reluctant grin. "Only if you help me put them back, I want to be finished."

"You know I always do."

We shake on it. Mom smiles at the two of us and holds out our wind chime so we can see the final product up close. Several shiny rows of flattened pennies hang from various lengths of thin gray strings. Mom drilled holes in a piece of driftwood we found on our recent trip to Lake Michigan for the top.

"I thought we could hang it up until the contest. Now that the leaves are gone it will give us something pretty to look at until the spring. How about you go find a good spot for it?" Mom asks.

"I'll find it," Em shrieks.

"No, I will! I know the perfect branch."

Emmeline and I both take a side and scramble up the tree. The tree bark feels cool against my palms as I grip the branches. On my way up, I pass the nest that we'd found earlier this summer and stop to inspect it as Em scurries past me. I leave the nest undisturbed, hoping the mom will come back next season.

I pull myself up onto a thick branch, shimmying over several smaller branches searching for a good place for our wind chime. I look to see if I can catch her but she's already way above me near the top.

"Emmeline, sweetheart, that's high enough. Do you see a branch you like? If not, I want you to come back down a little bit."

"Look Gem, I just found the perfect spot."

"Wait, but I just found a great spot too! Look at mine."

Emmeline looks down from several branches above. "That's the back of the tree. Don't you want to be able to see it from our bedroom window? If we hang it in my spot, we can look at it every day."

"Oh, you're right, I didn't think about that," I say, my hopes of finding the perfect spot diminishing.

Emmeline passes me on her way to go get the wind chime. Mom hands it up to her and she tucks it carefully under her arm. She pulls herself higher as she starts her climb back up the tree.

"I hope I can remember where it is," she says.

"You'll remember. Here, hand it to me. I'll hold it for you while you climb."

I follow closely below her. When she gets to parts of the tree where she needs both hands to pull herself up, she hands the wind chime down to me. We follow this pattern of back and forth as we go.

"I found it! Here it is," she says.

I stop at the branch just below her and she hands the wind chime back to me so she can climb out. She gets down on her stomach and hugs the branch, her arms and legs inching out until she finds the perfect spot. Sandwiched between two branches, I edge my way out below her.

"I'm ready. Hand it to me, Gem."

"Hold on, I'm going to swing it into those little branches on your right so you can grab it instead of trying to catch it," I say.

"Okay."

I try several times, unsuccessfully, until the strings finally hook onto a smaller branch near Em, and I let go. She reaches over with one hand and unhooks the wind chime, dangling it into the air. She shakes it, letting the strings untangle themselves. When they are unraveled, she takes the hook at the top and latches it to a sturdy branch that faces out to the back of our house.

"There! Safe and secure," she says proudly.

"You did it!"

"It looks so good, Em! It's just what our tree needed," Mom says, encouraging her from the ground below. "Come on down, girls so you can see it from where I'm standing."

Mom's beaming smile tells me she's proud of us and our wind chime. Emmeline slowly inches herself backwards on her stomach to the fork in the tree. Wedging one of her feet into the fork, she tries to stand but she slips and loses her grip, falling onto the branch below her with a loud and unexpected thump. The surrounding branches shake including the one I'm standing on. I can hear Mom's gasp from all the way up here.

"Em!" Mom yells to her.

She clings to the branch, I can see she's using all of her strength to pull herself back on top. Her feet dangle in the air just a few feet above me. I hold my breath, willing her to pull herself back onto her stomach.

"I'm fine, my foot just slipped," she says.

There's tension in her voice from straining to hold on. She tries to swing her leg up and over the branch to help pull herself back up, but just misses every time. After several tries, her toes finally connect and she shimmies up and over. She rights herself onto her stomach, taking a second to steady herself.

"You did it! Please hold on tight and go slow as you come down," Mom says.

"I will."

A wave of relief washes over me now that she's safely back on the branch. She starts backing up, and this time when she wedges her foot into the fork, she holds onto a bunch of smaller branches to help her balance. We take our time climbing the rest of the way down until she gets to the last branch where it's close enough to jump. She leaps onto the grass like a frog. Mom hugs her against her stomach as she runs her fingers through her hair. "Did that scare you?"

"A little bit, but I knew I could get back up."

"That's my girl, so brave and strong. Good thing you two are such strong climbers," Mom says, kissing the top of her head. "Come look at how beautiful it looks from down here, Gem."

I join them on the grass taking a few steps back from the trunk. The three of us stand together, proud of our shiny creation blowing gently in the autumn breeze. The sound of our pressed pennies clinking together breathes life into our sassafras tree.

"I love it so much," Em says.

"You were right Em, you found the perfect spot," I say, putting my arm around her. She leans her head down on my shoulder and we stand for several minutes admiring our work.

"Grandma's coming for dinner tonight. Do you think you two can finish the rest of the raking before she gets here? I'm going to make dinner."

I pick up my rake. "Yep. What are you making?"

"Mom's famous spaghetti and meatballs. It's one of Grandma's favorites," Mom says.

Em and I hungrily lick our lips. "Ours too."

"Can we make a special dessert for her when we're done?"

"Of course, she'd love that."

Mom walks in the house and Emmeline and I return to our raking. We take turns jumping over and over into the crunchy pile of leaves, pushing them back together after each jump. I take a running start and it feels like I'm flying until I disappear under the leaves. I stare up into the blue sky through gaps in the leaves as I sink to the bottom. Fragments of leaves swirl around the sides of my face—like I'm looking through a kaleidoscope.

Em stands with their back to the pile. "My turn!"

I climb out and push them together as she falls onto her back. She flaps her arms and legs up and down—her fall version of a snow angel, until she's completely buried.

TWENTY-FIVE

THE HAMPTONS

> Arrival still 3:00?

> Yep. The Jitney's nice!

> Glad you like it. Can't wait to see you.

> You too.

I smile and stare out my window. *I can't believe I'm about to spend an entire weekend with Miles.* The volume and speed of cars whizzing by on these multi-lane highways is utterly terrifying. It's a far cry from the farm lined roads back home. *I'm glad I'm not the one driving.* The view from my window is more cars than scenery so I pick up one of my books and start studying. I hope I can get everything done in the next two hours. I send a quick text to my mom, letting her know where I'll be for the weekend, and then get back to work, putting in my earbuds to focus.

    I occasionally glance out the window as the narrow field of asphalt and paint passes under the bus tires. The bright November sun feels good as it streams through the glass. The bus slows before exiting onto a smaller highway. I close my notebook and put my things in my tote bag so I can take in the scenery for this last stretch of the drive. About twenty minutes later, a green and white wooden sign appears that reads "Historic Amagansett Settled 1680." *We must be getting close.* I text a picture of the sign to Miles.

As the bus comes to a stop, I immediately recognize his strong and stocky frame through the windows on the opposite side of the bus. A trickle of lava swirls in my stomach. His hands are in his front pockets and he's leaning against the trunk of an old maple tree, wearing a green cable sweater. I stand and stretch my legs, waiting for the passengers in front of me to collect their things. I reach into the overhead compartment to grab my bag and wonder if he can see me through these tinted windows. A smile creeps across his face as he rakes his hand through his thick hair. *It's criminal how effortlessly handsome he is.* His hair falls just below his earlobes, perfectly accenting his dark olive skin and angular cheekbones. My legs go weak as I watch him through the window.

He gives me a small wave and I wave back. Now that I know he can see me, I scroll through my phone to avoid staring at him. *I wish this line would hurry up.* As soon as I'm off the bus, he reaches out to take the bags off my shoulder and pulls me against him into a hug. His arms feel tight and strong around me.

"How was your ride?" he asks, holding on to me.

"That was the nicest bus I've ever been on. I don't know what I was expecting, but it wasn't that."

"Are you hungry? I'd love to take you to lunch and show you around Amagansett if you're up for it?" he asks.

"I'd love a tour. I'm a little hungry now that you mention it. It was an early morning trying to get out here."

He smiles and takes my hand like it's the most natural thing in the world. "I'm parked right down the street." Warmth spreads up my arm as we walk past several parked cars until he stops beside a yellow Jeep Wrangler. He opens the back door and puts my bags on the bright and bold yellow and black leather seats.

"It looks like a bumble bee in here," I say.

He laughs, shaking his head. "I know, my mom got this car when my brother and I were deep into our Transformer era. She's never been able to part with it. We're kind of surprised it even still runs."

"Aww, that's the cutest. I love it."

"So does my mom." He opens my door and walks around to the driver's side to climb in.

"I wanted to take you to the Lobster Roll, but they're closed for the season. It's a Hamptons institution. I'll have to take you there this summer."

Summer plans? Eek. Let's see how the weekend goes.

"I know another little place with great food and a fun vibe. It'll be perfect for a late lunch."

"Sounds good, I'll let you lead the way."

He looks over at me, holding my gaze. His green and amber eyes look beautiful in this light. And good God, those thick and long eyelashes—it's enough already. My stomach fills with dancing butterflies. Unable to contain what I'm feeling, I look down, heat rising in my face.

Miles leans in, taking my chin in his hand, turning my face toward his. I lower my gaze from his eyes to his mouth. He has a bit of scruff, which accents his perfectly peaked, full lips. I look up into his kind eyes, realizing they're locked on mine. He pulls my face to his and kisses me, bringing back memories of our once-in-a-lifetime moment on the bridge. His lips feel like velvet against mine as his tongue meets mine with soft curiosity. I bury my hands in his satin-soft locks, pressing my lips more deeply into his over and over again.

I twirl his thick hair between my fingers, tightening my grip. The feel of his tongue swirling against mine, completely unravels me. Our intensity builds and I finally have to break away from his passionate, yet gentle kisses before my heart explodes. His sweet taste lingers on my lips and we press our foreheads together, lost in our post-kiss haze.

AFTER LUNCH he gives me a tour as promised. Amagansett is quaint and welcoming. Its brick buildings, taverns and old school crown molding storefronts give off a small-town feel.

"I have to say, this town feels like an upscale version of my hometown."

"Really, how so?"

"There's something about old-timey Main Street that just translates whether you're in a savvy city on the East Coast or a humble town in the middle of the country. It feels homegrown and well cared for," I say.

"Huh, that's a good way of putting it." He reaches over to hold my hand and we rest them on the console between our seats.

"Now that I've given you a tour of the town, do you want to head back to my mom's place?"

I nod, excited to see the house Mikayla has been raving about. "Sounds good, I'm looking forward to seeing it," I say.

"The house needed a lot of work when she bought it. As a single mom of two with a non-existent renovating budget, she did most of the updating herself, only bringing in contractors when it was absolutely necessary. She's got a great eye for these kinds of things."

"A DIY kind of woman. I like her style. I can tell how proud you are of her, it's nice hearing stories about her. Having a great mom is everything," I say.

"Are you and your mom close? What did you say her name is again?" he asks.

"Willow. Yes, we're very close. My mom is everything I want to be when I become a mom one day. She taught me love and kindness and the importance of inclusivity from a young age. She's the best of the best. I was raised by her and my grandma—two strong women who were never short on love and always long on patience."

Miles smiles warmly. "It sounds like we're both lucky in the mom department," he says.

I nod, looking out my window at the beautiful homes as they pass by.

"You must miss them since moving to New York," he says, as I nod.

"So much. We talk all the time but it's not the same."

"You're going to see them next month, right?"

He's a good listener. "Yep. After my semester ends. I'll be flying back in time for New Year's Eve, though. There's no place better to celebrate New Year's than the city."

"I have to agree. It's not even a fair comparison," he says.

"Mikayla and I throw a New Year's Eve party every year."

"That's right. She's invited me every year, but I've never been able to make it. I hope I make the list again."

"Odds are strongly in your favor," I say, squeezing his hand.

"Here we are," he says, pulling into a long pea-gravel driveway. There's something so soothing about the sound the tiny rocks make as the tires sink into them. *I bet that sound is nostalgic for him and his family.* He parks and opens the back door to get my bags.

The sun has already set so I can only see the front porch because it's lit by two large cylindrical light fixtures on each side of a robin-egg front door. Even in the dim light I can tell the house is that classic gray wooden clapboard so often seen in the Hamptons.

"Miles," my jaw dropping, "Your home is gorgeous. I mean—"

"Thank you. It's been my mom's labor of love."

He opens a modest gray wooden gate surrounded by dried hydrangea bushes on each side.

"I bet these hydrangeas are gorgeous when they're in season. They're my mom's favorite."

"Mine too. She's constantly making arrangements for every room during the summer."

The front yard is surrounded by a split rail fence, common on farms where I grew up. Two rows of thick slate squares separated by grass serve as steppingstones to their front door. The path is lined by mature boxwoods and more hydrangeas. It's obvious how much care his mom puts into her yard, it reminds me of my mom's love of gardening. Hanging from the ceiling to the left of the front door is a wooden platform bed suspended by four ropes. It's made up with blue patterned linens and pillows that complement the front door.

"What is that? A hanging bed-swing? I've never seen that before. Talk about an ideal spot for a rainy afternoon," I say.

"It's the perfect spot for a nap too. I know from experience. I can't tell you how many hours I've spent studying on that bed. My brother and mom call it my Hamptons office."

The porch is enclosed by a white wooden spindle railing that matches the trim of the house. *This just feels like a happy home.*

Miles unlocks the door, letting us inside. It's elegantly decorated and smells of cedar and an open fire. There's a giant woodburning Riverstone fireplace directly ahead, with a chunky floating wooden mantel. Above the mantel hangs an abstract oil painting of a field of red poppies.

The painting makes me do a double take and my body stills. It looks familiar, though I'm not sure why. My heart beats a little faster and I can't turn my eyes away. An overwhelming Deja-vu comes over me.

I force myself to look away from the painting and take in the rest of the room. All of the furniture is plush and white with modern pale blue and gray accents. The white furniture is a stunning contrast to the dark, hand forged wide plank wood floors.

"Your mom has exquisite taste. She could be a designer," I say.

"I'll tell her. She's always loved to decorate. She stages a lot of her client's homes."

Miles puts my bags down on the side table near the front door and I follow him past the rustic farmhouse dining table into the kitchen. The kitchen is on the smaller side and is bright and cheery with pale yellow cabinets and concrete countertops. A double porcelain farm sink sits below a wall of windows that look into the backyard.

"Tomorrow when the sun's out, I'll show you around the backyard."

"I'd love that."

"Do you want to go sit on the beach? It's only a five-minute walk. It's a clear night so the stars will be incredible," he says.

"Um, is that even a question? I absolutely love watching the stars."

"Let me grab a blanket, I'll be right back."

He runs upstairs and I show myself to the powder room near the front door. It's the cutest little bathroom decorated in playful Scandinavian print wallpaper with hand drawn clouds and teal birds. Several tiny glass succulent-filled terrariums hang from the pale blue ceiling on various lengths of jute twine. *This place is ridiculously cute.* I wash my hands and head back into the kitchen as Miles is coming down the stairs.

"Do you want an extra jacket? It'll be colder and windier down at the beach," he says.

"I think between my fleece, the blanket and you—I'm good."

He smiles, throwing an orange herringbone blanket over his shoulder and pulls me in for a long and gentle kiss. I run my fingers along the back of his neck while he wraps his arms around my back. Our bodies meld together in the dim light of the kitchen. With every second, our rhythm intensifies until he backs me into the counter, pressing himself firmly into me. He lets out a moan from the back of his throat and my insides tremble. *I just made him make that sound.* He pulls away, catching me off guard, and I recoil from where I was just leaning on his chest. He leans his cheek down against mine and whispers in my ear.

"We better take that walk now, or we won't be getting out of the house at all tonight."

I bite my lower lip and nod. I've suddenly lost all interest in a starry walk on the beach, but I follow as he takes my hand and walks us out a sliding glass door into the moonlight. The cool night air feels good on my face. I taste a hint of salt from the ocean air.

We follow a well-groomed wooden boardwalk until it eventually gives way to a sandy path. The tips of my Converse sink into the cool sand with every step. I walk carefully, trying not to kick sand into the sides and backs of my shoes but it's not working. I wiggle my toes and can already feel the grit from small piles of sand collecting between them. *I hate sand between my toes.*

"This part of Amagansett is called The Dunes. My mom chose it because it's a quiet community full of families and cottages. As a single mom, she said walking to the beach with two small kids while trying to carry everything was challenging, so the short walk was what really sold her."

"You've been coming to this beach for almost your whole life?"

"Yep. This place brings back so many great memories, I know these beaches like the back of my hand."

The path ends, putting us out onto a deserted beach. The only other inhabitant as far as I can see is the light of the moon's rippled reflections on the crests of the waves. Miles settles on a spot back from the water's edge and spreads the blanket onto the sand. He pats his hand on the ground, inviting me to sit down next to him.

"It's so peaceful at night," I say.

"Especially during the winter months. It's my favorite time of the year to come out here," he says, putting his arm around me, scooting closer.

"Look at all of those stars—there's not a cloud in sight," I say, marveling at the scattered starlight.

"They're really putting on a show for you tonight. I can't tell you how many hours I've spent out here just staring up at the sky. I made the decision to go to medical school not far from this exact spot," he says, his tone nostalgic.

I smile. "I can't think of a better setting for making life-changing decisions."

We sit quietly listening to the surf until a massive shooting star blazes above our heads.

"Did you see it?" he asks.

"That was so bright! It went across the entire sky!" I squeal.

Miles chortles. "You're adorable, Gemma. I love how excited you get just over a shooting star."

My jaw drops. "For the record, there's no such thing as *just* a shooting star. They're kind of a big deal." I nudge him, emphasizing my point. My cheeks flush, realizing I just screamed in his ear.

He throws me a look that melts me and lies back onto the blanket, gently pulling me on top of him. He flips the sides of the blanket, wrapping them around us. My hair falls into the sand, surrounding both sides of his face and he gently gathers all of my hair, bringing it to one side. "Fresh cut lilacs," he says, running his fingers through my hair.

His warmth beneath the blanket feels good against my body. He kisses me just below my ear and down the side of my neck, sending chill bumps up my spine. His lips feel warm against my skin as he leaves a trail of kisses along my collarbone.

I feel his heart pounding and wonder if he can feel mine too. He takes my head in his hands and leans up into my face, bringing his lips down firmly against mine. His tongue seeks mine and then pulls away, sliding back and forth in a tender game of give and take. We hungrily explore each other and I turn my head, moving slightly on top of him. He makes a guttural sound that sets fire to my soul. I try to hide the fact I'm panting and pull away from our kiss, burying my face in his thick curls. I lightly brush my lips against his earlobe and neck, breathless with desire for him. *I don't know how much more of this I can take—and I just got here.*

I prop myself up on one hand so I can look at him. I twirl his curls gently between my fingers trying to memorize the details of his face.

"You're beautiful, Gemma."

I smile as he pulls me back down, squeezing me tight. He rolls us over so he's on top of me, the back of my head pressed into the sand. We stare into each other's eyes, silently acknowledging the passion between us.

"What do you say we head back to the house?" he asks.

"Oh, I don't know—what if we spend the night on the beach? I kind of don't want to move from this spot right here."

I tighten my arms around his back in protest. He snickers and lowers his forehead onto my shoulder leaving it to rest there. He turns and his nose grazes my neck, "You've got a good point," he says, taking a deep inhale.

We lie in each other's arms for several minutes before Miles tosses the blanket off, unwrapping us from our beach cocoon. I whimper as he presses up onto his knees, letting the cold swirl in, instantly replacing his heat with chilly night air.

He holds out his hand and pulls me up. I feel his eyes watching me as I shake the sand from my hair. He picks up the blanket and we walk hand-in-hand back to the house. My shoes are so filled with sand, it's actually a nice distraction from being pressed against his tight body. It's all I can do to try and not think about where I'd like this to head when we get back to the house.

"I'm going to need a shower when we get home. I've got sand everywhere," I say.

"I think we can arrange that," he says, his eyebrows rising to his hairline. I laugh, pushing into his side as we wrap our arms around each other's waist. I'm a flood of conflicting emotions, the culmination of being alone with him all afternoon, our salt-kissed, moonlit evening on the shore, and the nagging voice that keeps reminding me not to get too close.

TWENTY-SIX

GEM & EM

"Grandma!" Emmeline and I shout at the sound of Grandma pulling up our driveway. We jump off the couch and run outside to greet her. She barely has time to stand before we throw our arms around her.

"We've missed you so much!"

"We made a special dinner for you," I say.

"Did you now?" she says, listening as we excitedly tell her about our special dessert. She's as happy to see us as we are to see her. It's only been a week, but a week is a long time for us to go without seeing each other.

"Hi, Mom," Mom says, as she appears behind us, coming to give Grandma a hug.

"Hey, my sweet girl! I've missed you all so much."

Mom holds onto Grandma. "We've missed you too. We got spoiled seeing you every day."

Grandma nods and smiles. "How about we have a Halloween sleepover at my house since it's on a Saturday this year?"

"Yes! Sleepover at Grandma's house," Em and I squeal.

"Girls, why don't we take Grandma to the backyard and show her the project you two have been working so hard on?" Mom asks.

Grandma closes her car door. "What's this? A new project?"

"Yep, it's for a contest at school. Mom thinks we might win." Em and I grab onto each other's hands, jumping up and down, unable to hide our excitement.

"Take me to it," she says, holding out both of her arms. Em and I each hold a hand and lead her to the backyard.

"Look way up there," I say, pointing to the top of the tree.

"Oh. . .wow, will you look at that. You two made that?" Grandma says, impressed by our work.

"Yep. We've been saving our pennies and pressed them on the railroad tracks. Mom helped us make a wind chime out of them. We just hung it today." Emmeline beams from ear to ear.

"Oh my goodness, girls, it's beautiful. Look how it sparkles in the sun."

The wind blows and the four of us stand together, listening to the delicate copper disks tinkle together as they softly brush against each other.

"It looks like a lot of love and hard work went into making it," Grandma says.

Em and I nod, smiling at each other, proud of ourselves and our project.

"It's getting chilly out here. Let's go inside, dinner should almost be ready. Girls, can you please set the table?"

"Sure, Mom."

"MOM, tonight the girls and I wanted to treat you to a special dinner to thank you for everything you did for us while I was in the hospital and when we were living with you. I can't tell you how grateful we are for you," Mom says, her eyes tearing up. She walks behind Grandma and rests her hand on her shoulder.

Grandma covers Mom's hand with her own. "Oh, sweetheart, you know there's no need to thank me. I loved taking care of you all. It made me so happy having you stay with me." Grandma squeezes Mom's hand and the two of them share a misty-eyed look.

Em and I come over to their side of the table and scoot in under Mom, holding onto Grandma on each side.

"We love you, Grandma!"

She kisses the top of our heads. "I love you both so very much. My girls. All three of them."

Grandma winks at Mom. "I'll say it as long as I live. No matter how old you get, that's just the way it is."

Something catches my eye in the backyard, and I run to the window over our kitchen sink.

"Look at the clouds," I say, pointing to a golden sky. Em and I run into the backyard for a better view. Mom and Grandma follow behind until the four of us gather once again, beneath our sassafras tree. The sunlight fades fast, clearing a path for the moon and stars. We watch as fiery orange and red hues reflect in the puffy clouds scattered along the horizon.

Grandma cups her ears. "Listen, it sounds like your chimes are applauding tonight's special sunset."

"Make a wish on our sassafras sunset girls," Mom says quietly.

Grandma looks at the sky and nods. "Sassafras sunset, I like the way that sounds."

"You make a wish too, Mom," Em says.

Mom pauses and looks down at us, smiling happily.

"All of mine have already come true."

TWENTY-SEVEN

THE HAMPTONS

We empty the sand from our shoes, leaving them by his front door.

"I'll make dinner while you shower," he says.

"*And* he cooks?"

"Me, cook? That's a bit of a stretch. My mom stocked the fridge with my brother's and my favorite dishes, so the credit really belongs to her."

"So thoughtful, just like her son," I say.

He smirks and takes my hand, leading me up an L shaped wooden staircase. The white walls and high-gloss black banister look elegant against the maple floors.

"My mom's room is here on the left and down the end of the hall is my brother's." He turns down a hallway to the right and flips on a light switch in the lone bedroom at the end.

"And this. . . is my bedroom," he says.

His room is on the smaller-side and the walls are painted a soothing dark navy. A queen-sized bed with a textured gray fabric headboard sits atop a shaggy ivory rug. Gray accents in his crisp white linens complement the flecks of gray in his headboard. Several tall windows line an entire wall, which must flood the room with natural light during the day.

"Your room is beautiful. Not exactly what I pictured after seeing your car. I'm kind of surprised there's no trace of the Marvel Cinematic Universe anywhere."

He looks around his room, nodding. "When we went to college, my mom redecorated both of our bedrooms and sent our superheroes packing. My brother and I were heartbroken to say the least."

"I can't even imagine," I say, patting his back.

Miles shrugs and walks around the dresser to his en suite bathroom. "Feel free to use my robe on the back of the door, and there are towels in the linen closet on the left. I'll get your bag," he says, turning for the door.

"I guess that means you'll be sleeping down the hall in your brother's room tonight?"

"I guess it means whatever you want it to mean." He shrugs and turns for the door. I wipe the smile off my face and walk around the corner to check out his bathroom. A black-and-white tiled floor nicely compliments his pale golden walls and wainscoting. I take down his heather gray robe from the back of the door. It smells of leather and citrus, just like him. I quickly hang it back on the hook, not wanting him to walk in and find me sniffing his robe.

"I'll just leave these here for you," he says, putting my bag on his bed.

I poke my head out of the bathroom.

"Thanks."

"Oh, and is there anything you don't eat?"

"Green peppers," I say, wrinkling my nose. "My mom and I both hate them."

"Got it. My brother can't stand them either."

He walks toward me, stopping half-way between us. "I'm going to go back downstairs or you're going to end up sharing your shower."

"Oh yeah? Don't be so sure about that," I say, biting my lip as I close and lock the bathroom door. I sit on the edge of the bathtub, pulling off my socks, freeing the gritty sand piles between my toes. As the shower heats up, I drape my clothes over the back of the tub and step into the marble glass-and-chrome shower.

It's hard to wrap my mind around the fact I'm in Miles's shower. My stomach flips at the thought of sharing the same space as his naked, muscular body. Being here with him, spending time at his house, it's more than a little overwhelming. I shampoo my hair, even the scent reminds me of him.

I'm impressed to find everything I need in the shower, including a razor. The mounting tension in my body starts to ease as the rain shower pummels my skin. My muscles are in knots and it's honestly nice having a moment to myself. I've never been so drawn to someone like I am with him, and it frightens me. I want it to last as long as it can, without me sabotaging it before it even has a chance to begin.

I finish my shower and towel off, excited, yet still guarded about where the night will take us. I look in several drawers but don't see a hair dryer. I wrap my hair in a towel and walk back into his bedroom to get dressed, pulling on my favorite jeans and a cream cardigan.

Something smells incredible as I'm coming down the stairs, and I follow the scent to the kitchen to find it empty. An opened bottle of pinot noir sits on the island, so I pour myself a glass and walk into the living room with the massive fireplace. The crimson poppy painting above the mantle that had drawn my attention earlier adds so much warmth and beauty to the room, and I stand underneath it to see the details up close. The artist's name is written at the bottom, but I can't quite make it out. It looks like it might start with the letter C, but I can't be sure. I hear steps on the front porch and turn around as the door slowly opens. Miles walks in, a stack of wood in his arms.

"How was your shower?" he asks, stacking the logs beside the fireplace.

"Relaxing, just what I needed. Great pressure, too. I might have to steal that bathrobe of yours."

He turns around and smiles. "I'm more than happy to share."

"Deal. By the way, your mom thinks of everything, there was even a bottle of conditioner in your shower and a razor, I'm impressed," I say.

"Oh, right. Huh—I didn't even notice," he says, in a way that makes me think it wasn't his mom who left it there. *Oh shit. Why did I even bring that up?*

While trying to clear my thoughts of the rightful owner of the conditioner and razor, I sit down on one of the oversized sofas facing the fireplace and pull a soft-knit throw over my legs. I watch as he lights the fire before joining me on the couch.

"The wet hair look suits you." He places his hands on my legs underneath the blanket—it's strange how familiar his touch already feels. I lean into him, and we watch as his handiwork builds into a roaring fire.

"Nicely done. On the first try, too."

"Another thing my mom taught me. Ready to eat?" he asks. "I'm reheating chicken enchiladas, they should be almost ready."

"That's what smells so good," I say.

DINNER IS FILLED with easy conversation and laughter. Not even nervous laughter, just regular old laughter because something's actually funny. This is the most amount of time we've ever spent together, and I was kind of expecting at least a few moments of awkward silence but that hasn't happened. After dinner we clean up and sit under the blanket in front of the fire.

My heart thumps wildly as I nuzzle in against him. I'm afraid my red flags have all turned green, and my nervous energy grows, wondering where this is all going to lead.

"What time is your tutoring session tomorrow? You said it was in the morning, right?"

I nod. "Good memory. It's at nine, why?" I ask.

"I'd love to take you out to Montauk Point tomorrow, maybe show you the state park too. It's about a fifteen-minute ride from here."

"That sounds great. I'd love to go for a run on the beach tomorrow morning before my session. Do you run?" I ask.

"I ran track in high school, but I haven't run in a long time. I'll join you—if you promise to go easy."

"I can't make any promises," I say, shrugging.

He laughs and leans into me, kissing my neck. I tremble slightly at the feel of his lips on my skin. I take my hand under his chin and tilt his face to meet mine, staring into his eyes. I could stay on the couch with him all night watching the fire. It feels like I've known him for way longer than a month.

"Do you want to go upstairs? It's getting late," he asks dryly, clearing his throat and sitting upright.

Um...what did I just miss? That wasn't the wink-nudge 'do you want to go upstairs' I was expecting. It sounded more like a record scratching.

"Sure?"

He must sense my confusion.

"I know you had an early morning getting out here—you must be beat."

I look at my watch and can't believe it's almost one a.m. I have to admit, I'm pretty tired from both the trip and my emotions from being around him.

"Tonight has been great. But you're right, we should probably call it a night," I say, slightly disappointed.

Miles pokes the fire, letting the embers fall to the sides until the last bits fade away. We walk upstairs and down the hallway to his room. I'm flooded by unwelcome thoughts as we climb the stairs. *That was just totally weird. What if he's seeing conditioner-razor girl?* I follow him into his room as he goes to his dresser, pulling out a pair of pajama pants and a faded t-shirt.

"I'll be right back. I'm going to take a quick shower."

He closes the bathroom door and when I hear the water start, I quickly change into my dark gray, long sleeve Henley nightshirt, needing to run this by Mikayla. I hop into bed, pulling the covers over my knees and text her.

> Hey Mika! How's work? You're right, this house is gorgeous. (Notice me not asking if you're feeling okay. Progress! Are you? 😜)

I look around his room, trying to distract myself from naked Miles on the other side of the bathroom door. I get up to take a closer look at two framed pictures on his dresser. The first one is of him and his brother at the beach in their wetsuits when they were young. Next to it is one of him with his whole family at his graduation from medical school.

His mom must be the one hugging him around the waist. *She's stunning.* She looks like a slightly older Eva Mendes and is meticulously dressed from head to toe. She looks every bit the fashionable New Yorker. The handsome older man in the picture must be his dad. Dark skin, dark hair, same build. Miles looks exactly like his father. A clone. *I wonder why the two of them aren't talking?* I walk back over to the bed and see a text from Mikayla.

> I'm fine! Beautiful, isn't it? I was there two summers ago at their end of season party. His mom throws the best parties, I try not to miss them.

> She sounds amazing. Btw, Miles isn't seeing anyone that you know of, is he?

> Stop. He wouldn't have asked you to the Hamptons if he was seeing someone. He's not like that.

I give myself a shake. She's right. I'm being paranoid.

> Okay, I got in my head for a second.

> You don't have to get in your head when it comes to him. Trust me enough to know you can trust him.

> I do. It's just. . . you know.

> I know. Have fun. Tell M hi. Love you.

I hear the shower turn off and text back:

> Gotta go. Love you.

I put my phone down on the nightstand and walk to the end of the bed, moving my bag to the floor. Miles comes out wearing a faded Columbia t-shirt and green plaid pajama bottoms.

"Aren't you cute?"

"Right back at you," he says, eyeing my nightshirt.

"Mika says hi by the way, we were just texting."

"Thank her for letting me borrow you for the weekend."

He walks over and puts his hands around my waist, drawing me close to him. He feels warm; the heat from his shower permeates his smooth skin. I turn my head against his chest, trying to absorb his warmth. He rests his chin on top of my head.

"You're so warm. I don't know if I'll be able to warm up in this big bed by myself."

He leans back with an expression I can't quite read.

"I'm more than happy to help keep you warm. Or I can just as easily take my brother's room. It's totally up to you."

"I'd like you to stay here with me, then. I mean—at least until my feet get warm." I smile up at him.

"Well, if you insist." He smirks and gives me a quick kiss before walking over to shut the bedroom door and turn out the light. I walk to the side of the bed where I left my phone on the nightstand and climb under the sheets. He closes the wooden blinds, as darkness blankets the room. His footsteps get closer to the other side of the bed and I can't help but feel giddy about the two of us sharing a bed.

He climbs in next to me and we turn toward each other, our bodies touching all the way from our chests to where my toes reach his shins. He whispers in my ear, "I'm so glad you're here, in my bed tonight."

I shudder in anticipation as he leans over to kiss me goodnight. I close my eyes and take in his fresh out-of-the-shower scent as he slowly pulls back, tucking his hand beneath his pillow. Really? I roll my eyes in the dark. *How in the world am I supposed to lie next to him all night and sleep?*

Thoughts of the two of us tangled between the sheets fill my head and then I remember the conversation Mikayla and I had about his wanting to take things slow when he's serious about someone. *I really hope it's that and not because there's someone else.*

I roll onto my side, away from him, to distract myself from my racing mind. He drapes his arm over my waist and pulls me closer to him, leaving his arm resting lightly on my stomach. *Not helping, Miles.*

I listen to the sounds of his breathing until they slow and eventually fall into a slumbered rhythm. I've been a bundle of nerves all day and my exhaustion kicks in. I close my eyes and start to drift. My heart feels happy and it's hard not to give in to it.

TWENTY-EIGHT

THE HAMPTONS

I wake up not knowing where I am. The course texture of the sheets rubs against my legs, reminding me I'm in the Hamptons. I've never slept on linen sheets before, I never even knew they were a thing.

It's still dark outside, no light trickles in through the slats in the blinds. I feel around for my phone, quietly prying it from the nightstand. Six twenty-five. I should take advantage of the break and sleep in, but I'm not tired. I may regret this decision later, but I'm too excited to go back to sleep. The opportunity to catch a glimpse of the sun's first rays is one that shouldn't be wasted.

Miles's deep breathing lets me know he's still fast asleep. Listening for the loudest part of his exhale, I roll to the side, waiting to see if he stirs. I lift the covers slowly and slide my legs out, over the edge until my feet are almost touching the floor. In one quick motion, I step down on the rug and lay the sheets back down, careful not to let the cold air sneak in and wake him up.

I turn on my flashlight, putting it on the dimmest setting and walk to the end of the bed. Digging in the bottom of my bag, I grab my running gear and tuck it under my arm. My phone's light leads the way to the door and I grip the doorknob. *Please do not creak.* With the age of this house, I'm thankful it's not one of those whiny, vintage glass knobs. His mom must have updated the hardware, because it's one of those sleek horizontal bars. *Kudos to her and her home improvements.*

Miles lets out a long breath that catches a few times and I make my move, pushing down on the handle, swinging the door open just enough for me to squeeze through. I hold the lever down, shutting the door behind me, only letting up when the latch quietly clicks into place.

I creep down the steps to the first floor and shuffle over to the powder room to change my clothes and splash water on my face. Parched, I quietly walk to the kitchen for a glass of water. After a long drink, I swish a sip around in my mouth to hopefully remedy any trace of morning breath.

While I'm grabbing a coat from the mud room, I write a quick note to Miles on their family chalkboard and grab a beach towel from a basket by the back door.

The mudroom door is deadbolted, so I walk to the sliding glass door behind the dining room table. *Oh shit. What if there's an alarm?* I look around for sensors and when I don't see any, I push the lock and slide the door open. *Phew.* Retracing our path we took last night, I walk barefoot through the cold, damp grass to the front of the house. I towel off my feet and throw on my sneakers. Other than birds calling out to one another, stillness fills the air. Witnessing the peaceful, hushed sounds of morning far outweighs any amount of sleep I'd be getting right now.

The city's hustle feels a million miles away and I soak in every drop of this tranquil moment. Turning down the boardwalk, I wander until my shoes sink into the sand. The moon is still high in the sky and the faintest glow of red light appears in a thin layer at the earth's edge. Several clouds moved in overnight, but a few remaining stars are still visible, twinkling in anticipation of the morning sun.

The ocean is calm, gentle waves lap the shore. I set my towel on the cold sand and sit, grateful for my front row seat. A subtle layer of red light grows bolder as it spreads up and out, hinting at the giant day star resting below the horizon. Shades of purple and pink transform the dark sky and I watch in awe as mother nature splashes her cloudy canvas with pastels of every shade. I take a picture and text it to Mom.

These quiet moments in nature always remind me of Emmeline. An image flashes of the two of us dangling our feet from the low branch of our climbing tree, watching a sunset. The memory fades along with my smile, as I watch the soft hues give way to deeper shades before disappearing altogether as the sun climbs higher into the sky.

It never ceases to amaze me how flawless the transition is from night to day and vice versa. One disappears, letting the other take their place, until it's time for their return. Two equally powerful opposing forces and their breathtaking, daily compromise since the beginning of time. I guess opposites do attract. *Except for the fact they never really spend much time together.*

Out of the corner of my eye I catch a splash and focus on the area. A pod of dolphins breaches the surface, their arched backs sparkle like diamonds, reflecting the sun's shine. I squeal and sit up taller, trying to keep them in my sight. I look around for anyone else who might also be seeing these majestic creatures, so we can share the moment, but the beach is empty. *You seeing this, Em? They're beautiful, aren't they?*

Needing a closer view, I stand and walk to the water's edge. The dolphins playfully rocket themselves out of the ocean so high, I swear they know I'm standing here watching. I clap and call out to them with every sighting.

The sun feels good on my face and I close my eyes, remembering how mom would lather us with sunscreen trying to protect us from its powerful rays. Our summertime freckles always had a mind of their own. My cold and sandy feet bring me back to the moment. I turn to head back to the house and startle, finding Miles sitting on my towel.

"Hey stranger," he says, a giant smile plastered across his face.

"How long have you been sitting there?" I ask, blushing.

"Long enough to know you're fluent in dolphin."

I cringe, knowing he heard me squealing.

"Did you see them?" I ask.

"I did. It was more fun watching you, to be honest."

I make a face. "The great lakes are freshwater, we don't have dolphins in Indiana. I've only seen them once before—the last time I was in the Hamptons, actually. It's like they knew and wanted to put on a show for the girl from the Midwest."

"I'm glad they gave you a good one."

He walks over and hugs me, lifting me off the ground. I bring my head back so I can see his face and he kisses me good morning.

"I woke up and you were gone. I hope it wasn't something I said," he says.

I shake my head, laughing. "I couldn't sleep and I didn't want to wake you. Besides, sunrise and sunsets are kind of my thing."

"Was it a good one?"

I pinch my fingers together and kiss them before tossing them away. "Perfection. I took some pictures, I'll show you. Did you see my message on the chalkboard?"

"I did. What time did you leave?"

"Around six-thirty. You should have seen me trying to sneak out of your room so I didn't wake you," I say.

"I'm sorry I missed it. Honestly, after working at the hospital, when I actually manage to get some sleep, almost nothing can wake me."

"You doctors and your lack-of-sleep superpower." I elbow him playfully.

We wander back to the house and Miles makes us breakfast including the best egg sandwich I've ever eaten.

"I thought I'd go for a run on the beach before my session. Want to join me?" I ask.

"Hmm. How far are you thinking?"

"Only two-three miles, easy pace," I say.

Miles nods, rubbing his chin. "You're on. I can't remember the last time I ran on the beach. I used to run out here all the time back in high school when I ran track. I can't tell you how many miles I've logged out there."

I finish cleaning up while Miles excuses himself to take a call. I head upstairs to brush my teeth and throw my hair in a ponytail for our run. While I wait for his call to end, I go check out his backyard.

To the left of the mudroom door is an enclosed outdoor shower in the same matching clapboard and white trim. Planted along the entire back of the house is a row of dried hydrangea bushes. The pool and hot tub are one sleek rectangle surrounded by tumbled stone and grass. What a little sanctuary they have back here. I feel like I'm on one of those yoga retreats at an outdoor spa. Not that I've ever been.

A variety of mature white pine, birch and red oak trees surround the entire property, making for a completely private oasis. You'd never know there were neighbors close by. I pick a spot directly in the sun at the end of the pool and sit down on an oversized wooden chaise with a plush, cobalt tufted cushion. I lie back letting myself sink deeper into the cushion.

It's nice to have a moment to decompress from my daily grind of law school stress. I stare up into the blue sky feeling like I'm in some kind of dream with my life's sudden turn of events. How am I even here right now, in the Hamptons—at this house? With him?

I run back inside to get my phone and at the top of the stairs, I see Miles is still on the phone in his brother's room. *Work? Conditioner-razor girl?* I roll my eyes at myself and start heading to his room when I overhear him saying, "Don't worry. You're right—Gemma doesn't need to know. I already promised you, I won't tell her. I don't know—I'll make something up if I have to." My foot freezes in midair.

What the hell?

My heart feels like someone just ran it through a shredder. I wonder if I've misheard him. *What don't I need to know?* He bursts out laughing and I quietly turn and run down back down the stairs, anger sizzling through my veins. *Is he laughing at me?*

My mind races with a plethora of scenarios—none of them good. Who could he possibly be talking to who knows me? The only person it can be is Mikayla. *Are they?* No. There's no way. She would never. What could they be talking about and why would they be hiding it from me? I wish I could text her but my phone is in his room and I'm not getting it now.

Tears sting my eyes as I take off through the back door. I don't want to be around someone who keeps secrets from me. Why did I even agree to coming here in the first place? I'm mad at myself for breaking my rules —for someone who isn't even truthful.

Needing distance between his lies and me, I run into the front yard, out the gate and down the path, angrily wiping tears from my eyes. I feel so foolish. Why did I trust him? I take off down the beach as fast as I can. I don't care that he doesn't know where I went. Let him come looking for me. When I get back, I'll pack my things and leave. Lesson learned. I'm never putting myself in this position again.

My sneakers pound the sand and I push faster. My coping mechanism for years—I'd almost forgotten how good it feels to run and cry. *Thanks for the reminder, Miles.* I shake my head at myself, disappointed I was even thinking about letting him in. My lungs burn as I pick up my pace. Faster. I've had enough emotional pain to last a lifetime, right now I just need to feel physical pain.

TWENTY-NINE

GEM & EM

Emmeline and I bolt out the front doors into the cool autumn air as soon as the long-awaited school bell sounds. It's the week of Halloween and I've been fidgeting in my seat all day, excited to see how much progress Mom has made on our costumes. We skip down the sidewalk and stand holding hands, impatiently waiting for the only stoplight on our walk home to change.

"If you could make one wish, what would it be?" I ask.

"Anything?"

"Yep, anything."

"That's easy," she says.

"What is it?"

"I wish Halloween could be every day. How about you?"

"I wish that we always love Halloween as much as we do now. Even when we're old."

The light finally turns red, and we dash across the road, down the hill to the start of our path home. The afternoon's light streams through the bare trees, signaling winter will soon be here. An eerie silence fills the woods; the only sound is from our footsteps crunching the dry leaves as we pass over them. I bend down to pick up a perfect sized walking stick and hear a strange, high-pitched sound in the distance.

"What's that noise?" I ask.

"What noise?"

"Shh. Listen."

Emmeline stops walking and puts her hand on her hip, brushing the curtain of blonde hair out of her eyes.

"There, did you hear it? It sounded like a cat," I say.

"A cat? I don't hear it."

I put my finger to my lips. "Wait. There it is again."

"I heard it that time. Where's it coming from?"

"I don't know, let's go find it."

Em and I walk softly, trying not to rustle the leaves as we search for the source. We turn off the path walking deeper into the woods, to follow the sound.

"It's a kitten!" Emmeline shouts.

"It's coming from in there," I say, pointing to a rotten, hollowed out log.

I peer inside, but it's too dark to see anything. We meow at the log's splintered opening until the kitten finally echoes one of our calls.

"Come here, kitty," I say.

"Here, kitty, kitty, kitty."

I pull my head back, my eyes wide. "Em, I just saw a face."

"Where? Move over so I can see," she says.

"Look back there, behind that pile of leaves."

"Awww, I see a little pink nose," she squeals.

"Here, kitty, kitty."

"It must be so scared," she says.

I reach my hand in further until I feel fur and whiskers. The kitten backs away. I lean in as far as my arm will go and grab the fur on the back of its neck, pulling it into the light.

"Poor thing is shaking," I say, cradling the gray kitten in my arms.

"It's okay, don't be scared," Em says gently.

"It's covered in dirt. We can't just leave it here."

"Let's take it home," she says.

I wipe some of the dirt off its back. "Do you think Mom will let us keep it?"

"I don't know. I hope so. Let's hurry so we can show her," Emmeline says, making a pocket out of the bottom of her green sweatshirt. I help her roll the kitten up to keep it safe and warm.

We turn back to the path and rush down the railroad tracks, Em carrying the bundle as gently as she can.

"It keeps crying. What should I do?"

"Maybe it's hungry," I say.

"Don't worry. We'll get you some food," she says, grimacing.

Em and I walk as fast as we can the rest of the way home, excited to show Mom. The tracks bend to the right and when our feet hit the gravel road, we start calling for her.

"Mom! Mom!" we both shout.

"Come outside!"

"Mom!"

We dash up the front steps as the front door swings open. Mom's frown is filled with concern.

"What is it?"

"Look what we found on our way home," I say.

Emmeline unrolls the bottom of her sweatshirt, revealing a tiny, crying fur ball.

"Oh my goodness! Where on earth did you find that?"

"In a rotted out log in the woods. It was so scared," Em says.

Mom picks up the kitten, holding it to her chest. "Oh you sweet little creature. There, there. You're okay."

"I think it's hungry, it won't stop crying. Can we give it some milk?" I ask.

"Milk can make kittens sick; they need a special formula."

"Can we go get some?" Emmeline asks.

"Mr. Paul rescued a couple kittens a few months ago, let me ask if they have any formula left. Can you get me a towel? We need to wrap it up to keep it warm."

Emmeline runs inside for a towel as Mom and I marvel at our furry friend.

"Is it a boy or a girl?" I ask.

"Let me see."

Mom holds the kitten up to inspect.

"It looks like this is a little girl," she says.

"It's a girl," I call out to Emmeline as she opens the door, a towel in her hands.

We smile at each other over Mom's discovery.

"Here, Mom," Em says, handing her the towel. Mom carefully wraps the kitten like a burrito with two little paws sticking out of the end.

"She's not crying as much anymore. Maybe she was just cold," Emmeline says.

"I'm going to run next door to Mr. Paul's. Hold her until I get back." Mom hands me the bundled kitten and runs down the driveway.

"Look at her little pink toes. They're so soft," Emmeline says.

We stare at her in awe, petting her dusty head.

"I hope Mom lets us keep her," I say.

"Me too."

"If she does, what should we name her?" I ask.

"I don't know. We have to think of something good."

"How about pumpkin? Since it's almost Halloween," Emmeline says.

"That's for an orange cat."

"How about Logan because we found her in a log?" I offer.

"How about Hazy? Hazy the Halloween cat."

A huge smile spreads across my face. "Wait! That's really cute! I love that name. She looks like a Hazy," I say.

Mom hurries toward us, a bag in her hand. "We're in luck, girls, Mr. Paul had two containers of formula and he also gave us a bottle."

"Aww, that's so cute. A kitten eats from a bottle. Can we feed her?" I ask.

"Of course. Let's go inside, I'll show you how."

Emmeline opens the door, and we follow Mom to the kitchen. We watch as she fills a mug of water and puts it in the microwave. When it's warm enough, she fills the tiny bottle and adds a scoop of powder.

"She's not shaking anymore, I think the towel helped," I say.

Mom takes the kitten from me, unwrapping her. She spreads the blanket across Em's lap and then lays the kitten on her tummy.

"She's so cute, Mom," Emmeline says.

"She certainly is. Okay, now when we feed her, we need to feed her like her mama would. Keep her on her tummy and hold her neck up like this."

A few drops of formula leak out and the kitten starts eating hungrily.

"Look, she likes it! She's eating so fast. Aww, that's the cutest sound," Emmeline says, imitating the kitten drinking.

"Let's only give her a little bit at first so it doesn't upset her tummy. It may have been a while since she's had anything to eat," Mom says.

"Can I have a turn holding the bottle, Em?"

"Okay, come sit next to me," she says.

We sit together, feeding the kitten until Mom says she's had enough.

I look up at Mom, giving her my best pout. "Can we keep her, Mom?"

"Please?" Emmeline pleads.

Mom looks at the two of us and then back at the kitten.

"She's pretty adorable. And so are the two of you," she says.

Mom puts a hand on her hip and smiles. *I think I already know her answer.*

"Please, Mom, please! We'll take good care of her."

"Oh, will you now?"

"We will! We will! We promise."

"I don't see why not. I think it was meant for you two to her find her." Mom takes a towel from one of the kitchen drawers and starts filling the sink. "Let's give her a bath, she's covered in dirt."

The three of us bathe her and then quickly dry her off so she doesn't get cold again.

"Emmeline wants to name her Hazy."

"Hazy the Halloween cat," she adds.

"As long as you both agree on it, I think it's the perfect name for her," Mom says.

"Where's she going to sleep?" I ask.

"Go into the garage and see if you can find a box that's big enough for her to walk around in," Mom says.

Em carefully hands Hazy to Mom and we run outside to the garage.

"How about this one?" I say, pointing to a medium-sized box filled with old towels near our bikes.

We dump out the towels and leave them on the shelf next to our helmets. Hazy's asleep in Mom's arms by the time we walk back in the kitchen.

"That's perfect. There's an old blanket underneath my bed. Can you go get it so we can put it down on the bottom for her? She'll sleep in here until she gets a little bigger," Mom says.

Em and I run to her room, returning with a fraying, patchwork quilt that was Mom's when she was young. We set the blanket in the bottom and Mom places Hazy down, still fast asleep, in a corner of the box.

"Can she sleep in our room tonight?" Emmeline asks.

"Yes, but if she cries and keeps you up, put her box in my room. That way I can feed her when I get home from work tonight."

I stick out my bottom lip. "You're working tonight? I was hoping we could carve our pumpkins."

"Sorry, my loves. I have Friday off, we'll carve them then."

"Okay," I say, disappointment running through me. "Are our costumes almost done?"

"Almost. Don't worry, they'll be done in plenty of time for your Halloween parade."

Em and I dance around in the kitchen, grinning ear to ear.

"I have to go get ready for work. I left tonight's dinner in the refrigerator along with some roasted broccoli. Just heat it up in the microwave. Should I have Grandma check in on you and the kitten tonight?"

"Yes! Then she can meet Hazy," Emmeline squeals.

"I'll call and see if she's free. Remember, both of you girls need to work on your science fair projects tonight. I want you to spend at least an hour on them. Okay?"

"We will, Mom," we promise.

Mom walks to her room to start getting ready for work while Em and I each take a side and carry Hazy's box to our bedroom.

"She's the most perfect kitten I've ever seen," Em says. "I just want to stare at her all night."

"Me too. I love her. I can't believe she's ours."

"Let's color the outside of her box for her," she says, reaching into our desk for markers.

"Em, did you ever think you could love something so fast?"

"No. We didn't even know Hazy when we woke up this morning and now, she's all I can think about."

"Me too. It's the three of us now, Hazy," I say, scratching behind her ears, as she purrs loudly.

THIRTY

THE HAMPTONS

Emotionally and physically drained, I reluctantly jog up the path back to his house. The anger I felt earlier isn't as intense—I left most of it in my footprints along the water's edge.

I let myself in through the back gate and glance at the clock in the mudroom. It's only eight-thirty. Relieved I didn't miss my tutoring session, I sit at the end of the pool to stretch. Now that I'm no longer punishing the sand—my anger at him for laughing at me slowly trickles back in.

A lone leaf falls from a nearby tree and I watch as it saunters lazily back and forth, floating carefree and weightless through the air. *Wait, is that what I think it is?* I look up to find the tree from which it fell, instantly recognizing the three distinct shapes. I pick the sassafras leaf off the ground, slowly tracing the spines with my finger. The fiery orange leaf floods me with bittersweet memories of home. I put the stem in my cheek as the sentimental taste of root beer fills my mouth. The familiar sweetness suddenly sours, reminding me of everything I've lost. My pain mixes with the heat from earlier, and tears fall down my face in frustration.

"If you're hungry I can get you a snack," Miles says.

I jump. I hadn't realized he was walking toward me.

"I'm good," I say, sitting back down so he can't see my face.

"Did you just get back from a run? I thought we were going together?"

"Yeah," I say, unapologetically.

"Oh. Um, okay," he says, sounding disappointed. He walks around to stand in front of me while I keep my eyes trained on the pool's edge, refusing to look at him.

"Is everything okay?" he asks, dropping to his knees. "Gem?" He gently lifts my chin and I turn away.

"Oh no, why are you crying? What's wrong?" He furrows his brows, worry and confusion filling his face.

"I don't want to talk about it. I've decided I'm leaving after my tutoring session," I say, dryly.

"You're leaving? Like—going back to the city? Why? What's going on?"

I refuse to look at him, not wanting him to see me cry.

"Did something happen when I was on my call? What am I missing?" he asks, trying to make eye contact. "Please look at me."

"Why don't you tell me? I seem to be the one who's been left out."

His goes to say something and then stops. I can tell he's completely baffled. "Left out of what? Gemma, this is—"

"This is *what*, Miles? I overheard your conversation. What is it that you're *not* going to tell me? Whatever it is, it sounds like you had a good laugh about it—at my expense."

He sits down next to me, leaning back on his hands, shaking his head. "I wasn't laughing at you. I'm sorry if that's how it seemed. But I wasn't." He puts his hand on my shoulder and I shake it off, scooting further away from him. We sit in silence, listening to the birds and the ocean in the distance.

"Gem," Miles begins, after a long sigh, "Next time you overhear half of a conversation, why don't you ask me instead of immediately assuming the worst and running off? Is that why you are out here crying? Because of what you heard on my call?"

"If this was reversed and you heard me saying 'Don't tell Miles' and then laughing about it, how would that make you feel?"

"It would make me wonder, I agree, but I would wait until you were off the phone and ask you about it instead of thinking the worst."

"Congratulations Miles, you're officially the bigger person." I scowl at him.

"Don't do that," he says, gently touching my arm.

I jerk my arm away. "I don't want to be around someone who keeps secrets from me." Secrets are my Achilles heel. Someone is always left out. *I can't be left again.*

"Why don't you call Mikayla, she'll explain everything."

"Why can't you just tell me?" I ask, trying to hide my hurt. *I wish I could stay angry, hurt feels so vulnerable.* I remember what my grief counselor told me so many years ago. "If you peel back the blanket of anger, you'll find hurt."

"Because I can't," he says, firmly. I stare at him, trying to read his response. It's not like him, or what I know of him at least, to give me such a rigid reply and not expand.

"So. . . Mikayla can tell me—and you can't? Or you won't?"

"I can't," he says, softly. And then it hits me. Mikayla's tests. She must have gotten her labs back by now. *Oh no.* What if she got bad news and wanted his advice? I need to call her.

"Wait, what time is it?" I ask, standing up. Miles pulls out his phone and hands it to me.

"My session is starting in five minutes, I have to go." I hand him back his phone and run into the house without looking back.

I FINISH my tutoring session in Miles's mom's office and check to see if there's a text back from Mikayla. Nothing yet. Worry daggers grow in my chest and I remember her words, reminding myself not to freak out. *Tragedy isn't as common as you may think.*

I take a deep breath and walk to the kitchen expecting to find Miles, but it's empty. I scan the backyard and look upstairs, but he's nowhere to be found.

Desperate for my post-run shower, I walk into his bathroom. As I'm taking out my ponytail, I notice a hair dryer sitting by the sink that wasn't there before. A pang of guilt twists my stomach. He must have gotten it out of his mom's bathroom and left it here for me to use. *Eesh.*

I see a missed call from Mikayla as I'm getting out of the shower. I play her voicemail while I towel dry my hair. "Hey Gem, everything okay in the Hamptons? I just got your text and two from Miles. I wanted to let you know my labs came back, they were normal. They're ordering a few more tests and I promise I'll tell you the results as soon as I have them. I just didn't want to worry you until I have more definitive information. It's most likely stress related anyway. Have fun with Miles. No need to call me back, I just got home from work and I'm going to sleep. Love you."

I stare into the mirror, suddenly regretting my harsh reaction. I dry my hair and get dressed in jeans and my favorite zip-up, sweater hoodie and walk downstairs to the kitchen. On my way down the stairs, I see Miles through the back windows, in his running gear, stretching by the pool. I grab two bananas from the fruit bowl on the counter and walk outside.

"How was your run?" I ask, hesitantly. He has every right to be upset with me.

"It was good. Great way to clear the mind," he says, coolly. I walk over to him, and hand him a banana.

"What's this, a peace offering?" he says, taking it from me. "I wasn't sure you were going to still be here when I got back."

"About that. I owe you an apology," I say, sitting down on the chaise lounge. "I shouldn't have reacted the way I did without knowing the whole story. I'm sorry." I look down at my feet as he sits across from me.

He peels his banana, taking a bite. "What was that about? Your reaction, I don't understand why you got so angry."

"It's just. I don't know—Miles. I'm scared, I guess." I look up at the sky, pressing my tongue against the roof of my mouth to stop me from crying.

"Of what?" he asks, tenderness in his tone.

"Of putting myself out there, of being hurt. Of getting close to someone and then losing them," I say, as my voice cracks. *I finally said it.*

He looks at me, and then gazes off into the woods behind his house. "I get it. It's scary putting yourself out there, but that doesn't mean because of one, or even a few bad experiences that you should stop trying."

I think he and I have very different definitions of 'bad experience'.

He rakes his fingers through his hair and lets out a long sigh. "My last girlfriend cheated on me with... someone close to me."

"Oof, that's brutal. I'm sorry." I shake my head, pulling my feet under me.

"Yeah, I wish I could erase it from my memory. But just because I was hurt by what she did, doesn't mean I'm not going to try again."

I nod slowly, wishing the two of us could bond over cheating exes, but my losing someone has nothing to do with a breakup.

He continues. "Her actions don't deserve to have that much power over me."

"You're right. They don't," I say, shaking my head.

"You met her. Well—at least saw her."

"I did?" I say, wondering when that could have possibly happened.

"The night of Ollie's show."

"Ohhh," I say, remembering the leggy brunette. "I wondered what that was about."

"I found out—" He shakes his head as his voice trails off.

"What?"

He looks at me and pauses. "I saw a text on her phone. From... my dad." I shoot him a confused look.

"Your dad?" I furrow my brow, waiting for him to continue, not connecting the dots.

A hurt look crosses his face. "It was his flight information. He said he couldn't wait to see her. That's how I found out they were seeing each other."

I feel like I just got the wind knocked out of me. "Your dad... was seeing your girlfriend?" I can feel my eyes bulging out of my head. "Miles... I'm—oh, wow. I had no idea. That's awful."

He nods. "They met when I'd invited her to join us for dinner one night when he was in town. Talk about trust issues," he says, looking down.

Stunned, my jaw drops and I quickly close it, not wanting to make him feel worse. "I can't imagine."

"I know. That's why we're not talking. Listen, I'm not trying to make this about me. My point is, bad things happen all the time, it's part of life. Sometimes we have to go through the bad days to get to the good ones. Life has a funny way of balancing itself out. No matter what we go through, it doesn't mean we shouldn't still try to find a way back to happiness."

Those may be some of the most profound words I've ever heard.

"That's a beautiful way of putting it." I sit silently, trying to wrap my mind around the fact his ex-girlfriend cheated on him with his *dad*. Yikes.

He stands and slowly walks over to me, taking my hands. His vulnerability and kindness soften the edges of my angry heart.

"Now, do you want to tell me why were you out here eating leaves? Was breakfast not enough?" He smiles softly, melting any residual of my indignance. My chest swells as I look up at him. I lead him over to where the leaf fell. "This—is a sassafras tree."

He shakes his head. "I've never heard of it."

"They're special trees, at least to me they are. They're the only tree that has three different shaped leaves; a mitten, an oval and this three-lobed leaf."

"Impressive foliage flex," he says, as I nod.

"I didn't know they grew in New York. Their stems taste like root beer when you chew on them," I say.

"Really?"

"Yep. Want to try?" I ask.

"To eat a leaf? Um, I've typically made it a practice to not eat things in the wild. Must be the doctor in me or something." I can't help but smile.

"No, not eat it. You just taste the stem, like I was doing. Trust me," I say.

"I trust you. But for the record, this is the first, and most likely, the only leaf I'll ever be tasting."

"Deal. Let me find you a fresh one, there aren't many left this late in the season."

I pull down a mitten shaped leaf and hand it to him. *The mittens were our favorite.* He puts the stem in his mouth and I watch as he tilts his head to the side and nods. "Wow, it really does taste like root beer. Now there's something they don't teach you in medical school."

The sight of him dressed in his stylish running gear, a leaf dangling from the corner of his mouth, it's almost too much for me to take.

"New York meets Indiana," I say, laughing.

"Does that laugh mean you're staying?" he asks, putting his arms around me. I nod.

"Glad to hear it. How about we start the day over?"

QUAINT SHOPS and restaurants line both sides of the street until the stores eventually fade away, replaced by dense greenery. The way the old trees hover over the road, shaped by the wind, you can just sense there's a promise of an ocean view ahead. We pass Montauk Point State Park and as we round another bend, a massive lighthouse with a black domed lantern appears.

"That's the Montauk Lighthouse in front of us. This is the easternmost point of Long Island."

My jaw drops open. "This is so cool!"

"I love how excited you get about things," he says, turning into the parking lot.

We bundle up and follow the path past the lighthouse, out to the top of the cliff that overlooks the Atlantic Ocean. The views are unlike anything I've ever seen.

"I've never been completely surrounded by the ocean like this before." His arms wrap around me from behind and I rest my head on his shoulder.

"The power of the sea always reminds me how small and insignificant we are. Let's go to the point and watch the waves," he says, taking my hand and leading me down the hill to an access point. It's such a rush listening to the thunderous waves crash against the boulders in their constant and unrelenting attack. Miles and I walk hand in hand, pausing to take a few photos so I can send them to Mom, Grandma and Mika. A cold wind blows, dousing us with the Atlantic's frigid spray.

"We'll have less chance of getting soaked if we move to the beach," he says, putting his arm around me, blocking me from the icy mist. We follow the path to the end, putting us out onto a rocky beach where sandy, green topped cliffs rise high above our heads.

I crane my neck to look at the tops of the steep rock faces. "I never knew a place like this existed in New York. It looks more like the pictures I've seen of Ireland or Scotland."

We climb up and over several boulders until we find two side by side and sit down to watch the waves.

"When Amos and I were kids, my mom would bring us here for bonfires and s'mores. The three of us would spend the whole night out here roasting marshmallows, building rock cairns and watching the stars," he says.

"What's a rock cairn?" I ask.

"That's one right over there," he says, pointing to a small tower of stones. "The term *cairn* is Gaelic and means heap of stones. People build stacks of rocks as offerings to people passing by, a thank you to the sea, or a memorial for a loved one. There are several interpretations, but I like to think of each stone as an intention. A way to send grace, peace, or forgiveness out into the universe. Building a cairn teaches the importance of patience and balance. It's still one of our favorite things to do when we're all together."

I grab his hand. "Well then—let's go build one. I could use a little more patience and balance in my life," I say, still feeling a little embarrassed by my earlier reaction. We climb down from the boulders until our sneakers hit rocky sand.

As I hunt for rocks, I think of what intentions I'd like to offer. Our arms full of stones, we pick out a level spot in the sand to start building our tower.

"Since this is your first cairn, why don't you start," he says, sitting down next to his pile. I sit beside him and place my flattest, biggest rock down firmly, moving it back and forth to make sure it's secure. My intention is forgiveness. Forgiveness of others is something that has always come easily for me.

The intention I'm setting is forgiveness of self.

I've been carrying a mountain of guilt around since I was twelve and it's time to lay it down. My bones ache with grief for my younger self and all she's endured. She has taken care of me for a long time, and now it's time for me to take care of her.

While Miles is balancing his stone, I place my palm on my chest and pat gently, soothing both of our wounded hearts. I've been walking a path of love and heartache long enough. Miles is right, it's time for me to find a way back to happiness.

We finish building and stand to admire our work.

I hope anyone who is also struggling to forgive themselves receives my offering.

"Thank you for teaching me about cairns, Miles. I have so much in my life to be grateful for. One of which, is you," I say.

He blushes but can't hide the smile crawling across his face. "You don't have to thank me. I love spending time with you."

He takes my face in his hands and kisses me tenderly, our hair blowing wild in the frosty gales of November.

THIRTY-ONE

THE HAMPTONS

"The Hither Hills Trail is a little over an eight-mile hike that takes around three hours. You up for it?" he asks.

"A chance to be surrounded by more of this for eight miles? Um. . . yes," I say, nodding. "Nature was one of my best friends growing up, this trip has been a much-needed reunion."

"I know what you mean. The city's great, but it's nice to be able see more trees than cement every once in a while. The trail is about a ten-minute drive from here, let's head back to the car."

I take a few pictures of our cairn, before walking hand-in-hand to the parking lot. He opens my door and I climb inside.

"Wait here a sec," he says, starting to close my door.

"Where are you going?"

"I left my water bottle, I'll be right back."

"I'll come with you," I say.

"No, it's okay. I know right where I left it, I'll be back before you even know I'm gone."

I give him a puzzled look as he leans in and gives me a long and deep kiss. I shut my door to keep out the cold and watch in my rearview as he runs down the road back onto the beach.

"THE TRAIL STARTS on the south shore and takes us up to the north shore and then loops us back to the beginning, so you'll get a good feel for both," Miles says, as we begin our hike. The twisting and rocky trail is narrow, so we walk single file with him in the lead. The trail's quiet; no one's out here but us. There's something cathartic about being completely surrounded by nature. Almost fifteen-minutes into our hike, two men dash by us. We try to move out of the way but they're running so fast they bump into us as they're pushing past.

"Hey, watch where you're going!" Miles shouts after them.

They don't even look back. I shrug and we brush it off, walking deeper into the woods. "We're in the middle of the Hither woods preserve now; there's nothing but trees and animals in every direction, as far as you can see." Miles pauses as we take in our surroundings. I hear someone shouting in the distance but can't quite make out what they're saying.

"Did you hear that?" I ask.

Miles shakes his head. "Hear what?" We walk a few more minutes and I hear it again. Someone is calling out for help and this time Miles hears it too.

"Call 911! Please. We need help!"

Miles sprints up the trail toward the voice and I follow closely behind. We run up the trail over leaves and exposed roots, following the winding curves of the dirt path. We climb a small hill and when we come down the other side, we find an elderly man kneeling beside a woman lying on her back. The man is shaking and has tears streaming down his face. Miles immediately bends down on one knee to get on his level.

"I think my wife's having a heart attack," the man manages between sobs.

"My name is Miles. I'm a doctor, I can help."

I move out of the way behind Miles and pull out my phone to see if I have cell service to call 911. No signal. Miles immediately drops to the women's side and checks for a pulse and any signs of breathing.

"I'm going to start CPR compressions on your wife. Gemma, can you run back to the road and see if you can get a signal and call for help?"

"Our sons just ran back to call for an ambulance," the man says, wiping his eyes.

My heart races as I stand frozen, not knowing what to do. Miles begins chest compressions on the woman as I watch in horror. I can't bear to look at the pain in the man's face, so I focus on Miles's movements counting the ratio of his compressions to breaths as he works to regain her pulse.

My mind flashes back to that fateful night and my arms and legs turn to jelly. Adrenaline surges through my veins, I want to run as fast away from here as I can, but my legs won't budge. My knees buckle and I sit down on a log, my breath ragged. The man's anguished cries snap me out of my trance, bringing me back to the emergency unfolding in front of us.

I remember what it felt like not having anyone by my side when I needed it most. I can't do that to someone, especially when I know the helplessness he's feeling right now. Desperate to do something—anything but watch what could potentially be this woman's last moments, I walk over and kneel beside the man, putting my arm around him. His sobs shake his entire body.

"Miles is going to do everything he can for your wife," I say, quietly.

Fifteen excruciating minutes pass by and I can tell by Miles's rapid breathing and reddened face he is exhausted but not letting up. There must still be no pulse.

I hear the thudding of feet on the path behind us and am relieved when a team of paramedics runs toward us, along with the two men who ran past us earlier. Miles tells them what he's been doing and for how long, and the team swiftly moves in, taking over his position. Everyone is asked to move back while they prepare her for the defibrillator.

I turn away to give the family privacy and Miles moves next to me, letting the paramedics take over. His breathing starts to slow as he watches the team work on the patient. After three tries with the defibrillator, they are able to restart the woman's heart. The medics quickly transfer her to a stretcher and rush her back toward the road, the rest of the family following behind. Just as fast as they rushed in, they're gone. I feel unsteady and sit down on a log and Miles sits next to me.

"Are you okay? That was a lot to witness," he asks, as I put my head in my hands.

I shake my head slowly, trying to unsee what just happened. My teeth start to chatter and my hands suddenly feel like two blocks of ice. "That poor man. Do you think she'll be alright?" My voice sounds fuzzy.

Miles puts his arm around me, pulling me into his warmth. "Here, drink this," he says, handing me his water. "There's unfortunately no way to know for sure. There are a lot of factors that will determine her chances for recovery. I hope she'll be okay, though."

I feel like I'm floating, his voice sounds so far away.

He turns my face toward his. "Gemma, look at me. I want you to take some long, deep breaths. Here, I'll do them with you." I watch his chest heave up and down as he guides me through several minutes of breathing. He rubs my hands until they feel warm again, and the blue tinged nails turns back to their normal color.

"More water," he says, helping me lift the bottle to my lips. He takes out a granola bar from his pocket, breaking off a piece for me.

"You jumped in so quickly, you just saved her life," I say, amazed by his calm demeanor.

"She's got a long road ahead of her. When these things happen outside the hospital, the chance of a full recovery is very small."

"Oh, I didn't know that," I say, looking down at the ground. I feel tears forming as Miles puts his arm around me again.

"You still feel like taking this hike? If you'd rather head back to the house, I totally get it," he says.

"I still want to go—I just. . . I need a minute. That was awful. I don't know how you do it," I say, shaking my head.

"How I do what?" he asks.

"Come to terms with not being able to control the outcome."

"Oh my, that's a long conversation," he says, taking a drink of water. "The short of it is, I know I'm trained to help save lives, but unfortunately, that's not always the end result. When it comes down to it, how many things in life can we actually control? The list isn't long. Nothing in life comes with a guarantee and my job's no different. Do I wish I could save every one of my patients? Absolutely. But is that reality? Of course not. Sometimes in life no matter how much we wish we could change the circumstances, they just can't be changed. There's no fault or guilt in that fact, it's just a part of life."

I let out a long and deep sigh. His words hit hard. *Why do I feel like he's speaking directly to all of my broken pieces?*

MILES PULLS into his pebble driveway at the end of our incredible day, and it feels like coming home.

"Thank you for making today so special," I say, putting my hand over his. "As terrible as it was witnessing what that poor family was going through, it was impressive to watch you and your life-saving superpowers in action. I hope she's okay."

"I do too. Great job rallying through an intense situation." He looks out the windshield and then back at me. "It was fun showing you some of my favorite spots out here," he says, leaning over to kiss me.

"How about we go inside and I'll make a fire to warm us up?"

I nod and lean down, kissing him lightly on his neck, pausing for a moment to breathe him in. He hands me the keys and I walk to the front door, letting myself in as he goes to gather wood from the side of the house.

Inside, the house is dark, except for a dimmed pendant light over the kitchen sink. I hang my jacket in the mudroom, leaving my shoes by the back door. I find a pack of matches on the counter, and light a few candles by the fireplace, leaving the lights off. Miles opens the front door, his arms filled with firewood, and pushes the door shut behind him. I sit down on the couch pulling a blanket around me so I can watch as he builds the fire.

"Do you have any music here?" I ask.

"Like vinyl?"

"I was thinking iTunes, but I like your style," I say.

"My mom has a sound system throughout the house, you can pick whatever you want," he says, pausing to hand me his phone.

I choose one of my favorite hotel lounge stations that Mikayla and I listen to when we want background music.

My eyes are drawn once again to the artwork on the wall. "The painting of the poppies above the fireplace is hauntingly beautiful. I can't get it out of my head. Is there a story behind it?" I ask.

Miles follows my gaze looking up. "Not really. I mean, I guess a small one. Many years ago right after my mom bought this house, she splurged and commissioned an up-and-coming artist to paint something for that spot. Poppies have always been her favorite flower and this artist was known at the time for her poppy series. My mom ended up buying a few more pieces for her house in Brooklyn, and they wound up becoming good friends."

"That's sweet. She's incredibly talented." I stare at the bold colors until something clicks. I know why it feels so familiar. "It reminds me a little bit of an old painting my mom has hanging in our hallway. Instead of a field, hers is a few poppies that are intertwined. The flowers all look the same—you have to look closely to notice their subtle differences. I'm sure the one my mom has is by a different artist, but the colors and mood are similar. Do you happen to know the artist's name?" I ask.

"I don't. I can ask my mom the next time I talk to her. Or if you want, I could get a ladder so we can read the back?"

"No, it's okay. I'm sure it's just a coincidence. As far as I know, my mom has never commissioned art pieces—umm, ever. But thanks."

Miles puts the final finishes on the fire and steps back to see if any adjustments are needed. Happy with his work, he comes and sits beside me on the couch, joining me underneath the blanket. He wraps his arm around me and I curl into him as we sit watching the flames hungrily devour the crackling firewood.

"This weekend with you has been such an unexpected gift."

"That's a great word for it." He tucks my hair behind my ear. "Today was incredible, but if I'm being honest, I couldn't wait for this—to be right here, alone with you," he says.

"Really?"

"Mm-hmm, really," he says as his hand softly cups my chin and tilts my face to his. I stare into his eyes with a want I've been holding back since the moment he picked me up from the bus stop. I grasp onto his wrist, inching him toward my lips but he moves back ever so gently, resisting my attempt to pull him closer. My insides quiver.

He smiles seductively, slowly running his tongue over his bottom lip. *Two can play that game.* I take his ear lobe gently in my teeth, letting the tip of my tongue graze his skin before releasing it. He lets out a throaty sound and I pull back, feeling the heat from his body. His fingers trail along my stomach, hovering just above the top of my jeans. My skin flushes feeling his hands on my bare skin and I lean back, my sweater rising higher. My heart pounds from his touch. He lightly brushes the side of my mouth with his lips as he turns and whispers in my ear.

"I want you, Gemma. I've wanted you since the first moment I saw you dancing on your kitchen counter," he says.

There's a hunger in his voice and I grip the back of his head as he moves on top of me. He brings his mouth down firmly onto mine and I open for him, our tongues seeking each other's with a ravenous passion. He kisses me over and over with painful urgency, making me ache for him.

I run my fingers down his spine, feeling the dents and ripples of his broad, muscular back. He presses his body against mine and I rise to meet him. He kisses my neck, trailing his lips over my shoulder, taking in a shaky breath. We lie entangled in each other's arms and legs before the light of the fire.

Our bodies have finally give in, surrendering to our pent-up desires. I feel as if I've been holding my breath this entire weekend. It's both a relief and deliriously satisfying. Miles props himself up onto one arm and leans back against the couch, putting space between us. He smiles down at me. Both of us have a look of surprise on our faces, stunned by the sparks that have taken over.

"Let's go upstairs," he says. This time, there's no mistaking his tone.

He scoops me off the couch, picking me up into his arms, leaving the roaring fire to fend for itself. I wrap my legs around his waist as he carries me to the stairs. His arms feel strong around me as he sets me down. He takes my hand and we quickly climb the stairs, my thoughts filled with being close again. He leads me down the hall to his bedroom and when we get to his room, he spins me around, kissing me passionately as he backs me against his bed. The moon's light fills the room and I peel off his shirt, my eyes taking in every detail of his bare and muscular chest. He takes his time undressing me, seizing every opportunity to leave a trail of kisses where a piece of clothing once was.

Completely undressed, we fall onto the bed, exploring each other's bodies. I want him with an unknown fierceness. I've looked forward to this moment for what seems like an eternity. Our bodies touch under the covers as his naked skin ignites against mine. *I need and want all of him.*

His tongue trails down my body and he caresses me softly with his delicate yet strong hands as I grip the back of his hair.

"Miles, I want you," I whisper.

A deep moan escapes the back of his throat and he pulls himself on top of me. Our bodies meld together in a perfect fit, consuming each other with a tender, but eager thirst again and again until our rhythm quickens and my body erupts, a wave of ecstasy washing over me, perfectly timed with his. We exhale deeply, both sweaty and out of breath. Miles takes my face in his hands and kisses me softly, each of us savoring every second. He moves onto his side, tracing my collarbone with his fingertips.

"I can't tell you how long I've thought about this with you. Every ounce of you and your perfect body. You're so beautiful, I wish I could paint you in this light," he says.

Miles holds me in his arms and for the first time in what feels like a lifetime, I feel completely safe. Protected. *The walls I've built around my heart are finally on shaky ground.*

THIRTY-TWO

THE HAMPTONS

I'm trapped in a forest of cadaverous shadows. Damp, musty earth buries my feet up to my ankles. I kick back and forth, trying to pull myself out, sinking deeper into the shallow graves. Sirens wail all around me as strobes of flashing blue and red streak across my ruffled, white nightgown. Broken ribs pierce my skin as their jagged edges puncture my lungs, replacing air with my own blood.

I tremble like a helpless prey, turning away from the hot, rancid breath that's inching closer with every second. A hooded black cape turns toward me revealing a cloaked skeleton, his wicked smile full of decaying, putrid teeth. My eyes widen in terror as I stare into the fiery, hateful eyes of evil. I put my arms up to shield myself as he raises his gleaming scythe above my head. His maniacal laughter fills the ice-cold, pitiless air as he lets it fall. . .

"NOOO. . . Please, no. Someone. . . anyone! Help—please, help us!

"Gemma, it's okay."

"No!"

"Gemma, wake up. It's just a dream, you're okay."

My legs kick and thrash, unable to outrun the inevitable.

"No! Emmeline. . . NO! Please. NO!" I wake to the high-pitched screams of a wounded animal howling. My hands fly up to my throat—raw from my screams.

"Gemma, I've got you. You're safe," he says over and over.

The sound stabs through the tranquil night and I sit up gasping for air, covered in sweat.

"I'm here. You just had a bad dream," Miles says.

I rock back and forth, unable to control my sobs.

Miles puts his arms around me and holds me tight. My throat hurts and I cough wildly as he rubs my back.

"I've got you. You're safe. It was just a bad dream."

"No, it wasn't, Miles."

"Yes, you're okay now."

"Miles, I'm not."

"Shhh, I'm right here, you're okay. It was just—"

I grab onto his arm so he won't say it again. "Stop saying that, Miles! It's not just a dream. *She's* not just a dream." I fall over on my side sobbing so hard I'm going to be sick. *Oh God, not now.* I run to the bathroom slamming the door behind me and throw up. I try and slow my sobs, but I can't control them. Miles knocks on the door. I grab a towel and throw it around me.

"Are you okay? I'm coming in."

"No, don't. I need a minute."

"No." He opens the door and immediately drops to his knees, joining me on the cold bathroom floor. He reaches out and rests his hands on my shoulders. I flinch at his touch.

"Miles, please. Just leave. I'll be fine."

"I'm not leaving you."

"I'm so sorry. You don't deserve any of this. I know this is hard to watch. Please... just leave."

"I'm staying right here." His tone is one of care and concern. "Please. Let me help." He stands, filling a glass of water from the faucet and sits beside me.

"Do you want me to call someone? Should I call your mom?"

"No!" I shout at him. *This beautiful and caring man.* I just yelled in his face. *I hate myself right now.*

"My mom has been through enough. I can handle this. It will pass."

"This isn't the first time this has happened?"

I shake my head and fold my arms across my chest, defeated.

"Please trust me. What is it?" he asks, tenderness in his voice.

Tears stream down my face, I feel so broken and humiliated.

"It's nothing. Please, I don't want to talk about it. Can we just go back to bed?"

"If something is upsetting you this much and it wasn't a bad dream, what was it?"

I take a sip of water and put my head in my hand as he holds me in his arms.

"I'm sorry you had to see this."

"Gemma, you don't have anything to be sorry about."

I slump over into him, giving in at last to his offer of comfort. He gently combs my hair with his fingers as we huddle together on the black and white tiles. The intense energy of the room slowly dissipates. I focus on my breath, slowing it down to match his, like earlier in the woods. I look up at him with tired eyes, he looks dazed.

"If it wasn't a dream, what was it? You sounded terrified."

I close my eyes, shaking my head.

He searches my face, warily. "Who is she?"

"Who's Emmeline?"

THIRTY-THREE

GEM & EM

"Girls, I'm leaving. Come kiss me goodbye."

We run down the hall to say goodbye to Mom.

"Hazy's still sleeping," Emmeline says.

"Kittens sleep a lot because they're growing." Mom ruffles the top of Em's hair. "Just like the two of you did when you were babies."

"When should we feed her again?" I ask.

"She'll cry when she's hungry. If she's sleeping, don't wake her to feed her. She needs her sleep right now just as much as she needs to eat."

Before Mom leaves, she takes out the measuring spoons and shows us how much formula to give Hazy, leaving a schedule and instructions on the counter.

"We'll take good care of her when you're at work, Mom." Em says.

"I know you will. Come and give me a hug."

We each take a side and squeeze her tight around her middle.

"You're both getting so big. Look at you, taking such good care of your first pet." She bends down kissing the tops of our heads.

"Thanks for letting us keep her, Mom," Emmeline says, as Mom nods.

"I know it's exciting to have a new kitten but don't forget to work on your science fair trifolds. They're due next week," she says.

"We will, we promise. Is Grandma coming over?" I ask.

"She can't. Tonight she's hosting a dinner for a friend of hers who's moving away. She said she's excited to meet Hazy though. Maybe tomorrow."

"Okay."

"Only six more days 'til Halloween!" Emmeline and I shout, chasing each other around the kitchen table.

"That reminds me I need to pick up some Halloween candy," Mom says.

"Don't forget to pick up a bag of Gem & Em's," I say, giggling.

"You two. My little peas in a pod. I love you so much."

"Love you. Have a good night at work," we say, following her to the front door.

She grabs her keys from the hook on the wall and kisses us once more before walking out the door. Emmeline and I run back down the hallway to check on Hazy, who's still fast asleep, tucked safely into the corner of her new home.

AFTER DINNER, Emmeline and I clean our dishes and work on our projects like we promised.

"Let's move Hazy in here so we can watch her while we work," Em says.

"Okay, I'll go get her." I lift her box carefully and bring her back into the kitchen, setting her on one of the empty chairs. As I set her box down, she starts to cry.

"She's hungry," Emmeline says.

I bend down and pick her up, snuggling her in my arms to help soothe her.

"When was the last time she ate?" I ask.

Em looks at the clock. "It was more than four hours ago."

"I'll heat up some water in the microwave, you measure her formula and put it in the bottle."

When I set her back in her box she starts to cry louder. Em and I quickly get her bottle ready and test it to make sure it's not too hot, just like Mom showed us.

"Can I hold her this time?" I ask.

"Okay." Em puts the blanket on my lap and I lie her down on her stomach, making sure to hold her head up while she drinks. Hazy chews furiously on the nipple, her cries instantly silenced. We sit giggling at her drinking sounds.

"It's so cute hearing her take her bottle," I say.

"Let me hold the bottle before it's all gone."

I scoot over to let Em have a turn. After her bottle, we hand her back and forth, listening to her purrs as we pet her, until she falls asleep. I put her back in the box, tucking the blanket around her and get back to work.

"Em, look. I just finished the twins. Does that look right?" I turn it around so she can see my two stick figures made of stars, holding hands.

"It looks so good! Which one am I?" she asks.

"This one," I say, pointing to the twin on the right. I'm almost finished. How much more work do you have?"

"Five more minutes." Emmeline brushes the hair out of her eyes, eyeing her work carefully.

"Oh, no!" she shouts, covering her mouth, her eyes wide. Her scream startles me and I look up.

"What?"

"Gem, tomorrow is our turn for the summer artifact show. We forgot to get the wind chime down!"

My mouth gapes open. Since the first day of school, Em and I have been counting down the days until our turn. I put my head in my hands.

"Oh no." A pained look takes over my face. "How did we forget?"

"I guess we've been too excited about Hazy," she says, sadly.

"We can't miss our day, the contest ends Friday! We won't get another chance, we have to go get it."

Emmeline scrunches up her face. "Now? What about Hazy? What if she cries and we don't hear her?"

"She'll be okay. Mom says she needs to sleep. We won't be gone very long, as soon as we get it down, we'll come right back inside."

"Okay," she says, hesitantly. "Maybe we can take turns checking on her."

"Sure, if it will make you feel better. C'mon, let's go."

After checking on Hazy one more time, we grab our fleeces and run outside. The air smells like fire—someone must be having a bonfire nearby.

"Can you see Gemini?" I say, searching the clear sky. "Does anything up there look like twins? I get extra credit if I can find them."

"Not really. Where should they be?"

"I don't know, somewhere up there."

"Do you think Hazy's okay?" Emmeline asks.

"She's sleeping and warm in her bed, Em, don't worry. We won't be out here that long."

"Can you see the wind chime?" Em asks, as a strong breeze blows. The two of us shiver, moving closer to help keep each other warm.

"No. Let's go get a flashlight," I say.

"They're still up there, right? Where could they have gone?"

I shrug and run into the garage for Mom's flashlight. I take it off the wall and rush back to Em and our sassafras tree, shining the beam into the branches.

"Oh no. Look, the strings are all wrapped around those branches," I say, worriedly. "What if we can't get it down?"

"Do you think we should wait until tomorrow when we can see better?" she offers.

"We won't have time tomorrow morning and besides, it's still dark out when we wake up. How about I shine the light and you climb up and untangle them?"

"Okay. But first I want to go check on Hazy."

"Em, she's fine."

"I know she is. I just want to check really quick."

I roll my eyes as she runs back into the house. She comes out with a smitten look on her face.

"She's so tiny and cute! I'm so glad we found her. Now she's safe and warm instead of cold and lonely in that rotten log."

"What was she doing?" I ask, unable to contain my smile.

"Sleeping. When I scratched behind her ear, she had a big stretch. Her little pink toes spread out and then she curled up again."

"Awwww. I already love her so much," I say, as Emmeline nods.

"I'm so glad Mom let us keep her."

"Me too."

"Let's go get our wind chime so we can go back inside with her. I'll shine the light while you climb so you can see where you're going."

"Okay," she says, as she walks over to the lowest branch of the tree and pulls herself up.

"Do you remember the way you took last time?"

"Yep," she says.

I watch from below, shining my beam on each branch as she climbs higher in the tree.

"You're almost there, Em."

"Tell me when I'm at the branch, I can't see it from back here—it's too dark."

"Okay, I'll tell you. Just a couple more."

Several minutes later, she reaches the branch near the top.

"That's it—that's the one, Em."

She lowers herself onto her stomach and inches herself toward the wind chime.

"Can you see it from where you are? Here, I'll shine the light back and forth from you to the wind chime to help guide you," I say.

"No, just keep shining it on the wind chime, so I can see where I need to go."

"Like this?" I say, spotlighting our shining pennies.

"Yep, keep it right there," she says.

Emmeline takes her time crawling out on the branch until she reaches our wind chime.

"It's really tangled." There's tension in her voice as she strains to free the strings. "I can't believe we forgot to do this when we got home."

"I know. It's Hazy's fault. Do you think you can get it down?"

"I'm trying," she says, frustration in her voice. "What if I can't?"

"Then I'll come up. We have to get it down tonight or we won't be able to be in the contest." I chew the inside of my lip, watching from below as she struggles.

She wrestles the smaller branches, bending them back and forth as gently as she can. I nervously watch as she frees each row, one by one. The tree finally loosens its grip from the last cord and our wind chime falls into place. I'm instantly relieved when I hear the delicate sounds of our tinkling copper pennies echo throughout our backyard.

"You did it, Em!" I shout to her, hopping up and down with excitement. My chest swells with pride. "You saved the day! We're going to win tomorrow, I just know it."

"Now we can go back inside and check on Hazy," she says.

"Yep. She's fine, though, you know she's just sleeping."

"I know, I just want to see her," she says. "I'm going to drop the wind chime down to you."

"Okay, I'll try and catch it." I put the flashlight down and walk closer to the trunk of the tree.

"Here it comes," she says, letting go. It lands with a crash in the damp grass. I pick it up, happy to see it's all in one piece after the long drop.

"We're ready for tomorrow, Em! It looks so good." I set it down and pick up the flashlight, shining its beam back on Em.

"I'm coming down." She hugs the tree branch tightly, edging herself backwards on her stomach toward the fork in the branch.

"Take your time. The hardest part is over."

She gets to the fork and slowly pulls herself into standing position. She wedges both of her feet in the fork of the tree, grabbing onto the branches on each side to help her balance. I aim my flashlight to the branch below her so she can see where she needs to step down.

"Gem, my feet are stuck."

"How stuck?"

"They won't move," she says, trying to wriggle them back and forth. "Not even a little."

I aim the light at her feet. "Try leaning to one side and see if that helps."

"I'm trying," she says, her voice strained. "They're just getting more stuck."

"Do you want me to come up?"

"No, hold on. I'll keep trying." She groans as she struggles to move her foot back and forth. "Nothing's working."

"Try taking off one of your shoes. That always works," I say.

"Okay."

Emmeline bends down to untie her shoe and manages to wiggle her foot out leaving both sneakers wedged firmly in the fork. I shine the light on her white sock as it searches for a branch below.

"Gem, I can't find the branch."

"Go straight down. Right there. Can you feel it?"

There's tension in her voice as she pulls herself back up to stand in the fork again.

"No. I can't find it. My arms are getting tired." I can tell from her tone she's frustrated.

"Sorry. Hold on, let me try from another angle. How about now?"

"Yeah. I see it now. Wait a sec, my hands are slippery," she says, bending down and taking turns rubbing each hand down the front of her jeans before trying again.

"Should I come up?"

"No, it's okay. Let me try again."

I watch as her white sock fumbles around in the night air until it lands on a branch below.

"Got it," she says, as we breathe a collective sigh of relief.

Her success is short-lived when she tries to bring her other foot down.

"Now my other shoe is stuck."

"Just push the empty shoe out so your other foot can move, like we always do."

"Okay."

I stand below, listening to her faint grunts as she tries to un-wedge her empty sneaker until it finally gives way.

A loud crack echoes through the air. Her screams pierce my eardrums. An empty sneaker and the branch holding my sister plunge from the tree, landing in a pile on the cold ground with a horrific, loud thud. And then silence.

"Emmeline!" I scream at the top of my lungs, dropping the flashlight and running over to where she's lying near the shed.

"Are you okay?"

No response.

My mouth goes dry. She's playing a trick. She has to be pretending. "Emmeline! Oh no. Emmeline!" My knees give way and my legs go numb as I kneel beside her pale face. A scarlet trickle from the corner of her mouth flows into the grass in a steady stream.

"Oh no, oh no, no, no. EMMELINE! NOOO!" The words burn my throat. Our backyard moves around too fast in front of my eyes, blurring my vision.

I lift the branch off of her and lie beside her, curling my arm across her chest. My heart is in my throat, a whooshing throb in my ears.

"You're okay. You're okay. You just hit your head. C'mon Em. Wake up. Please," I beg.

She doesn't move.

"We can go see Hazy now. Just wake up. Open your eyes, Em."

She doesn't move.

The world goes still. I open my mouth to scream again, but nothing comes out. A voice from behind me pierces the thick silence.

"Are you girls, okay?" Screams come from somewhere in the distance. Someone's hand is on my shoulder. When I look up, Mr. Paul is standing over me. He picks me up, moving me to the side so he can kneel beside Emmeline.

"She's okay, right Mr. Paul?" I whimper. "Right? Please, please say she's alright!"

When he doesn't answer my heart stops. It feels like giant hands are around my neck, squeezing tightly. I can't get out any words. Someone's high pitched wails fill the air. Streams of tears trail down my face and I stop trying to wipe them away and just let them mix with my strands of drool as they fall to the ground.

"She fell. We were trying to, , , her shoe was stuck. She's okay right? Is she—"

I keep hiccupping my words, swallowing air. "Is she. . . going to be okay?"

"Gemma, go inside and call 911 right now. Tell them there's been an accident and we need an ambulance. Give them your address. I'm calling your mom," he says.

The grave concern in Mr. Paul's voice sends ice through my veins. The roaring in my ears drowns out the screams as my chest pounds. A wave of nausea erupts and I feel like I'm going to be sick. I get up and run for the house but can't feel my legs. I fall down halfway and collapse again when I try to stand.

"Gemma, please hurry!" Mr. Paul screams urgently behind me, making every hair on the back of my neck stand. The terror in his voice gives me strength to push myself up and run as fast as my legs will carry me. I call 911 with the phone that Mom leaves for us on the kitchen counter and when the woman answers I search for the words, but they won't come. My voice gives way to sobs and every time I try to talk my cries won't let my words out.

"Sweetheart, can you please give me your address?"

Sounds stretched tightly from the hollow of my throat manage to spill out our address and she repeats it back to me. I get dizzier with every word; I feel like I'm going to pass out. The woman tells me to stay on the phone with her until help arrives. It sounds like she's in a tunnel. I hold on to the phone while I run back outside to be near Emmeline. As soon as I see her motionless body lying on the ground beneath the tree I fall to the ground and throw-up.

The woman's voice calls out to me from where I dropped the phone. I wipe my mouth with my sleeve and run to the trunk of the tree and lean against it, sliding slowly to the ground. Trembling, I pull my knees tightly to my chest. A cold sweat covers me. Something is very wrong, I can feel it in every part of my body. *Twins know these things.*

Saliva and tears soak the knees of my jeans while sirens penetrate the frigid and unforgiving October air. I stare at the flashlight's beam still shining in the grass where I dropped it—so I don't have to look at her small frame lying motionless on the cold ground. Her empty shoe sits beside me, next to the wind chime. Everything feels foggy, like I'm trapped in a dream. The worst kind imaginable.

My eyes blur to everything around me except for her shoeless foot. I sit memorizing every detail of the orange and yellow embroidered flowers on her sock. Her favorite pair. I keep my eyes trained on the flowers and the way her sock is bunched around her twisted ankle as a team of people rush over, crowding around her body. The ringing in my ears grows deafening as I rock back and forth against our tree. Someone is saying something to me but it sounds like they're underwater.

THIRTY-FOUR

THE HAMPTONS

"What did you just say?"

I sit on the cool tiles studying him closely. Frozen and unable to move, my mind struggles to make sense of what he's just said. I'm in a dreamlike trance and everything has slowed except for my breathing. My words hold an accusatory, almost defiant tone in their edges.

"I'm not trying to upset you—I want to be here for you," he says.

Hearing him say her name was a kick to the stomach and I swallow, fighting the bile rising in my throat.

"How do you know her name?"

I don't mean for them to, but my words come out in a snarled growl. I'm fiercely protective of her. She's a part of me that no one has access to, because I keep her locked away, deep in the other half of my heart. I try to conceal the hurt in my eyes but it's a losing game. I'm powerless over my tears as they race each other down my cheeks, falling into the folds of my towel wrapped tightly around me.

"You called out her name in your sleep. You're in so much pain—please talk to me."

There's an earnestness in his eyes, I feel his sadness and it makes me hurt for him. My heart pounds trying to knock down the door that stands between us. A cold metal vice clamps down on my chest until my shoulders slump in defeat. *I have to tell him about Emmeline.* He holds me tightly in his arms and I look up at his face, worry etched into the creases of his eyes. I know he genuinely cares for me; he would never judge me for what I'm about to say.

"Miles. I don't know how to. . .where do I even start?" I shake my head, feeling like I've aged decades in the last twenty minutes.

He tenderly brushes my cheek with his thumb, wiping away my tears. "Take as much time as you need. I'm not going anywhere."

I try my best to compose myself, knowing the dam will burst wide open from the weight of my next words.

"Miles, I lied to you. I lied—and I hate myself for it."

"Don't say that. What is it?"

I struggle to get the words out. "The night you took me to see your friend's show, you asked me about my family and I told you that I'm an only child."

He nods. "I remember."

"I'm not an only child. I have a twin sister. Her name is Emmeline. She died when I was twelve."

He closes his eyes and blows his breath out in a long and slow stream. I watch his reaction closely, searching for the slightest hint of anger or betrayal—my cue to run as fast as I can because this isn't about anyone but my sister and me. Confusion and compassion are all I recognize as he searches my eyes, not saying anything. We sit quietly as my words echo in my head. They're finally out.

He reaches for my hand. "I'm so sorry."

I abhor those words. He means well and I know it's what people say but that doesn't change the fact that hearing them still angers me. I silently nod and hang my head in shame. He pulls me to him and I lean into his chest, taking solace in between the beats of his tender heart.

We sit in weighted silence for several minutes. He gently rubs the back of my neck, offering me patience to talk when I'm ready. Tears stream down my face and I weep into his arms as I dig deep to find the courage to get the words out. My throat is so tight, they come out strangled.

"Who makes up lies like that? What is wrong with me?" I ask, repulsed by own my actions.

He shakes his head and closes his eyes. "Nothing is wrong with you."

I pull away. "I don't know why I haven't told you, or anyone before now. I'm embarrassed and so ashamed. It's like I'm trying to hide the fact that she ever existed. Who does that to their twin?"

"Come here." He gently pulls me back to him.

"I'm a monster for hiding her all these years. She doesn't deserve to be hidden. She deserves so much more than I've given her and that's something I'll have to live with for the rest of my life."

"You're talking about her now. It's okay."

I shake my head. "It's not okay. I'll never forgive myself for what I've done. It was my fault. I'm the reason she was up in that tree in the first place. I would give anything to go back and switch places with her. I was the one who should've died that night, Miles. Not her."

"Oh, Gemma." He rocks me back and forth as my words come out in a steady stream of ruptured consciousness. My silence has finally broken, freeing her at long last.

"She deserves to be talked about. She deserves to be remembered. She was the best of both of us and I love her with all of my heart. When she died, something broke inside of me. I've cried a lifetime of tears and yet there are always more. No amount of tears will ever be able to fill the hole of emptiness, regret and pain I've felt since the day I lost her."

I weep into his chest, my never-ending wave of sobs crash against him one after the other until I'm completely wrung out. I can't cry anymore. I'm exhausted and my head feels like it weighs a million pounds. My eyes are swollen, and my entire body is covered in sweat.

I'm completely empty and in some strange way, I feel as if the concrete block that's been sitting on my chest, holding me down, has finally been lifted. *I can breathe again.* I sit listening to the sound of my inhales and exhales working together as a team, trying their best to steady me.

Miles sits back; his careful and kind gaze reassuring as he rubs my back. He reaches over and hands me a box of tissues from the nearby shelf. I'm so embarrassed he is witnessing this devastating and raw moment. *I wouldn't blame him if he never wanted to see me again.* I blow my nose again and again, tossing each tissue onto the growing pile in the waste can next to my foot.

"That was probably a lot for you to hear... and watch," I say, rolling my eyes, dying a little inside.

He pulls me back to him and whispers into my ear. "Don't worry about me. There's no judgment. When it comes to grief, the only timeline is the one you set. You're the only one who can decide when it's the right time to talk about her. I'm sorry you've been holding all of that in for so long."

I nod my head, giving a thin smile and stare into his, calming emerald eyes. I miss the carefree and naive version of me who never had to think about any of this. Before grief sunk its vicious talons into my skin, tearing through my flesh and not stopping until they punctured the marrow deep within my bones. I would do anything to change the outcome. But no one has that kind of power. *Certainly not when you're twelve years old.*

"You're not a monster. No piece of you is. You're grieving. You have done all you can to survive up until now and that took a tremendous amount of strength. I can't begin to imagine the pain you've gone through losing your twin. I'm so glad you feel safe talking about her with me."

"Thanks, Miles," I say, looking down at the bathroom floor, humiliated and thoroughly spent.

He puts his finger under my chin and tilts my head up to look into my eyes. "You don't have to thank me. Not at all. I want to be the one you come to. For anything, especially for something as important as this. I hope you will be gentle with yourself. Emmeline would want that for you."

I know his words hold so much truth in them.

"I didn't realize how much pain and sadness I've been carrying around. I felt if I pushed her memory down far enough and never talked about her, then I wouldn't have to feel the pain of losing her again." I swallow hard. "As it turns out, it's *not* talking about her that has been keeping me up at night."

Miles nods his head reassuringly.

"I guess my nightmares for the last ten years have been a way of telling me that I need to talk about her. Either I talk about her, or my dreams will take it upon themselves to make her voice heard. I've always felt it was my responsibility as her twin to keep her memory alive, and by not talking about her, I've had to live with the crushing guilt that I've been letting her down all this time."

I gasp and the tears come again.

"That kills me. I was so proud to be her sister. I *am* so proud. Not talking about her makes me feel like I'm ashamed of her or something. It makes me so fucking sad. What if she thought the reason I didn't talk about her was because I was embarrassed by her? Oh my God. I can't, Miles. I just can't."

More sobs consume me as Miles holds me, rocking me back and forth.

"Of course you're proud to be her sister, it's obvious how much love you have for her. As your twin, she would know that better than anyone. You're not letting anyone down. You've been surviving. She would want you to take care of yourself in whatever way that looked like, to help you move forward. She wouldn't want you being this hard on yourself."

I sit for several minutes letting his words sink in.

"My head is pounding. I have such a headache the back of my eyes hurt."

He gets up and takes out a bottle of Tylenol from the top drawer, tapping two into his palm. He hands them to me and I take them with the glass of water next to me.

"It's the middle of the night. Let's go back to sleep, at least for however many hours there are left," I say.

He nods, fatigue and worry in his bloodshot eyes.

"I know you say I don't need to say it—but thank you for staying up and helping me through this. You don't get a lot of sleep at the hospital—and this was your weekend to catch up on your rest. I'm sorry I've kept you up."

"No apologies. My sleep can wait. Nothing was more important than this conversation."

He pulls me up from the floor into his arms. They surround me in such a solid and healing way that extends into my soul. He guides me back to the bed and I climb under the covers, burrowing in next to him, emotionally drained from our conversation. A kind of peace I haven't felt since I was twelve settles over me, and I drift off instantly in his arms.

THIRTY-FIVE

GEM

I wake with a jolt and sit up in bed searching the room and its unfamiliar surroundings. Then it hits me. I'm at Grandma's house. I've done this every day for the past week. The painful memory of Emmeline's accident comes flooding back and tears fall from my eyes as I reach out and touch the empty pillow lying next to me. *I wish I could go back to my dreams, being awake is too hard.* I hear Mom's voice on the other side of the door before she quietly inches it open.

"Hi, my sweet girl," she whispers. "I just went to get a glass of water. Do you want some?"

I shake my head and look over at Mom's red and swollen eyes, my second reminder that this is real and it wasn't just a bad dream. She sees me crying and immediately wraps me in her arms, sitting down on the bed beside me. So many tragic, unspoken words pass between our hearts. Our tears fall together and I hold on to her as tight as I can. *I never want her to leave my side.*

"My sweet, sweet girl. I want you to know I'm here for you and I always will be. I'm heartbroken and I know you are too. It's okay to be sad and to miss Emmeline. I miss her with all of my heart."

She barely gets out her last words—her tears choke them somewhere between her throat and her mouth. She holds my head to her chest. I stare directly into her favorite heart necklace, the one she never takes off.

The one with our initials E, G, F. *Emmeline & Gemma Forever.* I squeeze my eyes shut so I don't have to look at it.

"I'm sorry I wasn't home that night. I can't tell you how sorry I am."

She's been muttering the same words over and over for the last week. She's crying so hard, her bones rattle beneath her skin. I put my small arms around her and rub her back. My tears fall in a steady stream, soaking the front of her nightgown. *It's not your fault. You have no reason to be sorry.*

I want to admit to her that Emmeline's accident was my fault. I am the one who told her to go up into the tree when she wanted to wait until morning.

If I had one wish. . . I'd wish I could go back and have her hold the flashlight.

I'll carry that wish forever. Mom's shoulders shake so hard I worry she'll break in half. She looks so frail. A porcelain doll shattered on the inside. It hurts me to watch her suffering, especially because I'm the reason she's so sad. I'll never be able to forgive myself for the pain I've caused. The sound of a kitten's cries comes from a box near the closet. I look over and see Hazy's box with our drawings in the corner.

"Do you want to go pick her up?" Mom asks, wiping her cheeks. She reaches for a box of tissues and hands me one before taking one for herself. I blow my nose and nod my head, stepping down from Grandma's bed to get Hazy. She's curled in the corner surrounded by Mom's blanket, crying for her morning breakfast. I reach in and pick her up. Her cries get louder as I crawl back into bed with Mom.

"I'll go get her bottle ready. I'll be right back."

Mom hurries out of the room—the sounds of her blowing her nose echoes through the hallway. I sit staring into Hazy's eyes, thinking I would do anything to trade places with her. *She could be the broken girl and I could be the adorable kitten that everyone can't help but love.* Mom comes back with the bottle and a towel and I feed Hazy, watching as she hungrily drinks her breakfast. *It's not as cute as it was a week ago.* Feeding her just makes me sad. When she finishes her bottle, I put her on the bed between Mom and me and we watch as she clumsily walks around the sheets. I know I'm here sitting on this bed but it doesn't feel like it's really me. I'm not sure if I'll ever feel like myself again.

DEAR DIARY,

My counselor thought it might be a good idea to talk to you. I have a lot of time, so I'm going to give it a try.

It's been over a month and I haven't spoken a word since that terrible night. I wish I could, because I know my silence is upsetting Mom and Grandma, but I can't. My voice is gone, and I don't know if I'll ever find it again. Maybe the truth is—I don't want to find it.

I haven't been back to our house since the night of the accident. We've been living at Grandma's, and Mom told me yesterday she's going to put our house up for sale. They cleared our things out and put them all in Grandma's garage. Everything except our desk. Mom moved our desk into the room we're staying in, I guess to help make it feel a little more like our old one. I like sitting under it during the day and at nighttime, I've started sleeping there. Mom said she'd like me to sleep in the bed with her and every night we start out that way, but by morning she finds me curled up with my blanket beneath the desk.

I've spent hours looking at her name carved into the bottom. I run my fingers over the grooves of those eight letters—it makes me feel closer to her. I wish her name was longer so I had more letters to trace. Under my desk she's always right there with me. It's become our new place. It's the one spot that doesn't make me feel like I'm all alone.

Mom says I'm going to be changing schools to one that's closer to Grandma's house. She said maybe at the start of the new year or whenever I'm ready to go back. I've started seeing a grief therapist but our conversations are always one sided. I listen to everything he says so it's not like I'm wasting his time. I write my thoughts down for him or now and again he asks me to draw or paint, but I never talk to him. Sometimes I wonder if I'll ever talk again.

Hazy's growing and started eating regular food now. It makes me feel good to take care of her while helping Mom and Grandma at the same time. I try to find times when I know Mom will be gone so I can cry in my room. I see how much it upsets her when I cry so I hold it in as much as I can. Sometimes I can't help it and she always comforts me, but it's not fair for me to stack my sadness on top of hers. That's just too much sadness for one person.

When Mom's at school or work, Grandma and I've been spending time at the kitchen table drawing. I like drawing with Grandma. She hangs every one of my pictures, right next to the refrigerator. They take up most of the wall now, especially since Mom added all the cards we got at the funeral from kids in my school. She thought it would be a nice reminder that so many people are thinking of us, but I'd like it better if they didn't have to think of us at all.

Emmeline's funeral was a few weeks ago and I didn't want to go. I don't like being around so many crying people. Some of my school friends were there and I didn't know how to act. I just sat there feeling uncomfortable. When they tried to talk to me, I couldn't get any words out so it was embarrassing, and I counted the minutes until we could leave. Mom said it was important for us to say goodbye to Emmeline, but I don't want to. It just doesn't make any sense.

Since I don't go to school, I have a lot more time during the day and not a lot to do. Mom and Grandma help me with my homework now that they're sending it home for me, but once my work's finished, the rest of the day is long and boring. I play with Hazy when she's awake and she's great at keeping me company, but she sleeps a lot, so I spend a lot of time waiting for her to wake up. I try to find new things to do or read at Grandma's house, but most of the fun things are in the basement, and I can't go down there.

That was our place.

When Mom isn't here, I sit on my bed like I am now, staring out the window. I'll never get used to being by myself. I'd give anything to not have to.

We were a pair, Em & I, always together. I guess I never realized how much we were together because it was all I ever knew. Why would I ever think about how much time we spent together? It would be like thinking about how much air I was breathing. It never crossed my mind, because it was just always there. I can't remember a time longer than a minute we weren't together. Until now. That's all for now, diary. I have to go, Grandma's calling me. I'm not sure if I'll be back. Writing down my sad thoughts makes me even sadder.

"Hey, Gemma? Can you come down here, please?"

I climb down from the bed and walk downstairs. The smell of freshly baked cookies hits me when I'm halfway down the stairs.

I walk through the kitchen door and wave to her.

"Hi, my sweet girl. Whatcha doing up there? Playing with Hazy?"

I nod, even though Hazy's sleeping.

She comes behind me with a plate of cookies as I pull out one of the kitchen chairs and sit down.

I smile up at her, my new way of saying thank you.

"Chocolate chip, your favorite," she says.

I nod.

"I wanted to talk to you about something."

I look up at her as she pulls out a chair next to me.

"Your mom and I were talking earlier and I wanted to hear your thoughts about something."

I wait for her to tell me what they were talking about.

"How would you feel about trying out a dance class? One of my neighbor's sons takes dance lessons at a studio not far from here. They teach ballet, tap, jazz, all kinds of dance."

I shrug my shoulders.

"She said there are new students enrolling every month so you wouldn't be the only new kid."

She waits for my reaction and I just look down at the table.

"How about this, since your mom is out with her friend, would you like to go check it out just the two of us? That way you'll get a chance to see the studio and meet the instructors before you make your decision."

I look up at Grandma and all I feel is bad. *She's trying so hard.*

"I'll even take you out for a milkshake after we see the studio."

I shake my head.

"You don't want to go for a milkshake?"

I shake my head again.

"That's okay, sweetheart, we don't have to go for a milkshake. How about if we just go take a look?"

Indifferently, I tilt my head down, raising my shoulder, not wanting to disappoint her. Grandma reaches over and squeezes my hand.

"I love you so very much. Losing your sister has been devastating for all of us, but especially for you, Gemma. Your mom and I know how hard this has been for you. We want to help you any way we can."

I look at her and then look down at my feet.

"I miss Emmeline so much."

My eyes fly up at the mention of her name. Grandma's eyes fill with tears as her bottom lip quivers.

"It's not fair. None of it. I'm so sorry. I would give anything to be able to bring her back and it hurts so much that I can't."

I hear the pain in Grandma's voice, and I wish I could make it go away. She doesn't deserve to be this sad, none of us do. My eyes well up until my tears eventually spill down my cheeks. She pulls me onto her lap and holds me tightly in her arms while we sit and cry together. I reach down, taking her hands in mine, hoping she can feel just how much I love her. We sit like that for several minutes until Grandma takes off her glasses and dabs at her eyes with her handkerchief as I wipe mine on my sleeve.

"Sometimes talking about things helps, Gemma, and when you're ready, your mom and I will be here to listen to you. You take as much time as you need, my precious girl. Grandma understands."

I look into her kind face. *I'm so lucky she's my grandma.*

"Now how about we go and check out this dance place?" she says, as I slowly nod my head. I crawl down from her lap, following her to the back door to grab our coats. As Grandma and I walk to her car, I see Mom standing next to her car talking to someone. Mom looks upset. I watch as the woman puts her arms around her, pulling her into a hug. Mom rests her head down on her shoulder.

The woman must be going somewhere nice because she's all dressed up. Her dark brown hair is swept up into a bun and she's wearing a chocolate wool coat and pantsuit with high heels, and oversized black sunglasses on top of her head. *She looks like someone from one of those fashion magazines.*

Mom sees Grandma and I about to get into the car and pulls away from the woman, motioning for me to come over. Grandma waves to the woman and she waves back. I look up to Grandma and she nods, gently placing her hand on my back, nudging me toward them. I walk hesitantly down the concrete driveway.

Mom stops rubbing her hands together and pulls me beside her. "Gemma, sweetheart, I want you to meet a friend of mine," she says, wrapping her arm around me in a proud, yet protective way making me feel safe like only Mom's arms can.

"This is Miss Colette. She came down from New York to see how we're doing. Colette, this is my daughter, Gemma."

I watch her eyes as she smiles down at me. *I'm not exactly sure what her look says, but it's genuine. I can tell because her eyes are smiling.*

"Hello, Gemma. It's so nice to meet you. I'm an old friend of your mom's." Her voice is soft and comforting. I look up and she bends down so we're eye to eye. I've never seen her before, yet there's something familiar about her. Her eyes move in every direction, like they're searching for something in my face.

"My mom is taking Gemma to go check out a dance class," Mom says, as Miss Colette nods.

"I hope you like what you see. I danced when I was your age. Maybe one day you and your mom will come to New York, and I'll take you both to the ballet," she says.

A hint of a polite and shy smile creeps across my face and I look at my sneakers.

"Okay, sweetheart, Grandma's waiting. I can't wait to hear what you think. I love you." Mom kisses the top of my head, and I hug her around the waist. I traipse up the driveway and climb into the back of Grandma's car.

As she backs down the driveway, I watch Mom and Miss Colette out my window as they wave. *I wonder what they're talking about.* I press my palm against the window, leaving a foggy handprint on the cold glass.

THIRTY-SIX

THE HAMPTONS

Miles rolls over and the movement from his side of the bed wakes me. I can tell by his slow breathing that he's asleep. An image of me having a meltdown on his bathroom floor flashes in my mind. *Oh God.* I squeeze my eyes tight, trying to shut out the visual.

On one hand I can't believe that conversation finally happened, and on the other, I'm surprised it took this long. The vulnerable side of me imagines tiptoeing out of the house and heading back to the city before he even wakes up. Not that I don't want to see him again, it would just be nice to have some time to process everything before facing him. What happened last night can't be undone. It kind of changes everything from here on out. *If there was a before Gemma and Miles, this is definitely the after.*

I lie still, quietly reassuring myself that I have no regrets about our exchange. He was so patient and kind. Carrying my grief inside for so long has taken its toll. It was a relief to finally exorcise my demons, hopefully putting them to rest at last. My head still hurts, though not like it did a few hours ago, thankfully.

While Miles sleeps, I slip quietly out of bed to use the bathroom and splash cold water on my face to help the swelling in my eyes. Staring into my weary, moonlit reflection, I think back on our rock towers we built near the shore. I spent a lot of time searching for the perfect foundation stone, so it would be able to offer balance and strength to all of the other stones. That first rock is the critical building block, a kind of 'when all else fails, repeat step number one stone'. Forgiveness of self. I need to work on my foundation. For myself, for those I love—and for those who love me. I owe it to Emmeline to forgive myself so I can share her memory and let go of these heavy feelings of guilt and remorse.

A lonely tear falls down my cheek, but it feels more freeing than sad. I wipe it away and press my hand against the moonlit mirror, touching the reflection shared by the other half of my heart. My partner in the womb. She's still here with me; I see her in my own image. I look at our palms as they meet in the mirror and say to her softly:

"I'll love you for my entire lifetime, Emmeline. You're my best friend, my mirror soul. Your hand was the first I ever held. Your voice, my first sound. I miss you so much it hurts. But I'm strong. You've helped make me strong. Every ounce of love you gave me in our short time together has helped fill the cracks in my heart. You're forever a part of me and I want you to know I'm going to be okay. And when I'm not—I'll come find you here, in the mirror.

"You want to know something else? Every time I look up at the stars, I think of you. I know you've been filling your pockets with as many as you can, so that when I look up at the night sky, I know it was you who put them there for me. Thank you for always bringing so much light to my life, sister. You are every shooting star all rolled into one and I'm grateful to infinity and beyond that you are mine."

Slowly, I take my hand away from hers, watching as the space grows between our palms, knowing she'll always be with me because she lives inside of me. I turn, and walk down the darkened hallway, crawling back in bed with Miles.

"Good morning, beautiful," he says sleepily.

Surprised by his voice, I look over at him. "You're awake? It's three-thirty."

"I rolled over and your side was empty. I don't like this pattern we're in of me waking up and you're not here."

I snuggle into him, as he wraps me in his arms, warming me.

"I was just having a very important conversation."

"In the bathroom?" he asks, nonplussed.

"Yep, in the bathroom. To the mirror," I say.

"How are you feeling? Last night was..."

I sense he's searching for the right, words but I'm not sure there are any that would adequately capture what last night was.

"Our conversation was a big step for me. It's been something that has needed to come to the surface for a long time. As painful as last night was, it was a huge relief to finally tell you about her. I can't express to you how much it meant that you were there for me."

"I'm glad you trusted me. Thank you for sharing Emmeline with me."

It feels so strange to hear her name spoken so freely as part of casual conversation. And at the same time, it fills my soul.

"Hearing you say her name heals a piece of me."

"She would want that for you. I look forward to hearing more about her."

"I want to share more of her with you. I can't believe I'm saying this, but I'm grateful for my nightmare last night, because without it, I wouldn't have ended up telling you about my sister."

Miles kisses the top of my head as I lie my head on his chest, listening to his generous heart.

It feels strange being so unguarded, but it also makes me smile thinking about all the stories I want to share with him. And not just with him, with Mikayla—with the world. I've kept her hidden for far too long. I want to talk about her, share her stories so her memory can live on forever, because she is so much more than the hole she left.

A SHUFFLING NOISE WAKES ME, and when I open my eyes, Miles is walking into the room carrying a tray.

"Wait, what?" I sit up, rubbing my eyes. "What time is it?"

"I hope I didn't startle you. It's ten-thirty, we fell back asleep after our talk this morning. I just woke up and went downstairs to make us coffee."

I stretch my arms above my head, yawning. "I can't remember the last time I stayed in bed this late."

"I watched you fall back to sleep and have to admit I loved every second of it."

"Is that so?"

"Mm-hmm, that's so," he says, a warm smile on his face.

He sets the tray down on his dresser and comes to sit on my side of the bed giving me a tender good morning kiss on the forehead.

"Come back to bed," I say, lifting the sheets as he crawls in beside me.

"I was hoping you'd say that." He curls his arms around me.

"This weekend has been just what I needed. In so many ways," I say.

"This place has a way of knowing. I come here a lot to think. There's something healing about being this close to the ocean. I'm happy we were able to make this weekend work."

I nod. "It's so peaceful out here. I'm wrestling with the fact I'll be back in the city soon, sleeping in my own bed tonight. It feels a world away right now."

"No, don't say it. We still have a few hours left, let's make the most of them."

"What'd you have in mind?" I say.

He looks at me flirtatiously. "How about I show you?"

THIRTY-SEVEN

GEM

Grandma pulls into a big parking lot, and I stare out my window, eyeing several brick storefronts all lined up in a row. She parks directly in front of the dance studio as I sit taller in my seat, trying for a better look inside the huge glass window. There's lots of kids, all dressed in black leotards, holding onto a bar, stretching. My heart sinks. Seeing so many kids my same age makes me think of Emmeline and the fact she should be here.

It feels wrong trying something new when she can't try it with me. I immediately regret my decision and want to leave. Grandma must sense my hesitation because she gives me a reassuring look. "We'll just go in and take a look. You just watch, I'll do all the talking."

I look at her, filled with fear of the unknown. A father rushes by with his bundled-up son as Grandma slowly opens my door. My legs are shaky, making me second guess if I can trust them. I'd hate to fall in front of all these kids. This is the first time I've been in public since Emmeline's funeral and I feel exposed, like everyone knows she should be standing right next to me. *The girl who looks just like me is missing.*

Grandma takes my hand, and we walk through the front door of the warm, brightly lit studio. There's a large, mirrored wall at the front, and a long wooden bar that's attached to two of the four walls. Live music fills the room from a woman playing the piano.

We walk to a row of chairs along the back wall while the instructor leads the class through a series of stretches. A few of the kids look over at me and I train my eyes on the floor to avoid their stares. My worries about who might be staring at me are suddenly preoccupied with the wide pink-ribbon satin shoes tied around some of the girl's ankles. *How do they stand on their toes like that?*

As class goes on, the students eventually forget I'm here. I even forget I'm here. My foot starts to tap to the music as I watch the dancer's graceful movements with awe. The rehearsal flies by and before I know it, the dancers are running toward a sea of duffle bags, eager to take off their shoes.

Grandma leans over and whispers in my ear. "I'm going to go talk to the person behind the desk. Do you want to come with me or stay here?"

I grip the sides of my chair and Grandma takes the hint.

"Okay," she says, nodding a look of understanding, "I'll be right back."

I glance over at the students putting on their shoes. I recognize one of the girls, but I'm not sure how. I look back at Grandma and then shift awkwardly in my seat. When I turn my focus back to the students, the girl I recognized is walking toward me. Panicked, I look down at my feet and count to 100. *Maybe she'll leave if I stare hard enough.*

"Hey! Aren't you the girl we met at the tree fort?" she asks, brightly.

My heart squeezes seeing her face up close as well as her unforgettable ruby hair that's pinned tightly back into a bun. My face burns and I don't know where to look.

"My brother and I met you this summer. Remember? I'm Violet."

My throat tightens—it's taking everything to hold back tears. *Please don't ask me about her.* Grandma rushes over, I've never been so thankful to see her.

"Hello," she says to Violet.

"Hi," she replies, shyly.

"I got the information I needed, Gemma. Are you ready to go?"

A smile breaks across Violet's face. "Gemma, that's it! I remember now."

"Do you two know each other?" Grandma asks, sounding surprised.

"We met this summer at the fort near our house. Are you going to take dance lessons here?" she asks, directing her gaze back to me.

"She's thinking about it, we're just here to pick up some information," Grandma offers.

"You'll love it here! It's the best program in the area. The other dance studios are all so far away, and if I'm being honest," she drops her voice to a whisper, "they're not as good as this one."

"That's good to know," Grandma says.

"Yeah, my mom had me try all of them."

I nod my head before returning my eyes safely back to the ground.

"Let's go, Gemma. It was nice meeting you, Violet," Grandma says.

Violet waves. "Nice meeting you too. I hope I'll see you here again."

I give a half-hearted wave, vaguely in her direction. We pull on our coats and walk back to Grandma's car. The cold air feels nice after being inside the steamy studio.

She turns and looks at me from the front seat. "What did you think? It seemed like a nice studio, didn't it?"

I shrug as Grandma turns back around.

"The person at the front desk, suggested having you start private lessons with the teacher at first. That way you'll get to learn at your own pace," she says, as our eyes meet in the rearview mirror.

"She said when you're ready, she can add a few of the students to your lessons before joining the main class. Whatever makes you the most comfortable."

I nod, turning my eyes toward the sky as snowflakes begin to fall.

"There's a dance store not far from here; how about we go pick out a leotard and some shoes? You can pick whatever color you'd like."

Grandma's trying so hard, and it makes me feel awful. *Doing new things without her doesn't feel right, it's like I'm forgetting her.* Grandma leaves me to my thoughts and I leave her to hers. I know I'm not the only one grieving. *Losing Emmeline has been hard on all of us.*

THIRTY-EIGHT

GEMMA

The doors open and I climb the subway stairs unable to contain my glow from being immersed in nature all weekend. It was only four days, but there's a new bounce in my step. A small one, but it's there. My typical Monday morning walk to class feels different. In such a small amount of time, everything has changed. In me, in my surroundings, in how I look at the world.

Last night when I got back to the city, I told Mikayla everything. We had a long and tear-filled heart-to-heart about Emmeline—the source of my nightmares. I didn't spare her any detail of my ugly-crying breakthrough with Miles. She was so understanding and compassionate when I told her, just like I always knew she would be.

She told me she had a feeling there was a story behind my nightmares, but she also knew I would come to her when I was ready to talk. She gave me the space and patience that allowed me to tell her on my own terms—the mark of a true friend.

Mikayla thinks my nightmares were a prompt from my unconscious mind reminding me that my sister is a critical piece of me and sharing her is part of healing. I don't know why it took me so long to tell her, but that doesn't matter. I know I did what I had to in order to survive, and that brought me to the place I am now; ready to share her memory and forgive myself for not having done it sooner. My phone rings as I'm rounding the corner to my building entrance.

"Hey, Mom."

"Hi, sweetheart! How are you? I'm driving to work and wanted to see how your weekend was."

"I'm so glad you called. I miss you. My class is about to start, but I have a few minutes. We had a great time. It was just what I needed."

"I'm so happy for you. Your sunrise photo was beautiful."

"The photo doesn't do it justice. You would've loved seeing it in person. They always remind me of you—sunsets too. I have so much to tell you about our weekend, parts of it were totally unexpected. I can't get into it now, but it's important and I want to share it with you."

"I can't wait to hear all about it. How are you feeling about this guy, Miles? Is he going to be the one that breaks rule number three?"

She laughs and it makes me smile. *She knows me better than I do.*

"Ha, I don't know. Maybe? It's kind of scary how much I like him, Mom. He's smart, kind, hardworking and has so many interesting views of the world."

"That's how I felt when I met your father. It's the best feeling."

I stop walking and stare at my phone for a second before returning it to my ear. "Oh, wow, you never bring up my dad. I'd love to hear more about him when I'm home for the holidays—if you're up to it, that is."

"Sure, I'd love to tell you more—now that you're older." She sighs. "Our love story was cut short, but it was an unforgettable one," she says, wistfully.

My heart twists at the yearning in her tone. "I'll look forward to it, Mom. That would mean a lot to me." I chew my lip, hoping I haven't caused her pain, and I veer the subject in a safer direction. "How's everything with you and Grandma?"

"Work has been busy and Grandma and I have been spending a lot of time at the food pantry near her house. This time of year they need as much help as they can get. We both have been counting the days until you're home."

"I can't wait. Tell her I miss her."

"I will."

I lean my back against the front of my building. "Mom, I've been thinking a lot about you lately, especially after this past weekend. There's something I've been wanting to tell you."

"What is it, honey?" she says, concern in her voice.

The side of my mouth quirks upward. "You're such an amazing mom. You've been through so much and yet you were always there for me, helping me, making sure I was okay. You put me before yourself my entire life and I want you to know how much I appreciate you."

There's a beat of silence and I can hear sniffling from the other end of the line. "That's nice to hear. I'm so lucky to be your mom. I will always put you first, sweetheart. Nothing will ever come before you and your happiness."

"I don't want to say too much now or I'll start to cry. I just want you to know you've always been—my hero."

"Oh, Gemma! That just took my breath away. That's by far the nicest thing I've ever been told. Now I'm crying. Where is this coming from?"

"You've just been on my mind, and I wanted you to know."

"That means the world to me, thank you for telling me. I'm far from perfect, but I've always loved you fiercely. I've made choices in my life, some I'm proud of and some I painfully regret."

"Painfully regret?" *Those are strong words.* "You're too hard on yourself."

"No, I don't think so. As I'm getting older, I've had more time to reflect. Recently I've been looking back on my life and the decisions I've made."

I furrow my brow. "Is everything okay?"

"Yes. Everything's fine. It's better than fine, it's actually pretty great."

"You sure?" I say, not totally convinced, "I got worried for a second."

"No need to worry. I'm pulling into work and your class is starting soon. I didn't mean to start this conversation, but I look forward to finishing it when you're home."

"I miss our long talks on the couch, wrapped up under the blanket."

"Me too, love."

"I better go. Tell Grandma I'll call her soon. I have dance tonight so I'll call her later this week."

"Will do. Have a great day."

"You too. It was so good hearing your voice. I love you so much."
"I love you too. Bye, honey."
"G'bye."

I open the door and run up the steps to my class, and just as I'm about to sit down, I get a text from Miles.

> Good morning, beautiful.

His words make me smile.

> That's a nice GM. How's your shift?

> Brutal. How are you?

> Oof, sorry. Putting on my finals game face. Missing the ocean—and you.

> You're going to kill it. How about I steal you for another oceanside weekend after the new year?

> It's a date. Gotta run, class is starting.

I silence my phone and drop it into my bag. My conversations with Miles and Mikayla couldn't have come at a better time. I'm thankful for what this year has brought me and look forward to starting the new one, surrounded by those who bring so much light to my life.

AS I'M TAKING off my pointe shoes, I see a text from Mikayla from fifteen-minutes ago.

> In Chelsea. You done with dance?

> You still here?

> Yep. Wanna go see the windows?

A huge smile spreads across my face. *She knows the windows are exactly what I need right now.* Manhattan dressed up for the holidays is like walking around in the best dream you've ever had and being able to reach out and touch it. Mikayla tolerates them because she knows how much they mean to me. I text her back:

> Is that even a question? Rock Center in 20?

> Hopping on the E train, meet you in front of the tree.

> You're a true friend, Mika.

I bundle up and walk to catch a train uptown. The winter air feels good on my flushed cheeks, still beet-red from dance. *Tomato faces, Mom always called them.*

I GET off at Rock Center and walk three blocks to the tree. The holiday vibe is in full force. *No one takes decorating for the holidays as seriously as New Yorkers.* Mikayla's standing near the Channel Gardens next to the horn-blowing angels, in front of the renowned, multi-colored twinkling tree.

"Hey, you," I say.

"That was fast!"

I give her a hug. She doesn't seem to mind I'm still sweaty from dance.

"This city. Just—wow. How lucky are you to have grown up here?"

"Very. You know, I have to say, I'm surprised you like coming to see the windows as much as you do with how crowded it is." We join arms and start weaving our way through the packed sidewalk.

"Crowds have never bothered me. It was always the one-on-one I could do without. Present company not included, of course," I say, giving her a wink.

"By the way, my EKG came back normal. They are running more tests, but so far, so good."

I stop, making her turn and face me. "Wait a second, I didn't know you were having an EKG. They think it might be heart related?" My stomach sinks.

"Gem, you have a lot going on right now, I wasn't going to distract you with something that turned out to be fine, just like I knew it would."

"That's not for you to decide. Ugh, Mika. Please tell me next time, I want to know *before* you have any tests done."

"Why, so you can worry until I get the results?" She looks up to the sky, shaking her head.

"Yes. I just don't want to be blindsided," I say, my voice softening. "You know that's my thing. Just please—promise me?"

"You're right. I get it. Okay, I promise." She hugs me, as I try to push my worry aside so we can enjoy our night together. *Please let her other tests come back fine.*

We walk down 5th Ave. to watch the Saks light show. Lyrics of love and wonder play loudly over the speakers filling the jam-packed streets with holiday magic.

"This is what it's all about!" I shout to Mikayla. I can tell she's happy for me, even if she's not entirely thrilled being here. We cross the street and get in line to walk along the Saks side of the 5th Ave. windows.

The vivid imaginations of the creative minds who put together these brilliant, dream-inspired displays blows my mind. People come from all over the world to experience these windows. Droves of people standing in line, excited to watch something as simple as a light show in this day and age. It's an experience that's so uniquely NYC.

As a girl from a small town in Indiana, the splendor of the windows will always be a special memory for me. *Holiday magic in a brightly decorated city-globe.* Mikayla and I follow the line of people pressed shoulder to shoulder, marveling at the creations behind each window. When we reach the final window, it stops me in my tracks.

I stare in disbelief at the scene before me. Behind the polished glass, a whimsical four-foot-tall sparkling moon and sun stand on two legs, holding hands under a black velvet sky, amidst a field of wildflowers. Each carries a wooden bucket and, on their feet, giant rhinestone Mary-Jane platforms. Together they playfully tip their buckets over, spilling out mystical trails of silver and gold cosmic dust. The trails intertwine as they fall to the earth and then twirl upwards into a sparkly cyclone, transforming the night sky into a galaxy of twinkling stars. My jaw drops and I take a step back, putting my hand over my heart as it swells in my chest.

My sister. The moon to my sun.

THIRTY-NINE

GEM

The air is thick, it blankets me in a muggy cloud as I step out of Grandma's car onto the sweltering pavement. Coming to dance class five times a week has been my routine for the past eight months. It's the only place I've been outside the house, except for Mom's graduation ceremony. I'd felt bad I couldn't even pretend to be more excited for her on her special day.

Mom doesn't work at the restaurant anymore, which is nice because we get to spend more time together. She and Grandma have been taking turns tutoring me with my schoolwork. Mom got my Principal to agree to let me finish the year at home, allowing me to put off starting my new school—which I'm dreading.

I wave to Grandma as she pulls away, leaving me in front of the studio. It's been over nine months since the accident. Roughly 273 days since I've heard the sound of my own voice. I've realized something over these last months; time moves slowly when you sit in silence.

There have been a few times I've tried to talk when I'm alone in my room, but nothing ever comes out. Which is fine because I have nothing to say. My grief therapist called it psychogenic mutism, but I think it's something else. Emmeline and I shared a language and when she died, she took it with her, along with my voice.

My teacher moved me into a class with two other girls at the end of

February. I've been working hard to earn my first pair of pointe shoes. I spend hours practicing at home every day so my ankles get stronger. My teacher says I'm getting close and that's the first thing I've had to look forward to. I've wanted to wear those shiny satin shoes since the first day Grandma brought me to this studio.

Eventually, I'll be moved into the big class, but for now, I like our smaller group. I feel safer when there are fewer people around me. The two other girls understand that I don't talk, and though they say things to encourage me, they never expect me to respond. They've accepted me and my bubble of silence.

The truth is, I look forward to every one of my dance classes. A big part of me feels guilty for liking something so much. I wish I didn't, but I can't help it. *I love to dance.* Mom set up a bar and a big mirror for me in Grandma's basement. I never thought I'd go down there again, but as soon as she made an area for me to practice dance, I've spent every minute I can down there, stretching and working on my form.

The door swings open as a mom and her daughters rush out. I put my head down as they pass by and walk to the smaller room in the back for our class. My dance bag slides off my shoulder and I sit down beside it.

"Hey, Gemma," Violet says, walking toward me. She's one of the other girls in my dance group. When I first saw her at the fort, I thought she was much older than us, but it turns out she's just tall for her age. She drops her bag and sits next to me. I smile at her and quickly turn my attention back to putting on my ballet slippers.

"Do you want to come home with me after dance? I asked my mom and she said it's okay," she says.

I freeze, keeping my eyes locked on the X of my elastic straps. A few weeks ago, my mom invited Violet to come home with us—an attempt for me to have someone to hang out with, but it was more uncomfortable than anything else. We played with Hazy in my room and then her mom picked her up after an hour. I don't know what my mom was hoping for, but I think she sensed it hadn't gone well. The whole thing felt so forced. I never had to think of things to do before; it just always came so naturally with Em. *Going to someone else's house, though?*

"I thought we could go hiking in the woods, maybe go to the fort? You could stay for dinner too, if you'd like," she adds.

The flashback of Emmeline and I taking shelter high up in the tree during the tornado comes to mind. That was only last summer. *Back when she was still here.* The day of the tornado seems like yesterday and at the same time, a lifetime ago. Going to places we've been together sometimes helps me feel a little better. My grief therapist told me it's good that I find comfort in our spots. He had me write down all the things I enjoy doing that remind me of her, like sleeping underneath our desk and walking in the woods. *Spending time in our favorite places is when I feel her the most.*

My mind snaps to the present when I realize Violet's waiting for an answer. I had no other plans this afternoon except practicing dance and spending time with Hazy.

"Or we can just hang out at my house, we have a pool."

My eyes light up. *A pool. I've never known someone who has a pool.* It's so hot today, it would be nice to go swimming. If we have an activity to do, maybe it won't be so awkward. I take a deep breath and slowly nod my head.

"Yay! We're going to have so much fun. I'll call my mom and have her call your mom to see if it's okay. I'll make sure my mom tells her that you said yes. I can't wait for you to come over!"

VIOLET'S MOM picks us up when our class ends. She gives me a warm smile as I climb into their backseat. "Hi, Gemma," her brother Otis says from the front seat. I give him a slight wave and sit down, focusing my attention on my seat belt. Her mom asks how class went and Violet talks non-stop sharing every detail of our class. She talks so fast; I wonder how she can get so many words out at once. *Even when I was talking, I never talked this much.*

"Oh and, Mom! Gemma got fitted for her first pair of pointe shoes today."

Her mom turns around and smiles at me. "That's exciting. What a special day for you, congratulations."

I smile shyly at her, trying to hide the immense pride I feel inside about earning my first pair of those prized satin shoes. *I set out to do something, worked hard, and it came true.*

We pull into a long, winding brick driveway. Violet and her brother jump out and run into their backyard. I follow them down a stone path, through an iron gate. Their backyard is huge. In addition to a pool it has a wooden swing set with not one, but two slides. Violet sits down on the edge of the pool, kicking off her flip-flops, and waves me over as Otis takes off his shirt and shoes.

"First one in!" Otis screams as he cannonballs off the diving board.

"Put your feet in, the water feels so good," she says encouragingly.

I sit next to her and dangle my feet next to her.

"Do you want to go swimming, or go to the fort first? It's only about fifteen-minutes from our backyard."

I look at her and shrug.

"Why don't we go into the woods first and then we can jump in the pool when we finish our hike? By the time we get back, hopefully my brother will be out," she says, giving Otis the evil eye.

She stands and I follow her, nodding my head.

"Should we change out of our leotards now or when we get back?" she asks.

I shake my head no, holding onto the hem of my shorts. Changing in front of someone other than Emmeline just feels wrong. *That's for sisters.*

"Okay. Otis, tell mom we went to the tree fort and that we'll be back in a little bit."

He splashes water up at the two of us, just missing us as we walk out her back gate to pick up the trail. We swat at a cloud of mosquitoes that has been following us. I cover my ears to stop their buzzing.

"Let's run so they can't catch us," she says.

We run along the dirt trail, leaving the mosquitoes behind us. Most of the creek has dried up. Our whole town keeps talking about the drought—I can't remember the last time it rained. The cracked earth is littered with sticks, rocks and everything else you usually can't see when the creek is full. Everything's just hopelessly laying there, waiting to be carried away by the next big storm.

I follow her, running over the crusty graveyard until I see the fort up ahead. It looks totally different coming from this direction, but I can tell it's the same fort because of the hanging bridge.

My stomach drops. Memories flash of Emmeline and I jumping up and down on that bridge. I stop and put my hands on my knees to catch my breath. Violet sees I've stopped and runs back to me. I keep my eyes lowered, fighting back my big feelings.

"I'm sorry if I was going too fast. I'll wait up," she says.

I shake my head and motion for her to go on ahead.

"Are you okay?"

I nod, keeping my eyes down. She sits on the dusty, chalky ground beside me.

"Does it remind you of her?" she asks, timidly.

I look up at Violet, fighting back tears.

"My mom told me about your sister. I didn't want to say anything because I didn't want to upset you. I'm really sorry."

So she did know. My shoulders slump and I slowly nod.

"You must really miss her," she says.

I nod again as a tear falls down my cheek. I quickly wipe it away with the back of my hand.

"It's okay to be sad. I would be sad too, anyone would be. We don't have to go up there if you don't want to. We can go back to my house and go swimming," she says softly, kindness in her words.

I shake my head and walk to the ladder of the tree fort, putting my hand on the board closest to the bottom of the tree. I pull myself up onto the first rung and slowly climb until I reach the square opening of the landing. I grab onto the railing and pull myself up to where I can stand. Violet joins me and we look out in every direction into the woods. *I forgot how pretty it is up here.* The surrounding trees are lush with their mature, dark green summer leaves. Violet puts her hands on each side of her mouth.

"Hello!" she shouts.

"Hello... Hello... Hello!"

The woods return her voice to us in distant echoes.

"My mom says that an echo in the woods is a way for trees to tell their stories. Without an echo, they would always be silent. Until they fall, that is," she says.

Violet turns and walks through the wooden door frame as I follow her inside.

"Oh, look! Someone's been here. These weren't here last week when Otis and I were up here."

I look to the center of the room at a bunch of colorfully painted rocks in a circle formation, next to the stack of games. She picks up a brightly colored fish with teal and purple fins.

"Someone spent a lot of time making these," she says.

Several of the stones have words painted on them and we walk around the circle reading each one. Dream, Spread Kindness, Shine Bright, Love, Dance, Sparkle, Believe in Magic, Reach for the Stars, Be Brave. "Someone left these behind for us to find, that was so sweet," she squeals.

I pick up a bright green one that has a picture of a turtle on it and smile. *Emmeline loved her turtles*. I place it back down in its spot and look around to see if anything else in the fort has changed. A warm breeze blows through the window, and I walk over to look outside. I lean out and glance up to the sky just like I did the day of the tornado when I saw the black clouds swirling above, warning us that bad weather was coming.

Out of the corner of my eye I catch a glimpse of the wall behind the ladder. Goosebumps cover my arms and legs and my eyes open wide as I try to process the drawings in front of me. Flowers, trees and butterflies that Emmeline and I drew the last time we were here. I look down to her brown and green turtles, tracing my finger over the backs of their shells. I look to the signatures in green marker.

Gemma and Emmeline
Sisters, explorers and best friends forever.

I press both of my palms against those eight letters as the room begins to swim. A high-pitched shrill fills the fort. "EMM...MMM... E...LINNN...EE."

My vision clouds, giving way to a tunnel that slowly collapses on itself. *That's me. The sound's coming from me.* A giant curtain closes over my eyes blocking out every last speck of light until all I see is darkness.

FORTY

GEMMA

The wintry air sends a chill down my neck, and I tighten the collar on my coat. The holidays in the city can be chaotic and rushed, but also beautiful and serene if you know where to look. I've made an art of finding the quiet spots in the city.

Having just finished my last exam, I choose an empty bench and sit down. Fall semester of my last year of law school is officially in the books. The park is eerily quiet today. Though graduation still feels a light-year away, I know my time left at NYU is dwindling. I'm really going to miss this place and at the same time—I'm excited for what lies ahead.

People scurry along the sidewalks on their way to meet friends, loved ones or maybe do some last-minute shopping. I'm convinced it's impossible to live this close to the Times Square crystal ball and not feel the rush of excitement as December 31st draws closer. The closing of a chapter and the start of a new one.

There's so much I want to talk to Mom about when I get home. Our conversation is one that's been coming for a long time. She's been so patient with me and has never pushed me into talking about anything I wasn't ready for. I can't imagine how hard it must have been for her, grieving her daughter while at the same time doing anything that might help her other daughter survive another day. It hurts my heart to think of everything she's been through.

A text comes in from Miles:

> How'd it go?

I sniffle and smile. *Impeccable timing, Miles.*

> Grueling, but I think it went well. Officially on winter break!

> You deserve it. What time's your flight?

I told Miles I was going to fly home after my exams, he doesn't know my flight isn't until tomorrow. Butterflies fill my stomach, I sure hope he likes surprises.

> Not until tonight. I'm sitting in the park. Heading home to pack.

> I was hoping to see you before you left, I have something for you. I'll save it for NYE.

I look around the park one last time. *I'm going to miss you, NYC.*

MY TAXI SLOWS in front of a quaint and modern red brick hospital. It's located in a quiet residential neighborhood and a lot smaller than I had expected. I have no idea what part of the hospital he's in. I thought about texting him but didn't want to ruin the surprise.

I text Mikayla:

> Sorry we missed each other. Done with exams! Can you text Miles to see what time his shift ends?

I step out of my cab and pull my overnight bag over my shoulder. Miles's hospital is charming; it's such a different world for only being an hour outside the city. Trees line the beautifully landscaped paths in every direction. I follow the slate sidewalk through a set of stainless revolving doors and anxiously scan the atrium.

Mikayla texts:

> Sure. Why?

> I'm at Greenwich Hospital, I took the train up to surprise Miles before I fly out tomorrow night.

> You did WHAT? Look at you!

> Why? Is this a bad idea?

I'm suddenly second guessing myself and my idea. *I am not the kind of person who does spontaneous things like this.*

> Not at all!

> What if he's someone who hates surprises? You know that's a thing.

Oh no. I didn't think this through. Stepping into his world totally uninvited—that's not just a bad idea, it's creepy.

> STOP. He'll love it!

> I'm having second thoughts.

> Don't.

I'm sitting in the lobby with my overnight bag at my feet. It's giving stalker. We aren't exclusive, we've never even had that conversation. It's only been two months.

> What if he's talking to someone he works with? Maybe I should leave.

My phone rings and it's Mikayla. She's laughing when I pick up.

"Why are you laughing? I'm totally panicking. This was a bad idea."

"It's not a bad idea! I'm laughing because you're spiraling, that's why I called."

I pull on the ends of my hair, glancing around. "I know I am. I should have talked to you before I just jumped on a train to come see him."

"To my knowledge, Miles isn't someone who hates surprises. Especially when that surprise is *you*."

She always knows what to say to make me feel better. "What should I do then, text him I'm here? I feel weird sitting in this lobby."

"I have an idea. Is there a coffee shop around?"

I look around, my nerves growing and courage fading by the second. "Not that I can see. Let me go ask." I walk to the information desk, and they direct me to a cafe that's open, but closing soon. Mikayla overhears everything I'm being told.

"Okay, here's what we'll do. I'll text him saying I had a meeting in Stamford today and that I want to stop by before I catch my train back to the city."

"Do you think he'll believe you?"

"I don't see why not. I'm texting him now."

I sit waiting on the other end of the line, scoping out the room for the sixth time. "Thanks for doing this, Mika. If you hadn't texted me back, I might have left. How's your day going by the way?"

"Long. But this has made it much more interesting. When are you coming back? I want to see you before you leave."

I pick at my cuticle. "Tomorrow afternoon."

"Okay, good. I don't work again until tomorrow night. I want to give you your gift before you leave."

"I have something for you too."

"Hold on, he just texted me back."

My pulse races as I wait for her response. Why am I so tense? *Putting myself out there is terrifying.*

"He said he's wrapping up and will meet me in the cafe—to text him when I get there."

My stomach somersaults. "You're the best. What would I do without you?"

"It's a good thing we'll never have to know. How long do you want me to wait before I text him?"

"How 'bout fifteen minutes?"

"Got it. Let me know how it goes. Good luck."

"I will. Thanks, Mika."

"Happy to help."

I search the entire lobby as I walk to the women's restroom where I'll hide for the next ten minutes. My hands are clammy and I wring them together trying to warm them up. Surprises can go horribly wrong. I practice my 4-7-8 breathing, trying to calm myself and fix my hair in the mirror. Every time I look in the mirror, I see her. The dimple-less, older version. Just the thought of her helps calm me down. *Thanks, Em.*

I wash my hands and head toward the cafe. I'm equal parts nervous and giddy. I hope this goes well. The cafe has a glass door and as I'm opening it, I catch my first glimpse. He's dressed in a white lab coat and dark blue scrubs, sitting at a table staring into his phone. His back is to me and so is his unmistakable thick head of dark brown curls. My pulse is thumping as I open the door and walk toward him. I search for the right words to surprise him, but nothing clever comes to mind. *Witty has never been my thing.*

"Hi."

His head jerks around and his mouth drops open. I can see the genuine shock in his eyes as he springs to his feet and wraps me in his arms, burying his face in my hair.

"What are you—? How are you here right now?"

I lean back and smile at him, taking in his sweet expression. It's one I won't forget.

"You're supposed to be on a flight right now."

"Nope—it's always been tomorrow. Surprise?" I say, still questioning my decision.

"You just made my entire day!" *Phew!*

My nerves start to fade as he kisses me and pulls me to him. He feels so good, it's been too long since I've felt his arms around me.

"I can't believe you're here."

He gives me a look that says he's not totally convinced I'm standing in front of him.

"I'm here. Also, Mikayla says hello."

He throws his head back and laughs. "So, she wasn't at Stamford today?"

I shake my head. "Just the mastermind behind the surprise."

"I totally owe her," he says, putting his arm around me walking me out to the atrium.

My face hurts I'm smiling so hard. "I had a slight meltdown and almost ended up leaving. She convinced me to stay."

"Wait—why would you have left?"

"I don't know. Not everyone loves surprises. I felt like a stalker sitting in your lobby with my overnight bag at my feet."

He looks confused. "Stalker? Why?"

"I've never been here and you didn't know I was coming. What if you... I don't know. What if..."

His eyebrows knit together. "What if what?"

"What if there was someone else you were talking to?" *There, I said it.* I can tell by the look on his face he's hurt by my words.

"That's honestly what you were thinking?" he says, as I shrug my shoulders.

"I would never want to put you in an awkward situation, Miles. Which is why Mikayla had to convince me to not leave."

He shakes his head and reaches behind my neck pulling me to him so our foreheads touch. "You," he whispers. "I would have been so upset if you left. You're serious right now?"

I wrinkle my nose and nod.

"We can continue this conversation back at my place. Let me go finish my paperwork, I'm almost done. I'll meet you back here in fifteen minutes. And whatever you do—don't leave."

"I'll be right here."

"I like the sound of that. By the way, remind me to tell you a story when we get to my place."

I tilt my head, quizzically. He gives me a quick kiss and walks through two giant swinging doors, shaking his head as they close behind him.

I sit down and text Mikayla:

> He was totally surprised. In a good way.

FORTY-ONE

GEM

"Gemma?" Violet shouts, as she stands over me, a panicked look on her face.

"Gemma! Can you hear me?"

I nod my head.

"Should I go get my mom?"

"No," I say.

Her jaw drops and she stares at me, her eyes wide as saucers.

"Gemma! You're talking!"

I sit up and look around. I feel dizzy. It takes a second to recognize the sound of my own voice. *It's been so long.*

"Are you alright? I'm going to go get my mom."

I shake my head. "No, please don't. I'm okay."

Violet sits down beside me.

"My head hurts," I say, rubbing the top of my head.

"What happened? I was reading the notes on the painted rocks and you screamed. It sounded like. . . um, I think you. . .did you say your sister's name?"

I nod and stare at my hands folded in my lap. Violet turns her head to look at the drawings behind us. I watch as her eyes move down the wall to our names.

"Did you draw these together?"

I nod and reach out, softly tracing the letters of her name. "It doesn't make sense."

"What doesn't?" she asks.

"Her drawings are still here and she's not."

Violet gets a sad look on her face. I can tell she's uncomfortable.

"It doesn't. I'm sorry."

"Yeah, I know. Thanks."

The two of us sit quietly. Sometimes silence is better than talking.

She fans herself. "It's hot. Why don't we go back to my house and go swimming? That might make you feel better," she offers.

I stare at Emmeline's pictures, wanting to keep them in my eyes. "Sure."

"Also, maybe you should call your mom when we get back to my house."

I nod and follow her down the boards of the fort. I feel like I'm in a dream as we walk back to her house.

Violet and her mom exchange a look when we arrive back at the house. "Gemma, why don't you follow me into the study, you can call your mom from there?" I nod my head.

"Thanks," I say, softly.

I walk behind Violet's mom and she points to a chair for me to sit down. She hands me the phone and I press my mom's number as she closes the door behind her.

"Hello?"

"Mom?"

"Gemma? Oh my goodness, Gemma! My sweet girl. Your voice. It's. . .it's so good to hear your voice again."

She's crying.

Silence from me.

"Honey, are you okay?"

"Mm-hmm."

I'm trying my best to hide my uneven, shaky breaths, but it's not working. *Mom hears everything.*

"It's okay, baby. I'm coming over right now. Can you please put Violet's mom on the phone?" she asks.

A sound, rather than a word, comes from the back of my throat and I walk down the hallway to the kitchen, handing Violet's mom her phone.

I look over at Violet as our moms talk.

"Do you want to go swimming?" she asks.

I shake my head. "My mom's coming."

"Just until she gets here."

I shrug and follow her to their laundry room where she grabs two towels. "Here, you can borrow this," she says, handing me an orange and yellow polka dot swimsuit.

"You can change in the bathroom after I'm done," she says.

She waits by the backdoor while I change.

"Thanks for letting me borrow your bathing suit," I say, as I come out of the bathroom. She opens the back door and we walk out to the pool, laying our towels on the side.

"Watch this, Gem," she shouts. She takes a running start and jumps into the pool with a move that looks like a twisting cartwheel. Her long legs and arms flail about and it looks so ridiculous it makes me smile.

"Now you try!"

I shake my head and walk over to the pool and sit down on the side. The water feels good.

"I'll do it with you. Here, come with me."

She pulls herself up on the side and takes my hand. *It's nice holding someone's hand again.*

"On the count of three, let's jump together. Okay?"

I nod.

"One, two, three!"

The two of us run toward the edge of the pool and when she jumps I kind of just walk off the edge and sink to the bottom. The cool water is an immediate relief from the sticky heat. But it's more than that. I hover over the bottom. *Weightless.* We swim to the surface at the same time.

"Let's do it again!"

As we're pulling ourselves out of the pool, her brother does a cannonball off their diving board, sending a tsunami of water our way.

"Otis!" Violet screams.

The two of us jump back in and start splashing him. Otis struggles to defend himself and suddenly realizes he can't beat the two of us.

He screams, "I surrender!"

Violet jumps on top of him and pushes his head under water. The three of us laugh as he comes up and blows water out of his mouth like a dolphin. I look up and see Mom and Violet's mom watching from their deck above. Mom has her hand over her mouth and she has tears in her eyes. I wave to her, and she waves back.

"Hi, sweetheart. Do you want to swim for a little while?

I nod.

"You swim as long as you like, I'll just be up here."

She and Violet's mom sit and talk on the deck, leaving the three of us to play in the pool.

FORTY-TWO

GEMMA

"I still can't believe you're actually here," Miles says, shaking his head. I look up at the sound of his voice. He picks me up in a bear-hug twirl.

"My place is about a ten-minute walk from here. Are you hungry? We can pick something up on the way home," he offers.

We walk arm and arm to his apartment, stopping for take-out from his favorite Chinese restaurant. It feels bizarre seeing him in his Connecticut environment, walking the same path he takes to and from work every day.

"How'd you find this place?" I ask, as we walk up to his community filled with brick condominiums.

"A friend of mine told me about it. The location was key for me. It's a quick walk to the train station and the hospital. I don't have a car, so I needed a place where I could walk to everything."

When we get to his unit, he unlocks the door, letting me inside. It's an adorable and modern apartment with dark wood floors and a white Southwestern fireplace. We take our shoes off and I set my bag down, following him to the kitchen.

"This place is so cute! It looks like it's—"

He drops the bags of takeout onto the table and turns around, pulling me against him. His mouth is on mine before I can get the rest of my words out. He presses me back against the kitchen counter and lifts me into his arms. I wrap my legs around him as he sets me on the counter. We kiss each other hungrily, making up for the three long weeks.

"I've missed you. Your face, your hair, your smell. Everything. You are the perfect ending to my day."

He picks me up and carries me across the living room, down a hallway to his bedroom where we spend the next hour, showing just how much we've missed each other.

OUT OF BREATH and completely satisfied, I snuggle into him under the covers. I lean my head on his shoulder, bringing my leg up to rest around his waist. His warm skin feels soft against mine.

"Are you hungry?" he asks, kissing the top of my head.

I look up at him. "Didn't you ask me that, like an hour ago?"

We both chuckle as he trails his fingers down my back.

I suddenly realize I haven't eaten since breakfast. "I could stay right here all night—also, food sounds good."

"As long as you promise you're sleeping here tonight."

"Promise," I say, as he softly kisses me.

He slides out from the covers, pulling on a pair of jeans and t-shirt. "I'll meet you in the kitchen," he says.

"I'm right behind you."

I pick up my clothes and the condom wrapper strewn across his bedroom floor on my way to the bathroom. I put on his Columbia hoodie that's hanging on the back of his chair and meet him in the kitchen. He smirks when he sees what I'm wearing.

"It looks much better on you than it ever did on me," he says, gently tugging at the zipper, dragging his teeth slowly over his bottom lip.

"Food now, more of that—later," I say, giving him a peck on the lips.

"Well then, let's get this over with," he says, taking our reheated Chinese food out of the microwave, setting it on the table.

"So this is your Greenwich life, huh? I like it."

"Yeah?" he asks, as I nod.

"It's not very exciting. I'm hardly ever home, most of the time I'm at the hospital or the gym. Tonight was cardio. I guess I'll just have to count the last hour as the best cardio I've had in a long time. Possibly ever."

I feel my cheeks blush.

"It's super cute when you blush, you know."

"Stop—no. I hate that I can't hide it," I say, heat spreading from my cheeks into my neck.

He looks away, not wanting to make me uncomfortable. "I'm glad I get to see you before you leave for the holidays. Definitely the best gift this season."

Same, I think, smiling to myself. "I'm glad it worked out. What time do you work tomorrow?"

"I hate to say it, but I'm back at the hospital tomorrow morning at seven."

"Oof, early morning. I promise I won't keep you up too late," I say.

He reaches over, taking my hand. "I'd actually prefer it if you did." He takes a beat before continuing.

"Hey, I wanted to talk to you about our conversation earlier. Did you really think there was a chance I might be talking to someone else?"

"I wasn't sure. If you had been, I would've understood."

He frowns, looking insulted. "You would've?"

"Of course. Don't get me wrong, I would've felt like a total jackass, but that wouldn't have been on you. Listen, we haven't known each other for that long, and we haven't even seen each other in three weeks. It's not totally out of the question for me to think there was a possibility you could at least be talking to someone else."

"Well, I'm not. Are you?"

I shake my head. "No. That's not what this is about. You know my history and it shouldn't come as a surprise that vulnerability is really hard for me. Sitting in your lobby with my overnight bag, I felt so exposed. Usually when I start to feel that way I run as fast as I can, to avoid whatever is making me feel that way," I say.

He nods slowly. "I don't know how to show you, maybe only with time, but you're safe with me, Gem. I know it's been less than two months since we met, but in that amount of time, my feelings have grown so much for you. Do you not know that?"

"In my head I do, and I feel it when we're together, but this has nothing to do with you. This is about me getting comfortable with. . . all of this. We haven't had time to discuss what *this* even is."

Miles pulls me onto his lap. "We're discussing it now. I don't want to see anyone else. Okay?"

I nod, feeling reassured and then immediately apprehensive. "I don't either. The thing is, it's important for you to know, I hadn't planned on dating anyone, including you, until after I graduate and pass the bar. But in you walked with your suspenders and perfect teeth and here we are."

He leans his head back and smiles. "I see. Well, let's just see where it goes. No pressure—for either of us," he says, reassuringly, before tilting my face to his. He kisses me with such tenderness, the barbs around my heart loosen their grip.

"By the way, what was the story you wanted to tell me?" I ask.

He bends his head down and laughs. "My turn for the vulnerable seat."

"What is it?" I lean into his shoulder, smiling curiously.

"I can't believe I'm telling you this," he says, putting his head in his hand. "Talk about feeling exposed."

My smile softens. "What? Tell me."

"Remember that day I had a conference near NYU?"

I nod. "The neurology one, right?"

"God, this is embarrassing. Full disclosure?" he asks, his cheeks turning red.

"Now who's blushing? Yes—spit it out!"

"I may have googled to find a conference near your campus, hoping we'd be able to meet up. It was actually my day off and had nothing to do with the hospital." He smiles sheepishly.

"You did not!"

He keeps nodding while we both fall into hysterics. "So, one of us might be an actual stalker—and it's not you," he says, between laughs. My heart flips at the thought of him finagling a way to run into me.

I shake my head, grinning ear to ear. "I can't believe you just told me that. You're much braver than I am. . . I would've kept that one a secret for years. But I'm glad you told me."

"I hope I don't regret it later," he says, hesitantly.

"I have something for you." He stands and walks into his bedroom, returning with a small, wrapped box.

"I have something for you too." I retrieve his gift from my bag in the entryway. On my way back to the kitchen I find him sitting on the living room couch in front of the fireplace, his gift beside him.

"You go first," I say, handing him my bright yellow package. I watch as he peels back the paper. He smiles when he sees what's inside.

"This is beautiful. You took this?"

I nod.

The torn paper reveals a framed black and white portrait I took of our cairn. He turns the frame over and reads my inscription:

Intentions, stars and the sea. Montauk Point

Xo, Gemma

He leans over and kisses me gently, running his thumb across my cheek.

"Thank you. I love it."

My heart warms, watching him read the inscription again.

He laughs under his breath while propping it on the table beside him.

"What's funny?" I ask.

"No, it's nothing. Here," he says, handing me a small black and white box with a crimson satin ribbon.

I untie the ribbon and lift the top of the box. Inside is a smooth, flat gray circular stone on a brown leather cord. I pick it up to inspect it more closely.

"It's beautiful. And so me!"

"It's the top stone of our cairn we built together. It looks like we had the same theme this year." *This year.*

"It looks that way, doesn't it?" I say, smiling.

"Do you remember when we got to the parking lot, and I ran back to the beach?"

"I do. You forgot something."

"Yep. I needed a reason to run back and get the stone so I left something behind. I wanted you to have it as a reminder of our first weekend together."

I shake my head, stunned. "This is such a special gift."

"I have to give credit to my mom for the idea. She's taking a jewelry making class and showed me a gemstone cage she'd made and when I heard those words, the seed was planted. I found a crystal shop nearby and they drilled a hole in the stone and put a clasp on the cord for me."

My head spins at the amount of thought he put into my gift. *He just totally outgifted me.*

I hand him the necklace and turn around so he can fasten it around my neck. "I love it so much. Thank you." I reach up, feeling its cool, smooth edges.

"I hope it reminds you of our first cairn, and all of the intentions you set," he says.

"I'll never forget. What was your intention for this stone?"

He leans in, taking the stone between his fingers and shrugs.

"You're not going to tell me?" I ask.

He just shakes his head and smiles.

FORTY-THREE

GEMMA

The alarm goes off and I wake up with Miles's arms around me. I look at the clock on his nightstand; it's painfully early. I roll over to Miles who grumbles and turns off the alarm. The room is still dark, his bed cozy and warm.

"Can you explain something to me?" he asks, sleepily.

I groan. "This early? I doubt it."

"How is it that both times we've slept in the same bed, I've woken up to your side being empty. And now that I have to go to work, I wake up and you're right here next to me, making it impossible to get out of bed?"

"Sorry," I say, snuggling closer to him. "It's cold out there, I'm staying under the covers until the sun comes up," I say.

"So not fair."

He squeezes me tight, and I bury my nose into his neck.

"I'm going to miss you over the holidays," he says.

"I'll miss you too. Will you be in Brooklyn with your mom?"

"I'm working most of the holiday. Saving my time off for New Year's. What day do you get back?"

"I'm flying back on the 30th so I can help Mikayla get the house ready for our party," I say.

"Enjoy your time with your mom and grandma, I know how much you've missed them."

"I have. I can't wait to see them."

He runs his fingers up and down my arm. "I hate to say it, but I've got to jump in the shower. Stay here and sleep as long as you want. I'll leave a key for you on the kitchen table, just lock up when you leave."

He kisses my forehead and slips out of bed. I try to fall back asleep but I can't close my eyes while he's still here. I lie in bed listening to the sounds of his morning routine as he gets ready. He dresses in the dark and then sits quietly on the bed next to me.

"The key I'm leaving for you, take it with you for the next time you decide to surprise me. I'd like for this to become more of a thing."

"You would, huh?"

He nods. "Safe travels, let me know when you land. Miss you already."

"You too. Goodbye, Miles."

He kisses me goodbye and when he pulls away it physically hurts.

THE HOUSE IS empty when I get back. Mikayla texted to let me know that she ended up having to go into the hospital early. It looks like we won't be able to exchange our gifts until I get back. I sit down and write her a note:

Dear Mika,

I'm sorry we missed each other. Again. I've been thinking a lot lately about you and our friendship. Who would have ever thought that a cyclist leaving me bleeding on the pavement would end up being one of the best things ever to happen to me?

I know I make you crazy with how much I worry about you—but it's only because you mean so much to me. You're the first person I've let myself get close to and I wish I could keep you in a bubble because I don't know what I would do if anything happened to you. I could cry just thinking about it—so don't let it.

Meeting you has changed my life in all the best ways—and I want you to know how incredibly grateful I am for you. In my heart, I'll always know it was Emmeline who brought you to me.

Promise you won't work too hard while I'm gone (impossible ask, I know) and have fun with your parents. Something about you spending the holidays together in this house warms my heart. Merry Christmas Mika. The Clarence to my George.

Love,
Gem

I GLANCE out the window as my flight takes off from LaGuardia. It's funny how such a short plane ride opens the portal to another world. One where land is as abundant as air and there's an ease that's evident in the way people walk and talk. So many people back home thought I was crazy for moving to Manhattan, but I'm proud of myself for being able to straddle two totally different worlds. Each one is unique and have become a big part of who I am. At my core, I know I'll always be that little girl who grew up in the Midwest, alongside never-ending acres of golden cornfields.

Sprawling views of Manhattan come into sight as the plane climbs above the clouds. I take a few photos of the skyline and pictures from our weekend in the Hamptons pop up. I scroll through them until I get to selfies of Miles and me. The sweet look on his face makes me miss him. My favorite is one where I'm laughing and looking straight at the camera while he's staring at me from the side. It's like he didn't want to turn his eyes and miss seeing my happiness. I let out a sigh. *I guess rules are meant to be broken after all.*

The plane climbs higher, and I feel my shoulders start to relax. My heart skips thinking of how soon I'll be seeing Mom and Grandma again. I can't wait to hug them. I wonder what it is Mom wants to talk to me about. *Painfully regret,* she'd said.

Coming home always makes me think about what she'd be like today. Where she would live and what she'd be doing. There's a part of me that knows if she was still alive, I most likely would never have left Indiana and I'd never know the wonder that is New York City.

But we don't get to control any of those things. We can't trade our circumstances in order to avoid our pain. Losing Emmeline somehow gave me permission to leave home in search of bigger horizons.

I lean my head against the window and watch as drifting layers of clouds blanket the earth below as my eyelids grow heavy. It seems like ten minutes when the pilot announces we'll soon be landing. I peer out the window over the fields and farms of Indiana. A stark contrast to the concrete landscape of my new urban home.

My plane touches down and I text Mom, telling her I've landed. *Home for the holidays.* Mom, Grandma and me. And Hazy, I can't forget our beloved cat. I'm beyond grateful for all the love in my life.

FORTY-FOUR

GEM

There's a knock on Violet's bedroom door and when she opens it, Mom's standing there with a pensive look on her face. It's equal parts happy and sad.

"Hey, sweet girl, it's getting close to dinner time. How about you meet me in the driveway in fifteen-minutes?"

"Okay."

She smiles down at me. She looks happy and tired. I thank Violet's mom for having me over before walking out to Mom's car. She opens her arms and I fall into them.

"Come here. It's so good to hear your voice again. When did this happen?"

I cling to her, not wanting to let go. "We were at the tree fort behind Violet's house."

"The same one you went last summer?"

"Uh-huh."

"What happened?" she asks, searching my face.

Tears fill my eyes. Not wanting to remember, I shake my head back and forth.

"Do you want to talk about it? It's okay if you need some time," she says.

I wipe my tears with my shirt. "I saw our drawings. The ones we made together. When I saw her name at the bottom, I got dizzy and then everything went black."

"Oh no," she says.

"Violet said I screamed Emmeline's name."

Mom squeezes her eyes shut and draws me into her.

"I had this weird feeling when I was up there."

She pulls back, looking down at me. "What kind of feeling?"

"It's just. . . I don't understand how something she drew can still be here and she's not?"

Mom inhales sharply, holding it in, along with her tears.

"It doesn't make sense, sweetheart, and I don't know if it ever will. I wish I had an explanation for you, but I don't. There will always be things that remind us of Emmeline. In time, those things will bring us happy memories, but right now it just hurts because we miss her so much. It's okay to be sad. I miss my little moon so much."

We hold each other tight letting our tears fall, a gentle rain of loss and love.

"I'm sure it was hard for you to go back to that fort. I want you to know I think you're very brave," she says, squeezing me.

"You do?"

"I do, my love," she says, wiping her eyes as we get into the car to drive home. Mom's hugs are like a band-aid for my heart. *I hope my hugs help her like hers help me.*

I lean my head against my window, watching as the tops of the trees blur into one.

"Mom, it's okay if I want to be Violet's friend, right?"

She nods. "Of course. I'm so glad you made a new friend."

"Really?"

"Yes, really. Why?"

I pause, wringing my hands in my lap. "Because it makes me feel bad."

Mom glances over at me. "Being Violet's friend makes you feel bad?"

I nod slowly as my chin trembles. "I don't want to replace Emmeline, Mom. Not ever." Giant streams of tears roll down my face. Mom pulls over to the side of the road and takes me in her arms. She holds me against her chest so hard her broken heart thuds loudly in my ear.

"Gemma, darling. You're not replacing your sister. She will always be a special part of you. It's good that you made a friend."

"It is?"

"So, so good," she says softly.

"It feels weird. It was so easy with Emmeline."

"This new world must be so confusing. I don't want you to ever feel bad about making friends. She would want that for you."

I sniffle. "She would?"

"Yes, of course she would. Your sister loved you more than anything in this entire world. She would want you to be happy." I look up at her, a sad smile on her face.

I pause, thinking about what she's said. "Sometimes I don't know what to say to Violet."

Mom rests her chin on the top of my head, nodding. "Just like dance, making a new friend is something that will take practice. You and Em shared something that was so incredibly special. I'm glad you are telling me how you're feeling. It's important to get things like this out instead of keeping them inside. I want you to promise that you'll come to me when you have any questions or if there's something you don't understand. Okay?"

I hesitate as my chin trembles.

"What is it, honey? What are you thinking about? Please—talk to me."

I close my eyes and shake my head. "It's nothing."

Mom takes my face and tilts it gently to hers. "You know you can tell me anything, right?"

"I know."

My unsaid words hang in the air like lead balloons.

"I just really miss her, Mom. All the time, I miss her."

"I do too, my love. I miss her so, so much."

FORTY-FIVE

GEMMA

I wheel my suitcase to the curb and look for Mom. I see her car and raise my arm and wave. She pulls up in front of me and I run to her side before she even has time to come to a complete stop. She hops out, throwing her arms around me. I fall into her, hungry for the comfort only she can give. *She is my home.*

I breathe in her lavender scent. "I've missed you, Mom."

"I've missed you too."

I pull back to look at her. "What's all over your hair?"

She looks down at her paint-splotched hands and laughs.

"I've been painting a few of the rooms. I was hoping to finish the last coat before you got home but that didn't happen. Too much life happening at the moment. The walls might still be wet."

"I'll be careful. Can't wait to see how it looks."

"You know how I love changing my colors every couple of years," she says, as I nod.

I put my suitcase in the trunk before hopping into the passenger's seat.

She looks over at me and smiles. "I can't believe you're finally here! It's so good to have you home."

"It's been way too long. We have so much to catch up on. I don't even know where to start."

She puts her blinker on and eases into the steady stream of airport traffic. "How about your weekend with Miles? It sounded like there was something you wanted to talk about when we last spoke." Mom raises an inquisitive eyebrow.

"I do. It's kind of a long story," I say.

"Perfect timing for our long ride home then," she says, merging onto the highway.

I let out a deep sigh, wondering where to begin.

"You know the night terrors I've had off and on, right?"

"I do. You're not still having them, are you? I thought they'd stopped after you moved in with Mikayla."

"They did for a while—but they started again about six months ago. I didn't want to tell you."

Her face falls as she stares out the windshield. "Oh, honey, why would you keep that from me?"

"I didn't want to worry you. I thought it was just stress from my last year of law school."

"Sweetheart, it's not for you to worry about what I can or can't handle. As a mother, I will do anything I can to help you feel better. Having you come to me for advice or help is one of the best parts of being a mom. Please, I always want you to come to me. For anything. It will cause me more stress if you don't."

I look out my window so I don't have to see the hurt look on her face. "Alright. It's just, you've had so much—"

"Promise?" she interrupts, insistence in her tone.

"I promise."

She reaches over and rests her hand on my forearm, encouraging me to continue.

"First of all, I had the best weekend in the Hamptons. It was so good to be by the ocean. I have to admit, I thought Miles and I would run out of things to say, or it would be awkward at times. Turns out, he's really easy to be around."

Mom smiles warmly. "There's nothing better. I'm happy for you."

"It was all going so well. . . until Saturday night. I had a night terror and woke up screaming. It was awful." I shake my head, squirming at the memory.

"Oh no," she says.

"I had a complete meltdown on his bathroom floor and he was so great about the whole thing."

Mom's face looks pained. "What happened?"

I look away, avoiding her question while I build my courage. "Miles listened and comforted me. He honestly couldn't have been more understanding."

"That was sweet of him," she says, looking relieved.

I nod, nervous about telling her the details of our conversation on his bathroom floor. Fear grips my throat and I swallow hard. "I have to tell you something. I've felt guilty about it for a long time. It's what I was talking about when I was at my class the other day."

Mom frowns. "You feel guilty telling me something?"

I nod again and pick at my cuticles as my stomach fills with dread.

"I don't ever want you to ever feel guilty when it comes to me. What is it?"

My voice cracks. "It's just. . . it's hard for me to say to you."

"It's okay. Just say it. Sometimes things are much scarier when you hold them in," she says, trying to read my face while also keeping her eyes on the road.

I take a deep breath and choose my words carefully. *This has been a long time coming.*

"Something happened my freshman year at college I've never told you about."

Mom's knuckles turn white as she grips the steering wheel. My throat tightens around my words, contemplating whether or not to let them out.

"My first year away from home I was pretty open about sharing Emmeline's story. I'd always been so supported by you, Grandma and my counselors, I guess I had a false sense of security that everyone would be kind. Until one day I overheard a new friend make a rude comment to a group of people about the girl whose twin died."

Mom sits back abruptly in her seat, like she's been pushed. Her eyes stay fixed on the road, somewhere beyond the windshield. I know my words are as hard for her to hear as they were the day I heard them.

"I decided that day I wanted my own identity—one that wasn't tethered to my broken heart." I hold in my breath, blinking back tears. "Not talking about her eventually became habit. Ever since that day when people ask about my family, I've told them I'm an only child. I hate myself for ever having said that."

An avalanche of pent-up guilt and regret finally breaks loose as tears fall down my face. Mom shakes her head and reaches over, firmly holding onto my arm as tears fill her eyes.

"No—Gemma," she says, firmly. "You are everything that is good in this world. Please don't ever say that about yourself."

My chest feels like it's going to implode, it kills me to see her cry. "I'm sorry, Mom. I didn't mean to make you upset. Should we pull over?"

She shakes her head. "You don't have to apologize—this is important." She clears her throat and wipes her eyes.

"We have been through a tragedy so deep, our pain sometimes serves as a self-defense. It's good to protect yourself. I want you to set boundaries for yourself. Sharing your deepest wounds with someone you just met is terrifying. I get that. I've been there myself and have made comments that aren't true just to avoid the topic."

Every muscle in my body loosens with relief. How long have I been carrying this awful feeling? I take tissues out of the glove compartment and hand one to mom before taking one for myself. "You have?"

"Of course, honey. It's okay to wait until it feels safe before sharing the most fragile pieces of yourself. Especially when it's someone who may never become more than an acquaintance."

I dab my eyes. "Every lie I've told has only made me feel worse though. I was afraid you'd be hurt that I've been hiding her."

"No, sweetheart. Not at all. I understand. Listen, there is no right or wrong when it comes to grieving. Sometimes we do what we have to just to get by and that's okay. You love your sister. You've always been proud of her. No words, spoken or unspoken will ever change that."

I take a deep breath, trying to stop my voice from quivering. "You're not upset with me?"

She shakes her head. "No piece of me is upset with you. You don't owe anyone anything when it comes to talking about Emmeline. It makes sense you would be protective of her and her story. When it feels safe to share her, that's when I want you to talk about her. Please, I hope you'll let that in."

No one can steady my storms like mom.

I nod, the heavy weight of my guilt dissipating with every one of her words. "I didn't like lying to you. To everyone. I've never kept secrets from you—it's been eating me up inside—it feels good to finally get it out."

A faraway look suddenly comes across her face.

"Thanks for listening, Mom. I know this is hard for you, too," I say, gently resting my hand on her arm.

FORTY-SIX

GEM

I weave my way through a maze of stacked brown boxes as I walk out of my new bedroom down the hallway, looking for Mom. When Grandma learned from a neighbor that a house near her was coming on the market, Mom made them an offer before it even went up for sale. Grandma's house is only a five-minute walk, and I can be there in two if I'm riding my bike.

I walk down the stairs to the kitchen and find Mom wiping down the shelves in our refrigerator, before she unloads her grocery haul. I clear a path through piles of crumpled newspaper and empty boxes and pull out a chair at our kitchen table.

"How's the unpacking going?" she asks, her head buried in the back of our refrigerator.

I move a stack of bowls and sit down. "Two more boxes down, six more to go."

"Thanks for all of your help. I couldn't have done this without you."

"You don't have to thank me."

"I know, I want to." She winks, looking up through a glass shelf. "I still can't believe this is our house. It all happened so fast."

I kick my feet back and forth under the chair. "I really like our new house."

"Tell me what you like about it," she asks, briskly wiping dried food from the sides of the fridge.

"I've always wanted a yard with a fence around it. Now I can take Hazy outside to play. And stairs. I like climbing them like I do at Grandma's. Two bathrooms too, one for each floor. It's the perfect place for us," I say, quietly.

"That makes me so happy."

I pick up a huge pile of crinkled-up brown paper from our dishes and put it into an empty box on the floor. A letter and some photos cling to the paper before falling back onto the table.

Two photos. One of a family—a mom, a dad and a boy; and then a school photo of the boy.

"Hey, Mom?"

"Mm-hmm?"

"Who are these people?"

"What people?"

"I found these on the table," I say.

Mom looks up and quickly jumps to her feet when she sees what I'm holding. Paling, she reaches out and takes the letter and photos gently in her hands.

"They're friends of mine. We keep in touch and send pictures to each other every year."

"Is that the same person I met outside Grandma's house? Is she the one who talked about taking us to the ballet?"

Mom swallows and fidgets on her feet. "Yep, that's her. I forgot I introduced the two of you."

"I remember her." *She had a nice voice.* "How do you know her?"

"I met her shortly after you were born. We've kept in touch ever since."

"Did she know my dad?"

Mom closes the envelope putting it into a drawer by the sink. "No, the two of them never had a chance to meet."

"Oh," I say, softly. "Where does she live?"

"She lives in New York with her family."

"Do you ever go see her?" I ask.

"No. Not yet at least. It's far away, it's almost a twelve-hour drive."

"How old is he?"

Mom tilts her head and looks up, trying to remember. "I guess he's in seventh grade now."

"He's the same age as me."

"Yep, somewhere around there." She turns around and busies herself with stacking the plates in the cabinets.

"I never hear you talk about her."

Mom pauses, looking back at me, and then resumes stacking. "She helped me through some tough times. Even though we don't see each other very much, she's a good friend. She came and visited me in the hospital after my car accident."

"That was nice. Maybe someday we can go to New York to see her and go to the ballet, too. I'd love to see a real ballet."

I can tell by the dazed look on her face she's somewhere far away from these boxes and glass cleaner fumes.

"Mom?"

"Oh—yes, sweetheart. Sorry, what did you say?"

"I was just saying maybe we could go see her one day."

"Mm-hmm maybe one day we'll take her up on her offer. I'd love to see the ballet too. Speaking of dance, you have class in an hour, right?"

"Yep."

"Why don't you go make sure your dance box is unpacked and I'll finish unpacking in here."

"Okay. I still haven't found it."

I turn to leave and then something tells me to turn back around.

"Mom, is everything alright?"

She brushes my bangs out of my eyes. "Of course, why do you ask?"

I shrug. "I don't know. You look—stressed."

"I'm not stressed. Well, maybe a little." She smiles a thin smile. "I just want to finish unpacking. I feel unsettled with all of these boxes piled everywhere."

"Oh, okay."

"I want it to feel like our new home. A new start, you know?" she asks.

I walk over and give her a hug. I feel the heat from her breath on the top of my head as she sighs.

"You're getting so tall," she says. "Soon you'll have to bend down for me to kiss the top of your head."

I look up and she smiles at me warmly before I turn and take the stairs back to the stacks of boxes waiting for me in my room. Hazy follows and I close the door behind us.

The people we bought the house from left a full-length vintage mirror hanging on the wall next to my closet. Across the top, there's a crown of intricately etched flowers that have tarnished with age. *I wonder how many faces have looked in this mirror.*

The mirror is why I chose this room, even though it's a little smaller than the other empty room. I take a long look at myself and press my palm to the mirror, joining my reflection with Emmeline's.

"Hey, Em. What do you think of our new room? I wish you were here to see it. There's finally space for our desk and a bookshelf, just like we always wanted. Mom said I could paint one of my walls as soon as I'm done unpacking. Guess what I'm going to paint?"

A smile spreads across our faces. *She knows what I'm going to say.*

"I'm going to paint you the prettiest turtles you've ever seen. I can't wait to show you when I'm done."

FORTY-SEVEN

GEMMA

After a long dinner catching up with Mom and Grandma, I walk upstairs to call Miles and Mikayla. I leave them both a message, letting them know I made it home. I sit on the edge of my bed looking at the collage of posters plastered to my walls. Dancers and musicians I worshiped when I was a teenager, along with several of the NYC skyline. *Where did my obsession with NYC come from?*

It doesn't seem that long ago I was decorating this room when we first moved into this house. Souvenirs tacked up on my pale-yellow walls flood me with memories of our RV trips to the national parks. Ribbons from dance competitions hang in long rows reminding me of all the road trips the three of us took so Mom and Grandma could support me at my events.

I walk over to the mural I painted of three sea turtles swimming in the sea. *It took me months.* After living in Grandma's spare bedroom for the better part of a year, Mom wanted me to add my own personal touches so my room would feel like my own.

I trace the sunbeams shining on the turtle's backs beneath the water. Despite Mom's painting frenzy, it hasn't escaped my notice that she's left my room untouched. It's exactly as it was the day I left for college. I'm sure she couldn't bring herself to take down all of the memories. *These four walls are a time capsule of my childhood.* Even though this isn't the same house or room we once shared, being home always reminds me of Emmeline.

I pull open the middle drawer of my desk and find my diary. I'd forgotten I ever had a diary. I page through to find it's almost completely blank, except for one page. I read the entry and it reminds me of why I never wrote in it again. The words are too hard to look at, and I put it back, closing the drawer.

I lift a photo album from the bottom drawer, flipping through the years. Seeing myself at every stage of life is so surreal. There are photos of Emmeline and me from the time we were babies until we turned twelve. Halloween costumes, birthdays, first days of school, jumping in the leaves, all wearing the same clothes. Every season and occasion were always proudly captured by Mom.

I turn the page to a picture of my thirteenth birthday party. *My first birthday without her.* I'll never forget it. I wish I could reach into the photo and hug the little girl blowing out her candles and tell her she's going to be okay. My heart sinks remembering that day. Everyone was trying so hard to make it fun for me, but it was an impossible endeavor. The smile on my face is one of the saddest I've ever seen. It makes me hurt for my smaller self, knowing just how much pain I was in when this was taken. I shudder and turn the page.

Middle school dances, vacations, dance competitions, Hazy, and so many great ones of Mom, Grandma and me. I can't help but think of Emmeline's absence in them. *I forgot how hard it is to turn the page where it goes from life with her—to life without her.*

I never took a photo by myself until she passed away. Not one. It was always the two of us. Inseparable until we weren't. I didn't know how to take photos by myself. I remember freezing up every time Mom brought out her camera. Painful, forced smiles. A camera was a constant reminder that she wasn't in her spot, next to me.

I close my eyes, shaking my head, and close the album. A photo falls out and I pick it up. It's a picture of Mom, Grandma and me hugging in our kitchen. I'm wearing my cap and gown. A smile creeps across my face remembering this day. My high-school graduation was the first good day I remember having after Emmeline died.

I put the album back in the drawer. *Bittersweet memory lane.* I reach under the bottom of our desk, feeling for our names. Eight letters.

I start to trace them as my phone rings. Impeccable timing— it's like he knows.

"Hi."

"Hey! It's good to hear your voice," he says.

"Yours too. How's work?"

"Busy. I saw you called but I haven't had a chance to listen to your message yet. I'm saving it for later—like a reward. How are your mom and Grandma?"

"They're both doing well. We had dinner and I've been up in my room looking at old photos," I say, as memories of our family's story lingers in my head.

"You, okay?"

Hazy jumps into my lap wanting to be scratched. "Mm-hmm. Thanks. I like looking at them, but it's always hard to go from seeing pictures of the two of us—to ones of just me."

He sighs. "I can't imagine."

"Just being back in my room—it makes me miss her. What time does your shift end?" I ask, changing the subject.

"It's my long weekend."

"Oh, that's right. Well, hopefully Santa will still be able to find you."

The sound of his laugh makes me smile.

"I should go downstairs. Mom and Grandma are probably wondering where I went."

"Yes, go spend time with them. I should get back to my rounds. I just wanted to say hi."

"I hope you're able to get some sleep tonight," I say.

"Outlook doesn't look good, but I'll try."

"Goodnight."

"Bye, Gem."

I catch my goofy smirk in the mirror as I turn out my light. The hallway smells of fresh paint and I step carefully on the paint splattered sheets Mom spread out to protect the wood floors. *She's right, the pale lilac really brightens up this space.*

I poke my head in her room, flipping on the light to see what color she chose. Her walls are a beautiful shade of dark gray with violet undertones—a rich contrast to her white linens. Her room has a bohemian vibe, just like her. The macrame piece she made when we were young hangs over her bed and there are plants thriving everywhere.

Several pictures and mirrors from the hallway are laid out across her floor, waiting to be rehung when the paint dries. Out of the corner of my eye I see her poppy painting propped in the corner. It sparks my memory of Miles's mom's painting. I text him:

> Did you ever find out the name of the artist of that poppy painting?

I wait for his response as I go check it out. The background colors are vibrant shades of dark green and teal, which make the red and pinks in the poppies really pop. I've never noticed the detailed textures before. It's breathtakingly beautiful. I can tell the artist put a lot of care into every brushstroke. I search for a signature near the bottom but don't see one. *There's no way it could be the same artist.* I'm sure it's just a similar style.

I pick up the painting and sit down on Mom's bed, turning it around to see if I can find the artist's name on the back. The canvas has yellowed from age. *How long ago was this painted?*

There's a date written in the bottom left corner. The pen has faded over the years, making it hard to read. I shine my phone's flashlight on the numbers. It looks like our birth date. *Did someone give this to Mom for our birthday? Maybe Grandma?* A message is scrawled in the same pen on the upper right-hand corner of the canvas. I prop the painting up on my thighs so I can read the inscription.

My dearest Willow,

No words or gestures are significant enough to thank you for the gift you have given to my husband and me. Your generous heart has made it possible for us to become a family. There is no greater gift. You are the most loving mother and person I have ever known. I hope this painting brings you the enormous amount of love it was created with. Thank you is not enough for bringing him to me.

Eternally grateful,
Colette

WAIT. *What?* I read it again. And again. *Who is he? Who did mom bring to her?* I search the back of the canvas for any other words, but don't see any. I read it one more time just to make sure I read it right. *What the. . . Why is the date Emmeline's and my birth date?* There's a piece of hardened canvas at the top near the middle that hangs a little below the staples from where the canvas was stretched over the wooden frame. I fold it back, revealing the title of the painting that's written in the same handwriting as the note.

Trois—by Colette Berenson
Emmeline, Gemma and Finn

FINN? *Who the hell is Finn? And why is his name next to Emmeline's and mine?* My mind searches for any reason why our names would be grouped together. *This makes no sense.* I wrack my brain trying to think of anyone I know by that name. *Has Mom ever mentioned that name in the past?* Nothing comes to mind. I've never met anyone named Finn and I've never heard Mom say the name. *Not once.*

I sit desperately searching for an explanation. Why would someone give my mom a painting with these words? I reread the note a few more times as my palms start to sweat. Every time I read it, I get more confused. What did my mom give to this woman and her family that would warrant this level of thank you? *Eternally grateful?* That seems like an awful lot. My head spins trying to make sense of it.

A flash of Mom's locket comes to mind. Her favorite locket, the one she never takes off. Not even when she was in the hospital after her accident. The gold heart locket with our initials. E, G, F—Emmeline & Gemma Forever.

I knit my brows as my heart hammers in my chest. Hands trembling, I carefully put the painting back in the corner and leave her room, turning off the light. Mom and Grandma's voices echo down the hallway and I follow the sound to the top of the stairs. I tightly grip the railing, trying to wake myself from my stupor. My legs feel weak, and I grasp onto the banister until my feet touch the bottom step. I walk to the kitchen and lean against the doorway as Mom finishes the last of the dishes.

"Were you able to get a hold of—"

She turns from the kitchen sink, her smile quickly fading into worry. She runs over to me, casserole dish in her hands.

"Sweetheart, what is it? What's wrong?" she asks, her face filled with concern.

I search for the right words, but there aren't any. So I just come out and ask.

"Mom. Who is Finn?"

The dish slips out of her hands, hitting the tile floor sending an explosion of tiny shards everywhere. The sound of shattering glass makes me jump and I cover my ears to stop them from ringing.

FORTY-EIGHT

GEM

"Gem, honey, we're going to be late!" Mom calls to me from downstairs. "We want to take pictures before we leave."

"I'll be down in five minutes," I call down to her.

Staring back at me in front of my full-length mirror is my soon-to-be high-school graduate reflection. I feel so grown up wearing this gown. Seventeen feels like such a short time to be on this planet, yet also—an eternity. I walk over to Hazy sprawled across my bed and pick her up. I hold her to my face as we study ourselves in the mirror.

"Look at me, Hazy. I'm all grown up. I'm not the same girl I was the day we found you in that rotten log. And neither are you," I say, nuzzling her under her chin.

What a lifeline she's been for me. Her coming into our lives at the perfect time was no accident. She needed saving and though I didn't know it at the time, I would soon too.

"You're the best listener, you know that? No one knows my secrets, my fears, my hopes and all of my dreams better than you." I scratch her behind her ear before laying her back down. "Come sit in the sunny spot on my bed when you miss me."

She purrs as I bury my nose in her gray, velvety fur, just as I've always done in our quiet moments together. *She's helped heal me in a way only animals can.*

I walk back to my mirror, studying my face. "Hey, Em. Can you believe it? Today's graduation day. We're here. We made it." My smile turns serious the more I look at this person standing in her green and white graduation gown and yellow Converse. *I wish you were here with me today. I wish we were doing this together.*

A tear forms in my eye, and I blink it away. "I'm proud of us," I say, taking my hand away from the mirror. I walk over, picking up Hazy and my graduation cap.

"Sorry to disturb your nap time, I want some pictures of the two of us."

The soles of my sneakers squeak down every step on my way to the kitchen. Hazy squirms for me to set her down and I gently set her down on a chair and put on my cap. Mom, Grandma and Mom's new boyfriend, Jake are all in the kitchen finishing the final touches for my graduation party. Mom turns around and gasps, covering her mouth when she sees me.

"Gemm. . ." Her words get stuck, she can't get the rest of my name out before she starts to cry.

"Mom. No. Please don't. You're going to make me cry," I say, softly.

"I'm sorry, sweetheart. I just. . . It's just. You're all grown up. I'm so proud of you."

She hugs me tight, letting the unspoken language of our hearts do the talking. *She's thinking exactly what I'm thinking.* She pulls away, grabbing a tissue to dab her eyes.

"This is so nice. Thank you so much," I say, motioning to the decorations they've been busy hanging all morning.

"Today's a big day. We're excited to celebrate you and all of your hard work," Grandma says, blotting her eyes.

Mom and Grandma come stand beside me, hugging me from each side.

"Wait a minute, let me get a photo," Jake says, running to get his phone. He takes several pictures of the three of us and then I pick up Hazy and we crowd together for one more. *The four of us found a way through an unspeakable tragedy. Today is for all of us.*

"How are you feeling about your speech?" Mom asks.

"I'm a wreck. I've been practicing in the mirror all day," I say, nervously biting my bottom lip.

"Look at you being selected as one of the commencement speakers, what an honor!" Grandma beams with pride.

I wrap my hand around the back of my neck, feeling the tension. "I just hope I can remember all of the words."

Mom puts her hands on my shoulders and looks me in the eye. "You've got this. Just remember, if you lose your words, give yourself a moment before continuing. You'll find your way. And you'll have us cheering you on from the audience."

She gives me several squeezes, trying to help me relax.

"By the way, this came for you today," Mom says, handing me a letter.

"What is it?"

"I'm not sure, it looks like it might be from the University. Why don't you open it?" she says.

Everyone gathers around as I open the envelope. The postmark is from Ann Arbor, Michigan.

Dear Ms. Ellsworth,

Congratulations! We are writing to let you know you are the very first recipient of the Emmeline Luna Ellsworth Memorial Scholarship Fund. Through your resilience, hard work and determination, you have proven to be a student that our foundation would like to recognize and encourage to continue your educational efforts.

This four year, fully paid scholarship has been sent to the University of Michigan, to be used for tuition, fees or books, and should be treated as a scholarship of additional funds to you.

Our foundation wishes you continued success throughout your college career and beyond.

Sincerely,
Samuel Berenson

Director of Grants and Scholarship Committee
The Emmeline Luna Ellsworth Memorial Scholarship Fund

My mouth gapes open as tears fill my eyes.

"What is it?" Mom asks.

I hold out the letter with a trembling hand. As she reads, her eyes also fill with tears before she hands it to Grandma.

"Oh my goodness!" Mom says, hugging me tight. Grandma finishes the letter and joins our hug. The three of us stand together, holding each other up as a wave of emotions crashes down, like so many other times in our lives. Only this time—it's a happy wave.

"Did you know about this?" I ask, incredulous.

"I'm as surprised as you are," she says, a stunned look on her face.

"The only scholarship I applied for was the $1,500 dance scholarship and that was awarded at school," I say.

Mom and Grandma look dumbstruck, they're having a hard time finding their words.

"Do you think someone applied for it for me without me knowing?" I ask.

Mom looks as stumped as me. "I don't know, sweetheart. Whomever made this happen, it was very generous of them."

"So generous. I can't believe this. I have to find out who set this up so I can thank them. I've been so stressed about college tuition. This is a dream come true," I say, my heart overflowing with joy.

"It really is sweetheart. It makes me so happy to see your hard work being rewarded." She clasps her hands in front of her chest.

"It's someone who has to know us, right? How else would they know Emmeline's name?"

Mom shrugs, still stunned by the contents of the envelope. "I'm not sure. I'll look into it and see if I can find any more information for you."

"I don't think this day could get any better!" I say, cheerfully.

FORTY-NINE

GEMMA

Bits of glass cover the floor in every direction. Neither of us move. Grandma jumps up, taking a few towels from one of the kitchen drawers. Stunned and ashamed, Mom puts her head in her hands.

I stand not knowing what to do. I'm not even sure where I am right now. She looks so miserable, part of me wants to reach out and hold her and the other part of me just wants answers. I look to Grandma for any clues but she's on her hands and knees, cleaning up the wreckage. Mom reaches for my arm, leading me around the casserole ruins, to the kitchen table.

"I'm sorry, Gemma. I didn't want it to happen like this." She shakes her head.

"Didn't want *what* to happen like this? What is it? Please, you need to tell me. You've always taught me that no words are too scary, even if it feels like they are. Just say it."

She wipes her hands on her apron and sighs. The serious look on her face makes my stomach turn. It's one I've never seen before—I thought I'd seen them all.

She leans on the back of her chair before slowly sitting down. "I don't even know where to start. I can't tell you how many hundreds of times I've wanted to tell you, but the timing was never right. I want you to know, it was always my plan to tell you, but every time I felt ready, I could never find the words."

"Mom, tell me *what?* You're scaring me."

She looks away, guilt-ridden. "I don't want to scare you. I'm sorry for the shock of everything I'm about to say. I wish I would've had the chance to tell you on my own time, but by your reaction, I realize that's been selfish of me."

My eyes search hers for anything faintly familiar. Anything that will help make sense of what I've just read. This moment is so surreal, I push my feet down hard against the ground to make sure it's still there.

"I've made some decisions in my life that I regret. Decisions that once they were made couldn't be undone. This is what I was talking about on our last call."

"What decisions, Mom?" I demand, my tone unintentionally sharp. Grandma pulls a chair close to Mom and sits down. The knowing look in her eyes terrifies me.

"Before I get into the details, let me backup and give you some history," she says, taking a deep breath. I lean back and cross my arms, wishing she would just get to the point.

"The day your dad and I found out we were pregnant was one of the happiest of our lives. The two of us spent my entire pregnancy counting down the days until we would finally meet you. We were so excited for our future as parents. Our conversations were consumed with talks of how big you were getting and plans for the nursery."

I nod, my mind racing as time slows.

"The day I found out your father died was only two months before I gave birth. It was the hardest thing I'd ever been through in my entire life, and it happened at a time when I needed him most. I was grief stricken and overwhelmed with thoughts of being both a new mom and a widow. I was terrified and felt hopeless. It seemed like an impossible task to do everything on my own and do it well."

My heart cracks at the thought of how strong she had to be in just one lifetime. "My doctor never put me on bed rest, but for the remainder of my pregnancy I couldn't get out of bed, not even to shower. I spent the entirety of my days curled on my side drowning in sorrow over losing your dad. Grandma was so concerned she never once left my side. At night, I would wake to find her sleeping in a chair next to my bed." I look at Grandma—the pain of remembering on her face.

"When you were born, I was a young mother who was grieving the love of her life. I haven't told you about this before because the consequences that occurred from that pain are unbelievably hard for me to talk about."

Grandma reaches over and places her hand over Mom's protectively. My heart wants to break into a million pieces, seeing the sadness that's deeply etched into the creases in both of their faces.

"I'm sorry you found the painting. Reading those words must be so confusing. I never wanted you to find out this way, and if I could go back and change it, I would."

"Mom, just tell me. What do the words mean? Who is Finn?"

She takes a breath so big and long I'm not sure how all the air fits into her lungs. Then, after she lets it out, bit by bit, the words follow behind. "Gemma, you weren't just a twin. You were born a triplet. Finn is your brother."

FIFTY

GEM

I rub my hands together in an attempt to stop them from tingling while trying to swallow the growing pebble in my throat. As the crowd's applause for the previous speaker fades, I climb the steps to the stage. The sun is just starting its descent into the horizon and I'm thankful for the cool breeze on what is the beginning of another quintessential, steamy Indiana summer night.

I find my place behind the podium and cling tightly to the sides. Hundreds of faces look to me, waiting for me to begin. I've lived in this small town my whole life and it's reassuring to see so many familiar faces, many who already know at least some of my story.

Scanning the bleachers, I try to see if I can spot Mom and Grandma. My stomach twists when I can't find them. I wish I knew what section they were sitting. My heart thuds, and my mouth feels like I'm swallowing sand. I clear my throat and suck in a deep breath, hoping to settle my nerves. I've never spoken publicly before and certainly not to a crowd of this size. What's more terrifying than the amount of people here tonight, is the subject of my speech. I've spent so many hours preparing. I hope it's enough. *Please let this go well.*

I clear my throat. "Good evening, everyone. My name is Gemma and it's an honor to be standing before you, on this stage. Thank you for letting me tell my story on the biggest night of our lives.

"When Mr. Holland asked me to speak tonight about overcoming obstacles, I was hesitant. Public speaking is so far outside my comfort zone, it's in a whole other area code. But like my mom always says, you'll never know just how strong you are until you step outside your boundary of comfort. So, as we head into this next chapter, I encourage you to seize every opportunity you're given, because you never know—it may just be the one to change your life.

"Congratulations to my fellow graduates for earning your walk across this stage. Tonight is for you, your families—and every person who has helped get you to this day. Tonight and together, we celebrate all of us.

"Seventeen years ago, when I came into the world, I wasn't alone. I was born two minutes behind someone who looked exactly like me— only she got the dimples. Emmeline was my twin, my mirror soul, and just like socks, mittens or anything else that comes in twos, we were a pair. Then one day, the person who used to finish my sentences was gone and, in her place, deafening silence. I had no time to prepare for life without her and often doubted my ability to go on."

I clear my throat and dig my nails into the podium, taking a beat as every emotion bubbles to the surface. *Why did I think I could get through this?*

I breathe in sharply as my eyes start to water. "So how did I survive? How did I learn to go on without her? There was only one way:

"LOVE."

Feeling a newfound strength from somewhere deep inside of me, I continue. "I've learned many things from my experience with loss. The biggest thing being, when you have loving and supportive people by your side, in my case, my Mom and Grandma, there are no obstacles you can't overcome.

When grief swallowed my words whole and I couldn't speak for several months, they enrolled me in a dance class where ballet became my language. Dancing made me feel like I had some control at a time I felt powerless.

I'm going to continue to put one foot in front of the other, because I want to see what comes next. I know in my heart that bright and starry skies lie ahead for me. That's what she'd want for me. And while I begin to make a new life for myself—I'll never forget the magic that was my sister."

I blink several times, looking up at the sky. *Come on Gem, you've got this.* Regaining my composure, I look down and then out to the crowd, my heart racing.

"My high-school experience hasn't been a typical one, and because of this, there's a list of people I would like to thank who have helped and supported me every step of the way. I am deeply grateful for all of my tutors, teachers, counselors and therapists. Your understanding and compassion have touched my life in a way I'll never forget. Through your actions, I've witnessed firsthand the impact that caring and kindness can make on someone's life. As I begin this next chapter, you all have taught me that no matter how busy college and life beyond may become, there is always time for helping others.

"There are two people here tonight who deserve their own ceremony of thanks. They are the definition of saving the best for last. My guiding lights. They not only helped me, they saved me." I smile searching the audience.

"Mom and Grandma . . ."

My voice cracks and the pebble in my throat has turned into a boulder. I fight to hold back my tears, but it's no use. Chin quivering, I pause as tears roll down my face. *Oh no, this is what I was afraid of.* But I can't stop my emotions. They're too big and too filled with love.

Remembering Mom's advice I swallow and give myself a beat to collect myself. Out of the corner of my eye I see movement and look towards a stirring in the bleachers. It's then I notice two people in the middle section to my left standing amidst a crowd of seated guests. I know the moment I see their silhouettes in the fading light that it's Mom and Grandma. They are standing for me, supporting me, lifting me up and loving me fiercely, just like they've done every day of my life. My breath hitches in my throat as I smile at them through blurry eyes.

"Mom and Grandma, I would not be standing here today had it not been for your unwavering patience and nurturing support. You went to every length to ensure my childhood was defined by love, especially in the darkest moments. I love you both with all my heart.

"And to you, Mom—I will always be your sun. Thank you for teaching me how to shine through the rainy days."

"My fellow graduates, I leave you with one final and simple message. Celebrate your accomplishments. Open your heart and mind to new adventures because you'll never know unless you try. Go out there and dream your biggest dreams. My wish for you is that you achieve each and every one of them."

FIFTY-ONE

GEMMA

Disbelieving the words I've just heard, I shake my head slowly back and forth. "What? No. Mom—what are you even saying?" I lean back, trying to recognize this person sitting in front of me. This can't be real.

"It's true Gemma. I'm sorry. This is an awful way for you to find out, but it's the truth. You have a brother."

I wait for Mom's sentences to unscramble themselves into something I can understand. The three of us sit in silence for what feels like hours, her words playing over in my head, threatening every facet of my existence.

"Where? Where is he? Do you know where he is?"

"Yes. I do. I'll tell you everything."

"Wait a minute. Does he live near us? Oh my God, do I know him?"

"No sweetheart, you don't know him. Please, let me explain."

Mom walks over to get her purse and sets it down on the table in front of me. I look at Grandma to see if she can believe the words coming out of Mom's mouth and I can tell—she's known all along. Of course she has.

Mom unzips a side pocket of her purse, pulling a small photograph from the protective satin lining and hands it to me. My hands shake as I take it from her. The corners are well worn with age. The photo looks like it's been taken out and looked at every day for the last twenty-three years. There are several cracks in the photo, but the image is clear: Mom is sitting in a hospital bed holding three babies in her arms. The babies are wearing two pink hats and one blue. I look up to meet Mom's eyes.

"What happened to him? Why is he not in our lives?"

Mom takes a deep breath to settle herself before starting again.

"I had just turned twenty-one when I had the three of you."

I still can't believe I'm hearing these words. *Three of us.* I'm holding the proof in my hands, yet there's no way this is true. It can't be.

"I was deeply depressed and struggling after I gave birth. The death of your father almost killed me. I was consumed in my own grief on top of trying to navigate my new world of postpartum depression. I knew there was no way I could manage taking care of three babies. Every day I felt like a failure with no promise of doing better the next day. Eventually it got to the point where I lost my will to live.

"Grandma didn't know what to do, she was already helping me so much, but as days turned into weeks, it was too much for her to take on. Finn had several back-to-back respiratory infections when he was born and needed extra care. Care I wasn't able to give to him. He was having trouble gaining weight and was so frail and ill. Every second of the day was filled with his screams, but the nights were the hardest. Those long nights nearly drove me mad. Nothing I did worked. I felt I was failing not only him, but all of you. I spiraled into a deep depression, back when people didn't talk about these things.

"Grandma agreed to take care of Finn for six months in the hopes it would give me time to heal while I learned how to be a mom with the two of you. We both thought in time I would be ready to take him back. But I didn't heal. My depression worsened. After six months, I couldn't ask her for more time, I had already asked so much of her. She and I had many conversations about Finn and the life I wanted for him. I knew I couldn't give it to him. I was still barely getting by with the two of you. I had to make a decision. I had to do what was best for my son who deserved a life filled with care and love."

I flinch. Hearing Mom say the words "my son" is like forcing a piece of a puzzle that doesn't fit. *It just feels wrong.* Who is this stranger sitting in front of me who has lied to me my entire life? I blink several times, trying to make my old Mom reappear. My skin feels hot from the flood of anger and betrayal pulsing through my veins. Mom is the one person I've trusted more than anyone in the world and now it seems as if I've lost her, too. I wish she would stop talking. Listening to this story is like picking a scab, the more she tells me, the deeper and more scarring the wound.

"I spent hours searching for a family for Finn. After researching foster programs in the area, I realized I had to do what was best for him and give him up for adoption."

My eyes widen. I feel like I've jumped into someone else's life. I grab the back of my chair to make sure it's still there. Another physical reminder this is real.

"I spoke with several adoption agencies until I found one in New York that felt right. I knew from our first conversation that they were a caring organization that also wanted to find the best family for Finn. The agency sent me information on several families, and every day in between nursing the three of you, I pored over each file. It took a long time, but one woman stood out. She sent me a letter through the agency telling me about herself, her beautiful love story with her husband and the struggles they'd faced trying to conceive a child. She'd lost several babies and they desperately wanted to be parents. She never judged me. She understood that my wanting to give him up for adoption was because I loved him with all my heart."

Mom's voice cracks at those last words. I can feel the painful truth inside of them. She puts her head in her hands and weeps. I reach out and put my hand on her knee. I hate seeing her this heartbroken. She has already had so much pain in her life. *How much can one person take?* Mom wipes her eyes before continuing.

"Finn's mother was a great listener at a time I desperately needed it. We had so many conversations that eventually, she became more than Finn's adoptive mom, she became a friend. She always made herself available for me back then and she still does over twenty years later. She was a great comfort to me during an incredibly difficult time in my life. She, more than anyone else, understood how important choosing the right family was to me. I chose her because she showed me kindness and love at a time when I hated myself."

Mom touches the locket around her neck with what I now realize is *all three* of our initials.

"This necklace was a gift from Finn's mother. She gave it to me the day of the adoption, and I've rarely taken it off. It was a way of keeping him close to my heart, even though he would be raised hundreds of miles away."

My eyes move slowly back and forth from the locket to her eyes. I'm still desperately trying to make sense of what she's saying, yet nothing is ringing true.

"Part of our agreement was that if she and her husband adopted Finn, they would send me letters with updates on him every year. She's always kept her word. Receiving her letters made me feel like I was still a part of his life and I've saved every one. You came across one of them when we moved into this house. I'm not sure if you remember."

I look up and nod, vaguely remembering.

"Have I ever met her?" I ask.

Mom nods. "Briefly. She came to see me the year Emmeline died, when you'd lost your voice. You met her in Grandma's front yard. She and Finn also came to see me shortly after my accident when we were still living at Grandma's. It was summer and you and Emmeline were standing on our front porch as they were leaving. Colette has been a huge source of support and strength for me when I needed it most. I honestly feel in some strange way that your father sent her to me."

Dabbing her eyes, Mom lets out a slow, deep exhale. I can't imagine keeping all of that inside for as long as she has.

"Mom, I can't imagine how hard it must have been for you. You were so young. It makes me hurt seeing you relive all this pain," I say.

"It's been a long time coming."

I can't keep the words in any longer. Adding to her pain is the last thing I want, but I still need answers. "Mom, I'm trying, but it's just hard for me to believe there was never a time before now to tell me. Not even after Emmeline died?" I say, as tears spill down my cheeks. I feel so unbelievably vulnerable right now, in front of the one person I never felt I needed to protect myself from.

Mom sits quietly as I blurt out every question in my head, and there's so many more, it's possible I'll never reach the bottom. The reality playing out before me is so warped. It feels like one of those dreams that's so vivid and real, that even when you wake, you're still stuck in the other world and can't believe the one you've wakened to is the real one. *Only this is real.*

"I'm sorry every day of my life for not telling you sooner. Please know that. I just didn't know how to tell you. I kept putting it off for the right time, but there was never going to be a right time. After Emmeline died, I wanted to tell you but the grief counselors thought it would be even more devastating for you. The last thing I wanted to do was to cause you—all of us, more pain. We were barely surviving as it was."

A jolt of anger flashes through me, unbidden. "After I lost my sister, don't you think that learning I had a brother out there somewhere might have been a huge comfort to me? Maybe even made things a little easier?" I ask, knowing my words must feel like knives in my mom's heart.

She shakes her head. "Not if you couldn't meet him, Gemma. You would have had to experience yet another loss and I couldn't do that to you. My agreement with Finn's parents was that I would not contact him. When Finn's mom and dad adopted him, I gave them a letter and they promised to give it to him if and when, he ever asked about his birth mother." She takes a breath. "His mother just recently gave it to him."

Mom pauses to gauge my reaction, studying me to see if I'm okay. *Always putting me first, even during the most painful moments of her life.*

"I know this is a lot of information. I've wanted to tell you for so long. I don't expect you to understand and I don't expect you to forgive me. I'll never be able to forgive myself for keeping this from you for as long as I did. I'm so sorry. You deserved to know. I hope one day you'll understand and be able to forgive me."

Tears roll down her face. Grandma gets up and gets a box of tissues, placing it in front of Mom as her sobs fill our kitchen. I can tell by the look on Grandma's face, her heart is breaking for all of us.

My initial feelings of anger and sense of betrayal start to soften. I know who my mom is. She's carried the trauma from her decision for far too long. She deserves to finally lay it down. I'm angrier with the brutal hand my mom has been dealt than with her for not telling me about Finn.

"There isn't one day that goes by that I don't think about the consequences of my decisions. Some nights I wake up and can't stop thinking how different our lives might have been if I'd raised you all together."

She's crying so hard her shoulders shake. I get up and kneel next to her, holding her hands in mine. She's in so much pain, and I can't take seeing her like this. It's too much. For her, for me, for all of us.

"Mom, I can't imagine what you went through. Our birth should have been one of the happiest times in your life, and instead you were drowning in grief over losing the love of your life. It's no one's fault, and it's certainly not yours."

Mom squeezes my hand and looks into my eyes for a moment. "My sweet girl. Please don't try and make this easier on me. That is my burden to carry and mine only. I've always thought losing your sister was some kind of cruel punishment for the decisions I've made."

I feel like I've been kicked in the stomach. "No, Mom. That's a terrible thought to have, please don't ever say that, or even think it. You're no more to blame than I am."

I pause, looking down and then quickly push my words out before I lose my courage. The trap door bursts open, and I cry with a rage I've never known.

"I still blame myself for Emmeline's death. I was the one who convinced her to climb the tree that night, remember? After she died, I thought you secretly blamed me, but couldn't say it because you're my mom. I have always wondered if you ever wished it had been me that night."

The words that have haunted me for years.

Mom gasps as if I've struck her. Her chest heaves in and out, wracked with sobs. "Oh, no, no, no. Never once have I ever thought that. Never. Don't ever, *ever* say that again."

Her shoulders tremble as she lets out several high-pitched cries. We hold onto each other sobbing in each other's arms until our cries slow, and then fall away.

Grandma wipes her eyes and stands behind us, wrapping us in her arms. "You've both spent so much time and energy blaming yourselves and it's time to stop. It's what she would want and you both know it. Neither of you deserve these words and it does you no good to even think them." Grandma hugs us as tightly as she can. The three of us stay like that for what feels like an hour.

Their arms are my sanctuary.

IN THE SHORT amount of time I've been sitting at this kitchen table, everything has changed. I feel dizzy with this new information. Mom looks over at me, scanning my face.

"Do you forgive me? I know what I did was wrong." she asks, somberly.

I close my eyes, tipping my head back. "Yes, of course I forgive you." It suddenly hits me that she was a few years younger than I am now, when she made these decisions.

"I might have done the same thing, had I been in your shoes. Who knows? What I do know is I love you and I'll always love you. You're my mom and nothing will ever change the amount of love and respect I have for you. You've had to make sacrifices I could never begin to understand." I squeeze her hand. "You are the light in all of us and every day I'm thankful you are my mom."

She sits quietly. I'm hoping she's letting my words sink in. Her eyes are red and swollen—she looks so tired. *A lifetime of tired.* I focus on the ticking of the kitchen clock above the sink, there's something soothing about its sound. *Time, the great healer.*

"Wait. You said Finn's mother gave him the letter. Has he reached out to you?"

She nods.

"Last month, just before Thanksgiving. When I saw his name in the return address, I couldn't believe how long I'd waited for his letter to come, yet I was terrified to open it. I wasn't sure what he thought of me or what he would say, or if he hated me. But he was so kind, Gemma. It's such a beautiful and thoughtful letter. I'd love for you to read it if you feel you're ready to?"

A dog barks outside, and the hum of the refrigerator seems louder than usual. A letter. Words my own brother has written. *What would it feel like to read that?* I stare ahead, my eyes glazing over.

"I knew from his carefully chosen words that he has been raised by loving and supportive parents," Mom continues. "His parents have given him a wonderful life. One that I couldn't. Finn and I've exchanged a few letters and his words have helped heal me. He told me he doesn't hold any hostility towards me, though I wouldn't blame him if he did. I expected him to. I've been waiting for it. The only thing he's shown me is understanding. Something I never thought I deserved."

I close my eyes, grateful he has been kind to her. "Does he know about Emmeline and me?"

She nods.

"Colette had a long conversation with him about the two of you after he'd read my letter and before he reached out to me. He told me that learning about you and Emmeline was one of the reasons he wanted to reach out to me."

"He did? Have you seen him? Does he want to meet you?"

"He hasn't mentioned meeting yet. I'm going to let him bring it up. Whenever he's ready. I'll go anywhere to meet him."

"Where does he live?" I ask.

Mom pauses. "New York."

My heartbeats pick up their pace like they're racing each other.

"New York? Where in New York?"

"He lives in the city. He's in his third year of law school at Fordham."

My eyes widen.

"He lives in the city?"

Mom nods her head.

"He's a law student?"

She keeps nodding. What if I've passed him on the street? Shared a subway car or an elevator with him? What if he's sat next to me at a restaurant? *My small world keeps getting smaller.*

"Where do his parents live? Are they also in the city?"

"They are. Finn's dad is an investment banker and his mom is a well-known artist."

Three intertwined poppies flash in my mind.

"The painting," I whisper.

Mom nods.

"She painted that for me when we were just getting to know each other. She gave it to me along with the necklace the day they adopted Finn."

Mom and Grandma watch closely as I put my head in my hands and think about everything I've just learned. My mind swims from the unexpected turn my life just took. Talk about blindsided.

I have a brother.

FIFTY-TWO

GEMMA

I wake up in the same bed I've woken every Christmas morning for almost ten years, but this year feels different. Hopeful. Hazy's curled up at the end of my bed and I feel her stretch and then wrap herself around my feet. I've missed the warm, familiar feeling of her. Light pours through my side window but I'm not ready for daylight's nudge just yet.

Mom and I stayed up late talking after Grandma left. I'm still coming to terms with everything she told me. It still doesn't feel real. I had a dream about Emmeline last night and thankfully, didn't wake up screaming. I haven't had a night terror since my weekend with Miles.

I roll onto my side, away from the light. Facing me, illuminated by the first rays of the morning sun, are Emmeline's turtles. Three of them. One for each of us. *Merry Christmas, sister.* I can only imagine what we'd be saying to each other right now if you were here. *We have a brother.*

My mind swirls with so many unanswered questions. What's he like? Does he look like us? Ripples of excitement skitter through me. I've always focused on wishing I could rewrite the past. Now I have an opportunity to write a new future, with a brother I never knew I had. Part of me wonders if my fascination with NYC from when I was young was because, on some level, my soul knew a piece of me was there. *Multiples—we can sense these things.*

AN HOUR LATER, I'm still trying to force my sleepy self out of bed. I turn my phone over on the nightstand to find a text from Miles.

> Merry Christmas! Still at the hospital, call me when you wake up.

I sit up and Hazy comes over, burying herself in my lap. I scratch behind her ears as her comforting purrs vibrate against my legs.

"You and your purrs are the sweetest things to wake up to." She cranes her head and looks back at me. Her eyes stare deep into mine, with an understanding only she knows. I'm convinced animals are the purest form of love on earth. Their only motive in life is to love and be loved.

"You're such a gift, Hazy girl. I love you so much."

I smother her in kisses, remembering the day we found her in that rotten log. That was ten years ago. Ten years she's been gone. A lot of life has happened since then. I'm hit with a sudden impulse and return to my phone screen. The only photo I've seen of Finn is the one of my mom holding the three of us in her hospital bed. I type the words *Finn Berenson* into the Google search bar and click the images filter. Nothing comes back. I try Finn Berenson New York City.

Still nothing.

I type in Finn Berenson New York City Fordham University. Images of a familiar face pop up on my phone and I cover my mouth. It's him. It's strangely her too. I suppose there's some of me in there too. His smile is all hers though. A wave of excitement rushes over me as I stare at the photo of him standing in the middle of his ultimate frisbee team. Finn is average height with blonde hair and a stocky build. *He looks so much like our dad.* I search for more photos of him and his parents as my phone rings. *Again with his incredible timing.*

"Hey there."

"Hi. It sounds like someone just woke up."

"Yep, just now. Hazy and I are sitting in bed, cuddling."

"What I'd do to trade places with that cat right now," he says.

I smile warmly. "That would be a Christmas miracle. Merry Christmas, by the way."

"Thanks. Merry Christmas to you too. How's it being home?"

"It's been. . . oh my. . .where do I? It's. . . well, it's been great seeing Mom and Grandma. I've missed them so much."

"There's a lot to unpack in that response. Everything okay?" he asks.

"Yes. Everything's fine. No, it's pretty great, actually."

"Okay, good. I wasn't sure. Oh, by the way, my mom got back to me with the name of the artist of that painting. It's Colette Berenson."

I glance up at my mirror, a knowing smile on my face. "I thought it might be."

"Why? Is it the same artist as your mom's painting?"

"It is."

"That's funny, my mom didn't think it would be. Your mom's is an old painting, right?"

"Mm-hmm. Twenty-three years to be exact."

"That's strange. My mom said Colette only sold locally back then because she was just getting started. She only started shipping her work in the last ten years. I thought you said the first time your Mom and Grandma visited the city was last summer."

"You're a good listener."

"Well—that depends on who's doing the talking."

I can't help but smile.

"Yeah, the first time they came to see me was this past June."

"Well then how did your mom—"

I interrupt him before he can finish. "It's a long story. One I still need to process. I'll tell you all about it when I get back."

"Sounds interesting. I like long stories, especially when you're the one narrating. I gotta run, rounds are calling."

"I hope the hospital isn't too hectic for you today."

"That would be a true Christmas miracle. I'm grateful our paths crossed, Gem. I can't wait to spend New Year's Eve together."

"I have to admit, Clark, you've been an unexpected yet pleasant surprise."

"Ha, ha. I'm off to save the world. Or at least, make it through the day. Enjoy your day with your mom and grandma."

"I will. Talk to you later."

"Bye-bye."

I sit contemplating the fact that two totally random, yet significant men have suddenly come into my life out of the blue. *What are the odds?* I feel protective of my new discovery about Finn and also protective of Mom's decision to withhold his information from me for as long as she has. For now, knowing I have a brother is just for Mom, Grandma and me.

FIFTY-THREE

GEMMA

I walk downstairs to find Mom curled up on the couch with her coffee next to the Christmas tree. She still gets a fresh one every year and decorates it with ornaments that Emmeline and I made, along with several others from our trips.

"Merry Christmas, Mom. The tree smells so good. Whatcha doing?"

On her lap and stacked at her feet are several photo albums.

"Merry Christmas, love. I've been going through old photos. It's one of my favorite things to do, especially on a day like today."

She stands as I give her a big hug.

"Want coffee?" she asks.

"I'd love some. You sit down, I'll go grab a cup. I want to see what you're looking at."

She nods and sits back down, pulling the blanket over her while I go make myself coffee. I dig to the bottom of my purse on the counter and pull out her gift. I tuck it into the pocket of my pajama pants and walk back to the family room, scooting in next to her under the blanket.

She flips a few pages and I point to a picture of a blonde-haired man holding Mom in his arms. "I've never seen this one before. He's got a beautiful smile. Look at his dimples," I say. "That's where Emmeline must have gotten them."

Mom nods. "I loved his smile." A wistful look crawls across her face.

Having just seen Finn in my Google search, I decide that he and my dad could pass for the same person.

"Are you okay to talk about him? I honestly don't know much about my dad. I remember a long time ago someone told me he wanted to be a lawyer," I say, as Mom nods.

"That was the plan. I've always loved that you chose to study law. It's like you're following in the footprints he was never able to make. He'd be so proud of you." The corner of her eyes crinkle. "Now that you're older, it makes sense you'd want to know more about him. Talking about him doesn't make me sad like it used to. I've actually been looking forward to having this conversation with you."

"You have?"

"I have. It's a long one, so get comfortable," she says, as I snuggle into her.

"We were so young. Your dad and I met right after I graduated from high school. He was a year older than me and had just finished his freshman year at Purdue. I met him during summer break when he was visiting his best friend, Evan. They came into the restaurant I was working at the time. The second I saw your dad I just knew. I'd never had that feeling before.

Hmm... interesting.

"Harrison was the kindest, most considerate man. There was nothing he wouldn't do for those he knew and loved. Your dad was my world. The love we felt for each other was so intense and powerful, there was no stopping it for either one of us. We hated being apart and dated long distance while he finished his political science degree at Purdue. I was working, living with your grandma and taking clinical sociology classes at the community college.

"Harrison and I talked about marriage and made so many plans for our future. We hadn't planned to get pregnant, but it must have been written in the stars for you three to be born. We found out we were pregnant in the fall of his senior year. And then shortly after, we found out we were having triplets."

Mom pauses, raising her eyebrows and I do the same.

"I can't imagine," I say, shaking my head.

"We were shocked, excited and absolutely terrified. We set a date to get married after graduation, right after the babies were to be born. Our life together was everything I'd ever wanted. He was my best friend. Grandma absolutely adored him. The two of them would sit and talk at the kitchen table for hours. He was always helping out around the house with whatever needed fixing."

My heart fills with love for the father I've never known.

"My pregnancy was surprisingly easy, considering we were having multiples. Your dad would drive up from school so he could be with me for my milestone doctor visits. He'd make a list of questions beforehand and read them off to the doctor as they measured my stomach. There were times he would drive to the appointment just so he could be there and then turn around and drive right back to school. Every weekend he could, he'd come home to see me and feel the babies. He loved putting his hand on my belly and feeling you all kick."

She holds her eyes on me, making sure I'm okay. I put my hand on her wrist giving her a soft squeeze to continue.

"It was springtime, and I was almost eight months pregnant. Harrison had less than two months until he graduated. After a full week of midterms, we'd made plans for him to drive up for the weekend. Right before he was supposed to leave, his friend Evan's car broke down and your dad loaned him his so he could go to work that night. Harrison was going to leave the next morning, but that night there was a fire at the house. Back then, smoke alarms weren't mandatory like they are now. Evan came home to find the house engulfed in flames. He tried to save him, but it was too late." Her voice cracks and she stops to take a breath.

"I was so heartbroken, so angry. At first, I wanted to blame Evan, and then anyone and everything—even your dad. It felt good to sit in my anger. Grandma never once left my side, listening, letting me cry on her shoulder. She helped me understand it wasn't anyone's fault. It was just an awful tragedy, one that had no reason, answer or explanation.

"Evan came to see me, right before you were born, apologizing. This is a small town, people had said some cruel things to him, blaming him for your father's death. He'd had such sorrow in his eyes. I knew he was struggling too. It felt good to help him. Helping him was the only thing that made me feel a little better during that time."

"It's pretty amazing with everything you were going through, you had the ability to even think about his pain."

Mom smiles softly. "My entire life I'd only known love and understanding. I'm who I am because of Grandma and your dad. They loved me fiercely. Helping Evan, your dad's best friend, helped me. Plus, there was no room to hold on to anything that pulled me further down."

I shake my head, thinking about all that my mom has gone through in her life.

"Helping Evan planted the seed that grew into me wanting to get my master's in social work."

I look over at her, placing my hand over hers. "You know what I think?"

"What's that, sweetheart?"

"You're one of the greatest humans I've ever known."

"Oh, I don't know about that. As you know, I've made plenty of mistakes. But I do know that forgiveness is one of the most powerful gifts you can give yourself," she says.

I reach up and rub my cairn stone hanging from my neck. I lay my head on her shoulder, breathing in her lavender scent.

"I have a little something for you," I say, taking out the small, wrapped box.

"You didn't have to get me anything," she says.

"I wanted to. I saw these at a market in a park near my campus and they made me think of you. Open it."

She peels back the silver paper exposing a pair of raw gemstone earrings in the shape of a sun and a moon. Mom draws in a quick breath. "They're beautiful. My moon and sun, in your birthstone, too. I love them, thank you."

GRANDMA, Mom and I are sitting at the kitchen table well after our dinner when there's a knock at the door.

"I'll get it. You two sit," I offer.

I open the door and I'm surprised to find a familiar face on the other side. "Mr. Collins! I haven't seen you in so long. Merry Christmas."

"Hello, Gemma. Merry Christmas to you as well. Please—call me Theo."

"Oh, wow. That feels so grown up. My twelve-year-old self is squirming right now."

We both snicker.

"How are you doing? How's law school going?"

"It's going well, I'm in my last year. Please, come in. It's freezing outside."

He stomps the snow off his boots. "I won't stay long, I just wanted to drop something off for your mom," he says.

I open the door and let him in as Mom walks up behind me.

"Theo! What a nice surprise. Merry Christmas." She gives him a warm hug.

"Merry Christmas. I won't stay long, I'm on the way to meet my son, but I wanted to drop this off for you." He hands her a poinsettia and a small, wrapped box.

Mom blushes. "You're the sweetest. Thank you."

Why do I suddenly feel awkward? Like maybe these two could use a moment alone? What's even happening?

"I'm going to go help Grandma in the kitchen. It was nice to see you . . . um, Theo."

He smiles and nods. "Likewise. Good luck with school."

"Thanks."

The conversation Mom and I had when I was grocery shopping suddenly pops into my head. I've been so preoccupied since learning about Finn that I totally forgot to ask her about the fact she mentioned he came for Thanksgiving dinner. I pull out a chair at the kitchen table and sit down next to Grandma.

"Do you remember Mr. Collins, my grief therapist from several years ago?"

Grandma nods her head.

"Why is he here?"

"I believe he's here to see your mom," she says, a curious look on her face.

"Really? That's all you're going to say?" I ask.

"You'll have to talk to her about him. He's a very nice man."

"I know how nice of a man he is, Grandma. I poured my heart out to him for the entirety teenage years. He's the best. Why's he stopping by with a gift on Christmas to see Mom? Wasn't he also at your Friendsgiving?"

She raises her eyebrows and nods.

"Grandma!" We both start laughing as Mom walks into the kitchen.

"What's so funny?" she asks.

"I was just asking Grandma why Mr. Collins, err, Theo just came to see you on Christmas night, with a gift. She's not giving me anything."

Mom looks over to Grandma and smiles.

"Is that right, Mom?" she asks.

Grandma shrugs. "I told her she should ask you."

"You two are the worst," I say.

Mom and Grandma laugh, and it brings me back to the days when the two of them were both in on something and were trying to keep it from us. It's like one of those family jokes—no matter how many times you hear it, it's still funny.

"What's going on, Mom? I totally felt like I was interrupting something back there," I say.

She shakes her head. "You weren't. It's funny, I hadn't spoken to him since the night of your high school graduation. Then about three months ago, I referred someone from my office to him and he called to thank me. He wanted to hear how we were doing and how you were liking New York. When I got the letter from Finn, I confided in him. He's a great listener."

"The best. Um, cute too—don't forget that."

"Yes, I'm aware." Mom laughs and looks over at Grandma who's smiling ear to ear.

These two.

"So... what are the two of you?"

"Officially, you mean? Oh, I don't know. We're taking it slow. But I'm starting to have feelings for him, if you must know," Mom says, blushing.

"You're turning red! What are you, twenty again?"

She shakes her head. "Ha, no. I'd never go back to those years. I'd take age and wisdom over youth any day." She reaches for her locket, gently sliding it back and forth on its chain.

"I'm in a great place, Gem. I'm the happiest I've been in a long time."

FIFTY-FOUR

GEMMA

I'm sitting in O'Hare airport in the middle of a blizzard, waiting to board my flight back to New York. The weather forecast had been calling for snow, but nowhere near this amount. Even the meteorologists were caught off guard. Mom dropped me off three hours ago, and my flight keeps getting delayed. She said she'd come back and bring me home so we could try again tomorrow, but I don't want her driving on these roads. I text Mikayla:

> We keep missing each other. How's your family? Stuck in Chicago. Hoping to get out tonight, not looking good.

The conversation I had with Mom about Finn is on repeat in my mind. I wonder if she would have told me about him while I was home if it hadn't been for the painting? I guess I'll never know.

An attendant walks behind the counter of my gate and I walk over. "Hi. Do you happen to know if the four-thirty p.m. flight to LaGuardia is getting out tonight?" I can tell by the look on her face it's not good news.

"I'm just about to make an announcement. All flights have been grounded due to weather. We'll let you know as soon as we have more information on rebooking for tomorrow."

My hopes fall. "Oh, okay. Thank you." It looks like I'm sleeping in the airport tonight. I text Mikayla again:

> Bad news. All flights are grounded. Hopefully I'll be able to get out in time to help you decorate.

She texts back right away:

> Slammed at work. Sorry about your flight. No worries, I'll get it set up. Can't wait to see you. Text me your flight info.

I text her my flight number and reach into my bag for my charger so I can plug in my phone. It's not there. I frantically dig through my bag searching the side pockets and my coat and then I remember, I never unplugged it from the side table next to my bed. Ugh. I walk to see if there's a store open that carries chargers, they're all closed. *This night just got that much worse.*

My phone rings and it's Miles.

"Hey."

"Hey there. I was hoping you didn't answer. I take it you're not getting out tonight?" he asks, sounding disappointed.

"Wait—how do you know that? Did Mikayla just tell you?"

"No, I just saw it on the news. It looks like the entire Midwest is getting hit with this storm. I was hoping you got out before they closed the airport."

I let out a frustrated sigh. "Nope. I've never slept overnight at an airport before—this should be interesting. What are you up to? Are you still at work?"

"No," he chuckles, "I'm on a train to your place right now. It was supposed to be a surprise."

"Are you serious right now?"

"Yep. I told Mikayla I'd help set up for tomorrow night while we waited for you."

"You did?"

"Mm-hmm. Have you talked to her?"

I detect a hint of concern in his voice. "No, we keep missing each other. Why?"

"No reason. She left a key for me. You mind if I crash in your bed tonight?"

I smile at the thought of him sleeping in my bed. "I can't believe you're going to be in my bed—without me. I'm glad you'll be there to help her, it's definitely a two-person job."

"We'll get it done. Then tomorrow morning I'm going over to my mom's place to help her set up for her party."

"Mikayla told me about your mom's parties—they're legendary."

He laughs. "I don't know about *legendary*, but they're always a good time. This year, she's throwing it at her house in Brooklyn. She's combining her NYE party with an art fundraiser for a few of the schools near her."

I watch as a dad tries to console a three-year-old crying and screaming on the ground, kicking his legs. I'd like to throw my own tantrum right now for forgetting my charger. "I can't believe I'm stuck in Chicago—in a blizzard."

"You'll be here soon," he says encouragingly.

"Wait—your mom's throwing an art show fundraiser tomorrow night?"

"That was a delayed reaction. Can you hear me okay?" he asks.

"Mm-hmm, I'm sorry. I got distracted people-watching. It's going to be my main form of entertainment for the unforeseeable future. What were you saying?"

"Nothing much. Just that my mom decided to combine her NYE party with a fundraiser that she and her artist friend throw every year."

Artist friend.

"That sounds fun." I chew my bottom lip as something stirs in my stomach. "It's not the same friend whose painting I asked you about, is it?"

I hold my breath, hoping I sound casual.

"Colette? Yep, same one."

"So, she'll be coming to the party?"

"They're co-hosting, so yeah. By the way, you never told me how your mom got ahold of one of her paintings."

I let out a lengthy and tired sigh.

"Gem, are you there? Can you still hear me?"

"I'm here. There's something I need to tell you."

"Uh oh. That doesn't sound good. Everything alright?"

"Everything's fine. I wanted to tell you in person, but I don't know when I'm getting home and honestly, I can't keep it inside anymore. I've been wanting to tell you and Mikayla since the moment I found out."

"Found out what?"

I pause for a moment. I can hardly believe what I'm about to say to him, how can I expect him to?

"It's complicated. . . I don't know where to start so I'm just going to come out and say it. When I was home, I learned that I have a brother I never knew about."

"What?" He sounds shocked.

I pull my knees up under me on the chair. "I know. It's still hard for me to say, let alone believe—but it's true. My mom told me about him the first night I was home. I wanted to be in person when I told you."

"You're serious?"

"I'm serious."

"Where is he? Is he older or younger than you?"

I take a deep and steady breath. *This is the first time I'm saying it out loud to someone.*

I look around, making sure no one's around. "Miles, I was born a triplet and I never knew it until a few days ago. I've lived my entire life not knowing he even existed. It's all been a lot for me to process to say the least, but it feels good to finally say it to someone. To say it to you."

There's a long pause. "Wow."

He sounds lost for words. *I know the feeling.*

"You know my father died a few months before I was born, right?"

"Yes, you mentioned that before."

I take a beat, wanting to phrase this the best way I can. I'm so protective of Mom and her secret she's kept buried in her heart for so long. I know he would never judge her, or anyone for that matter.

"This is hard for me to talk about," I say, tears burning my eyes.

"I can hear it in your voice. You must be feeling a million different things right now. Is whatever you have to say too upsetting to talk about right now? Would you rather wait until you're back?"

I smile through my tears. He's the most thoughtful man I've ever known.

I dab my eyes with the bottom of my sleeve. *Now I'm the crying airport entertainment.*

"No. It's okay. I need to get this out."

"I'm here. I'm listening."

"There are a lot of details to what I'm about to tell you, but right now isn't the time to go into all of them."

"Tell me as much as you want."

I look around again, seeing if anyone is within earshot before I begin.

"When I was born, my mom had just lost the love of her life. On top of grieving his loss, she was also suffering from postpartum depression. She was barely able to take care of herself, let alone three newborns. She ended up giving my brother up for adoption when he was about six months old. I only found out about him because I read an inscription on the back of my mom's painting the first night I was home."

"What painting? The one you asked me about? Colette's painting?"

"Yes, Colette's painting."

I pause again, searching for the right words.

"Colette, the artist of both of our paintings, is also my brother's mother. She gave the painting to my mother as a gift the day she adopted him."

There's a long pause. "Wait a minute. Finn? Finn is your brother?"

My eyes fly open at the mention of his name. The room spins and I stare at the floor trying make it stop.

"Wait. You know him?" I say, incredulous.

"No, I wouldn't say I know him. I've met him a few times. Colette always brings her family to my mom's parties. I think Mikayla's met him too."

My mind races from all of my colliding worlds. I'm trying to put all of these moving pieces together, but everything is moving too fast for me to keep up. I feel sick to my stomach. *Miles and Mikayla have met my brother.*

"Gem, are you okay?"

My Achilles heel flares as I sit, speechless. Why do I suddenly feel hurt? Like I'm the one who's been left out of the secret? *Again.* I want to curl up in the fetal position and cry.

The line goes quiet for a moment. "I'm sorry. I shouldn't have blurted it out like that," he says.

I put my head in my hands, fighting back tears. "No, you have no reason to be sorry. I'm just frustrated. Frustrated at this storm, frustrated I wasn't able to tell you about this in person, and frustrated that I feel like I'm always the one being left out. I'm so tired of people hiding things from me because they think I can't handle it."

I dab my eyes on the sleeve of my jacket.

"My mom and Grandma have been trying to protect me from knowing I have a brother my entire life. Mikayla hides her test results from me because she doesn't want me to worry. As if the truth would break me. I'm a lot stronger than people give me credit for. I've had more trauma and grief in twenty-three years than most people have had in a lifetime and yet—I'm still here."

I shake my head and stare out the tall windows at the driving snow.

"And what I really wish is that we could be having this conversation face-to-face instead of sitting on a cold metal bench at the airport, crying in front of a bunch of strangers."

I laugh because there's honestly nothing more I can do. I wait for his response.

Silence.

"Miles?"

". . . Are you there?"

No answer.

I turn my phone around. My battery is dead.

FIFTY-FIVE

NEW YEAR'S EVE

My flight touches down on a snow-lined runway of LaGuardia airport. It feels good to be back in New York and just in time to ring in the new year. There's no place in the world that knows how to celebrate New Year's Eve better than this city. I could really use a sparkly celebration right now.

I've gone through every emotion since learning about my brother. Having no phone and nothing but time on my hands, I've done a lot of thinking over the last twenty-four hours. My mood seems to change every ten minutes, but right now I'm hopeful. Maybe sleeping on a row of metal chairs in a chilly airport all night brought a little perspective.

With everything I've been through, learning that I have a brother—though wildly unexpected and jarring—is something to be grateful for. A new chapter lies ahead and it's one I never saw coming. Not in my wildest dreams. *And I've had some doozies.*

I borrowed a charger from a passenger next to me on the flight and was finally able to charge my phone. I turn my phone on to find several missed calls and texts from Mikayla and Miles. I put in my earbuds and listen to a voicemail from Mikayla as I'm waiting for my turn to get off the plane.

"Hey, Gem. Sorry you're stranded. I'm on my way home from work but wanted to call you to let you know I just finished meeting with the neurologist Miles referred me to. I tense, my pulse picking up.

Apparently, and this won't come as a surprise, I work too hard and stand on my feet for far too many hours of the day—all of which we already knew. What we didn't know is that I'm severely deficient in vitamin D which, combined with the other two, makes me prone to passing out. The good news is—it's treatable. I'm going to be fine. More on this later—I just wanted you to be the first to know. Love you. Bye-bye."

The first to know. I smile and breathe a huge sigh of relief as I grab my bag from the overhead compartment. *She's okay.*

I glance at the exhausted passengers behind me. We are a sad bunch. Sleeping in an airport is such a bizarre experience. Complete strangers stranded together, taking refuge from an icy storm. Stuck in a moment, totally isolated from the rest of the world. None of us wanted to be there, yet we were trying to make the best of our situation. There's a shared, unspoken bond that we got through it together. In a blink, we were off to our destinations and most likely will never see each other again. It's such a strange, short-lived camaraderie.

My night in the airport was a small example of how life's experiences, even the most random ones, can have such an impact on your life. I can't help thinking of the pieces that brought me to where I am today. A random introduction that led to a painting. A painting that would change my entire world as I once knew it. *What a surreal happenstance.* There's no way this is all a coincidence.

I read Miles's last text:

> You haven't responded to any of my texts. I hope you're not upset with me. I'm here when you're ready to talk.

I'm ready to talk, I just needed a minute. *A minute for the storm to pass.*

I walk shoulder to shoulder with the rest of the weary passengers to baggage claim to wait for my bag. As I'm coming down the escalator, I see a familiar stocky frame leaning against the back wall, hands tucked into the pockets of his jeans. Miles. *He's here.* My heart swells as he looks up at me. In such a short amount of time this man has moved in and set up camp in my heart and I never really had any say in the matter.

There is so much I still need to come to terms with, but for right now, I'm going to focus on enjoying every second of these fleeting moments of the year. A warm feeling washes over me. I'm home.

OUR HOUSE IS PACKED with people in their finest fashion, dancing like it's the last night of the year. New Year's Eve is New York City's night to shine, and nobody does it better. Several mirrored globes hang from our ceiling, sending facets of bouncing light in every direction. It looks like a galaxy of twinkling stars in here. The anticipation for the new year is palpable.

Mikayla and I bounce to our favorite song. She looks so beautiful in her cobalt-blue velvet pantsuit, gold dangling earrings and her signature scarlet lipstick. Her long braids flow behind her as I twirl her under my arm. She looks blissfully happy. *Good for you girl, no one deserves it more.*

I feel a tap on my shoulder and turn around to find someone requesting my dance partner. I look over at Mikayla and she gives me an approving wink before reaching for his hand. I shoot her a smile and turn away, giving the two of them room to get close.

There are only a few minutes left in the year. What a year it's been. Tomorrow is a whole new beginning and I'm excited for everything it will bring. Including meeting my brother. *Those words are going to take some getting used to.*

I make my way through the crowd looking for Miles until I see his achingly beautiful smile. His rugged and handsome looks are in an entire class of their own. His olive skin glistens in the room's dim light against his plum suit. A rush of energy shoots through me—I know his smile is for me.

After a few turns and twists through the dance floor, we finally meet in the center of the room. He leans in and kisses my neck, sending shivers down my arms and legs.

"May I have this dance?" he asks, handing me a glass of champagne.

I hold out my hand and twirl into him, letting his hand fall around the small of my bare back.

"You're radiant tonight," he says, trailing his fingers up my spine as we sway back and forth. My stomach quivers, feeling his warmth pressed against me. My emerald sequin halter dress sparkles as he spins me, adding to the glittery vibe of the room. It feels decadent to be so dressed up after spending the entirety of last night sleeping on a row of plastic airport chairs, in sweatpants. It's true what they say, whoever they are: *what a difference a day makes.*

"One minute to midnight!" someone shouts.

The room erupts with cheers as Miles and I hold each other in a perfect moment. I wrap my arms around his tight waist, feeling the definition of his muscles beneath his shirt. I never would have imagined that next to him would be how I'm spending my last moments of this wild ride of a year.

He leans in, raising his glass. "Cheers to the most beautiful woman in every room."

I beam at him as we clink glasses, tasting the final sips of the outgoing year.

"Cheers, handsome."

The entire room shouts out the countdown...

...5 - 4 - 3 - 2 - 1!

Happy New Year!

A volcano of confetti explodes over our heads as noisemakers squeal out from every corner of the room. Miles holds my face softly in his hands and my heart pounds as he pulls me closer. We cling to each other as bursts of swirling confetti surround us in an orchestra of celebration. He bends down slowly, inching closer until I feel his warm breath on my skin. His lips softly brush against mine before he pulls them away, making me ache for him.

I narrow my eyes as he presses his full lips to mine, hungrily kissing me with an intense desire, sending a jolt of electricity through my skin. It feels like we're the only two people in this crowded room. I know with absolute certainty I will remember this New Year's Eve kiss for as long as I live.

"Happy New Year," he whispers in my ear, kissing my earlobe.

"Happy New Year, Miles."

The crowd sings Auld Lang Syne as we hold onto each other and sing our hearts out. A slow song comes on and he places his hand under my chin, tilting my face to his. His expression turns serious.

"There's something I want to say to you," he says, holding onto both of my hands. He pauses for a moment letting two people pass behind us.

"Everything changed the moment I saw you dancing up on that kitchen counter. I haven't been able to stop thinking about you since that night. I smile whenever I think of you and I miss you until I see you again. When you were upset last night at the airport, it crushed me hearing the sadness in your voice knowing I couldn't be there for you. It made me realize how much I want to be the one you come to for all your moments; the happy, the sad and all of the in between."

He stops for a moment, contemplating his next words. I know he's choosing them carefully and I squeeze his hands, encouraging him to go on.

"Nothing makes me happier than watching your eyes light up when you tell a story or hearing your laughter fill a room. I want you to know, as long as you're with me, I promise I will always protect your heart."

I hold my breath and blink away the sudden tears.

For so many years I've been in survival mode, trying to save myself from ever feeling the pain of loss again. I'm scared of hurting again, but what scares me more is letting my fears lead me down a path that doesn't include him. His words make me want to try. I've learned the hard way there are no guarantees in life. Not even tomorrow. But I'll never know unless I give him—and us, a chance.

"Miles. . ." I mutter, tears filling the corners of my eyes. "Those are the most beautiful words anyone has ever said to me. These past two months have been the brightest of my entire year. You've made me feel things I've never felt before. I can't think of anything I'd rather do than to spend more time laughing with you. That night you held me on your bathroom floor, you healed me in ways I can't even begin to explain. Not only have you helped me find my smile again, you've lit a candle in the darkest part of my heart."

He pulls me into him for a tight hug, burying his face into the back of my hair. The wall of barbs around my heart loosens and slowly falls away, breaking into a million tiny fragments. For the first time in over ten years, I feel open and light. Instead of regrets about not being able to change the past, my thoughts are filled with excitement for the future. Not only my future with Miles, but also the one I look forward to creating with my brother. After all these years, I'm finally going to meet him.

Happiness. That's the intention I'm setting for the new year. I glance around, taking in the shimmering glow of our post-midnight dance floor. It looks like someone took the lid off a mason jar, freeing an entire sparkle of fireflies. I extend my hand toward the giant disco ball dangling above our heads, as hundreds of tiny mirrors reflect my sister's hand back to me, covering me in her embrace.

Happy New Year, Emmeline. Your heart is all over this. I know you are the one who gathered the stars and aligned them one by one, just for me.

EPILOGUE

I check the subway map again to see how many more stops before Fordham. Three. I take a seat and try my best to occupy my mind.

Finn and I have been trading emails for the last few weeks and finally found a date that worked for both of us. The weather in New York has been abysmal lately and meeting him has given me something to look forward to. *My bright spot.*

My stomach has been in knots all week. I have this overwhelming want—who am I kidding, I *need* him to like me. I talked to Mikayla and Miles about it and they've tried their best to comfort me, but I won't be able to shake my anxiety until I finally meet him. I feel pressure to make a good impression not only for myself—but also for Emmeline. I can't let her down, not with something as important as meeting our brother.

It feels bizarre to be meeting someone for the first time, who shared the same womb with me. We kicked and rolled over each other for nine long months.

The number of hours I've spent thinking about what he'll be like, it's a miracle I've been able to get any work done. These past two months have felt like two years. My nerves are through the roof and I'm glad today's finally the day. All of my questions about him will soon be answered.

Finn's also in his last year of law school, which will give us a lot to talk about if the conversation lulls, which I highly doubt. But you never know. I've prepared a bunch of topics just in case things get awkward. My stomach turns over and I take a breath of stale subway air. I'll feel better once I'm outside and can breathe properly. I wring my hands and wipe my sweaty palms on my jeans.

I wonder if Finn's going to be a super savvy, refined New Yorker? I glance down at my jacket wishing I'd gone with my long, plaid wool coat instead of this slicker. This one is better for the cold and wet weather, but it's not very stylish.

I can't stop myself from second guessing myself and it's not helping my current state. I fiddle with my jacket's zipper and then fold my clammy hands together in my lap, looking at my watch. Less than five minutes to my stop.

I wonder if Finn played sports in high school? I wonder how he brushes his teeth at night and how he holds his fork and knife? I wonder if he's left or right handed? I'd love to know if he's ever stared into the eyes of a toad and thought they had the most beautiful eyes. I wonder how often he sees his parents? I have to be careful not to overwhelm him with a barrage of questions. Breathe in... five, six, seven... breathe out. . . just like your new therapist taught you.

I must have changed my outfit a hundred times. After approving at least twenty of them, Mikayla had to force me out the door or I'd still be trying on sweaters in my closet. I had a long talk with Mom and Grandma last night and they're on standby. They want me to call them as soon as I leave our meeting.

What if Finn and I have nothing in common? What if he regrets agreeing to meet me? What if he's resentful of me and Emmeline for being the ones Mom raised? Ouch. I didn't think of that until now. *Why didn't I think of that before?* I don't think he would have agreed to our meeting if he was resentful. Our emails have been very friendly, borderline formal. I'm not a formal person, I wonder if he is? Maybe he'll want to keep his distance, which I would completely understand. I hope not, though. I hope he wants to have a relationship with me and not just meet this one time.

The train slows as it approaches my stop and I double check the map on the side once again, just to make sure. The doors open and I climb the stairs putting me out on 59th St. It's about a five-minute walk, and I pull my waterproof jacket tightly around me, breathing in the wintry air.

I hurry along the snowy, wet sidewalks following my phone's directions until I see the blue bottle logo on top of the storefront window. *Finn has excellent taste in coffee.* This is one of my favorite coffee shops; there's one near school and every now and then I treat myself.

I open the door and the warm ambiance and delicious smell of brewing coffee welcomes me. I look around but don't see anyone in here that looks like it could be Finn, so I place my order and grab an open table near the windows. Trying to get my jitters under control, I take a few deep breaths, but not even Wim Hof himself could calm me down right now. My phone buzzes and I take it out of my coat pocket and see it's from Miles. A flash of relief comes over me. Thank goodness it's not Finn canceling.

> Good luck. Text me when you're walking back to your train. It's going to go well. I know it. I'm a doctor, I know these things. ;) Xo

I smile at Miles's winking emoji. Someone from behind the counter calls my name and I walk up to grab my coffee, sitting back down at my table. It's eight fifty-eight, two minutes before the time we agreed upon. I weirdly have never been in a situation where I don't know the person I'm meeting. I've never gone on a blind date or met someone online and that's what this kind of feels like, even though this couldn't be farther from it. Finn and I have history that goes way back. Twenty-three years to be exact.

The door opens and I turn to see who it is. In walks a man wearing a fashionable, gray herringbone peacoat with a pale blue scarf loosely tied around his neck. *I knew I should have gone with the other jacket.*

He looks to be about my age. It's him. He has shaggy blonde, medium length hair and he looks. . . he looks like he could be—my brother. *Mom's third sassafras leaf.* My heart pounds in my chest as he glances over at me. I slowly raise my hand and wave, taking in every detail. He walks over to my table. *Please hold it together.*

"Gemma?"

I stand up, fighting back tears, and smile.

"Hi, Finn."

I hold out my hand to shake his and he pulls me in for a hug. The way his arms fall around my shoulders—it's been so long since I've hugged a sibling. It's been so long since I. . . since I've hugged Emmeline. Tears spill down my cheeks and onto his jacket. He pulls away and sees I'm crying. I'm mad at myself for already making things weird, but I can't help it. I can tell he doesn't know what to say. He reaches into his coat pocket and takes out a pack of tissues, handing me one to dab my eyes.

"I told myself I wouldn't cry. It's just. . .it's. . .I just. *Breathe.* Your hug—it reminds me of hers."

"Gemma, it's okay. Please, take your time. This has to be hard for you. I understand."

"I'm alright. I just didn't know what to expect or how it would feel to finally meet you."

He gives me an understanding smile and there's something eerily familiar about it. It takes me a second to realize what it is. His dimples. *They're her dimples.* His smile is a perfect copy of hers.

"Thanks, Finn. Seeing you is a little. . .overwhelming. For you too, I'm sure."

"Yes, more than a little. I have to admit I've been nervous about meeting you," he says.

"You have been?"

He nods. "Ever since I first learned about you, I've been curious."

I know the feeling.

"I have a million questions, I hope you don't mind," he says.

I smile inside. "No, not at all. I have so many questions for you, too. I'm so happy you wanted to meet."

His shoulders relax a couple of inches. "I've been looking forward to meeting you since the day my mom told me about you and Emmeline. She wanted to come today but thought it might be a little too much seeing us both at once."

"I'm looking forward to seeing her again—it's been a long time. She's been a great friend and a tremendous source of support to my mom," I say.

"She feels the same about your mom. She asked me to give you something." He pulls an envelope from his inside coat pocket and hands it to me.

"Should I open it?" I ask.

"Please," he says, encouragingly.

I open the envelope and pull out two tickets to the ballet along with a handwritten note. I immediately recognize the handwriting from the back of the painting.

> Dear Gemma,
> Many years ago I invited you to the NYC ballet. I hope you enjoy the show.
> With love,
> Colette & Samuel

Tears fill my eyes as love fills my heart.

"Your parents are so thoughtful. This means the world to me. Please thank them for me and let her know I remember," I say, tears glistening in my eyes.

"She'll be happy to hear it. You two are going to have a lot to talk about, I can already tell. I'm going to go grab a coffee, I'll be right back."

The knots in my muscles loosen as I breathe out one of the most healing exhales of my life. He's kind. He's patient. He's already trying to make me feel better. Just like she would be doing, if she were still here—right next to me.

END

ACKNOWLEDGMENTS

Thank you to my readers for taking a chance on Gemma's story, and on me. As a debut author, I am humbled and grateful to have you read my words. There are a number of people I would like to thank, for without them, Secret Of The Sassafras would not be the story it is today.

Jessica Ryn, thank you for your guidance and brilliant advice as my editor. You are a gem. Your infectious positivity encouraged me every step and I am thankful I found you. Bia, my talented and patient cover designer—working with you was a pleasure. Thank you for bringing my vision to life with your beautiful artwork. Brooke, my gifted artist, thank you for drawing my sassafras leaves. Leslie Ann and Scott, thank you for showing up like family does—through the good, bad and everything in between. Anthony, Dre and Alex (birth order) what a blessing to have you join our family. The bond you share and the love you have for one another was one of the inspirations for this story. Sabrina, thank you for taking time out of your busy days as a corporate trailblazer to beta read my novel. CB. What can I possibly say? You've always been, and always will be—The One. Thank you for continuing to take my breath away. Also for your late nights editing from halfway around the world, distributing, moral support, believing in me—all while loving me fiercely. HB and BB: my teachers. I love you endlessly. Zuzu, thank you for the thousands of hours you spent cuddled next to me on the couch throughout the entire writing process.

A heartfelt thank you to each and every one of you for joining me on this wild ride of a journey. This novel is a testament it's never too late to dream big dreams.

Much love,
O.S.

ABOUT THE AUTHOR

Olivia Sparrow is an emerging author. Her debut novel, Secret Of The Sassafras, is her love story—to New York City, and to the person the stars destined she would marry. A professional portrait photographer for fourteen years, this novel is her story-telling transition from behind the lens to the page. For the first time, she's revealing the untold stories and family secrets of what lurks just beneath the surface of blissful and often contrived smiles.

When Olivia isn't writing, you'll find her in one of the national parks or hiking Big Sur with her family and dog Zuzu.

Olivia can be found online at OliviaSparrow.com, @OliviaSparrowAuthor on Instagram, and at Facebook.com/OliviaSparrowAuthor

Made in the USA
Middletown, DE
01 July 2024

56658877R00187